ACCLAIM FOR
CANE RIVER

"Strongly written . . . [a] proud saga of survival."
   —People

"[Celebrates] the resourcefulness and resilience of people trapped in a system perversely dedicated to destroying those very qualities."
   —Washington Post Book World

"A remarkable and unusual story . . . pulls us powerfully into the life of a family . . . . With a clear vision, and a beautiful, straightforward style, Tademy avoids the temptation to make her tale polemical. Not that she doesn't score political points with smooth, deft prose."
   —Philadelphia Inquirer

"Frank...fascinating."
   —Publishers Weekly

will haunt you long after you've shared their stories of suffering, abuse, joy, love, separation, reunion, hard work, survival, triumph."
    —San Jose Mercury News

"A compelling story! A powerful book!"
    —Billie Letts

"[A] remarkable debut . . . absorbing and moving . . . . These characters come to vivid life . . . captures the intricate rhythms of plantation life in all their harshness and beauty . . . [and] faces head-on the realities of black racism."
    —New Orleans Times-Picayune

"Gripping."
    —BookPage

"An incredible accomplishment . . . insightful."
    —BookBrowser Review

"Tademy re-creates the tale of the Cane River women . . . . In telling of their strength, courage, and heartbreaking choices, [she] reclaims the complexity and beauty of their lives."
    —Honeymag.com

CANE RIVER

LALITA TADEMY

WARNER BOOKS

An AOL Time Warner Company

Thanks to Father Victor Vead of the St. Augustine Catholic Church, for permission to reprint the portrait of Augustine Metoyer and the Church of St. Augustine on page 5.
Thanks to Trident Press International, for permission to reprint the image of General Banks's army crossing Cane River in 1864, which appears on page 259.

Warner Books, Inc., 1271 Avenue of the Americas, New York, NY 10020
Visit our Web site at www.twbookmark.com.

 An AOL Time Warner Company

Printed in the United States of America
Originally published in hardcover by Warner Books, Inc.
First Trade Printing: April 2002
10 9 8 7 6 5 4 3 2 1

The Library of Congress has catalogued the hardcover edition as follows:

Tademy, Lalita
    Cane River / Lalita Tademy.
        p. cm.
    ISBN 0-446-53052-2
        1. Cane River Region (La.)—Fiction. 2. Afro-American families—Fiction.
    3. Afro-American women—Fiction. 4. Louisiana—Fiction. I. Title.

    PS3570.A248 C36 2001
    813'.6—dc21   00-043682

Book design by H. Roberts Design
Cover design and illustration by Honi Werner
ISBN: 0-446-67845-7 (pbk.)

Dedicated to my mother,
Willie Dee Billes Tademy

ELISABETH'S DESCENDANTS
Seven Generations

ELISABETH and Marse, Virginia

ELISABETH b. 1799 and GERASIME b. 1802

YELLOW JOHN b. 1813, Virginia and DORALISE DERBANNE b. 1810

PHILOMENE and CLEMENT

PALMIRE b. 1821

SUZETTE b. 1825 and EUGENE DAURAT b. 1813, France

PHILOMENE DAURAT b. 1841 and NARCISSE FREDIEU b. 1825

GERANT b. 1839 and MELANTINE b. 1840

"BET" b. 1859

THANY b. 1859

EMILY "TITE" FREDIEU b. 1861 and JOSEPH BILLES b. 1840, France

ANGELITE and DENNIS

EUGENE b. 1866

Baby FREDIEU b. 1868 d. 1868

"NICK" b. 1872

HENRY b. 1875

"JOE F" b. 1877 and FANNIE

Baby JOSEPHINE b. 1878 d. 1879

"MATCHIE" b. 1880

ANGELITE b. 1879 and JACQUES

THEODORE "TO" BILLES b. 1881 and GENEVA BREW b. 1892 m. 1911

JOSEPHINE b. 1885

JOSEPH "MAN" b. 1887

MARY b. 1890

NARCEASE b. 1903

GURTIE b. 1905

JOSEPH "BUCK" b. 1897

ERNEST b. 1904

JOSEPH LEE b. 1912

THEODORE b. 1913

HENRY EARL b. 1918

I.V. b. 1919

WILLIE DEE BILLES b. 1921 and NATHAN GREEN TADEMY JR. b. 1919

THEODORSIA b. 1941

JOAN b. 1943

LEE b. 1944

LALITA TADEMY b. 1948

AUTHOR'S NOTE

My great-grandmother Emily died in bed at her Louisiana home at the end of the summer of 1936, with $1,300 in cash hidden under her mattress. Although she passed away twelve years before I was born, her presence is firmly imprinted in our family lore. Neither my mother nor her brothers ever talk about Emily without a respectful catch in their throat, without a lingering note of adoration in their tone.

I've been told that Great-Grandma 'Tite (Emily's nickname, rhymed with "sweet") was very beautiful, and this is verified by the four photographs I have of her, two of which hang on the wall of my home in California. She was full of life into her seventies, dancing alone in the front room of her Aloha farmhouse on Cornfine Bayou to the music from her old Victrola, high-stepping and whirling to the cheering-on of family gathered on Sunday visiting day. Always, at the end of her performance, she would arch her spine and kick back one leg, little booted foot suspended in air beneath her long dress until the clapping stopped. It was her trademark move. My mother and all of the other surviving grandchildren remember this vividly. Laughter and fun surrounded Grandma 'Tite, they say, describing the flawless skin, thick chestnut hair, high cheekbones, thin sharp nose, and impossibly narrow waist. My mother has said to me often, each time with a proud, wistful smile, "She was an elegant lady, like Jacqueline Bouvier Kennedy."

I always found this last statement impossible to embrace. I now know that Emily Fredieu was born a slave in 1861, lived deep in the secluded backcountry of central Louisiana, dipped snuff, and drank homemade wine every day, insisting that all visitors, even children, drink along with her. She bore five children out of wedlock over the thirty-plus-year span of her liaison with my great-grandfather, a Frenchman. Interracial marriage wasn't against the law for all of the time they were together, but it was dangerous and against custom for a colored woman, even if she did look white, and a white man to be together. My great-grandmother Emily was color-struck. She barely tolerated being called colored, and never Negro. My mother, the lightest of the grandchildren, with skin white enough to pass if she chose, was a favorite of hers. It is difficult to reconcile these facts and confirm my mother's judgment of "elegant."

I was always unsympathetic to the memory of Emily because of her skin color biases, although I never dared say so to my mother. But at the same time I was envious of Emily's ability to stare down the defeats of her life and aggressively claim joy as her right, in ways I had never learned to do.

Emily fascinated me for years, an untapped mystery, but my life was too busy to dwell on impractical musings with no identified purpose. I loved my world, jolting awake every morning, impatient to begin the day, savoring the next deal, the next business to build or turn around, the next promotion. For two decades I had hoisted myself upward, hand over hand up the corporate ladder, until I was a vice president for a Fortune 500 high-technology company in Silicon Valley. The position brought all-consuming work, status, long hours, and stock options. But every so often, while reviewing strategic businesses in small, airless rooms, I found myself secretly thinking about Emily, who she was, how she came to be. During budget reviews my mind would drift to Emily's mother, Philomene, about whom I knew so little, only as a name in a brief two-page family history written twenty years before by a great-cousin and sent to me by my uncle. I began to develop a nagging and unmanageable itch to identify Philomene's mother, to find out if she lived on a plantation as someone else's property, a slave, or if she had been free.

In 1995, driven by a hunger that I could not name, I surprised myself and quit my job, walking away from a coveted position for which I had spent my life preparing. Crossing back and forth from California to Louisiana, I interviewed family members and local historians, learning just how tangled the roots of family trees could become.

I scanned documents until headaches drove me from moldy basements where census records or badly preserved old newspapers from the 1800s and early 1900s were stored. In assorted Louisiana courthouses I waded through deeds, wills, inventories, land claims, and trial proceedings. Joining the Natchitoches genealogy society led me to some private collections, including letters. The search for my ancestors moved beyond a pastime and became an obsession.

A series of discoveries challenged what I thought I knew about Louisiana, slavery, race, and class. I thought Creole meant mixed-race people, black and white, but was informed in clipped tones that Creoles were only the white French-speaking descendants of the early French settlers, a snobbish distinction that clearly separated them from the black families the Creole men created "on the side," as well as elevating them above their lower-class French-speaking Cajun cousins. I discovered that most plantations were not like the sprawling expanses of Tara in *Gone With the Wind* but were small, self-contained communities, surrounded by farms that were smaller still. I discovered that the horrifying institution of slavery played out in individual dramas as varied as there were different farms and plantations, masters and slaves.

As I tightened my search for Philomene's mother, the trail led to Cane River, a complex, isolated, close-knit, and hierarchical society whose heyday was in the early 1800s. It was a community that stretched nineteen miles along a river in central Louisiana where Creole French planters, free people of color, and slaves coexisted in convoluted and sometimes nonstereotypical ways. In Cane River the free people of color, or *gens de couleur libre,* had accumulated a great deal of land and wealth and were just as likely to be slave owners as their white neighbors.

As a child I had spent many muggy summers in Colfax, a small country town not far from Cane River where both my parents grew up. The road trip there took days, with me sandwiched in tight between my brother and sisters in the backseat of our 1951 Ford, riding cross-country from California to Colfax for our annual two-week stay in July. In 1978 my father and I took a *Roots* trip to Louisiana, my first time to go back by choice. My mother sent me off with a "must talk to" list for her side of the family, and it included an elderly great-cousin living in Shreveport, Louisiana. My father drove us the hundred miles from Colfax, and we were eagerly welcomed into the home of a

Gurtie Fredieu, circa 1928. Said to look like her grandmother Philomene.

large, light-skinned woman with dark, piercing eyes. I still remember those eyes. Cousin Gurtie lived alone and radiated something almost touchable—a relish for life, an intensity, an undefeatable spirit. She was chatty, but her mind wandered, one minute talking about her shoelaces and what she had for breakfast, the next spinning tales of distant ancestors, grisly murders, suicides, and forbidden love. I assumed she exaggerated for effect, but I was hooked. It wasn't until sitting down to write this author's note twenty-two years later that I realized she was the same woman who had produced the two-page typewritten family history I relied on so heavily in trying to re-create my family's past. She had not exaggerated.

When I quit my job in 1995 I hired a genealogist to help with the search for Philomene's mother. It took her two years before she found the bill of sale in a private collection of French plantation records that positively identified Suzette as Philomene's mother. Only then was I sure that my ancestors were not free people of color. They were three generations of slaves owned by Françoise Derbanne, a Creole widow whose husband left her a medium-size plantation in Cane River, Louisiana. It was then that I resolved I would not allow Suzette or her family to be lost from memory again.

Revealed bit by bit from mounds of documents and family stories, I connected the line backward between these women of my family, daughter to mother. From Emily, back to Philomene, to Suzette and Elisabeth. They were not Mammy or Jezebel or Topsy, the slave images made safe and familiar in *Gone With the Wind* tradition. They were flesh-and-blood women who made hard choices, even in oppression.

Emily's mother, Philomene, came to life before any of the others. She visited my dreams, urging me to tell their stories. No, "urging" is too tame a word, too remote. Philomene *demanded* that I struggle to understand the different generations of my family and the complexities of their lives. She made it unacceptable that any of them be reduced or forgotten. It defies description in words, this bond I have with Philomene and her ability to reach across four generations to me with such impact. There were demanding days in the beginning when I feared her, a shapeless apparition, usually in the aftermath of her unrelenting hand at my back and the unnerving certainty of her voice in my ear. But the fear was always tempered with respect.

This book is a work of fiction deeply rooted in years of research, historical fact, and family lore. The details of Cousin Gurtie's accounting weren't always supported by other documents I uncovered. Some dates were off, some facts twisted, but I found that each precious line of her carefully typed history had at its base at least a grain of truth, and a family story had arisen around it. Many official and historical documents had inaccuracies in them as well. The challenge was to marry all of the data. In piecing together events from personal and public sources, especially when they conflicted, I relied on my own intuition, a sometimes intimidating undertaking when I felt Philomene's judgmental presence over my shoulder. There were gaps I filled in based on research into the events and mood of the place and time. I presupposed motivations. Occasionally I changed a name, date, or circumstance to accommodate narrative flow. I hope I have captured the essence of truth, if not always the precision of fact, and that liberties I have taken will be forgiven.

I hope you can put some of these things
together better than I did, you may have
heard that my Brother or I did not finish
School or no one tought me one thing about
Typen but that I know I know it, Smile. My
God have blessed me to be here my three
scores and ten.

        --Cousin Gurtie Fredieu, in a letter
           recording our family history written
           in 1975

CONTENTS

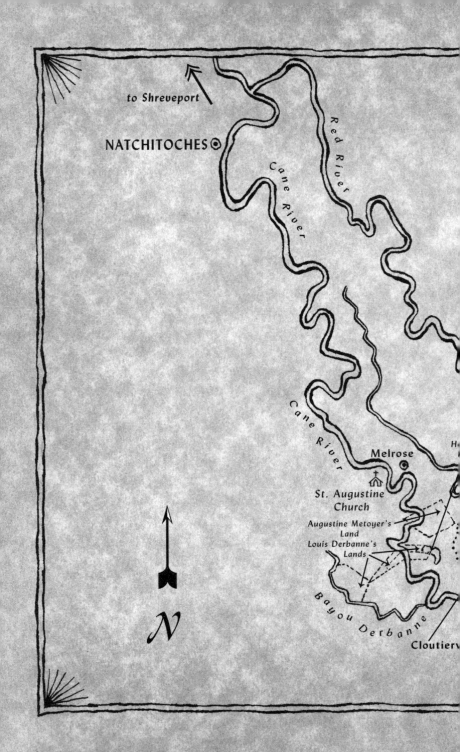

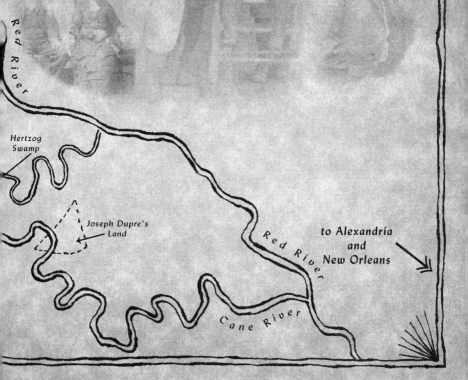

Cane River

(before 1868)

0 miles 5

Red River

Hertzog Swamp

Joseph Dupre's Land

Red River

Cane River

to Alexandria and New Orleans

PART ONE

Suzette

ELISABETH AND GERASÍME
Descendants

```
                    ┌──────────────────────────┐
            ELISABETH                      GERASÍME
             b. 1799                        b. 1802

  ┌──────────────┬──────────────┬──────────────┐
PALMIRE       APPHIA        SUZETTE       SOLATAIRE
b. 1821       b. 1822       b. 1825       b. 1826
```

1

CANE RIVER, LOUISIANA—1834

On the morning of her ninth birthday, the day after Madame Françoise Derbanne slapped her, Suzette peed on the rosebushes. Before the plantation bell sounded she had startled awake, tuned her ears to the careless breathing of Mam'zelle above her in the four-poster bed, listened for movement from the rest of the sleeping household, and quietly pushed herself up from her straw pallet on the floor.

Suzette made her way quickly down the narrow hall, beyond the wall altar, and past the polished mahogany grandfather clock in the front room, careful to sidestep the squeaky board by the front door. Outside on the gallery, her heart thudded so wildly that the curiosity of the sound helped soften the fear. Her breath felt too big for her chest as she inched past the separate entrance to the stranger's room and around to the side of the big house where the prized bushes waited.

Barefoot into the darkness, aided only by the slightest remnant of the Louisiana summer moon, she chose Madame's favorite, a sprawling rosebush with delicate pale yellow flowers and visible roots as long as her father's fiddling bow.

The task didn't take long, going and coming back, and Oreline's breathing was still soft and regular when Suzette slipped back onto her makeshift mattress at the foot of the bed. The only evidence that Suzette had been gone at all was a thin, jagged scratch on her bare arm from a thorn she hadn't seen in the darkness.

The day before had started with midsummer Louisiana predictability, so smotheringly hot that the spongy air seemed to push down on Suzette as she hurried to the cookhouse after church. Once there, she slipped a clean apron over her good dress, a loose-fitting dark calico with a yoke neck, one of Oreline's last-season castoffs her mother had altered to fit the girl's small body. Her mother had left room in the dress for a growth spurt. Every last item of Suzette's clothing from undershift to leggings and shoes had first belonged to her mam'zelle. Although the girls were the same age, Oreline was taller than Suzette by half a head. They made an odd pair, the pale white girl, long legged and gangly as a young colt, and her tiny cocoa-colored nurse, Suzette, with skin like strong coffee after the splash of cream. Suzette's eager smile showed off a gap between her two front teeth. The space was almost the width of a full kernel of corn, and Suzette used it to give more force to her whistle. It came in handy for calling chickens or pigs or for impressing Oreline and Narcisse when they ran the woods together in play.

The added heat from the blazing cookhouse fires made Suzette's dress stick to her as she worked the paddle of the butter churn. Built at a distance from the main house because of the risk of fire, the cookhouse belonged to the Derbannes, along with the cotton and cornfields, the swamplands, the facing rows of eight slave cabins in the quarter, four on each side, and every other living thing on Rosedew, their plantation along Bayou Derbanne.

Suzette looked over to her mother Elisabeth's strong, quick hands as she pulled a gray white dough ball toward her, kneading air into biscuits for the master's breakfast table. When her mother finished the cooking, it was Suzette's job to run the food to the big house while it was still hot and to serve the table.

Der-banne. Fre-dieu. She silently practiced her speaking voice in time to the paddle, hoping her mother would make conversation.

Elisabeth hummed as she worked, her tune deep, slow, and plaintive. Suzette wasn't sure of her mood. Her mother had never taken to Creole French, even the rough version they spoke in the quarter. Elisabeth never achieved the same slurry rhythm that everyone else from the house used.

"How was church?" Elisabeth finally asked.

"St. Augustine was beautiful." *Belle,* Suzette pronounced carefully, wrapping her lips around the word, hoping her French sounded as refined as Oreline's, imagining her words flowing as smoothly as those she had heard this morning at the church. "Old Bertram and I stood outside, but he found us a place where we could see into the sanctuary." *Sanctuaire.* "M'sieu, Madame, and Mam'zelle sat behind a row of *gens de couleur libre.*"

Augustine Metoyer and the Church of St. Augustine.

Suzette could still feel the wonder of the morning, the long ride in the wagon pressed between Oreline and Narcisse Fredieu, seeing for the first time the broad bell of St. Augustine above the vestibule, the shimmery waves rising off the sun-baked tiles on the gabled roof, the brightly colored glass. But mostly the clusters of people. White, colored, Negro, free, and slave, all dressed fine, all in one place.

Elisabeth grunted. "The free people of color who built that church own more slaves than the Derbannes. They go by their own rules," she said.

"I saw him, *Mère*. When he came outside, I saw Augustine Metoyer himself. I was as close to him as I stand to you now. You should hear him talk. More proper than M'sieu Louis. And his top hat was silk."

Suzette closed her eyes to bring back the images of the morning. Augustine Metoyer was the most famous of all the *gens de couleur libre*. The closest she had ever been to Cane River royalty before was her godmother, a free woman who had married into that famous family.

"I wanted to go inside. Old Bertram went in for a few minutes and took communion while I waited." Suzette was sorry her mother had never seen St. Augustine, that she and Old Bertram were the only slaves who had been allowed off the plantation.

"Just do your work, Suzette," Elisabeth said. "We have ten to feed this morning, and I still have Mam'zelle Oreline's birthday supper to make."

"Mam'zelle promised to leave some of everything on her plate for me tonight since it is almost my birthday, too."

Elisabeth said nothing, began to hum again.

Suzette wished her mother would send her on an errand, away for a time from all of the eyes that sought her out night and day. She would slip off her shoes and walk, with the rich Louisiana soil under her feet and between her toes, and carry back a pail of fresh cow's milk without spilling any, or bring in more wood for the fire, or gather green beans from the big garden to string and snap later. She was eight years old today, would be nine tomorrow, and she was meant for the house, not the field. Everyone, white, colored, and Negro, told her how much pride there was in that.

On good days Elisabeth would tell Suzette interesting things, mostly about cooking or preserving or flavoring, and sometimes she would compare Rosedew with the plantation she had come from in Virginia.

"This big house is puny next to some," Elisabeth would declare. In Virginia, her mother said, the big house had an upstairs, a downstairs, and thick white columns in the front. There were separate servants for every task, and each one of them had assistants. The big house on Rosedew was slung low, a one-story house of wood and brick frame, stuccoed in white, and topped with a long, sloping roof. There were six rooms that Suzette helped clean and a special bedroom for visitors, the stranger's room, with its own separate entrance from the outside for passersby on the river who might need a place to stay overnight. More often, as when the entire Fredieu family stayed over, it was used for the Derbannes' relatives who came calling by the day or week or month.

Beneath her madras *tignon*, Elisabeth's broad, dark face was streaked with a mixture of sweat from the heat of the cookhouse fires and a film of fine white flour from her morning baking. The sleeves on her long calico summer dress were pushed up above her elbows, and Suzette could see the old leathery burn marks on the brown skin of her mother's arms from her many years as cook, from boiling kettles and the big smoky fireplace and sizzling skillets. Suzette looked down at her own skinny arms, wishing they were pale and white like Oreline's instead of the color of cocoa.

"Mam'zelle and I went down to the quarter yesterday."

For Suzette there were real smells in the quarter no one tried to mask, loud sounds no one tried to quiet, and large motions no one tried to subdue. Weekdays only the smallest children were there, along with those too old for the field, the sick, new mothers, and the old woman who took care of all the little ones. Everyone else was gone, working sunup to sundown. After dark everyone was usually too tired from the day in the field to do much more than prepare their evening meal of ground cornmeal and their ration of bacon. A handful of meal, a little water, a pinch of lard, into the ashes to cook, and fall into bed exhausted after eating. But Saturday, after half-day labor, the quarter came alive with each household working their own patch garden, washing clothes, trading gossip, and bringing back fish or game along with stories of how they had caught it. Children mixed at will, white and black, broadcloth and homespun, nearly masters and nearly slaves not yet fully grown into their roles. Suzette's family lived in the quarter, including two sisters and a younger brother. There were moments when she wondered what it would have been like to live there instead of the big house.

"Papa made up two songs. One for Mam'zelle's birthday and a different one for mine."

Her father, Gerasíme, never gave Suzette hard looks when she used her house voice, unlike some others in the quarter. He was coppery brown, small framed, and always glad to see her, no matter how tired he might be. With his booming laugh, he called her his "big-eyed gal." Gerasíme's wild mane of springy black hair couldn't decide whether to stay down or curl up, so it did both, and his face was so smooth that he didn't have to shave like the other men. When Suzette had asked him about it, he'd said it was because he was half Indian. Her father was a favorite in both the quarter and the big house because he played the fiddle, and Louis Derbanne often got requests to rent him out for the frequent parties held up and down Cane River.

Suzette grew quiet when Madame Françoise Derbanne swept into the cookhouse, the silk of her pale green visiting dress rustling. Françoise's heavily corseted build was typical of well-fed Creole ladies, and her fading brown hair had been darkened with coffee-grounds water and upswept in calculated curls. Both her pointed nose and chin were inclined slightly, and her feet were nestled in black high-top shoes with leather-covered buttons. Usually she had Elisabeth come to her in the dark back room of the big house to decide on the menus for the week. But from time to time she appeared in the cookhouse unannounced, being careful not to let anything touch her or her fine clothes. It was an old ceremony between the mistress and her cook, and they had been acting it out since Elisabeth had come to the plantation fifteen years before.

"Elisabeth," Madame said, crinkling her nose as if she had caught wind of something slightly foul, "I've just talked to Oreline, and I want today's supper to be special. I have promised her a birthday treat of her favorites. There will be ten of us in all."

"Yes'm, Madame Françoise," said Elisabeth, eyes still on her worktable, hands never stopping their rhythm.

Suzette tried not to smile as she watched the two women, one tall, with skin the color of day-old grits, the other short and dark. She had already told her mother each of the choices she and Oreline had decided upon.

"We will have chicken and *tasso* jambalaya, sweet-potato pone, green beans, *cala* with the gooseberry preserves we put up last year, and peach cobbler," Françoise instructed.

"Yes'm."

Suzette was surprised Madame could not smell the peaches hidden in the pantry. Their aroma still lingered in the air of the cookhouse, competing with the sharp yeast smell of the starter sponge for *cala* they had concocted the night before, holding the promise of the rice fritters to come. She had peeled the potatoes for her mother and had been careful to watch how Elisabeth combined the boiled potatoes, cornmeal, flour, and cooking soda and left it in the night air to ferment before mixing in the boiled rice to make the sponge. Just before mealtime would come the flour, eggs, butter, and milk, the stiff batter to beat, the dropping of the *calas* by the spoonful onto the blistering skillet.

"I give you my permission to go to the smokehouse after breakfast and get the ham and one jar of preserves," Madame said with a slight nod of her head.

"Yes'm."

Madame Françoise walked a few steps toward the doorway and then turned back. Her tone had a scolding edge.

"You used far too much sugar in your last peach cobbler, Elisabeth, and Monsieur Derbanne got an upset stomach. Use less sugar this time."

"Yes'm."

The last time Suzette had served her mother's peach cobbler, she had spent half of that night cleaning up after Louis Derbanne. Elisabeth herself had told Suzette that M'sieu was ill because he had drunk too much bourbon. Her mother had done nothing wrong.

Suzette stood to her full height, the butter paddle still in her hands.

"Madame," she said eagerly to Françoise Derbanne, "it was the bourbon that made him sick, not the sugar."

Suzette's words fell into the damp, dead air and hung there. Each of the three stood rooted in the cookhouse, the white woman's lips reducing to an astonished slim line, the black woman's face turning in on itself, her eyes closing briefly, and the suddenly uncertain little cocoa-colored girl letting her arms fall limply to her side. A fly buzzed sluggishly toward the open doorway.

Françoise Derbanne's eyes flickered hot. She turned, took three quick steps toward Suzette, and slapped her hard with her green-gloved hand across the right side of her face, fingers spread wide.

She squinted at Elisabeth. "I won't be contradicted," she said, her voice wavering slightly. "You need to teach the girl her place." She wheeled around and walked deliberately out of the cookhouse.

Françoise Derbanne had never slapped Suzette in the face before, and it took a moment for her to start to cry. After the first startled tears, she looked toward her mother, who continued working the ball of dough.

"I didn't mean to be bad, *Mère.*"

Elisabeth sprinkled more flour on the worktable and roughly pulled down the rolling pin. "Your little-girl days are done." At first her tone provided no opening, but then it softened. "Come over here, Suzette."

Suzette obeyed slowly, sniffling.

A single plump tear stood perched on the high ridge of Suzette's cheek, refusing to drop to the red outline below where Madame had slapped her. Elisabeth reached over and with her broad thumb pushed the wetness away, leaving a thin trace of white flour in its place.

"*Mère?*"

Elisabeth had returned to her dough, humming.

Suzette felt the stinging on her face, the heat of the fires, the stickiness of her shift against her skin. She stared at the old burn spot shaped like a quarter moon on the inside of her mother's exposed arm, fascinated by how perfectly the tips curved in toward each other. She was tempted to reach out and touch it.

"How many times have I told you to keep that mouth from running?" Elisabeth said. "There's lots worse than slapping." She didn't often look angry, but now she pounded at the dough as if she were scrubbing clothes on the washboard.

"It wasn't fair," Suzette said stubbornly.

"There is no fair. Just do your work, Suzette."

Suzette went back to the churn. Der-banne. Der-banne. The paddle resisted more with each movement until she had butter. She spooned it out, rocking herself in place where she stood, her face settling into a dull ache, while Elisabeth's big wooden rolling pin gave out stubborn squeaks with each pass over the dough.

"*Mère,* I finished the butter."

"Is the table set?"

"*Oui.*"

"Then come watch," Elisabeth said. "Your time's coming soon enough to make the biscuits."

This seemed like safer ground to Suzette, and she held on to it. "Can I help you today if Mam'zelle Oreline doesn't need me?"

Elizabeth showed the beginnings of a rare smile, partially exposing the gap between her two front teeth, a gap that matched Suzette's own.

"I'm going to make you a little secret peach cobbler for your birthday tomorrow. No telling anybody else, even Mam'zelle." Elisabeth reached out and touched Suzette's arm, insistent, the almost smile fading. "Understand?" she said. "Not even Mam'zelle."

Suzette nodded. "Should I run and get more peaches?" she asked.

"First use those young legs to go get me some more sugar. One extra cup and we'll make sure this peach cobbler bubbles up nice and sweet for Mam'zelle Oreline."

The ache had faded from her cheek by the time Suzette served the breakfast of tamales, tortillas, sausages, blood pudding, and biscuits to the Derbannes and their visiting houseguests. They were ten around the long dining room table, and the adults seemed in high spirits. She dished the sausages out of the platter for everyone around the table, coming last to Oreline's cousin Narcisse Fredieu, a pudgy boy with light brown hair thick clumped in waves hugging his head.

Suzette stayed close to the table, hoping to hear the Derbannes and the Fredieus talk about St. Augustine. For a long while the breakfast conversation meandered lazily from the price of cotton and old people's ailments to the poison grass creeping up from the marsh, what the weather was likely to be, and the heavy responsibilities of the planter class. She'd heard all of that before.

"I tell you, brother, the seating arrangement is improper at St. Augustine. White sitting behind colored," Narcisse's mother complained. "We were meant for better."

Suzette waited to see what would happen next. Oreline had told her that the Fredieus were not exactly *de la fine fleur des pois,* not the most select blooms of the sweet-pea blossom, and the marriage of Narcisse's mother to a Fredieu had been below her place. On many of their visits Suzette had overheard Narcisse's mother, a Derbanne, talk about her family's quality, with history and distinction in the bloodline. She passed on her family stories, bold and proud tales of the original French settlers in Louisiana. She was silent on the subject of the Fredieus' background.

"They reserve the eight rows for their betters, sister," Louis responded. "Only Augustine's family is in front. He did pay for the church, after all."

Françoise cleared her throat to speak. "We should go to the Natchitoches church," she said, and her voice rose slightly. "It dismays me to have to consort so closely with the *gens de couleur libre.*"

Suzette knew she really meant her godmother, Doralise. Even the mention of Doralise Derbanne could trigger an ugly mood in Françoise. Louis Derbanne had freed Doralise when she was still a nursing baby, acknowledging her so openly as his daughter that she had taken his last name as her own, even in public, making it impossible for Françoise Derbanne to deny the obvious, as she had done with the others. Suzette's godmother, her *marraine*, occupied a middle place, not as high as the white Derbannes or the Fredieus and not as low as any of those she sponsored as godmother from the house or the quarter. She was a woman of color, and free.

All eyes at the table shifted from Françoise to Louis Derbanne. He looked the part of the older-generation Creole French planter, from his pomaded thinning gray hair to his black suit and riding boots. The role had been handed to him whole on the day he was born. "We have had this conversation before," he said. "I will not drive all the way to Natchitoches when there is a perfectly acceptable chapel on the river."

Françoise gave ground in the face of opposition from her husband. "With the infidel Creoles around Cane River, we were lucky our eight rows were half-full."

"I understand your discomfort, my dear, but the best church is a church nearby." Louis waved Suzette over for more blood pudding, and she hurried to his place at the head of the table.

"At least St. Augustine draws the best of the *gens de couleur libre*," Françoise conceded. "They do have the proper respect for whites so crucial for the smooth running of a community. Thank goodness they don't consider themselves white, but they certainly don't consider themselves Negro, either."

The children at the table, including Oreline and Narcisse, sat quiet, as demanded, listening to the adults talk, joining in only for the singing after the meal.

Midday the Fredieus left Rosedew to return to their own plantation.

Later that evening Suzette helped Oreline undress for bed.

"Mam'zelle Oreline, would you teach me reading?"

"I cannot, Suzette. You must stop asking. You know as well as I do that you are not allowed. Besides, it is no good for you to try to learn something so hard. Your ideas are wicked."

"Just a few words? My name?"

"I will not," Oreline insisted.

"What if we don't tell?"

"No. Aunt Françoise would be very angry if she found out. Why would you want to read, anyway? Even Aunt Françoise doesn't know how."

Suzette stopped to consider. The Derbannes had taken Oreline in when her parents died, and Oreline would never disobey either Françoise or Louis. Still, she persisted. "In church today, I could not follow what the priest said."

"He talks most of the time in Latin," Oreline said. "Nobody understands."

"But I want to take communion. Old Bertram went inside the church today, like everyone else."

"You do not have to know how to read to take communion. I can ask Aunt Françoise to give her permission for you to take classes when I do. Besides, I will always be around if there is something to be read."

Oreline gave Suzette a secret, reassuring side glance when Françoise came in to lead the two girls in bedtime prayers. "Aunt Françoise, can Suzette take communion with me?"

Françoise looked from one girl to the other. "First communion is not until you are twelve, and requires serious study to get ready."

"I would help her," said Oreline.

"Your behavior today did not show you as a very good follower of Christ, Suzette," Françoise said. "You have failed to be properly obedient."

"I can be good, Madame Françoise. I do want to take communion, like Mam'zelle Oreline. Old Bertram told me he was confirmed when he was a boy."

"We will see how you conduct yourself." Françoise sat in the cane-bottom chair beside the four-poster bed, perched tentatively, as if prepared for any turn of events. "Oreline, tonight you will start to learn the Lord's Prayer."

Oreline repeated each passage after her aunt, and then Françoise kissed her niece lightly on the forehead. "When you are ready to be confirmed, you will wear a beautiful white dress and a veil, and I will get you your own rosary beads." Françoise looked to Suzette, standing near the foot of the bed. "And you, Suzette. If you apply yourself, you can rise above your mother and the others in the quarter." She straightened her skirts and prepared to retire to her own room. "Time for bed. Good night."

Suzette made her rounds of the big house, pulling the drapes, emptying the spittoons, and gathering everyone's dirty laundry. She checked on each member of the household to see if they needed her for anything before she returned to Oreline's room, where she blew out the candles and pulled out her pallet from under the bed.

Early the next morning, on her ninth birthday, before the household stirred, she made her way to Françoise Derbanne's favorite rosebush.

2

CANE RIVER, LOUISIANA—1837

Suzette felt the weight of the rosary alongside her lucky strip of cowhide, safely sheltered in her apron pocket. If her hands hadn't been covered with butter, she would have taken a moment to finger the beads again, memorizing their shapes and sizes. She stood opposite her mother across the worktable in the cookhouse, her hands almost as fast as Elisabeth's as she greased several baking pans.

"That dress turned out fine," Elisabeth said, and smiled. "Change right after breakfast."

It was as if her mother were the one who had just had her first communion, not Suzette. As if it were Elisabeth who had studied the Lord's Prayer and the catechism side by side with Oreline and Narcisse and twenty-one other twelve-year-olds from Cane River at the hands of unforgiving nuns to prepare for this big day.

"I wish you could have seen me at St. Augustine, *Mère*," Suzette said.

Elisabeth sniffed. "Plenty to do here."

"All the girls had on long white dresses and veils, and all the boys had on black suits. My dress was just as good as the others. Outside, in front of the church, Madame Françoise gave Mam'zelle Oreline and me our own rosaries, with pretty white beads and a silver chain. I get to keep it always, she said so. And the bishop came all the way from New Orleans to give us our first communion, and he had a big ring on his finger, and we marched into the church in a line with our candles lit, and I got to go inside the church along with everyone else, at the back, and the bishop came down to the altar rail and gave us the body and blood of Christ, and I took the wafer under my tongue just like we practiced, and didn't spill any of the wine even though I shook a little, and I was so nervous, but I did it perfect, and—"

"Slow yourself down, girl," Elisabeth said. "You have the whole day for telling while we get the place ready for the food and dancing tonight."

"It's called a *soirée dansante*, *Mère*. Remember, I told you before?"

Even her mother's deliberate refusal to call things by their proper names could not interfere with Suzette's outlook on the world today.

"Separate whites and yolks of about six of those eggs," Elisabeth said, using her apron to wipe the beads of perspiration from her forehead. "Who was there?"

"M'sieu and Madame. M'sieu held Madame's arm as

they went into the church, but it was more like she was holding him up. They told me that I had grown into a respectful young woman."

Suzette was so preoccupied with her cooking and the telling that she didn't see her mother push her lips together tight.

"And the Fredieus were there for Narcisse. And the Mulons came for Nicolas."

"I see how you look at the Mulon boy. Don't get to thinking they'll mix with us."

Suzette felt her cheeks go warm, thinking of the scrap of cowhide pushed deep into her apron pocket. "Nicolas has always been nice to me," she said primly.

"There's nice that's how neighbors do and nice that you can hang some part of a life on. Even if Nicolas had a pull in your direction, his family wouldn't stand for it."

Suzette could not pinpoint exactly when it was that her mother had turned so full of doom, but some days it was almost impossible to listen to her and not talk back. As if Suzette didn't know the *gens de couleur libre* chose free women to marry so that the children would be born free. Nicolas was different, more like her godmother, Doralise. They were both free people of color, but they never looked past her as if she were not really there.

Whenever she saw Nicolas it was as if everything around her drifted out of focus except for him, and she had a difficult time doing the simplest things. Nicolas was following in his father's trade of shoemaker, and she saw him when he made the deliveries to Rosedew or when they met at St. Augustine to study for first communion. She had known Nicolas since they were both children, but in the last few months something had changed. When she asked him how he made shoes, he had brought her a small scrap of cowhide to show the untanned leather he and his father worked from. Since it was a discard, he'd let her keep it. Now she found herself at odd moments wondering what it would be like to run her fingers over the freckles that criss-crossed his cheeks or to dance the waltz with him, which would mean she would be so close that she would have to tilt her head just so and look up at him. Nicolas always spoke kindly to her at St. Augustine or when she saw him on his horse on the road. She had to put forth a great deal of effort to speak to him, and afterward she always felt as if she had embarrassed herself somehow, or at least had not shown herself off very well. Nicolas's very presence made her voice small and her knees unpredictable. Suzette knew her mother couldn't possibly understand. She didn't understand it herself.

"*Marraine* Doralise wasn't born free," Suzette said, "but she's free now and was married in a church."

"M'sieu had his own reasons to make her free and set her up to marry."

"You asked her to stand up and be my godmother when I was born, and she did," Suzette persisted. "The *gens de couleur libre* are not all the same."

"Pay attention to your work. We don't have time to let those rolls rise again if you mess them up now." Elisabeth pursed her lips and shook her head. "Who else was there this morning?"

"*Marraine* Doralise and Monsieur Philippe were there for Elisida, and *Marraine* came over to congratulate me when Madame stepped away. I told you she is not like the rest."

Elisabeth let it pass. "How did Philippe look?"

"He did all right in the chapel, but after the ceremony he followed Doralise out to the road and screamed in her face, in front of everyone. His brother had to pull him away. Nicolas says Monsieur Philippe acts the fool even in front of white folks now. Elisida looked like she was going to cry. I felt sorry for her, even if she does think she is better than everybody else."

"Don't be so eager to judge, Suzette. You can't tell how heavy somebody else's load is just from looking. The Lord doesn't give us more than we can carry, but he's putting it to the test with Madame Doralise. A shame, with M'sieu Philippe coming from such a good family."

"Even Narcisse was nice to Elisida after that," Suzette said.

"That boy always has been a puzzle," Elisabeth said, "both sides of a coin at the same time. Sweet and helpful, or spoiled and full of himself. No telling which way he'll turn out."

"Mam'zelle Oreline said in the wagon on the way back that we should think about becoming nuns," Suzette said.

Elisabeth cocked her head to one side. "Mam'zelle doesn't know what she wants."

"I know what I want." Suzette thought of Nicolas. "I want to stand up in St. Augustine in a white dress and get married the way *Marraine* Doralise did." Daydreaming about the white dress always brought Nicolas to mind, standing next to her. "But it doesn't matter," Suzette said petulantly. "What could I do anyway if Mam'zelle wanted something else?"

Elisabeth wiped her hands on her apron and looked hard into Suzette's eyes.

"You do whatever you can think of to protect you and

yours. You're better than most at getting along with the folks up to the house. Too good, maybe."

The two worked in silence for a while.

"Those dresses came out fine," Elisabeth began again in a conciliatory tone. "You should let Gerasíme see how you look."

"You just want me to go down to the quarter."

"The big house isn't all there is. Your people are in the quarter."

"It is too dirty down there. Papa can see the dress tonight at the party. Mam'zelle is going to wear hers, too."

"Suzette, you'll be serving, not dancing. Your gingham will do."

"Madame Françoise already said I could wear it."

Elisabeth stopped whipping the eggs in the bowl and leaned across to Suzette, speaking slowly and deliberately, each word snapping like bedsheets drying on the line in a biting wind.

"I'm glad you're getting on so well with the Derbannes, but you have a mother and a father both, and they don't live up to the house. You come on out of your head and see how things really are. Any of us could be sold tomorrow. Praise the Lord it hasn't happened yet to our family here on Rosedew, but that doesn't mean it can't."

Suzette kept her head down and her tongue quiet, but she seethed inside at how her mother was purposely trying to ruin her big day. She didn't understand why her mother couldn't see that she wanted something better. That she had the chance to be more than her father, sisters, and brother, who were already getting ground down going into the field every day. More than her mother, who didn't practice the way that Suzette did to sound like the Ones with Last Names, who still clung to her old-timey religion when no one was around. Just today Suzette was the only slave from Rosedew to take first communion in a real church, one of only a handful from Cane River who was-n't either white or free, and she had marched into St. Augustine with the rest. Couldn't her mother see she had a bigger future in store?

Elisabeth had not finished. "You only have one family, and not everybody gets that. Think about where you want to put trust. Reaching too deep into something not meant for you is full of pain. Figure out what you can have and work on that. *You only get one family.*" Her mother looked fierce. "Now do your work, Suzette."

*　*　*

Sunday night was perfect for the Derbanne party. It was dry and crisp, lit up bright by a full moon, lanterns, and high spirits. The first flurry of guests arrived, their cheeks flushed from the cold and anticipation, shedding their overcoats and wraps, eager to show off their party finery. Elisabeth and Suzette had fixed a double pot of steaming gumbo, and a whole pig in a pit had been slow roasting since the night before.

The dancing began in earnest soon after the food was served. Wide cypress planks had been laid down in the barn as a dance floor, and the boards strained under the weight of Creoles young and old dancing to Gerasíme's tunes. Suzette watched from the sidelines as the carefree couples spun, her feet aching to join them as she circled the room to serve food or drink or clean up spills.

It was too cold to stay outdoors, and the house was not large enough for all of the friends the Derbannes had invited, so the party was held in stages, from the big house to the barn and several points in between. The guests danced set after set of the quadrille waltz, until only the most hardy were able to negotiate the dance floor.

The week had been filled with hundreds of big and small orders coming Suzette's way, from Françoise, Elisabeth, and Oreline as well as the priest. It had been exhausting and thrilling, practicing for first communion, the ceremony in the church, all of the planning for the big party tonight, the cooking, scrubbing, helping Oreline practice the steps to the quadrille waltz, getting her confident enough to make a public dancing appearance. Oreline had kissed Suzette on the cheek earlier that afternoon and declared herself ready.

Just a few feet away, Suzette watched Narcisse and Oreline taking their place among the young adults of French Cane River society. Narcisse was on his most exemplary behavior tonight, pulled between two of the things he loved best, food and dance. He had grown taller and thinner in the last few months and was playing the perfect gentleman with his cousin Oreline, initiating small talk, making sure she danced, bringing her food and punch.

As the party wore on and the night turned cooler, Narcisse gestured Suzette over to where he stood surrounded by his cousins in the barn.

Her heart skipped, and she rushed over to them.

"Girl, go get Cousin Azelie her wrap. Don't dawdle."

Suzette stood a moment too long, unmoving.

"Go on," Narcisse said, his voice impatient.

Girl. As if they had never played together and shared secrets. As if they had not all taken their first communion together that morning.

Suzette glanced over to where Oreline sat, but Oreline

had fixed her gaze to a spot on the opposite wall, as if she couldn't hear.

Gerasíme played another quadrille. Sounds of excited talk and laughter mixed with the steady patter of metered feet on the cypress planks.

Suzette turned toward the house. There was nothing to do but fetch the wrap.

They had cleared out the minor furniture and pulled up the rugs to make room for dancing inside, pushing small tables toward the wall for checkers, backgammon, dominoes, ramps, and *maroc*, especially for the older men whose dancing days had wound down. The guests were mostly the usual from Cane River, extended family and neighbors, but there were a few fresh faces.

The star of the evening was Eugene Daurat, newly arrived from France. He was short and neatly dressed, had startling black eyes and the smallest feet Suzette had ever seen on a man. His dark brown hair was slicked down to one side and tucked behind his tiny ears, and he smiled at everyone he was introduced to, as if it gave him the greatest pleasure to be alive in a world that had dancing in it. He was a curious fellow, his pale skin the dull white of goat's milk. He seemed to Suzette to be a little doll man. He was some sort of relation to Françoise from the Rachal side. To Suzette, Eugene was brand-new. She found herself pulled to wherever he was, to try to get another look at those eyes without seeming to look at him directly.

Louis was an impressive host, welcoming everyone, full of good cheer. Suzette circled around one more time in the front room with her tray of special hors d'oeuvres, and Louis called her over.

"You better try one of these crab cakes," he announced to the collection of men gathered around him. "Our girl Suzette makes the finest dipping sauce this side of the Mississippi River."

He turned and spoke another language to a tall, thin man with light hair and a wispy beard, a distant cousin of the Derbannes' from Virginia, and the two men had a private laugh. The bearded man could only smile and gesture to the others, and he stayed close to Louis, the only one among them who could talk with him in English. The cousin reminded Suzette of her older sister Palmire, deaf and dumb since birth, neither of them able to make themselves understood in a group except through signals or translators. Still, the man seemed to be enjoying himself, drinking and dancing with the rest.

"What other delights have you and Elisabeth cooked up?" Louis asked Suzette.

Suzette could tell by his tone, but even more by the flush in his cheeks and the color of his nose, that Louis was in the mischievous stage of his evening drinking.

The doll man looked directly at her and grinned, a white, dazzling smile that showed his square, even teeth, and he held her gaze. Suzette took her tray of crab cakes and backed out of the room to cover her confusion.

When some of the older men retired to their brandy and cigars around the backroom fireplace, Suzette followed to serve. It was less painful than going back outside where Oreline and Narcisse were. These men had done their obligatory turn on the dance floor and now were settled in for camaraderie and companionship with other French Creole planters, leaving the more active entertainment to their children, grandchildren, nieces, and nephews. Both the doll man and the English-speaking cousin had been invited to sit with them.

Louis Derbanne settled into his leather chair and called for cigars, which Suzette retrieved. Suzette lit Louis's cigar first, watching his spotted hands, always in slight motion the way the highest branches looked in the pecan tree when the trunk was being shaken to get the nuts to fall.

"You'll see the sense of our ways, the advantages of how we do things, after you've been here awhile, Eugene," Louis said, continuing some earlier conversation. "The plantation is the fulfillment of God's design."

Suzette knew what came next, having heard so many of Louis Derbanne's monologues that her mind could fly ahead to the pauses. By the tone, she knew this was his "our burden is heavy" speech, but she listened carefully anyway in case there were clues about the doll man.

"You're a merchant at heart, Eugene, too new to this country to understand our way of life yet. We have a responsibility here that we take seriously. The Lord almighty blesses our system, and we do what is best for everyone. Our black family could not survive on their own. We have to protect them, as much from themselves as from others. We feed and clothe them, and take care of all their needs when they are too young, too old, or too sick to work.

"Slavery is the only workable system for cotton production, as good for our Negroes as it is for the whites. We took them out of Africa and lifted them up. The planters set the tone for the rest. Our burden is heavy."

Louis shook his head sadly.

"There are some who do not exercise good sense,

treating their Negroes worse than their oxen, but that's just a handful, ignorant enough to damage their own property. Not one of mine ever gets more than twenty lashes without my permission. Not like on McAlpin's place, where one of his boys almost bled out from the beating he gave him last month. The church teaches us they have souls, and they have to be faithfully led."

They talked as if Suzette were not in the room, refilling glasses, stoking the fire, emptying spittoons. She felt Eugene Daurat's bold eyes on her, so she made herself small, careful not to make any response or acknowledgment of his stare.

A little before midnight Eugene called for the wine he had brought for his host. Suzette carried the gift bottle and eight fresh glasses on a silver tray to the circle of planters, placing them in front of the doll man. Earlier in the evening he had uncorked the bottle with great fanfare, and now he waved her away, choosing to do the pouring himself.

It was an 1825 Bordeaux, Château Lafite Rothschild, a vintage wine of early harvest that he had brought from France. Eugene poured, and Suzette took the silver tray around to the men in the room until each held a wineglass.

"To new beginnings in a land of opportunity," Eugene toasted, and they all raised the wine to their lips.

Suzette turned to tend the fire as they once again fell to casual conversation.

"So, Eugene, as a well-traveled man, what do you think of this wine?" Louis Derbanne asked contentedly, balancing the half-empty wineglass in one hand. "I confess to being more of a bourbon man myself."

Eugene directed his attention to his host, raising his

eyes from twelve-year-old Suzette's back as she poked at the red embers of the fire and added another log to the failing flames.

"This Bordeaux caused a great deal of excitement in France," the doll man said. "Look at the lovely color." He held the wineglass closer to the lamp, allowing the flame to bring out the intensity of the crimson liquid.

"It has a ravishing bouquet, and a flavor to match. I confess an 1825 Lafite may still be a bit young, but sometimes it can be difficult to wait," he said.

Christmas Day was dry and chilly. The crop had been a good one this year, in a succession of very good years, and the talk of the quarter for the prior two weeks had turned to what the gifts would likely be. It was certain that there would be the big contest for the best cuts of beef, and one bottle of liquor for each man, and new blankets, but they couldn't guess the surprise. They speculated that whatever it was would be store-bought since no one from the house or the field had had a hand in its preparation. Maybe broad-cloth for new trousers or seed for their gardens.

The week between Christmas and New Year's would pass without any heavy fieldwork. Only music and food, singing, dancing, and drinking. Visiting, fishing, courting, and sleeping-in until after the sun was already up. Friends and family gathering in the light of daytime. Mothers nurs-ing their babies according to the baby's need instead of the plantation bell. Traveling to other plantations to see family. The luxury of planning. Planning the flow of each day for one full week.

No cotton would be planted, hoed, or picked. When the plantation bell sounded, it would mark the passage of time, but it would not begin the march to the north field before sunrise. No backs stooped over this week except to work a personal patch or bend over a checkerboard. No long sack hung around the neck to drag between endless rows of cotton plants. No weighing of each basket at twilight to measure performance against quota. No bold script recording one hundred and seventy-five pounds next to the name *Palmire* in the big plantation book. Two hundred and three for Gerasíme. Forty-six for Solataire, just starting out at the age of eleven as a one-quarter hand.

Suzette wiped her forehead with the back of her sleeve while she threw pine chips into the cookhouse fireplace. The flames spat and burned hotter.

"Christmas morning, and we're the only ones working," she grumbled under her breath.

"Don't try to match up one misery against another," Elisabeth said. "Field or house, we're all in the same web, waiting for the spider to get home."

Elisabeth never broke her rhythm as she stirred the batter for griddle cakes. She had spent the night down in the quarter with Gerasíme and was in a very good mood. "Besides, that's no talk for Christmas," she went on. "This is the Lord's day."

If Suzette was cheerful, her mother's response was likely to be full of gloom. If Suzette was sulky, it would be something full of false hope and cheer. But even as she was complaining, Suzette's heart wasn't really in it. Tonight was the big quarter Christmas party at Rosedew.

Some of the slaves owned by their smaller neighbors would be coming, including the three from François Mulon's farm. Suzette wished that Nicolas would come, but the *gens de couleur libre* kept to their own for social occasions. It seemed to Suzette that Nicolas saved his smiles for her since their communion classes, and she certainly saved her thoughts for him. She still kept the scrap of cowhide he had given her close at hand, most times in her apron pocket or hidden beneath her pallet. Nicolas had dreams, planning to have his own place along Cane River by hiring himself out. But Nicolas or no, Suzette intended to have fun tonight.

Only thirteen, Suzette had already sold some of her baking along Cane River. She had even been rented out once to the Rachal place for one of their big parties. She sometimes sneaked her cooking to her family, but tonight they could enjoy their treats out in the open, without the risk of being caught.

Determined to make this Christmas feast the best yet on Rosedew, she and Elisabeth had been cooking for days. They would serve up portions for the Derbannes separately, but the rest was for the tables that had been set up in the barn, where the entire quarter would gather. On Christmas Day everyone could have as much to eat as they wanted.

Suzette did a few sample steps of the waltz with an elaborate dip at the end in her mother's direction. Elisabeth laughed, and peace was restored.

"Can I wear my first communion dress for the party?" Suzette asked.

"I hope it still fits," Elisabeth said. "You're growing more curves every day."

"I heard M'sieu Louis talking to M'sieu Eugene Daurat,"

Suzette said. "He said the week off between Christmas and New Year's is just a way to make the hands more manageable the rest of the year. To let them blow off steam so they don't get ideas about running."

"Let *us* blow off steam," Elisabeth corrected. "We're all in the same web."

"Anyway, he invited M'sieu Eugene to come to the big contest."

"Suzette, I want you to stay away from that little man as much as you can. Try not to be alone with him."

"He means no harm, *Mère*."

"The man already struts around this place like he owns it. Like everything here is his for the taking. Tell me you'll take care."

Eugene had been nice to Suzette, always had an easy smile for her.

"Yes, *Mère*."

"We're ready," Elisabeth said, making one last inspection of the griddle. "Let's go on up to the house."

There was a small crowd from the quarter outside of the big house. Gerasíme, hair wild and eyes alert, drew his jacket tighter around his body against the chill. He had chosen a place nearest the front door to stand, and his children, Palmire, Apphia, and Solataire, flanked him. Suzette and Elisabeth headed toward them.

"First light come and gone," Gerasíme said when he saw Elisabeth. "They're starting late."

As if on cue, Louis, Françoise, and Oreline came out onto the front gallery still in their nightclothes. Louis rubbed his eyes and yawned.

"What are you all doing here?" he asked gruffly.

"Christmas gifts," they shouted back in one voice.

"Surely it isn't Christmas already?"

Gerasíme spoke up. "M'sieu, it surely is."

Louis looked doubtful and slowly drew his fingers through his hair.

"I may have something I could find to give," he said at last, and with a great flourish he drew the cover off the makeshift table set up against the front of the house.

Underneath were forty-eight Christmas stockings, each filled with nuts, oranges, apples, pecan candy, and a ten-hole harmonica for each hand over the age of five. As they came forward to receive their stocking, Louis greeted each by name. All men got a jug of whiskey, each woman a length of muslin and gabardine, and everyone received their new blanket for the year.

Suzette and Elisabeth slipped away while Louis was still handing out gifts and began to serve up the breakfast of scrambled eggs, smoked ham, flapjacks with cane syrup, and café noir. There was to be an uninterrupted flow of food of every description all day long, and it would be considered a sad failure if anyone left the tables hungry.

By the time Louis, François, Oreline, and Eugene Daurat made their appearance at the annual celebration in the quarter, dressed in their finery, the party had been going for some time. By custom they knew not to stay too long. Heaping platters of meat, vegetables, breads, and sweets were arranged on makeshift tables. Gumbo waited in the heavy black kettle steaming over an open fire. Old Bertram carved pieces from the crackling porker barbecuing in a deep pit.

"Time for the big contest," Louis announced, leading the way to one side of the barn. "Who's first?"

"Old Bertram's the oldest," came the shout back.

They cleared a path, and Old Bertram came forward. Louis handed him a bow and arrow.

Outlined on the side of the barn in charcoal was the crudely drawn picture of a cow, and Old Bertram drew back the arrow and let it fly. The point made a soft *thunk,* landing near the top of the cow image's tail.

"Looks like Old Bertram gets tail stew," Gerasíme said, laughing.

"I call that close enough for rump roast," Louis said.

Old Bertram looked very pleased with himself. He would get to keep a piece of the meat from that section of the cow to be slaughtered the next day.

"See if you can do better," Old Bertram sniffed, giving up the bow and arrow to Gerasíme.

Gerasíme took aim, and his arrow tip landed squarely in the center.

"Short loin!" Louis called out, and the crowd whistled and cheered.

Some of the men had gotten such a head start on the whiskey, they had trouble hitting the target at all on the first try.

After the big contest, Gerasíme picked up his fiddle and the dancing began. Suzette watched her mother with delight. Elisabeth danced in the clearing with the others, her good lace scarf pulled across her shoulders and tied neatly in front of her ample chest, first flying up and then falling down with each movement. Eyes wide and full of spirit, she picked up her long skirt to give her feet more maneuvering room, looking at her partners but more often over at Gerasíme, playing his fiddle under the oak tree. Elisabeth smiled and winked at Gerasíme, broadly, in front of the entire quarter, in front of the Derbannes and their guests, and Gerasíme winked back.

Suzette found herself responding to the gaiety of the music, finally getting her chance to dance. She pulled first one and then another into the center of the dance floor, teaching anyone who didn't know the steps and wanted to learn. She danced the quadrille waltz and the *fais do do,* while her father played the fiddle. The *fais do do* was her favorite, with six couples taking the lead from Gerasíme as he called the figures in French faster and faster in a contest between dancer and musician.

The dancers leaned on one another in exhaustion when the number was over, laughing and panting, hearts racing, adrenaline left over. Suzette closed her eyes, and she could see herself in her white dress in the chapel at St. Augustine with Nicolas beside her. When she opened her eyes, Eugene Daurat was staring at her fixedly, familiarity in his gaze, as if there were some secret between them. Suzette pulled her eyes away from his, her confusion laced with a trace of shame, although she knew she had done nothing wrong. The music started up again, and her little brother, Solataire, tugged at her hand to dance.

After the set finished she decided to take herself away from the noise and closeness for a moment. The party would go on until almost dawn.

"You are a wonderful partner, brother," she said to Solataire with a fond smile. "I am counting on another dance as soon as I return." She had not felt so free since she was a child.

It was a crisp December evening, cold enough for Suzette to see traces of her own breath on the frosty air, but she had worked up a sweat. She headed off dreamily through the woods to cool off and to think in peace about the things tugging at her mind. Her family. Nicolas.

It was a relief not to be under the watchful eye of so many masters in the big house, and for once Suzette felt grateful to be surrounded by people who looked like her. Living in the big house had made her forget this other self. She had been ashamed by the way her mother talked, the coarse clothes her sisters wore. All the distance and embarrassment had been forgotten tonight, until she'd looked over Solataire's shoulder and caught herself in the mirror of Eugene Daurat's eyes.

She walked sure-footed through the thick mass of pine trees, all the way down to her thinking rock on the bank of Cane River, a place she had found a few years past, after Oreline grew into more confidence and stopped pulling at her every minute.

As Suzette looked off across the river, standing by her rock, she heard the soft squish of boots against mud, signaling a man's approach. Someone had followed her to her secret place.

"Ah, *ma chère,* I thought you would never stop walking," Eugene Daurat said as he emerged from the woods, slightly out of breath.

"I'm going right back." Suzette glanced nervously in the direction of the party, as if she could wish herself back to the center of the dance floor, surrounded by other people. "I just came away from the party to cool off."

"And are you so cool already?"

"It felt good to walk, M'sieu Eugene."

"Better for the young than for those of us who are older, I'm afraid," he said. "That's a pretty dress. A little thin for this time of year, but you make it look just right. If you are cold, I could lend you my coat."

"I think I should get back now, M'sieu." Her voice sounded thin and tinny to her own ears.

"Just stay here with me for a little bit until I catch my breath. I might not be able to find my way back without you."

The frightful pounding behind Suzette's small breasts would not slow its pace. She wanted to run but was afraid of insulting such a close friend of the master and mistress's. And he had said her dress was pretty.

"The music will guide you back."

"Just give me a minute, Suzette."

He sat on the rock, in no particular hurry.

"You seem different tonight than you do in the house," Eugene said. "Why is that?"

"Mam'zelle Oreline and I practiced the steps of the quadrille for the soirée last summer. I hadn't had a chance to dance them so much before."

"I see. You dance them as well as any I've seen. Even in France."

"Really?"

"*Oui*. When I saw you dance, you reminded me of my home in France. A town called Bordeaux. I miss it."

Suzette was curious. "Why would I remind you of France, M'sieu Eugene?"

"In France, they are full of life. You are full of life." Eugene patted a spot next to him on the rock. "Come, sit next to me for a moment."

What was she supposed to say? What was she supposed to do? Was he making fun of her? Did the Derbannes know he was here with her, talking like this? Suzette edged closer toward the rock. "It isn't right, M'sieu Eugene. I can just stand."

"Nonsense," Eugene said. "You're cold. No more discussion. Come here."

Suzette cautiously balanced herself on the far flat edge of the rock, sitting but leaning away from the doll man.

Eugene moved closer to Suzette and put his coat around her. "I think you are so vibrant, Suzette. So full of joie de vivre. You make me forget myself."

She was trembling and could think of nothing to say.

"The Derbannes say you are a good Catholic girl. Maybe you weren't thinking so much of the church when you were dancing tonight, eh? You have babies yet, little Suzette?"

"No, M'sieu." Babies? Babies were for after she and Nicolas Mulon made plans.

The moon's rays shimmering on the water's surface broke in odd places, confusing her. She felt rooted to this spot, Eugene now sitting by her side on her special rock, his arm around her shoulder. It wasn't real, being talked to in such soft tones by a white man with a last name. He shifted his position and rested his hand on her knee, as if it were his right. Would it show poor upbringing to protest? To run? Suzette stared at Eugene Daurat's little feet, unwilling to bring her eyes up any farther than that. Casually he reached under her dress, under her bloomers, his hand cold and deliberate against her bare skin. She heard the sound of his jagged breathing and smelled the sharpness of liquor as it oozed from his pores.

"Lay back, Suzette."

"I am a good girl, M'sieu."

"Yes, I am sure you are."

His voice didn't sound the same, as if it were coming from somewhere lower and deeper as he pressed her back onto the unforgiving rock. He moved above her, making strange noises in his throat while he undid the buttons of his britches with his free hand. He was heavy for a man so small. Everything was moving slowly, as if it had nothing at all to do with her. Like during a bad storm when the water rose on the river so fast that you could only watch it spill the banks, and nothing any man did could stop it. He moved back and forth, back and forth, pinning her, and she froze in the inescapable certainty of the moment. Nicolas, she thought unexpectedly. Nicolas should come and pull the doll man away, take her back to the party, ask her to dance; but try as she might she could conjure up only his name and not the kindness of Nicolas's face. Eugene's knee pried her open and he pushed into her, delivering pain to a central place. He stayed on top of her, dead weight grinding her hip and shoulder into the rock, catching his breath as if he had run a long race, forcing her to breathe in the flat smell of brandy and cigars that escaped from him as she could not.

"*Merci, ma chère,*" he said raggedly, but he still didn't move.

When at last he got up from her, careful not to get mud on himself, he looked away and busied himself straightening his clothes.

"You'd better go back now and join the party," he said.

It was over. Suzette looked down, and even in the dull moonlight she could see that her beautiful white dress was streaked with traces of scarlet. She would need to wash it out in secret, she thought, make sure her mother never saw the stains. She needed to figure out how to change her dress and go back to the party before she was missed, what to do next. She wanted to ask the doll man his advice. The cold of the night pressed in as she waited for him to initiate some further connection, but he made no move toward her, had nothing else to say. Uncertain, with Eugene's back still to her, she forced herself up and started to walk in the direction of the music, listening for a sound, any sound, that would tell her the proper thing to do. There were party noises in the distance, festive sounds. She heard night calls from the woods, skittering creatures out prowling for food or trying to avoid becoming some bigger prey's next meal. There were river noises, gentle and soothing, as the edges of the water lapped at the red banks of the shore in a centuries-old ceremony of give-and-take.

But all that Suzette could make out was a sound just this side of hearing, like dreams drifting out of reach, slight as a soft spring wind.

The March winds arrived with an abrupt ferocity, buffeting the land and the workers in the field with equal determination. Before daybreak each morning the quarter emptied out and labor gangs split off and headed in separate directions, some holding down their hats, others with the wind whipping at the hems of their long, threadbare skirts. A set went off to the east, leading the oxen to lip up the cotton lots and to prepare the new season's beds for corn and potatoes. Another took off to the west to burn logs, shrub, and cut down last year's cornstalks. Even the quarter hands and half hands were pressed into service until dusk to pick up and clear the spent cornstalks or gather the manure behind the animals. By first weeding four weeks later, a hint of the coming warmth had begun to work its way inside the chill of the heavy Louisiana air.

Suzette stayed low in the bushes and watched her sister

Palmire and the other hoe women off in the distance, trudging out to the fields, balancing their heavy hoes over their shoulders. First light from the rising sun glinted off the heads of the hoes, broad as shovels and hammered out of pig iron. The tool took tremendous strength to lift and skill to manage, and her sister was considered one of the best. Deaf and dumb was not a liability in clearing weeds and thinning the newly sprung cotton seedlings.

A sour odor rose from the mass at Suzette's feet, threatening to wrench her stomach again, and she pushed herself up. It was the fourth time this week she had been forced out to the bushes before the plantation bell rang. There was breakfast to prepare, but all she wanted was to lie down right where she was, close her eyes, and sleep.

A morning breeze helped center her. Eugene Daurat was coming again today. He had become a regular visitor of the Derbannes, bringing her small things from time to time and giving them to her in the woods: a leftover piece of cloth from his store for a kerchief, a hard candy, the stump of a candle. In the big house she was invisible to him.

Since the quarter Christmas party, he sought her out whenever it struck his fancy. He would tell her to meet him after supper at the rock or to wait for him beyond the edge of the piney woods in the afternoon, and she would go. He barely spoke, and he did not expect her to do much of anything except lie or stand until he was finished with her. Each time they were together in that way, he would say, *"Merci, ma chère."*

Suzette tried to figure out what the doll man meant by those words. If he was thanking her, did that mean he thought she had a say in whether or not to obey his instruction to meet him? That she could say out loud that she did

not want to lie down in secret while he fumbled and sometimes hurt her? *Ma chère*. No matter how often she played
back the words, trying to hear a new tone or emphasis, his
true intent was just beyond her grasp. Was she dear to him?
When she went to him she transported herself to the smooth
rhythm of shelling peas while her mother hummed in the
cookhouse or the sleepy-eyed reassurance of Nicolas
Mulon's face. Just until he stopped moving on her and it was
time to get back to work.

Questioning him was unthinkable. He was a grown man,
a white man, and a close friend of the Derbannes'. She
couldn't talk to her mother. She couldn't talk to Oreline,
who prattled on about her older cousin Eugene's visits, how
interesting he was, how entertaining. The secret rendezvous
were not like the prickly tingling Nicolas Mulon could set
off in her. Those feelings scared her, too, but they had been
full of possibilities. This was heavy, like the old rotted oak
tree she had seen fall across the road near the front gate that
took days and many men to carve up and move aside. She
thought about talking to Palmire about the tangle of hope,
despair, and emptiness that came to her whenever she saw
Eugene Daurat or even heard his name, but there were no
signs in the language they had created between them to
describe these feelings. What could her sister tell her, even if
she could speak? Palmire had her own worries with Louis
Derbanne's nighttime visits.

It was months before she stopped puzzling over the hidden meaning of Eugene Daurat's *"Merci, ma chère."* The
words meant only that he was done with her and it was time
for her to go away and resume her chores under Françoise's
watchful eye in the big house or her mother's in the cookhouse. But her daily routine had come to seem small and

meaningless next to this other thing that was spreading out and taking hold of her body. She wondered if either Françoise or her mother, who both seemed to be able to see the smallest thing out of place in the big house, could see this, too.

When her birthday month came around again in the summer she would be fourteen. She could still recall the delicious taste of turning nine, when it was possible to strike out in a direction of her own choosing, and Oreline and Narcisse would follow, open to whatever came next. It had begun to feel like a suspect memory that must have happened to someone else.

"Pay attention to what you're doing," Françoise snapped, catching Suzette on the side of the head with her knuckles.

Lately she was getting as many swats, slaps, and pinches as Palmire used to when she worked in the house, before she had been banished to the field. Suzette burned the bread. She scorched one of Louis Derbanne's shirt collars and mixed up the salt and sugar. The delicate blue-and-white figurine in the front room that Eugene Daurat had brought as a gift from France had smashed into so many pieces when she dropped it that there was no hope of repair. She forgot to clean out the wall altar in the Derbannes' bedroom.

Her life had traveled far beyond her understanding. The picture in her mind of standing in front of St. Augustine with Nicolas Mulon and being married by a real priest was obviously hopeless. Try as she might, she couldn't create an image of a future with Eugene Daurat in it. He could never marry her, even if he wanted to. Not only was it against the law, it was unspeakable. She had no new dreams to replace her old ones.

The longer she hid her secret, the greater the distance between her and everyone else, as if they were all on the close side of Cane River and she were on the opposite bank, alone. The thought of the baby frightened her but gave her comfort, too. It was a concrete thing that belonged only to her.

Suzette let each day drift, holding on to time. Shortly after the cotton reached a foot high in the field, Elisabeth cornered her in the cookhouse.

"Looks like you're eating for more than one, Suzette."

"Uh-huh," Suzette answered from her faraway place.

"Who's the man?"

Suzette brought herself back, eyeing her mother cautiously. "Wh-what do you mean?" she stammered.

"You can't hide it. Who's the man?"

"I did not want to, *Mère.*"

"Is he white?"

Suzette tried to speak and found she could not. She stared down at her hands.

"The world didn't start with you, Suzette. I've been through it. In Virginia, with the Master's son, before coming here." Elisabeth put down the rolling pin. "It's Eugene Daurat, isn't it? Looking at you like you're some new Louisiana sweetmeat to try."

"Yes," Suzette said in a small voice.

"Did he hurt you?"

"Not much after the first time. I don't know. He chose me."

Elisabeth let out a low moan, a strangled sound steeped in resignation. "Oh, baby girl," she said.

"What do I do now?" Suzette asked.

"Your stomach twist up in the morning?"

"Yes'm."

"This baby is already caught. We wait for the quickening, to make sure it's going to stay caught."

Elisabeth came around the worktable and pulled Suzette close, wrapping her big arms around Suzette's shoulders, rocking her slowly from side to side. Suzette stiffened, but Elisabeth didn't let go. After a time Suzette sank into the warmth and smells of her mother, and they rocked together.

"This is what our life is, baby girl. It didn't stop me from loving those babies of mine in Virginia."

An urgent coldness shot through Suzette. She did not want to hear what had happened to her mother. She pushed herself away, picked up the sharp kitchen knife, and busied herself chopping the okra, separating the hard green caps from the stalks on the cutting board.

Elisabeth turned to stir the stew simmering in the kettle. "If I can see your condition, it won't be long before others do, too. When that Frenchman comes at you again, you tell him about this baby, that he should be leaving you alone now. We need to make sure that Madame knows it wasn't M'sieu. You turn up with a high-yellow baby without warning, there's no telling what she could do. It's bad enough trying to keep Palmire away from her. You just do your work. I'll go to her tomorrow."

Françoise left a trail of damp footprints as she came into the stranger's room, where Suzette had just finished scrubbing the floorboards. Françoise stared openly at the beginnings of a gentle rounding under the fabric of Suzette's thin gingham dress.

"Elisabeth came to see me," she began stiffly. "You were brought up better. We did not give permission for you to start a family yet. Who is the father?"

Suzette hung her head.

"You hear me, girl? I didn't bring you up to the house so you could slide back and be like Palmire. Who is the father?"

Françoise's tone had become loud and insistent, and she grabbed Suzette's arm. They were alone in the room, and Suzette was suddenly afraid.

"It was M'sieu Daurat. He told me not to say anything," Suzette said quietly.

Françoise gripped her more tightly. "It wasn't anyone from Rosedew?"

"No, Madame, I'm sure."

"Has there been anyone else? Do not lie to me, or I can get you put out to field like your sister." Françoise's narrowed eyes were menacing.

"There's only been M'sieu Daurat," Suzette said, her voice small and timid.

Françoise loosened her hold. "Another little mulatto mouth to feed." Françoise spat out the word *mulatto* as though she had gotten hold of one of the bitter herbs she used for doctoring. "We gave you every opportunity, Suzette. This is not the Christian way. You people cannot help yourselves, I suppose."

"*Oui*, Madame."

Suzette had trouble concentrating on her work for the rest of the day, afraid of what would come next. She was jittery throughout the evening, just wanting to lie down on her pallet without having to face anyone else, answer any more questions.

"You are so quiet, Suzette," Oreline said that evening when the two girls were alone in the bedroom. "Is anything wrong?"

"No, Mam'zelle."

"You have been acting odd of late. You can tell me. I tell you everything."

"There's nothing, Mam'zelle."

"It's first Friday," Oreline said conspiratorially. "Are you ready?"

"Yes, Mam'zelle."

Oreline became solemn. Unsmiling, she extended her bare right foot and touched the flat of her heel to the wooden base of the four-poster bed, closing her eyes.

"Today, the first Friday of the month, I place my foot on the footboard and I pray the great Saint Nicholas to make me meet the one I am to marry," she recited soberly. Then she jumped into her bed without touching the floor, lay down on her right side, her hand over her heart, and made herself still so she could fall asleep without talking, without laughing, without moving.

Suzette lowered the mosquito bar over her and blew out the candles.

The next morning, as Suzette came back from the cook-house, she almost ran into Françoise in the narrow hallway coming out of Oreline's room.

"Suzette," Françoise said tautly as she brushed past, and Suzette dropped her eyes and curtsied.

Oreline was standing beside the armoire, and Suzette went over to help her tighten the stays in her corset, trying to gauge Oreline's mood. Oreline seemed sulky and silent, anger collecting in her face as if it were building up to a storm.

"Aunt Françoise told me about the baby," she said, her words clipped.

There was nothing for Suzette to say. She removed Oreline's gray-and-black-plaid dress from the armoire.

"Why did you go with him?"

"I can only do what I am told, Mam'zelle."

"How long has it been going on? Since he came to Cane River?" The on-the-edge pitch Suzette recognized from childhood was mixed with something new.

"He found me alone at Christmastime," Suzette said tiredly.

"What did you do to make him come to you?"

"He followed me. I did nothing. I was wearing my christening dress." Suzette didn't know why she had added the last part. As if what she was wearing mattered.

"Did you want to make a baby with him?" Oreline pushed.

"No."

"Did you tell him that?"

"No."

"If you didn't want this to happen, why didn't you say anything?"

"I don't know."

"Why didn't you tell me?"

"I don't know, Mam'zelle."

"I tell you about everything important that happens to me." The new tone again. "I could have helped you. I have always been the one to help you."

"What could you have done?" Suzette asked, her tongue heavy and dull. "What could anyone have done?"

"You didn't even tell me. Aunt Françoise knew before I did." Oreline's voice broke, midway between a whine and an accusation. She turned her face away, and several minutes passed before she spoke again.

"Don't think for a minute that now that you've been found out you can come to me for anything," Oreline said haughtily. "I need for you to get my bonnet. I'm going out visiting with Aunt Françoise today."

Suzette was dismissed from Oreline's heart.

Suzette carried the full coffee service into the front room and set it down with care on the sideboard. Her belly jutted out bigger and rounder than the ripe watermelons they cracked open in summer, and cramps had stitched her in waves all morning. Slowly, with effort, she moved across the room and placed freshly pressed white linen napkins in the laps of Oreline and Françoise.

"We'll have to bring Apphia in soon to replace Suzette," Françoise remarked to Oreline. "Louis won't spare Palmire from the field."

Suzette began to pour steaming coffee into the fragile cups, allowing her thoughts to linger on the pleasing idea of thirty days away from the big house in Palmire's cabin after the baby came.

Oreline gave a sideways glance at Suzette. "You know, Aunt Françoise, I intend to miss Cousin Eugene desperately when he leaves. He is my favorite dance partner."

Suzette listened, as she knew Oreline intended her to. She knew nothing of Eugene Daurat leaving. Oreline no longer confided in her about the comings and goings of Cane River's Creoles.

"He'll come back to us when he finishes his business in France," Françoise said, leaning forward to settle her sewing kit on the side table. "With wonderful presents, no doubt."

Suzette watched Françoise's napkin slide in a deliberate line from her lap to a tangle near her feet. With an awkward twist she bent toward the floor to retrieve the cloth. Deep inside something shifted, and Suzette felt a warm gushing down her thighs.

"Ohhhhh." The sound escaped before she could stop it. "I think it's my time," she moaned. Panicky, she looked up at Françoise.

Françoise sprang to her feet, ordering Oreline to get Old Bertram and the wagon.

Suzette remembered being taken down to Palmire's cabin in the quarter, she remembered waiting for the midwife to arrive, and she remembered the curious taste of the cloves and whiskey Françoise offered. More than anything else, for the next twenty-four hours Suzette remembered the pain.

Afternoon dragged into evening. They lit candles and waited, the midwife next to Suzette wiping her forehead and neck with a damp rag and Françoise sitting on a straight-backed pine chair by the fireplace, her shawl gathered around her shoulders. Overseeing the birth of slaves was her responsibility on Rosedew, and she took her role seriously. Elisabeth brought a simple supper for the two women and a pot of copal moss soaked in boiling water for Suzette. Françoise poured whiskey in the pot, and the women got Suzette to drink it down. They waited. Suzette's screams pierced the dark night of quiet in the quarter, and still the baby had not come with the ringing of the plantation bell the next morning. A little before noon a baby boy finally emerged in a spill of earthen color, dappled with red. They wrapped him in his new blanket and handed him to Suzette. His name will be Philomon, from the Bible, Suzette thought, but she could focus on his buff-colored face for only the briefest moment before she descended into an all-consuming sleep.

The sun had gone down by the time Suzette woke. She smelled the biting scent of laurel leaves on Elisabeth's hands as her mother shook her firmly by the shoulders, and she struggled to open her eyes. For a moment, as Elisabeth's dark and unchanging face came into focus, Suzette felt safe. Palmire was near the fireplace, just in from the field, sweat and tiredness still clinging to her. She moved heavily on her feet as she ground a corn paste for ashcakes, her belly bulging. Palmire's own child would be coming soon.

Suzette stared at the whimpering bundle next to her on the cot. "Time to feed your boy," Elisabeth prodded, opening the front of Suzette's shirtwaist and settling the fretting baby at Suzette's breast. He fussed for only a minute before finding Suzette's nipple and pulling at it greedily.

"His name is Philomon," Suzette announced weakly, looking down at the contorted face, stroking the fine dark hair plastered to his head.

"They going to call this one Gerant," Elisabeth said. "Madame already gave him the name."

"But he's mine," Suzette said shakily.

"His out-loud name is Gerant," Elisabeth repeated deliberately. "That has to fit him."

Elisabeth crossed the room to the fireplace and tapped Palmire on the shoulder to get her attention, then made a drinking motion with her hands. Palmire nodded, poured steaming liquid from the small dented pot over the hot coals into a cup, and handed it to Elisabeth. Elisabeth came back to the cot where Suzette nursed the baby.

"This laurel tea will do you good, and Palmire will have supper up directly," Elisabeth said, bringing the cup to Suzette's lips. "You must be starving." She tucked the blanket around the infant. "We love all our children in this family, no matter how they come to us. You be careful not to roll over that baby. Palmire will show you what you need to know. I can't stay."

Long after she left, Suzette stared through half-shut eyes at the closed door until Palmire took the baby away and brought the ashcakes.

For the next few days the constant thread weaving in and out of Suzette's wake-sleep was Gerant, always crying. Suzette cried, too. It became difficult to tell the difference. She couldn't walk or sit up in bed in the same position for long, and the thoughts that had always chased one another around in her head were gone. There was only sleep, pain, nursing, rocking, and more crying.

Her sister's cabin became a meeting place, and she had visitors from the quarter and from the big house, bringing advice, food, or a sweet tit for Gerant. Even Oreline came, a worried look on her face, repeating over and over that everything would be all right, holding Suzette's hand as she drifted back to sleep.

Voices drifted in and out of her awareness, advising her how to tell the difference between this cry and that cry, but Gerant's wailing vibrated deep to her core and communicated nothing but endless need. He accused her with each breath he took. Whenever he pushed away her breast, Suzette knew that he wanted someone else more worthy to be his mother. Exhausted, Suzette slept through much of it.

She resisted the talk around her, but whispers pierced the cushion of her sleep and she heard them anyway. "All that fancy talk and dress, up at the big house acting like she belong there, but she's come home to her own," they said.

Elisabeth came every night and walked with Gerant,

humming familiar lullabies. Palmire used her strong arms as if she were swinging the hoe and wordlessly rocked Gerant into peace. Suzette fell deeper into her failures, heavy-hearted in the face of how she had disappointed everyone.

For the first three weeks after Gerant's birth, life was an expanding panorama of ruined dreams and expectations.

Suzette got down on her hands and knees to scour underneath the dining room table with a stiff brush and sudsy water, taking care to clean between the floorboard cracks. Louis Derbanne had taken to dropping his food and drink wherever he happened to be, and there seemed always to be a wet spot or hardened crust Suzette needed to get to before Françoise found it. It seemed as if everything had changed in the sixty days since Gerant was born. Every minute of her day was filled with someone pulling at her, trying to take possession of her hands, her breast, her mind, or her heart.

Louis had been an old man for a long time already, but he seemed more fragile to Suzette now, like one of the Derbannes' fine cracked dishes that had to be handled with extra care because it was too good to throw out. It fell to Suzette to put him on and lift him off the bedpan and to wash him. She hand-fed him special foods that he could chew and keep down. He seldom rode out to the field anymore, preferring to sit on the front gallery with his bottle of bourbon, nursing a tumbler full of the dark brown liquid, and she cleaned up after him when his weakened stomach rebelled.

Oreline entered the dining room in a flurry of impatience. "There you are. I can't find my lace gloves," she complained to Suzette.

"They're up on the top shelf of the armoire, where they're supposed to be, Mam'zelle," Suzette said. Her hands stung from the hot water.

Oreline paused, as if in a debate with herself. "It's good to have you back. I know she's your sister, but Apphia didn't have good house sense," she said in the soft, accepting tone of long ago. "She never got my hair right."

"I'll find the gloves," Suzette said. She got to her feet and put the pail aside.

Oreline followed Suzette back to the bedroom, and Suzette used the stepstool to reach the gloves.

"If you don't need me further, Mam'zelle, it's been three hours."

"Go on, then," Oreline said, indulgence edging her tone. "Do your business."

Suzette hurried down the path to the cookhouse, and she heard Gerant's loud, blustery cry before she got to the door. He was hungry. A staccato whimper meant he was uncomfortable, a rolling howl begged for attention. Elisabeth was chopping vegetables at the worktable when she came in. She looked up at Suzette and went on with her work.

Suzette sat down and brought Gerant to her breast, mother and son in their quiet time. Her thoughts turned to her own mother. Since Gerant, Suzette had begun to think of Elisabeth as the strongest link in a growing chain. Blessedly, her mother was still strong and healthy and in firm control of the cookhouse.

Eugene Daurat returned from his three-month trip to France just as the persimmons were ripening red orange on the south field trees. He brought back a delicate figurine for

Françoise to replace the one Suzette had broken, a bottle of Madeira for Louis, and a fashionable bonnet with festive green streamers for Oreline. The Derbannes gave a party to celebrate his return to Cane River, and Suzette served.

Each day flowed into the next, and Rosedew returned to its routines. On a late summer day, when Gerant was nearly a year old, Eugene caught Suzette alone out behind the spring-house as she was carrying back a pail of water for the house.

"Suzette, go to the rock this afternoon after supper. I will meet you there." He used the honeyed voice of possession, but Suzette had fallen out of the practice of considering her trysts with Eugene to be part of her duties on Rosedew.

"M'sieu Daurat, I have to get things ready for the soirée tonight. There is no time. Madame Françoise is waiting on me. It is impossible to get away today."

The mention of Françoise's name put him off, but she knew it was only a postponement. Her mother had gone to Françoise once to ask for her help. She could not go again. It was up to Suzette from now on.

It reminded her of cats with the mice they caught around Rosedew, toying with their food before they ate it. After the first capture they would pretend to let the mouse go on its way, pulling back just enough to encourage hope. Only then would they shoot out the fast paw or deliver a quick nip to the neck, trapping it once again into the game. She had once watched an old tomcat get careless near the smokehouse. The mouse had dashed to freedom, damaged, probably easy game for the next predator, but it had gotten away. Escape was unlikely, but it was possible.

5

Suzette almost envied Louis his contentment. He liked to stare out for hours while he sat on the gallery in his rocker, cup balanced in his hand, at one with the motion of the chair. He seemed to lean his mind into the landscape, his eyes scanning the scope of Rosedew, the muscles around his mouth locked in an expression of permanent amusement. From time to time he would push himself out of the rocker with his frail arms, carelessly dropping the tin cup they had decided to give him after so many broken glasses. With a great sense of purpose he would first stand erect, testing the uncertainty of his knees, and then limp away stiff legged on his own beyond the boundaries of the house. No one ever knew where he was going or why he was in such a hurry to get there. Suzette supposed he was answering a special call that only he could hear. Perhaps he was on his way to meet some cronies for a friendly smoke and a drink, or off to give instruction on the running of his plantation. But before long he would forget why he had started out or where he should go next.

Everyone on Rosedew and on the surrounding plantations had become used to seeing Louis alone and seemingly bemused, suddenly appearing in new and unexpected places. Before his mind had gotten so clouded, he would turn most often toward the quarter and the familiarity of Palmire's cabin, whether she was there or not, but that phase passed and he branched farther out. Once he got as far as Henry Hertzog's barn. Whoever found him would lead him back to the big house on Rosedew, turning him over to Suzette. He seldom resisted or argued and was content with whatever companionship was offered on the leisurely journey back to where he had started.

His wandering lessened as arthritis settled in his knees, and the time came when Louis Derbanne never left the front gallery at all. As he approached the seventh decade of his life, they all had to face the reality that he was dying. It was as if a protective cloak had been pulled away from the plantation and exposed the temperamental nature of the delicate machinery underneath. There was not a single position that would be the same without the continued labored breath of the master of Rosedew. It had been years since Louis had ridden across his land, tall in the saddle. The day-to-day affairs of the field had long been turned over to a succession of overseers, and life in the quarter was grinding and capricious. But Louis Derbanne's presence on the front gallery of the big house still had meaning, defining an imaginary point below which things could not sink.

He died in his sleep with his affairs in order, leaving a respectable sum for the Catholic Church, as well as declaring his love and recognition of his faithful and loving spouse,

Françoise Rachal Derbanne. All of his goods that remained after Françoise's death were to be divided among Oreline and two of his other favorite godchildren. It was the other story that spread quickly through the quarter. Louis Derbanne had freed three of his slaves in his will. One was an old family servant inherited from his father, beyond working age, and the other two were his own natural children by a slave woman who had died years before. But he had not freed his three children by Palmire.

Françoise took to her sickbed for two weeks after the reading of the will. Without Louis on Rosedew, she was just one more unschooled widow along Cane River. Without Louis, Oreline had lost yet another of the male protectors she needed to marry well and take her place in Cane River Creole society. And without Louis Derbanne, dreams of promised freedom and humane treatment in the quarter died a quick and suffocating death, like a sputtering fire that can't get enough air to keep itself burning.

Eugene proved to be a pillar of strength for Françoise and Oreline. He stayed on Rosedew for four weeks after Louis died, helping Françoise adjust to running a plantation as large as Rosedew alone. She could neither read nor write and was without the youthful enthusiasm to take on new challenges. As was the way along Cane River, the extended family formed a tight protective circle around the widow. Between the Derbannes, Fredieus, and Rachals a steady stream of visitors came daily to Rosedew to keep her company, play cards, bring gossip, and help oversee business affairs.

Suzette had done her best to avoid being alone with Eugene, trying to keep out of his way. She made up one excuse after another why she could not meet him when he

early 1840
Natchitoches Parish
The succession of **Louis Derbanne** opened, consisting of a
number of documents:

4 March 1830, Testament: I, the undersigned **Louis
Derbanne** of the parish of Natchitoches, in the state of
Louisiana, declare that I am Catholic Apostolic, and
Roman, that I wish to die in the religion of my ancestors,
which I wish while I am of sound health and body to reg-
ulate my affairs. I will and ordain that the present be my
testament, expressly and formally revoking any other
testament or codicil that I may have previously made
before the present testament, and that it be the only
valid one. As a Catholic I give to the Church of St.
François de Natchitoches the sum of 10 [piasters] "un
fait payée." I pray that Messieurs Embroise Lecomte and
Dassis Bossie will wish to be my testamentary executors,
without them having to make bond, yet still to make a
judicial inventory, as soon as possible after my death.

I give and bequeath to my godchildren [plural] and
niece [singular] Marie Aimé Lavespere, Seraphine
[Seraphim?] Chaler, and Marie Oréline Derbanne, all
my goods that remain after the death of my faithful
spouse, Marie Françoise Rachal. I wish to give testimony of my love and my recognition to my faithful and
loving spouse, Marie Françoise Rachal. I leave to her
the enjoyment and use of during her life only, all of my
goods. I expressly dispose of any security to my heirs and
until the death of my said wife, she has the right to
enjoy and hold possession of my goods.

I ordain that three of my slaves be freed after my
death: Jeanne, Negress; Marie Pamela, griffe [mixed
black & Indian]; and Marie Apoline, mulatress. These
three slaves are to be free by my [3 illegible words].

Made and passed at my domicile this 4 March 1830.
/s/L^S Derbanne. "Neveriteur" C. E. Greneaux, Parish Judge.

Succession of Louis Derbanne.

wanted, but he was such a regular on Rosedew now that she could not always keep her distance. Their rendezvous were less frequent, but over the months his insistence was impossible to escape. Suzette approached her meetings with Eugene Daurat with the same state of mind she had when cleaning the outhouse. The task had to be performed from time to time, and when finished she could go on to other things she didn't mind as much. She no longer looked for hidden signals or explanations, and the fewer words exchanged the better. By first picking, Suzette knew another baby was due in the spring. Eugene's mood for starting something new seemed to follow the schedule for the planting of the new cotton crop.

On a sunless, soggy day in September, Eugene commanded her to meet him in the barn after supper. This time she didn't try to avoid him.

Suzette set out into the beating rain and got to the darkened barn first. She swung open the wide door and closed it carefully behind her. The horses and mules were already bedded for the night, but the wind and rain made them edgy, and they pawed at the earth in their stalls. A small hole in the roof off in the far corner let in a steady dripping of rain on the hay beneath. She waited for Eugene there in the dark, hoping no one was looking for her. The moldy scent of the damp hay was sickening, and the barn was drafty and cold.

When at last the barn door swung open, she made out a shapeless form slipping inside furtively. Only when the door was fastened again did Eugene light the kerosene lamp he had brought. He struck a matchstick against the match safe, and the horses whinnied nervously.

He turned the wick on the lamp down low, dimming the flame, and set the lamp down near the door. "Where are you?" he called out.

Suzette squeezed out her courage. "M'sieu Eugene, it's about the boy, Gerant."

Eugene grunted, giving her no encouragement. He began loosening his pants as he moved toward her.

"If you freed him now, he could have a different life. He's your blood." The wind made a shrill noise as it thrust the rain against the roof. "And there's another child on the way."

Suzette watched Eugene's hands freeze on his trouser buttons. His face clouded.

"Who says it's mine?" he got out at last.

As if anyone would want her as long as he had his mark on her, Suzette thought. "It's yours, M'sieu. Another boy, I'd say, by the kicking." He hadn't even noticed her rounding belly. "They both could be bought out as soon as this one is born, and raised free. I've seen it happen."

Eugene didn't answer, staring at her. He hesitated for only a few moments, and then he nimbly buttoned his pants back up. Without a word he picked up the lamp and went back out into the rain, leaving Suzette in the darkness.

From that day forward her prayers of the last two years were answered. He left her alone.

Suzette asked Françoise on a Friday to be allowed to go to early mass the following Wednesday, promising to make up her chores later. Indifferently, Françoise gave her a pass to attend St. Augustine alone.

Before the plantation bell rang, Suzette put on her checked calico josie and set out for the long walk in the dark. Mass had started by the time she arrived, and Suzette quickly picked out her *marraine* Doralise's sorrel mare and brown buggy. She stood quietly, waiting for the service to end. At last the church began to empty out its early morning worshipers, and she saw Doralise coming toward the buggy with her daughter, Elisida, and Azenor Metoyer, the *gens de couleur libre* Elisida was engaged to marry. Suzette was relieved that Doralise's husband, Philippe, was not there. There was something about him that frightened her.

Even with downcast eyes, Suzette managed to admire her godmother's profile as the three approached the carriage. Doralise was a dignified, well-bred woman, everything Suzette wished she could be. As Doralise got closer, she turned stiffly toward Suzette in welcome. Suzette quickly looked away from the expanding circles of puffy dark flesh that formed petals around one of Doralise's eyes. The gossip must be true, that Philippe had taken to beating Doralise so often and acting so strangely that even his own high-and-mighty family was considering locking him up somewhere. Doralise's face reminded Suzette of a ripe peach she had once found on the ground in the big garden, seemingly so perfect until she'd picked it up and exposed an oozing, rotten wound on the underside.

"Good morning, Suzette. I wouldn't have expected to see you here. Did you need to talk to me?" Doralise asked.

The bruise distracted Suzette. Stammering, she began anyway. "*Marraine* Doralise, I'm going to have another baby. I want to ask you to be his godmother."

"Another baby?" Doralise asked with some surprise, but not unkindly. "Is it the same circumstances as before with Gerant?"

Suzette felt herself go hot. "Yes, Madame," she forced herself to say. She would have liked to turn around and begin the long walk back home, but the baby had to come before her pride. He would need more protection than she could give. Doralise was a free colored woman, one of the Ones with Last Names. She had land, money, and slaves of her own.

"I think this is another boy," Suzette offered.

Doralise turned her head slowly, and her breath caught as if with pain.

"Suzette, you must be more careful. This is your second baby, and you are what? Fifteen, sixteen?"

Suzette pricked the bubble of bitterness before it had a chance to rise. As much as she loved Gerant, as much as she would do to protect the new life inside her, their making had nothing to do with how careful she was allowed to be.

"I'll be seventeen come harvest. I do what I'm told, Madame. I can't do more. This baby is coming, and he needs someone who can help him, like you promised my mother you would help me before I was born."

Doralise's face softened. She gave more of a grimace than a smile.

"Yes, I will be godmother to your baby, Suzette."

There was nothing else for them to say. Elisida was already high above them, waiting impatiently in the buggy with Azenor Metoyer, carefully looking away from her mother and the girl-woman slave. They were clearly waiting for Doralise to finish talking so they could go home to their own life, a very different life.

"*Merci*, Madame."

Suzette backed away and began the five-mile trip back home to Rosedew. If this baby could not have a last name, at least it would have protection from someone who did.

Suzette and Elisabeth were in the cookhouse together when the contractions began to grip Suzette's body.

"*Mère,* this one's in a hurry," Suzette said.

Elisabeth gloved her hand and moved the heavy kettle from its hook to another farther away from the hottest flames in the fireplace. She took Suzette by the arm and walked her slowly down the path to the quarter. They stopped whenever the contractions came again. It was early afternoon and almost everyone was in the field. By the time they got to Aunt Jeanne's cabin Suzette was panting heavily, unable to let go of Elisabeth's arm. Aunt Jeanne sat on her pine stump on the front porch, an infant asleep in a wooden box at her feet. Three small children looked up from playing in a muddy puddle.

"It's her time," Elisabeth said to the old woman, nodding toward Suzette. "Send one of the children to let Madame and the midwife know."

A light-skinned little boy in a shapeless shirttail smock trailed Elisabeth and Suzette as they made their way farther down the row to Palmire's cabin, built a small distance away from the others at Louis Derbanne's command.

"Why are you going to my house, *Mémère?*" the boy asked as Elisabeth helped Suzette inside the empty cabin.

"Go on back to Aunt Jeanne, Paul," Elisabeth said. "We have women's business. And you stay out of sight when Madame comes down here."

There were two cots in the room, one for Palmire and the other for her three children. Suzette eased herself onto Palmire's cot and pulled the blanket over her, waiting for the next contraction. There were several split logs and some kindling inside, and Elisabeth started a fire in the fireplace.

"I'll be back directly," Elisabeth said to Suzette, turning to go out again. "I need to get some copal moss to brew you tea for the pain."

"Don't leave me, *Mère*," Suzette begged. "Please. He's coming now."

Elisabeth propped up Suzette's knees where she lay on the cot, fanning back the blanket to get a better look. "He sure enough is," she said.

Gerant's birth had been all exhaustion and pain, and by the time he came out into the light Suzette had been sliding into a darkness of her own. With this second child, it was as if the process were in reverse. It was the baby who took the lead, and when it emerged headfirst Suzette was alert and wide-awake.

"Not a boy at all," Elisabeth said. "Quick as lightning and you got yourself a girl."

Elisabeth brought the baby up close to Suzette's face and placed her in Suzette's trembling arms. Suzette saw the thick blue cord of life that connected her to a girl-child.

"What's wrong with her?" Suzette could hear the hysteria in her own voice. The baby was gray.

"Don't worry," Elisabeth said. "The color will turn. We just don't know what direction yet."

From outside came sounds of a buggy and voices. Françoise and the midwife arrived breathless at Palmire's cabin almost at the same time.

"Philomon already got here," Suzette said to Françoise as soon as they came through the door. She looked down at the face of the little gray baby with tiny blue fingernails and dark matted hair that clung to her head like a helmet.

"Philomon is a boy's name," Françoise said.

"Philomene, then," Suzette said with as much faith as she could muster. "That fits a girl."

Françoise nodded. The name held.

This girl was Name Phelman Dorrod Some
spelled it Fellerman Door Rod.
--Cousin Gurtie Fredieu, written family
  history, 1975

14 May 1843
Natchitoches Parish
Baptism of Phylomene, born 1 November 1841 to Marie
Louise [sic], slave of **Widow L. N.** [sic] **Derbanne.** God-
parents: Lois Rachal and Marie Doralise Derbanne.
[Immaculate Conception Church, Register 10, Baptism
of Slaves 1831–1846: unnumbered 1843 entry.]

Baptism of Philomene. [Mother's name in error.]

Suzette drowsed one Saturday evening as she breast-fed
Philomene in Palmire's dark cabin. The space was cramped,
overflowing with life. She and Palmire slept together on the same
cot, nose to toe, each with her nursing infant girl. They had put
Palmire to work in the west field closest to the quarter after her
lay-in month, and she was allowed to come back three times during the day to nurse her own baby daughter, Melantine.

The three boys were already asleep on the other cot, a
tangle of arms and legs. Gerant, who was almost three, got
along well with Palmire's boys—Paul, four, and Solais,
two—but Gerant had taken to clinging to Suzette all of the
time, unused to having his mother so available. She tried not
to think about how it would be after the month was up and
the Derbannes owned her time again in the big house.

She was still amazed that Gerant and Philomene had
come from her. She tried to identify a future in their expres-

sions that could carry them beyond a two-footed ox for the field or an invisible breeder who would disappear into a big house. They didn't look alike at all. It was too early to tell how Philomene's features would fix themselves, the final color of her eyes or hair or skin, but already Suzette could see that, in appearance, at least, Philomene favored Eugene Daurat. She had thin fingers and delicate features, a high-yellow baby with a sharp nose and a full, thick head of wiry hair that stood up at peculiar, spiky angles.

Outside the cabin, a small group gathered, eager to share evening gossip, and she picked out the low hum of familiar voices. Her sister Apphia; her brother, Solataire; Eliza; and Old Bertram. Their voices drifted in and found her.

"He beat up on her one too many times, almost killed her twice. After he pulled the knife, she went on up to the Natchitoches courthouse and asked for what they call a divorce. That puts the marriage to the side, official."

"They wouldn't give a colored woman leave to quit her husband. No matter how crazy M'sieu Philippe is."

"I tell you they gave her papers to carry back, papers that say she's not married to him anymore."

"Go on. White folks aren't going to side with a colored woman. I don't care if she is free."

"She had help."

"What kind of help?"

"From a white man looking to take Philippe's place, but without it going through any church this time."

"Who?"

"Eugene Daurat, that Frenchman always coming around here."

Suzette came fully awake. Her godmother Doralise and Eugene Daurat? How could that be?

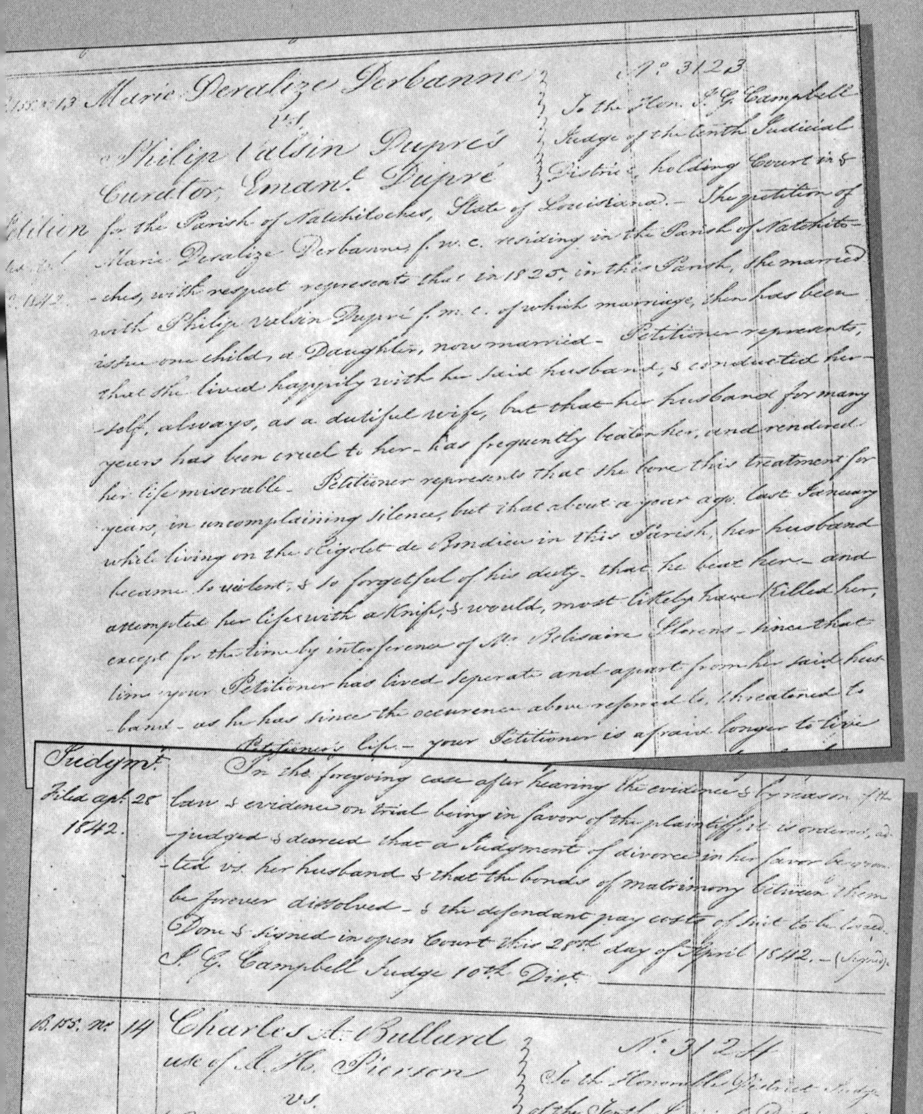

B.115. № 13 Marie Doralize Derbanne
vs.
Philip Valsin Dupré
Curator, Emanl. Dupré

№ 3123

To the Hon. J. G. Campbell Judge of the tenth Judicial District, holding Court in & for the Parish of Natchitoches, State of Louisiana. – The petition of Marie Doralize Derbanne f. w. c. residing in the Parish of Natchitoches, with respect represents that in 1825, in this Parish, she married with Philip Valsin Dupré f. m. c. of which marriage there has been issue one child, a Daughter, now married – Petitioner represents, that she lived happily with her said husband, & conducted herself, always, as a dutiful wife, but that her husband for many years has been cruel to her – has frequently beaten her, and rendered her life miserable. Petitioner represents that she bore this treatment for years, in uncomplaining silence, but that about a year ago, last January while living on the Rigolet de Bondieu in this Parish, her husband became so violent, & so forgetful of his duty, that he beat her – and attempted her life with a Knife, & would, most likely have Killed her, except for the timely interference of Mr. Belisaire Llorens – since that time your Petitioner has lived seperate and apart from her said husband – as he has since the occurrence above referred to, threatened to Petitioner's life. – your Petitioner is afraid longer to live

Petition
Filed
1842.

Judgmt.
Filed apl. 28
1842.

In the foregoing case after hearing the evidence & by reason of the law & evidence on trial being in favor of the plaintiff, it is ordered, adjudged & decreed that a Judgment of divorce in her favor be granted vs. her husband & that the bonds of matrimony between them be forever dissolved – & the defendant pay costs of suit to be taxed. Done & signed in open Court this 28th day of April 1842. – (Signed)
J. G. Campbell Judge 10th Dist.

B. 115. № 14 Charles A. Bullard
use of A. H. Pierson
vs.
George W. Lewis et al

№ 3124

To the Honorable District Judge of the Tenth Judicial District of the State of Louisiana, sitting in and

Doralise Derbanne divorce decree, 1842.

6

Françoise pushed herself up higher against the pillows in the middle of her four-poster bed, listening to the steady drone of Oreline's voice as her niece read aloud to her. She wasn't well, hadn't felt truly well for years. In mind and body she was as brittle as the two thinning plaits of white hair that Suzette brushed out and rebraided for her every morning. Her hands were busy with her needlework, but her mind had trouble keeping up with the passages as Oreline spoke them. The overseer had requested an audience with her this morning on a matter, he had said, of grave importance, and she dreaded the intrusion, anticipating the worst. She silently cursed Louis for leaving her alone with too many responsibilities, for allowing the plantation's slide that had started long before he died.

Rosedew still straddled Bayou Derbanne and stretched across both sides of Cane River as far north as Old River, but the plantation had steadily shrunk. It infuriated her still that during the flush times her husband had given pieces of their land away to his freed mulatto children, including Doralise, and had sold even more in the Panic of 1837. After Louis died, Françoise had been forced to sell additional parcels just to make ends meet. Now there was less than eight hundred acres left and fewer than thirty slaves.

At first, after Louis's death, Françoise had tried to take charge of everything that needed to be done, to run the fields and the house, to maintain the religious and social calendar of Rosedew, to visit in the community. But by the time her girl Suzette came back to work after her second child, Françoise had retreated, had begun to live her life from her bedroom. It was more than she could manage to respond to all of the requests that came flying at her from all directions, demanding decisions.

"A pity," they said in front parlors up and down the river. She knew how they spoke of her. "Poor Françoise never did get over Louis's death."

Rosedew had taken blows that Françoise did not know how to reverse or correct. Each year seemed to bring a new set of problems. One year the rains came too early. The next, poison grass choked out part of the crop. The cotton gin broke and cost $300 to repair. They never seemed to have enough money from one year's crop to breathe into the next after paying for food, clothes, seed, machinery, and tools, and the times were against them. When their troubles were at their worst, the banks had stopped lending money to almost everyone. Françoise had relied on Louis to take care of running the business at Rosedew, and he had in turn relied on her to keep the house running smoothly. That arrangement had suited Françoise's sensibilities perfectly, but she was too old and unprepared to take on Rosedew all alone.

Other plantations along Cane River weathered five years of sacrifice and uncertainty, outlasting the depressed cotton prices and tight credit aftermath of the Panic of 1837, and eventually cotton prices crept back up and the banks made cash available again for those felt to have a future. Their neighbors bounced back to prepanic levels of production, and king cotton reigned supreme. Relatives and neighbors reverted to their old ways, entertaining, holding soirées and hunts and horse races as if the money worries of the last few years were too far away for anyone to remember. Cane River became truly joyous again. Except for Rosedew.

There always seemed to be too many things to worry about. Françoise looked over to Oreline, her niece's small bow mouth moving with concentrated intensity, her voice pleasant enough. She had proven to be a devoted companion and a great comfort, attending Françoise through mourning, melancholy, and illness, trying to shoulder some of the responsibilities of Rosedew. But she was too tall and too plain and had no land to attract a proper beau, as was essential at her age.

Her age, Françoise thought. Oreline was getting older, twenty, not yet married, and lovesick over a boy whom she had lost to a more spirited girl. He had been the only suitor Oreline encouraged, a seemingly sincere young man who turned out to have *le coeur comme un artichaud,* a heart like an artichoke, with a leaf for everyone. He had paid court to a girl in Cloutierville at the same time he charmed Oreline and had recently announced his engagement to the other girl in the spring. Françoise could understand that her niece needed time to let her heart mend, but time was not on her side. If she reached twenty-five unmarried, her chance to be a bride was most likely gone. She might as well throw her corset on the armoire, prepare herself for the spinster's life. Françoise would miss Oreline's soothing presence when she married, but she wanted to see her safely matched and starting her own life. She determined to talk discreetly to her friends to unearth a suitable husband for Oreline. Françoise was more confident about her success in this arena than in dealing with the overseer.

No doubt the overseer's requested audience today would be another in a constant string of complaints about surly Negroes, or missing livestock, or how much food each slave consumed, or broken tools. What was she to do about any of that? It was too overwhelming, the constant appeals and recitations of petty wrongs. The whole business of having to deal with an overseer was unseemly to begin with and contrary to her upbringing. After a time, she had left this latest one to his own devices or waited until her nephew Narcisse Fredieu or kinsman Eugene Daurat came by and asked one of them to handle whatever needed looking after. For anything official that required writing, she sent word to Eugene Daurat, and he took care of it. She was grateful that her kinsman had come to Cane River, and although she did not approve of how he consorted so intimately with Negroes, she ignored that unpleasantness. She trusted him with her business affairs, and she enjoyed his company.

She had stopped making the overseer account to her for punishment meted out in the field. If he had to give more than twenty lashes in order to ensure obedience, why should she question it? Monitoring the overseer's activities had been Louis's way, but Louis had died and left her alone. She did not want to know about these things.

In some ways it was a blessing that she did not get outside much anymore, to see how the cabins needed white-washing or the barn had begun to lean at a curious angle or how her beloved roses lost their petals early and meandered unsupervised. But she saw the evidence of leaks in the roof, when the constant dripping into the catch pots in the corner of her own bedroom disturbed her sleep, and she could count the dwindling number of times meat was part of the meal.

From time to time Suzette approached her on behalf of someone in the quarter, pleading a case for this one or that one, about some specific injustice or cruelty. Françoise often felt that she was in the middle of squabbling children, each insisting on giving his or her particular interpretation of the same event, an event that didn't really matter anyway. All she cared about was that within her own household the girl knew her place and the work got done. The day-to-day running of the house and grounds was left to Elisabeth, Suzette, and Old Bertram. It was the best she could do.

"The overseer's here, Madame."

Her girl's voice sounded wary. A stumpy man holding a soiled and misshapen hat in his hand followed Suzette into the darkened room.

Françoise had a strong distaste for the overseer. He was uncouth, with a face chapped rough by the sun, an unwashed odor that preceded him, and no family connections to speak of. She didn't want him inside her house, let alone her bedroom. She would have rather had Narcisse or Eugene deal with him, but the overseer had been insistent that he speak to her immediately.

Françoise heard Oreline quietly close her book. Her niece remained seated in the chair by the bed. Suzette disappeared.

"I hope your health is improved, Madame," he began,

standing a respectful distance from the bed but filling the room nonetheless.

"As well as can be expected, but my vitality comes and goes. You had an urgent matter that required my personal attention?"

"Yes, Madame. The bank won't extend any more credit to us. We already let part of the south field go last year. We need seed now, or we miss this planting, too. I have a way out of our problem."

"I'm listening," said Françoise, impatient with her dependence on this man.

"The deaf and dumb girl has three mulattos that would bring a decent price. If we sell them, we save the season, without losing any workers."

Oreline gasped. "Aunt Françoise, there must be some other way," she said, interrupting, her voice shrill. It was unlike her. "Not Palmire's children."

"I can get two hundred dollars for the oldest. With such a shortage on Cane River, even the little ones are fetching a good sum," the overseer continued as if Oreline had not spoken. "They're banking on the future," he said with a wink. "If we don't do this, we put the whole plantation at risk."

Françoise could picture their faces, two boys and a girl, mulattos carrying Louis's features. They used to try to hide the children from her when she went to the quarter, but she had seen them.

"Most of the worth of Rosedew is tied up in the quarter. All you have to do, Madame, is give me the go-ahead," the overseer pressed. "I can take care of the rest."

And so, without wanting to remember their names, Françoise authorized the sale of first Paul, age five, then

Solais, three, and finally Melantine, age two, away from Rosedew.

Once the slave sales began, the slow but steady outflow continued, one or two from the quarter each year, but Rosedew couldn't right itself. The smokehouse was never more than half-full, and rations were reduced in both the big house and the quarter. Grass completely reclaimed the south field.

The year that cotton fell to less than seven cents a pound, Françoise managed to arrange a match for Oreline to a poor young farmer from lower Cane River. Her niece was twenty-two.

Two weeks before the wedding Françoise and Oreline sat in Françoise's bedroom, stitching items for Oreline's trousseau. Françoise began to cough, a long series of clipped strangles that seemed to feed on themselves, and Oreline threw aside her handiwork.

"It pains me to go away and leave you," she said, easing Françoise's upper body forward and rubbing her back in firm, circular movements. "I'll be so far away."

"Only downriver, no farther than your cousin Narcisse," Françoise replied. "It is important to embrace the chance to marry when you have it."

"Monsieur Ferrier thinks I could learn to be a good wife to him. He says he enjoys my company." Color dotted Oreline's pale cheeks. "But it doesn't seem proper to leave you on Rosedew alone."

Françoise looked at the young woman she had raised. Oreline was a plain-featured woman, but devoted and as close to her as any daughter who would have been born of her own body. It was difficult to think of her niece paired to a man who worked with his hands, but the union was preferable to having Oreline adopt the hooded bonnet of spinsterhood, with ribbons that tied under the chin. Joseph Ferrier was a tall, long-limbed man, a welcome fit for Oreline's height, an outdoorsman with sure movements and sandy hair that fell into his eyes. He seemed good-natured and was solicitous of his mother, both good signs, and he had appeared at once to be attracted to Oreline's quiet, obedient ways. At least someone found the girl attractive, Françoise thought. She didn't want to dwell on the fact that Ferrier was a small-time farmer, overreaching.

"My time is past," Françoise said. "Now we must secure the best position for you that we are able. Once I am gone, Rosedew will have to be sold. Perhaps your portion will allow you and Monsieur Ferrier to better your lot."

"*Oui*, Aunt Françoise," Oreline said respectfully. "I promise to come back to visit every week."

The wedding was a modest affair. When the ceremony was over, Oreline moved away from Rosedew to Ferrier's small farm, a bumpy step down from plantation life.

Only Françoise Derbanne was left in the big house on Rosedew, Françoise and her visitors and her servants.

Ⅰn the ten years following the death of Louis Derbanne, everyone on Rosedew had learned to adjust to the
hard luck that kept to the heels of the plantation like a
mean-spirited dog.

Suzette endured, always standing, waiting to serve, without complaint. She had spent her entire life taking care of
people who could not take care of themselves. She pretended to care about the knot of infirmities that tightened
around Françoise. She pretended to care that Eugene Daurat
brought little candies and trinkets from his store for Gerant
and Philomene. As the children grew older, Eugene even
gave Gerant a real carpenter's awl, the handle nicked and
worn and the point dulled but still serviceable, and he often
brought bits of calico for Philomene to patch a skirt or sew
up a new josie. Suzette pretended to care each week when
Oreline confided during her visits how homesick she was for

Rosedew and how worried she was about Françoise's physical decline. Since the birth of her children and the selling of her niece and nephews, Suzette had become unflinchingly certain about what mattered.

All she really cared about now was her own family.

Outside Françoise Derbanne's bedroom, Suzette drew Gerant and Philomene close to her. She stooped low and whispered so only they could hear. "Philomene, you stay where Madame can see you in case she wakes. If she starts to fret, send Gerant to come find me."

"You know you can count on me, *Maman*," Philomene said in the matter-of-fact way she had. "I can handle Madame by myself, get her to calm down and do whatever I want."

Suzette stared at her daughter's serious face, then pinched her hard on the arm. "That is dangerous talk, and you must never say anything like it again."

Philomene looked surprised but not sorry. "Yes, *Maman*," she said at last.

Suzette hurriedly left the big house by the back door.

Despite the gauzy shadows of haze across the evening sky, the full moon lit the way for Suzette's nightly journey to the quarter. As she began her walk, she reached into her apron pocket. Her fingers found the items she carried with her everywhere, the rosary Françoise Derbanne had given her over a decade before and the stiff scrap of tanned cowhide, a present from a young boy to a young girl who still had dreams.

Only a few steps down the path, she suddenly turned and began to run back to the house, almost stumbling on a loose stone in the dark.

"Gerant, Philomene," Suzette whispered urgently into

the stillness of the back room, opening her arms wide. They came to her, and she clutched her children, pressing them to her as tightly as she could. The boy smell of Gerant mixed with the odor of wax from his lighting of the candles, and the sharp scent of lye soap from the supper dishes had found its way into Philomene's braided hair.

"My babies," she said. Then, loosening her grip, she stepped back to put distance between herself and them. To Philomene she said, "Why can't you understand the danger?"

"I will send for you if Madame stirs," Philomene said. "Please do not worry, *Maman*."

Suzette felt their eyes looking after her as she went out again into the night. Sometimes she couldn't get enough of Gerant and Philomene. Other times she couldn't attach herself to them at all, as if they were already gone. Her children were house raised, she thought. Maybe she could keep them safer than Palmire's children.

Suzette was still small, and she was still pretty. It was easy to trace in her facial features and body proportions the African ancestors on her mother's side and the stray drops of Caddo Indian from her father. For a time, the spicy snap of her name and the way she had been brought up had tricked her into believing that she was also partly colored Creole, immune. At twenty-five, she saw more clearly now. The open-faced sweetness of her youth had been replaced by a nagging vagueness that came and went of its own accord, and although she still claimed a child's distinction of soft brown eyes too big for her face, the shimmering of possibilities was no longer reflected there.

The few chickens stirring around the henhouse scattered as she walked into their domain, and she clucked at them softly. They were used to her. The straw pricked at her fingers as she felt around in the setting beds. She took only two eggs, putting them in her apron pocket. After pulling the door shut behind her and fastening the latch, she kept on the path to the cookhouse. Three buttermilk biscuits were hidden in the pantry where she had left them this morning, wrapped in a white rag. She put those in her other pocket, along with a jar she had filled with molasses and a small kitchen knife.

Instead of the footpath that would take her past the overseer's house, Suzette cut through a small patch of pines to approach the quarter from behind.

She went to see her father first, careful to step around the rotted plank on the porch. The place held the tight, close odor of mold and waste. The cabin had not been white-washed for three planting seasons, and the floors had not been limed for well over a year.

"How is he?" Suzette whispered to Elisabeth as she came through the door.

A small fire burned in the fireplace and threw patterns of light and dark around the room, highlighting the spare furnishings. There were two pallets at opposite corners and three seats at a small table set with wooden plates and several drinking gourds. Only Gerasíme, Elisabeth, and Solataire lived in the cabin now. Gerasíme breathed loudly, his head protruding from a ragged gray blanket on the pallet, his hair long and wild, tangled and sweat soaked on the log pillow. Elisabeth sat by his side on a pine stump.

"Better," Elisabeth said. "I salved the cuts, and he's able to sleep now. This overseer's meaner than the last. Five stripes this time." She lightly wiped Gerasíme's face with a damp rag. "If he doesn't get back out to the field tomorrow, there'll be more lashes on top of these. I'll make sure he doesn't miss the morning bell."

"You need to get some sleep, too," Suzette whispered as she unwrapped the rag from her pocket. "I brought an egg and biscuits. Where is Solataire?"

"Trying to hunt up some meat."

"I'll be going to sit with Palmire a little, then."

"Move around careful," Elisabeth warned. "Even Madame may not be able to help if the overseer finds eggs in your apron."

"I'll say it's for the house."

Suzette continued down the line of cabins in the quarter. Several men and women holding gourds waited their turn around the small hand mill to grind their corn ration for tomorrow's dinner in the field. They stopped talking as she neared.

"Good evening," Suzette said, slowing a little.

"How is Madame?" one of them asked.

"Still poorly," Suzette answered. "Mam'zelle Oreline comes back to Rosedew tomorrow to stay until Madame is better. With her son."

The group nodded tiredly, and Suzette kept moving along the line of cabins, almost to the end.

Young Clement and his mother, Eliza, ate their evening meal outdoors on the elevated porch of the cabin next to Palmire's. Suzette waved. Eliza was Suzette's age, and Philomene and Clement were inseparable whenever she allowed her children to come down to the quarter.

"Has Madame picked up any?" Eliza called out.

"Still about the same," Suzette said in passing, and tried to continue on, but Eliza motioned her in.

"What's to come of us when Madame dies?" the young

woman asked with urgency, and although Clement sat quiet, he listened hard, as if Suzette's words could make the future.

No matter how many times someone asked Suzette the question, the pain was raw and caught her fresh. She surprised herself with her outward calm, walking, talking, performing her chores, all the while on the edge of a consuming terror.

"I don't know, Eliza. The talk is they will sell the place."

"Can you say something about me and the boy going together?" Eliza implored.

"There's nothing I can do," Suzette said, turning away. "I have to see to Palmire."

No light came from her sister's cabin, no smoke from the chimney. A sadness engulfed the small dwelling, an emptiness that flowed from the inside out. The door was open, and Palmire sat motionless on her pallet. Suzette almost expected to see Paul's chubby legs pumping as he ran to greet her, Solais behind his older brother, and Melantine in the corner, blowing bubbles to amuse herself. It had been seven years since the children had been sold from Rosedew, and Suzette still thought of them as babies. They were as grown as her own two, and although she knew they were still on Cane River, they belonged now to some other place.

Suzette walked over and touched Palmire's shoulder. Palmire looked up, lines etched deep in her forehead and around her eyes.

"You must eat, sister," Suzette motioned, and unwrapped the last of the biscuits and the other egg.

She lit a fire in the fireplace and waited for the flames to take hold, gathering up Palmire's small skillet and wooden plate. Suzette took the covering off Palmire's weekly ration of bacon in the corner, cut off a small piece with the kitchen knife she brought, and put it in the skillet to fry. When there was enough grease in the pan, she cracked the egg and fried it up, too, and scooped it all out onto the wooden plate alongside the biscuits and molasses.

She sat stiffly in Palmire's pine chair, watching her sister listlessly swallow the food. When Palmire finished, Suzette wiped the skillet and dishes as clean as she could, and the two of them sat in the childless cabin wrapped in silence.

Suzette finally got up. She needed to get back to the big house to make sure Françoise had not called for her. She touched the door and pointed out toward the moon.

"Tomorrow night," Suzette motioned to Palmire.

Palmire nodded.

No amount of punishment, reward, or deadening routine could ease the growing dread that reached from the big house to the quarter and into the fields. In more ordinary times it was the season to be totally absorbed in the fourth and final picking of the cotton harvest and the brief, sweet lull before the planting of the new crop. Instead all hands waited anxiously for word from the big house. The overseer had lost some of his power to an even bigger terror, and the lash on the backs of the dispirited slaves now had the opposite effect of what he intended. The more he whipped, pushed, and demanded, the slower the tempo in the field became, the more hoes and pickaxes and oxen's yokes turned up mysteriously broken, the more twigs appeared in the swelling baskets of fluffy white at the end of each row of cotton. The questioning pop of the lash and the answering human refrain could be heard most days now as the overseer performed his work unchecked.

In the big house visitors still called, but their stays

became shorter as Françoise became less responsive. Narcisse Fredieu was among those who came most often, and Eugene Daurat traveled sometimes by boat and sometimes by horse the six miles between Rosedew and the farm downriver he now shared openly with Doralise Derbanne.

In the end, it was the women's job to tend to the dying. Suzette and Oreline often found themselves alone in the dark back bedroom with the weak, shrunken Françoise. Her skin had taken on a strange translucent quality, and after long hours with no relief, Suzette sometimes believed she could see the blood straining to squeeze through the raised ropelike veins of Françoise Derbanne's hands.

"Have you talked to M'sieu Ferrier again?" Suzette began hopefully in a whisper, careful to tamp down any insistence in her tone. "Will he buy all of us together?"

Oreline looked nervously at the supine figure of her aunt, who in troubled sleep drew ragged, raspy breaths.

"This is not the time to discuss it," she whispered back.

It was bad news. Suzette knew Oreline well enough to recognize when she was trying to avoid something she did not want to face.

"But it will be your money when they sell Rosedew. It comes to you, not M'sieu Ferrier."

"Sometimes I think I tell you too much, Suzette. Monsieur Ferrier is my husband. He is the one to take care of such matters. I have given you my word that we will buy both you and Philomene. He has agreed to that much. But he cannot see his way clear to buy Gerant. The boy is too young to be of the kind of help he needs in the field, and Monsieur will not move from his position. We are not rich. We only work a small farm, and we need someone for planting right now. Perhaps Eugene Daurat can help with Gerant. I can talk to him on your behalf."

Suzette knew pushing any harder would force Oreline into defending her husband, taking his side against hers. She clamped down hard on her bitterness, as if it were a metallic bit set in her mouth. What kind of man needed to be shamed into buying his own son?

"I would be grateful if you would talk to M'sieu Daurat, Mam'zelle."

Suzette busied her hands folding linen, letting time pass before beginning again. "Mam'zelle, if it's help with planting you're after, my sister Palmire can do the work of a man in the field. She's the strongest hoe woman on Rosedew, and she can pick two hundred pounds of cotton a day. Deaf and dumb doesn't stop her from being a good hand."

"I can make no promises, Suzette, but I will try. I don't think you appreciate how much I've done for you already. This isn't proper talk with my aunt on her sickbed. Let's hear no more about it."

The days passed in dreary repetition, grinding down all three of the women in the back room, until Françoise began to use the short spurts of strength that came to her to fight against life. The curtains stayed tightly drawn at her request. She refused to sit up, and she choked on the food they brought to her bedside. After a time she refused to eat or be fed at all, pushing away anything they brought like a petulant child. She slipped in and out of consciousness.

The more Françoise's condition worsened, the less useful Oreline became, until Suzette was forced to take hold of the situation.

"Mam'zelle," Suzette said gently but firmly, "you should send for the priest. She can't last much longer, and she would want to die in grace."

"*Oui,*" Oreline said. "Send Gerant for Father Blanc."

The priest and Gerant returned together, Father Blanc on his chestnut bay and Gerant on the Rosedew mare. Still smelling of haste and horse sweat, the priest went directly in to Françoise without stopping for his customary pleasantries and set about the task of performing last rites. After he finished they served him café au lait, and the three mourners waited respectfully for Françoise Derbanne's spirit to depart. When she neither died nor regained her senses, Father Blanc rode back to St. Augustine at a far less hurried gait than when he had arrived.

And still Françoise hung on.

Suzette thought it must be true what they said. *Creoles pas mourri, ils desseche.* Creoles don't die, they dry up.

Françoise Derbanne finally died on a Thursday, two weeks after receiving last rites, with Oreline sitting at her aunt's bedside, holding her limp hand, and Suzette cleaning up after the mess of the attempted morning meal. It had taken Françoise a long time to die, just like her husband, Louis. Unlike in life, in death she passed without drama or instruction. She just stopped breathing.

Suzette said a quick prayer, made the sign of the cross, and got up off her knees. There was much to do. Her red-rimmed eyes burned and her back was stiff, the result of her having sat up most of the last three nights tending to Françoise, and she refused to embrace the sentimental scene of the niece's final farewell to her aunt. She let it pass through her without sensation, unwilling to be weighed down with the dead when the living were at risk. Her gingham dress clung to her, and her cocoa skin was slick, even more from the dread that had settled down deep within her than the familiar wet heat.

"Mam'zelle Oreline . . . Mam'zelle . . ." Suzette spoke to the pale, trembling woman in the same tones she had heard her father use when steadying a high-spirited horse, more importance in the tone and continuity than the words themselves.

"First we'll say a prayer for Madame Françoise together," Suzette crooned, "and then I want you to go to the front room and sit down while I take care of everything in here. I've brought your rosary. We'll send Gerant to fetch back M'sieu Daurat. They know him well enough on Cane River, you don't even have to worry yourself writing out a pass. We should send for Narcisse Fredieu, too. You need family around you right now. Philomene will get you some nice sassafras tea while we wait for them to get here. We'll wait together. I'm still here, Mam'zelle. Aren't I always here when you need me? Come on with me now. I'll take you myself and get you settled in the front room, and I'll be back to sit with you directly after I do a few things. You're a Derbanne, Mam'zelle, and you can get through this. I'll help you."

Oreline offered no resistance, allowing herself to be guided toward the front of the house, away from the still-warm body of her aunt.

"Look at those roses, Mam'zelle Oreline. Still pretty. Those flowers know how to keep on blooming year after year whether they're looked after or not."

Suzette had cut some of the roses from the yard and arranged a cluster of soft yellows and salmons and reds in the cut crystal vase Louis had brought back from France so many years before as an anniversary present for Françoise.

Even though Suzette had pulled back the heavy drapes at

the window and thrown open the windows, the house still had the closed-in smell of infirmity and deterioration. She had spent each spare minute of the last few weeks cleaning walls, floors, and windows, bringing in pails of soapy water. As though by scrubbing she could hold back the moment when everything she held dear could be torn from her, the way she knew it had from so many others.

Suzette saw Philomene appear silently in the front room, as if she had called out loud for her. "Philomene, there you are. Go get Mam'zelle some tea, and send Gerant for Eugene Daurat and Narcisse Fredieu. Madame has passed."

An unspoken signal passed from mother to daughter. *And make sure the news gets to the field that she's dead.*

Suzette kept Elisabeth's words in the front of her mind to keep herself from wavering. "You do whatever you can, whatever you have to, in order to protect you and yours." She knew the Ones with Last Names could buy those she loved, if they chose. Eugene Daurat. Oreline Derbanne. Doralise Derbanne. Narcisse Fredieu.

In the days following Françoise's last rites, the panic had come in waves, threatening to overpower Suzette unless she practiced her appeals over and over. She had repeated them to herself so many times that they chased each other around in her head, appearing in wake and in sleep in random order. She had begun to wonder if she would be strong enough now that the time had come, terrified that her pleas might not strike the right chords. That they would turn a deaf ear because she would sound as if she had forgotten her place.

Would anyone else know how valuable they were? Her fiddler father, Gerasíme? Her deaf and dumb sister Palmire, whose remaining senses allowed her to see her three children taken from her and sold? Her clever Gerant, who at the age of eleven already showed signs of being able to make anything out of wood? Her mother, Elisabeth, whose breeding years were at an end and whose tongue still stumbled sometimes over her French words, but whose cooking was second to none? And Philomene. Her little Philomene with her thick wavy hair and creamy skin, who did not know how to bend enough, yet. Whose expectations were even higher than Suzette's own at that age. She needed more time with Philomene to get her ready.

Leaving Philomene to watch over Oreline, Suzette hurried to the cookhouse. There would be many mourners visiting Rosedew today, and grief would not overpower the need for hospitality or nourishment.

"*Mère* Elisabeth, I have to try to catch M'sieu Eugene and M'sieu Narcisse alone when they come. I'll send Philomene in to help with supper as soon as I can."

Elisabeth nodded, her face hard as she continued to stir the contents of the heavy iron pot suspended over the fire.

Suzette picked up her skirts and ran to the front of the house to see if anyone had come yet. There were no horses. She hurried around to the back door and entered the house, passing down the hall to the front room, and motioned Philomene away from Oreline's side.

"Go down and help *Mère* Elisabeth," she whispered. "But be ready to be useful in the house, too."

"Yes, *Maman*," Philomene said gravely, and headed for the back door.

Suzette took her position again in the front room with Oreline, and they waited.

Eugene Daurat was the first to arrive.

"Cousin Oreline," he said, arms outstretched as he

strode in through the front door. "Françoise Derbanne was a good woman."

Oreline held fast to him for a moment, and then they sat together on the settee. Eugene stayed close by her side for the next two hours.

Shortly before supper was to be served, Eugene took up his hat to go outdoors for a smoke. Suzette followed him quietly, and when he stopped to light his cigar just out of sight of the house, she assumed her humble pose, eyes downcast, making small noises with her feet to let him know she was there.

Eugene turned. "Suzette?"

"M'sieu Daurat. If I could just talk to you. You're a gentleman, like Louis Derbanne was. And he freed his children. Look at what he did for Doralise."

It was the wrong beginning. Suzette knew it, but the words she had rehearsed were taking a crooked course of their own. She spoke in a rush, needing to get it out while she had this chance.

"M'sieu Derbanne recognized blood ties," Suzette said. "He did the right thing for his own flesh and blood."

She tried not to think of Palmire's children, sold one after the other by the Widow Derbanne. *Because* they had Derbanne blood. She circled Eugene quickly and dropped to her knees, head bowed, in front of where he stood. A small sharp stone cut at her knee, and she rocked herself on it to clear her mind.

"He treated you like a son. He would want you to look out after Gerant and Philomene. He would say it was your responsibility. M'sieu, please."

Suzette forced herself to stay on her knees, staring at the eyelets of Eugene Daurat's shoes as she talked, willing the crisscross pattern of the laces to hold her together. Something dangerous and wild was threatening to lift her up, to set her clawing at the doll man's throat. Even through the material of her dress and undershift she could feel the soft, warm pulsing and the stickiness around her knee where the blood had been loosed. She ground her knee down harder on the rock.

"Gerant has been trained in the house. He knows how to be around people of quality. He's clever with his hands. He could help you around your own house, or in your store. You've seen yourself how he can make tools out of wood, and fix things better than grown men. If you don't step in, he could end up on the McAlpin place, where they whip their Negroes into early graves. I'm begging. I never asked you for anything for myself. You can figure out a way to free him."

Suzette knew she had pushed in the wrong direction, but she couldn't seem to stop. It used to be that Eugene would make vague promises about freeing his children, but any talk of freedom now just set his jaw. She didn't have to see his face to feel the tightening of his body, like a cornered loggerhead turtle pulling its head into its shell.

"Or buy him for yourself. Save him. I'm begging you, save him. I'll do anything you want, just don't let him be sold away from Cane River."

Eugene backed away from her, leaving her there, and turned to walk back toward the house.

"I'll do what I can for the boy," he said over his shoulder, and with quickened steps he hurried away.

Even with her eyes closed and the stale taste of dust in her mouth, Suzette could still see the crisscross of his shoelaces, long after he was gone.

*   *   *

Narcisse didn't arrive until midafternoon. Suzette listened for his approach and went out to him as he rode on to Rosedew atop his sorrel mare.

He looked prosperous in his dark broadcloth suit and new riding boots. He had recently married and bought land downriver near the parish line, close to the farm where Oreline and her husband lived. Suzette had been lent to both of them to cook and serve for their opening parties.

This time, she promised herself, she would say the words as she had practiced them. "M'sieu Narcisse. I am so sorry for the loss of your aunt."

In front of her was an aspiring young planter sitting high on his horse in his stiff black jacket and tie, but Suzette could still see the pudgy little boy trying to order her and Oreline around in the piney woods behind the big house.

Suzette did not look directly at him. "You know us here on Rosedew. You spent time in my mother's kitchen. She always thought high on you. More than any of the other cousins who came to visit. She always told me that you would make something of yourself, even when we were little. She knew you had a good heart. A kind heart."

The lies were second nature. They were expected and easily accepted.

"Our family was always faithful to the Derbannes. My father was born here. My mother has been cook for thirty years. You must need good workers you know and trust. Take Elisabeth and Gerasíme together. They would be grateful and work hard for you. You've tasted my mother's cooking. With Mademoiselle Tranquillin being so new to marriage, Elisabeth could help her get the house set up and running smooth. And Gerasíme is a steady hand in the field. He handles an ox as well as he plays the fiddle."

Narcisse's heavy brows pushed together toward the center of his wrinkled forehead in a gesture Suzette knew well. He was anxious to get down from his horse and get inside out of the drizzle, but he was also drawn by the idea.

"*Oui,* Suzette, I know your family," Narcisse said uncomfortably, "but I can't afford to buy two more slaves now no matter how helpful they might be."

"M'sieu Narcisse, they need to be sold together to a good place. The kind of place you would run. They've been together for over thirty years on Rosedew. Already they'll be separated from all of their children and grandchildren. They'd work harder if they were sold together."

"I can't go into debt trying to keep the two of them in the same place. It's likely they'll both end up on Cane River somewhere and they can visit each other Sundays."

Narcisse spoke into the distance as if Suzette were not standing close enough to the sweating mare to feel the heat pouring off her.

Narcisse paused. "But I could use someone for the house who would give Tranquillin a hand with the cooking," he said, as if the notion had just appeared out of the sky. Just as quickly he was finished with the subject. "I need to go in to Cousin Oreline. See to it that someone takes care of my horse."

He swung himself easily off his mare, splattering mud on Suzette's dress as his boots landed in a small puddle. He threw the reins in Suzette's direction without looking back and disappeared into the house.

Suzette had wanted to do more than plant a seed with Narcisse Fredieu, but a seed planted was better than nothing.

Suzette asked Oreline for permission to go to mass the

next morning to say prayers for Madame Françoise, and Oreline wrote the pass. Suzette set out on foot before day-break to get to St. Augustine by six o'clock. Doralise Der-banne would be there, as she always was on Wednesday mornings. Suzette listened to the mass from outside on the gallery. St. Augustine had risen in status since its struggling early years and no longer allowed slaves inside the sanctuary for any reason.

Doralise was one of the first out of the church. She looked calm and steady, older than Suzette remembered, with fine lines around her eyes, and the corset couldn't hide the thickness around her middle. But she was still the por-trait of refinement to Suzette, and the few gray strands in her hair only made her more stately. Doralise might be colored, a woman, and her *marraine,* but she was still one of the Ones with Last Names. Suzette had to be careful.

"Suzette?" Doralise said, surprised.

"Madame, I have come to see you," Suzette said. "Rosedew is finished, and they are going to sell all of us away."

Doralise reached out and touched Suzette on the arm, nothing more than a moment's contact. Suzette reminded herself that this was the woman now living with the father of her children.

The words poured out too hot and fast and random. "You're a mother. You understand. Have mercy on us. What if your daughter, Elisida, was in danger of being sold away from you and there was nothing you could do? You have a part in this family. They're planning to sell Gerasíme and Elisabeth and Palmire and Apphia and Solataire all to differ-ent places, and our children somewhere else altogether."

Suzette took a deep breath. This was too important to let get away from her. The thought of the fleeting touch steadied her. Doralise was listening, even sympathetic. She began again.

"Mam'zelle Oreline has promised to buy Philomene and me together. But that leaves Gerant. Mam'zelle Oreline can't get M'sieu Ferrier to buy in an eleven-year-old boy. It's no use, his mind is set against it. If you or M'sieu Eugene could buy Gerant, he'll be treated right. M'sieu Eugene told me he would free them both, but now he doesn't say anything at all except that the times aren't the same as they were before. Please. Please. Think about what could happen to my boy. Help M'sieu Daurat do what is right. I talked to him already, but he didn't say what he's going to do. Gerant could get sold away from Cane River."

Suzette began to sob. "I don't have anything but my family, and now even my children could be taken away from me. Madame Doralise, if you help me now, I'll always do anything I can for you. Always."

Doralise shook her head slowly.

"I do not have as much power as you think, Suzette." She reached out to her again, and Suzette felt the smoothness of the soft gloves wrapped around one of her callused hands. "But I will try to find a way to help. Now I must go."

With each step of the long walk back to Rosedew from St. Augustine, Suzette felt the tiredness spread beneath her skin and lodge itself deeper than muscle or bone. She had done what she could. Nothing was certain. Nothing was settled.

The girl came to Elisabeth one afternoon in the cook-house. The wind had been howling for the better part of the day, an unearthly screeching sound that made Elisabeth restless.

"*Mémère* Elisabeth, I cannot talk to *Maman*," her grand-daughter began without preamble. "She is . . ." Philomene paused and looked away. "She is nervous again."

"Then talk to me," Elisabeth said.

"I've had two glimpsings." Philomene made the announcement as if this were an everyday occurrence.

Elisabeth looked closely at Philomene, staring deep into the intensity of her buttermilk-colored face. She swiftly crossed to the door, leaned out, and spat in the dirt out-doors.

"Tell me about both of them, quick."

Philomene sat in one of the cane-bottom chairs, her feet

swinging free, not reaching the floor. "On wash day, *Maman* was telling me the story of her white dress and St. Augustine. I heard her voice, I saw the steam from the washtub, but all of a sudden there was a different picture in my head. It was like floating, being in two places at once. I was the one in the white dress, with flowers in my hair, and Clement and I were in front of a priest, grown. Heavy drops ran down the side of Clement's face, as if he just came in from working bareheaded in the sun. I thought maybe we were taking first communion, the way that *Maman* did, but then this morning, the second picture came."

"Go on," Elisabeth urged.

"Clement and I are sitting inside a cabin, and each of us is holding a baby. Both the babies are the same size, and they are ours. I know this."

Elisabeth allowed herself to grin. "That gives you meaning, bringing a child into life. It looks like you're glimpsing yourself some good."

"Both of the pictures feel happy, *Mémère*," Philomene went on, "but in the first glimpsing, Clement's hands are too big, thick and rough and bright white, and he has a long split up his back."

"Were the pictures clear or dim?" Elisabeth asked.

"They came to me for a long time, *Mémère* Elisabeth, long enough for me to study. Clement has those big white hands, and he looks scared. And I don't know why he is in two pieces up the back. What could it mean? Should I tell Clement?"

"I don't know what each part means, Philomene, but at the heart, it seems you and Clement are going to have some life together. The rest will come to you in time, if it's meant. Store away what you don't understand for now. As for Clement, what do you think will happen if you tell him?"

"He might turn scared of me, the way some people are, or nervous, the way *Maman* gets."

"Have you told him about the other things you've seen?"

"Always. He listens, and asks me questions, like you. He hasn't been scared yet. But this time, he is in the glimpsing. That never happened before." Philomene pulled at her hair, coiling the tip of one braid around her finger. "You know *Maman* doesn't like me to talk too much about Clement."

"Philomene, sometimes Suzette gets beside herself over color. His brown doesn't make him bad, and your yellow doesn't make you good. Your mama follows her road, your path may be different. You go on and tell Clement everything you can, for as long as you can. See what he's made of. There are things so hard that they refuse telling. Not this."

"What hard things, *Mémère?*"

Elisabeth shook her head. "You glimpse the best that can happen to a woman, and it takes me back to the worst."

"The worst?" Philomene asked.

Elisabeth looked beyond her granddaughter's young face into the depths of her old-soul eyes. She judged Philomene strong enough. "Other people can tell you that you're nothing, that you have nothing, not even your own flesh and blood."

"Like Aunt Palmire's children?"

"Yes." The shrill wind dared Elisabeth forward. "Before I came to Louisiana, I lived on a big plantation in Virginia, working in the big house there, too. I wasn't long past girlhood when the young Marse got to pestering me. He was older, and whenever his mother wasn't around he came after me. I didn't want him fooling with me, but there was no need fighting. There's no winning against what white men take into their heads to do on their own place.

"So I became his thing when he wanted. And it wasn't so long before I had a boy-child.

"I named him John and just kept on. The boy had light eyes from the beginning, even when he was struggling just to keep them open. They made me laugh at this little person I had made. He was mine. Wasn't nobody else going to claim a blood tie.

"The Mistress turned against me then and whipped me for dropping the bread, for looking at her wrong, for anything that came into her head, but I still had my John. I loved that little baby, and at first I kept him with me whenever I could. It didn't take long to figure out that whenever she saw me with him it put her in the mind to reach out and hurt me, or worse, John. It made the Mistress a little crazy to see that pale baby peeking out of those blankets, or in my arms.

"I started to leave him down in the quarter then, looked after along with the rest of the babies by whoever could tend him. I got down there when I could, especially to nurse him. I got whipped for that, too, when I wasn't where they wanted me to be.

"The young Marse kept away from me for a while, and his mother got him married, but he still looked to me when he was feeling a certain way. I nursed John as often and for as long as I could. They said in the quarter that nursing kept you from the next baby. It worked. I didn't come up caught again until after John finished nursing. He was almost two. I had another boy, and this time the Mistress and the new wife got together and said they were going to remove temptation. They sold me away from both of my boys. I didn't have much time to get to know the second one. I named him Jacob. That name was in the Bible, too.

"John and Jacob."

Elisabeth moved stiffly to the fireplace to put another log under the kettle. Philomene sat quietly until her grandmother started talking again.

"They sent me straight to Cane River from there, without giving me a chance to say good-bye, not even to my babies, although Lord knows they wouldn't remember me. They put me on a boat in the hands of a friend of the family, and sent me to New Orleans. I had already been sold to someone they knew here, to Louis Derbanne's father, Pierre Derbanne. Both of those were French Creole men you never knew, here and gone before you were born. I didn't know any French at all, and that's all they spoke. They put me in the kitchen because of my baking in Virginia, and when old Pierre died, I got passed around to his son, Louis, and came on here to Rosedew. I was blessed to meet up with your grandfather Gerasíme. Lord, that man had to be patient, I was so torn up. When the babies started coming again, I thought I couldn't have any more boys. But I loved my girls and watched them grow. First Palmire, deaf and dumb from the birth and special, then Apphia, and your mother, Suzette. And finally a boy, Solataire. I got to be grateful for every season that passed and we were still together. I saw them all grow up, and now there are grandchildren. The Lord gives us what we need sometimes."

Elisabeth managed a fragile smile. It never went beyond her mouth.

"I don't know what happened to either one of my boys I left in Virginia. They would be your kin, your uncles.

"You find all the happiness you can with Clement,

Philomene, and you bring us children when the time comes.
Family stays family no matter where they are or who they are.
I can see the truth of your glimpsings. Go find the boy. Talk to
him as straight as you talk to me."

The assessors arrived in waves over the course of the
next two weeks. They set about with great purpose, never
alone. They came on horseback, riding the length and
breadth of Rosedew on both sides of the Cane River, first
looking in this direction or that, taking out some metal
instrument, consulting one another, checking and recheck-
ing. Then, seemingly satisfied, they made marks in their
books. They visited all of the structures on the plantation,
the smokehouse, cookhouse, barns, springhouse, toolsheds,
corncribs, quarter cabins, marking them off one by one.
They handled each piece of equipment from the large to the
small, inspecting the condition of the cotton gin and the
gristmill or the balance of the weighing scales. They ran their
colorless hands over the tools and harnesses as if they were
getting ready to use them, but they never did. Inside the
main house they went from room to room as if they were in
pursuit of a secret, their boots tracking in mud from outside
that Elisabeth knew either she or Suzette would have to
clean. She watched them feel the smooth dark mahogany of
the armoire, count the bedsteads, eye the silver, and finger
the intricate patterns of the fireplace mantels, all the while
scribbling notes in their journals.

They left the slaves for last, as they tallied up the life of
Louis and Françoise Derbanne, gathering them in early from
the field one day, before twilight, and instructing them to
wait under the ancient oak at the edge of the big house. The
spread and grandeur of the tree made them look small, old

and young huddled together. They had been given double rations for the last few weeks, and the overseer had been ordered not to mete out any fresh lashes before the sale.

The assessors worked from the inventory that had been taken ten years before, after Louis Derbanne passed away. All they had to do was add the names of those who had been born in the last decade and subtract those of the ones who had died or been sold since. They didn't have to guess at the slaves' ages again or the spelling of names. Not one new slave had been bought in the last ten years. Times had been too lean.

The assessors sat behind a makeshift table, four grim-faced white men selected with great care, whose job it was to estimate where the bidding should start for each of the lives passing in front of them.

The slaves clustered together in their family groups, glancing over at the assessors behind the table with the big journal. Elisabeth and Gerasíme formed the center of one of the groups, their children fanned out around them. Suzette brought out Gerant and Philomene from the big house and took her place with her mother and father as they waited. Elisabeth's second daughter, Apphia, held tightly to all three of her children. Laide clung to her mother's dress, too old at eleven to suck her thumb but mouthing the back of her hand. Apphia carried infant Florenal high on her hip and with her free hand held on to three-year-old Euphemie. Solataire, Elisabeth's youngest, talked quietly to those around him. His wife and children were on the Greneaux plantation, and Elisabeth knew he was praying to be sold there. Palmire had come alone in silent surrender. Her three children had already been taken from her. What difference could it make what they did to her now?

The assessors were ready. After conferring among themselves, they nodded to the overseer to begin.

"Get yourselves old to young. First men, and then women. Old to young," the overseer called out loudly from behind the table.

There was confusion, as if they had been torn apart from each other already. They looked to one another for understanding. This wasn't even auction day yet.

The overseer moved menacingly toward the clumps of families under the oak tree. He caressed the coiled whip at his hip next to his flask but did not remove it from its place.

"Are you deaf? Line up old to young. Don't force me to put you in line myself."

Gerasíme was the first to understand. Elisabeth watched her husband as he moved quickly toward Old Bertram, whose clouded eyes and swollen leg made it difficult for him to move. Gerasíme led him slowly by the arm to the assessors' table and then plunged back into the knotted group to find Athenase, the next oldest man on the plantation.

"It's just getting into a line for today," he said under his breath to everyone he passed, "and then you go back to your families."

They sorted themselves by looks and by remembrance.

"I was picking a hundred pounds a day when he was still sweeping cow paddies out the road," said one.

"I'm older. I remember the drought of '22," said another.

All of the men went first, oldest to youngest.

Then it was the women's turn. Only mothers with babies in their arms were allowed to come before the assessors' table as a family group. The process went smoothly, carefully, once everyone understood what was expected. A dollar figure was suggested and debated among the assessors. When they came to agreement they marked it down in the book. A special notation was made for any defect, physical or mental. On auction day it was honorable to provide full disclosure among gentlemen, seller to buyer, of any damaged merchandise.

Elisabeth heard each of her children assessed, as well as herself and her husband. The overseer winked and smiled at his betters behind the table, proud to display his knowledge.

"A strong, healthy buck. Prime field, no injuries. Strong as an ox. No defects. No less than fifteen hundred dollars. . . .

"He has the hernia, pulls up now and again. Past prime, but useful to get others to work. With the fiddling, he should bring twelve to thirteen hundred. . . .

"Auntie's getting slow, but good for the house and cooking. Eight hundred would be fair. . . .

"Deaf and dumb, but you won't find better with a hoe. The lash gets her attention, if there's need. Bidding should start at nine hundred dollars. . . .

"The uppity one is set aside, she and her daughter both."

The assessors kept steadily at their work until each one of the slaves was accounted for. They finished as the sun disappeared behind a dense thicket of pine trees to the west.

The slaves avoided looking at one another after the inventory. They trudged back to the quarter against the murky darkness in silence, shoulders hunched and jaws slack. Even the children did not speak.

They made fires and quickly prepared the evening meals. Some hardly ate at all, wanting just to go to bed and close their eyes until the morning light.

Elisabeth and Gerasíme lay down on their narrow pallet pushed up against the far corner of their one-room cabin.

"We have dollars on us now," Gerasíme said.

"We always had dollars on us," Elisabeth said.

"This is different. The sale is certain."

They lay on the pallet without speaking, Gerasíme's chest to Elisabeth's back, his knees tucked up behind hers under the threadbare blanket. Finally Elisabeth thought he had fallen asleep, until she heard his voice punch through the darkness.

"You been a good wife. If we don't end up on the same place, I don't want another."

"I'm through, too."

"We made some fine children, wife."

"We did, husband."

When the plantation bell rang out the next morning, they were still folded together in the same position.

9

Eugene Daurat wiped at his puffy eyes. He had slept fitfully the night before, dreading the arrival of the second day of the auction, but he took his role as executor to the Rosedew estate too seriously to waver now. The day was cold and soggy, like his spirits. Rain had come down in sheets for most of the night, raising the river to dangerous levels and leaving the ground soft and yielding. The heaviest rain had eased its pounding after sunup, but already the day had seen several driving showers. Despite the weather, the turnout was a good one. Most of those who attended were locals from the different communities along Cane River who had known the Derbannes. They came from Natchitoches, Cloutierville, Isle Brevelle, and Côte Joyeuse. But they also came from beyond Cane River, from as far north as Campti and as far south as Monette's Ferry and Point Coupée.

There had been endless details to take care of, contracting the assessors, advertising the upcoming sale in the *Natchitoches Chronicle* for the required thirty days, and setting up the property for sale. Eugene had been consumed for weeks with preparations. Although he considered himself very capable in the art of trade, he had not felt up to the challenge of peddling human beings himself, so he had hired an experienced auctioneer from Natchitoches. There were twenty-nine slaves to be auctioned off before the day was out, and his devotion to the memory of Louis and Françoise Derbanne obligated him to get the best price for each one.

He had Solataire put planks down across the cypress-lined entrance of Rosedew to keep the wheels of the carriages and wagons from sinking into the mud, starting at the front gate and ending at the barn. Chairs and benches had been placed around the big house, but it quickly became clear that the day was so stormy, they would have to squeeze into the barn. They crowded in as many chairs as they could, but there was only enough space for the ladies to sit.

The opening day had gone as well as could have been expected. Rosedew itself, along with the house and all of its outbuildings, had been sold to Henry Hertzog, a no-nonsense neighboring planter with a wide, solid face and stocky build.

Eugene pulled out his watch. The auction was scheduled to begin at three o'clock, but people had started arriving shortly after dinner, coming early to get a closer look at whatever particular Negro they had in mind to buy, or to visit with the neighbors they knew would attend. Buyers and spectators exchanged pleasantries, waiting for the start.

Everything was ready, except that Dr. Danglais had not yet arrived. If he didn't come soon, they would have to begin without him. The sooner the auction got under way, the sooner it would be over.

Eugene kept to the front of the barn near the partially open door, where he could view both the packed-tight crowd inside and any late arrivals. Women and men formed separate groups. Several branches of the Rachals were represented, Emanuel Rachal from Cloutierville and Antoine Rachal from Isle Brevelle from the white side of that family and Jacquitte Rachal from the free colored. The Widow Greneaux sat and chatted with Oreline and Tranquillin, Narcisse Fredieu's new young wife. Eugene noted that Henry Hertzog had not come back for the second day, although his brother, Hypolite, stood with a small clump of men that included Narcisse and Joseph Ferrier, Oreline's husband.

Doralise and her married daughter, Elisida, stood off toward the back of the barn. Doralise was stone-faced, hard-edged, and detached, and Eugene was careful not to exchange glances with her in this mixed crowd.

Dr. Danglais made a noisy arrival through the open front gate, his horse's hooves drumming against the wooden planks and churning up sodden clods of mud. Eugene went out into the light rain to greet the doctor, helping him dismount. Eugene did not want to go back into the barn but knew that he must.

The barn had the dank, sour-damp smell of decomposing hay, wet horseflesh, and bodies packed too close.

Eugene escorted the doctor to the back of the barn, weaving past the seated ladies and the groups of standing men. They stepped behind the quickly erected barrier of corded hay where the slaves waited. Old Bertram separated himself from the others and stepped forward.

Dr. Danglais gave Old Bertram a tight-lipped nod. "I do

not forget how you looked after me when my father died," he said.

Eugene looked behind Old Bertram at the Rosedew slaves gathered, some looking frightened, some dazed. Pressed close together against the side wall of the barn were Suzette, Gerant, and Philomene.

Gerant was his only son, Philomene his only daughter. The boy had Eugene's small ears and a sprinkling of freckles across the bridge of his nose. Suzette had called Gerant clever with his hands, and it was true, the boy had a gift. He could work with wood, carving complicated and pleasing shapes as well as figuring out how to take odd pieces of wood and put together a chicken coop, carve a butter paddle, or craft tools. But he always seemed withdrawn and shy.

Philomene was another matter entirely. Eugene found his chestnut-haired daughter unsettling, sometimes even frightening. Philomene's jaw, when she concentrated, set along exactly the same lines as those of his mother's. Her long hair was a springy explosion around her head, making her look too fierce for a nine-year-old girl, and her eyes were hard and flat.

Eugene pulled Suzette to the side. Keeping his voice low, he told her, "I will be buying in Gerant."

Even as Eugene saw the relief catch hold in Suzette's face, Philomene dropped Gerant's hand, stepped over to them, and motioned for Eugene to stoop so she could whisper in his ear.

"My name is Philomene Daurat," she said in her high little-girl voice. "I already saw you choose Gerant instead of me to live with you." She swallowed hard and went on, "And you will leave all of us in the end, even Madame Doralise."

Eugene stared at Philomene for a long moment, as if

frozen, and then took Dr. Danglais by the sleeve and walked him out toward the front of the barn. Suzette was too meek to put the idea into Philomene's head that the girl could take his last name. Where had that come from? And those other things she said. He would never leave Doralise. He didn't know what to make of this strange girl, his daughter.

Eugene had not planned it to turn out this way.

At one time he had really meant to free the children, but Gerant and Philomene had seemed to be doing just fine on Rosedew whenever he visited, and the years had slipped past. He had been preoccupied with his own affairs and his obligations to the Widow Derbanne. But he did think about them, he did bring them gifts. Gerant would accept them shyly, but Philomene would reach out for them without hesitation, as if they were her due. By the time he looked seriously into what it would take to give them their freedom, the rules had changed. The laws discouraged even his inquiries. If he could get around the new decree that slaves could not be freed until they reached the age of thirty, they would still revert to being slaves if he did not move them out of the state within one year. And even if he managed to buy them and take them out of the country, what would he do in France, starting over again with two mulatto children?

How had everything become so complicated?

Eugene settled Dr. Danglais into the front of the crowd and gave the auctioneer his nod to open the proceedings. They brought Old Bertram out first.

There was a carnival tone in the air. Auctions were serious business, but they were community entertainment as well, social gatherings not to be missed. A few of those in the barn looked away discreetly as Apphia pleaded for her daughter Laide, sold away to a planter from upriver. When Amandee, a man who could lift a two-hundred-pound bale of cotton, began to sob loudly as the mother of his children was loaded into a wagon, leaving him behind, many in the crowd were unmoved. It was business. It was necessary.

Mothers and fathers were the most likely to be separated. Brothers and sisters were sold in different directions. Sweethearts could only hope they would still be within walking distance of one another.

The spectators embraced what they considered to be the kindnesses of the day. Mademoiselle Landry buying Dick and Lucy as a pair. The benevolence of Joseph Ferrier and his wife, Oreline, taking in the cook's daughter and one of her children and her deaf-mute sister as well. Old Dr. Danglais buying Old Bertram, long past his prime, for his own house. Jacques Tessier buying Eliza and her son, Clement, together. Monsieur Plaissance buying Auntie Jeanne, close to eighty and nearly blind, for $25, just because she had been his wife's wet nurse.

The auction was considered a success. All of the slaves were sold, most above the opening bid. There was a brisk market for slaves in 1850. Once the bidding started, bargains were quickly struck, money changed hands, mortgages drawn up, payment schedules arranged. Eugene signed off on the proceedings and gathered together the papers sealing all the transactions of the last two days.

The estate of Louis and Françoise Derbanne was officially dissolved.

For a long time Eugene Daurat and Doralise Derbanne both pretended they were asleep in their bed that night, not touching, facing opposite walls. Neither wanted to talk about the day.

Gerant was spending his first night away from Rosedew, sleeping in the back of Eugene's storeroom. He was their new houseboy and would help in the store. Doralise had taken supper out to him earlier and stayed away talking to him for quite a while. When she returned she was unsociable, with few words for Eugene, and she went to bed early.

Cane River society had considered Eugene an eligible suitor when he first arrived among them, and he had been thrown together with any number of acceptable and available Creole daughters of French planters. Instead he was living with Doralise, a free woman of color who filled his days and frequented his dreams at night. Doralise Derbanne, with her smooth hazelnut skin and dark, silky eyelashes.

He would have married Doralise if he could, would have made her Doralise Derbanne Dupre Daurat. But that was against the law, a white man and a free woman of color. Like was only allowed to marry like, white to white, or free color to free color. Mixed could only pair up, and they paid a heavy price for their defiance. But he wanted her so badly that he had bribed the courts to grant her a divorce from her crazy husband, a *gens de couleur libre* who had tried to kill her with a knife one morning as she was fixing his breakfast. And he went down to the courthouse again to gift her his land and his house, to convince her just how sincere he was.

His white neighbors were not as friendly as they had been to him before he moved Doralise into his house, and he could not take her into the homes of any of his white friends or relatives; but they had an active social life among the *gens de couleur libre*.

At last Eugene heard soft breathing that signaled Doralise had fallen into a disturbed sleep. The entire business with the sale had created a strain between them. The few times they talked about his children openly and frankly, she seemed disappointed in how he discharged his responsibility toward Gerant and Philomene. Doralise reproached him now, even in sleep.

Each time Eugene closed his eyes, he saw a vivid picture of the three of them in the dripping rain that afternoon. Suzette was mouthing words he could not hear as she clutched the two small figures gathered in her skirts. Gerant's tears mingled with the drizzle, his mouth open. Only Philomene was dry-eyed, staring openly at Eugene with a look he could neither identify nor erase.

Unable to lie still any longer, he got up from the bed and found the papers he had left on the table. He had already started to prepare one of the duplicates he would file with the courthouse, copying out in his cramped handwriting his day's work. The weight of the single page of the original record felt insubstantial as he held it. He would have to prepare yet another copy tomorrow before he was finished with this business, before he could place this one with all of the other plantation records, signifying the end of Rosedew.

The room was too dark for him to read the ink on the page. He didn't want to light the lamp and disturb Doralise, and he could recall each entry from memory anyway, each transaction a permanent part of him now. Eugene ran his fingers across the page, guessing at the areas toward the bottom on the paper that contained the names of his children, the lines that described their individual fates.

5 February 1850, sale of community property of Louis Derbanne and Françoise Rachal: To Henry Hertzog for $15,275: a plantation whereon deceased resided on both sides of Cane River, containing 778.76 acres, with all buildings and improvements, bounded on the left bank above by Henry Hertzog, and below by Ambroise Lecomte; on the right bank above by Old River and Alexander L. DeBlieux and below by the Widow Françoise Mulon, free woman of color (fwc).

(sale adjourned until following day)

6 February, 1850

Slave, BERTRAM, Negro age 70, health not guaranteed, sold	to Doctor Danglais for	$ 345
Slave, ATHENASE, Negro man age 60, not guaranteed,	to Mr. G. Guy	$ 105
Slave, BERNARD, Negro age 55, not guaranteed,	to Emanuel Rachal	$ 350
Slave, DICK, Negro man age 50, fully guaranteed,	to Madame T. Landry	$ 510
Slave, GERASÍME, Negro age 45, not guaranteed,	to Hypolite Hertzog	$1,305
Slave, IGNACE, mulatto age 43, fully guaranteed,	to Azenor Farron	$1,005
Slave, FRANÇOIS, Negro age 40, not guaranteed,	to Antoine B. Rachal	$1,025
Slave, AMANDEE, Negro age 25, fully guaranteed	to Jacquitte Rachal (fmc)	$1,555
Slave, AZENOR, Negro age 25, fully guaranteed	to DeBlieux brothers	$1,565
Slave, SOLATAIRE, Negro age 23, fully guaranteed	to Mrs. Eliza Greneaux	$1,560
Slave, MARIE JEANNE, Negress age 75, not guaranteed	to Bertrand Plaissance	$ 25
Slave, LUCY, Negress age 55, not guaranteed	to Madame T. Landry	$ 605
Slave, LAFILLE, Negress age 40, not guaranteed	to J. B. Charleville	$ 885
Slave, ELIZA, Negress age 27 and son CLEMENT, age 10	to J. M. Tessier	$1,615
Slave, CAROLINE, Negress age 24 and SEVERIN, age 2	to François Gascion	$1,030
Slave, MARGUERITTE, Negress age 25, fully guaranteed	to Joseph Ganier Sr.	$1,190
Slave, ELISABETH, Negress age 48, not guaranteed	to Narcisse Fredieu	$ 800
Slave, PHOEBE, Negress age 30	to Benoist Lavespere	$ 900
Slave, EUGER, Negro age 11	to Hypolite Hertzog	$ 750
Slave, SUZETTE, Negress age 26, & child PHILOMENE, mulatto age 9	to Joseph Ferrier	$1,400
Slave, GERANT, mulatto age 11, fully guaranteed	to Eugene Daurat	$ 975
Slave, APPHIA, Negress 28 & children PHEME, 3, & FLORENAL, 8 mo.	to Madame Elisida Metoyer (fwc)	$1,400
Slave, LAIDE, age 11, fully guaranteed	to Antoine Radish	$ 900
Slave, PALMIRE, Negress, deaf and dumb, age 30, not guaranteed to Joseph Ferrier		$ 950

Witnessed and signed by Eugene Daurat, executor of the last will and testament of Françoise Rachal, widow of Louis Derbanne

Derbanne plantation bill of sale, 1850.

The longing for each member of her family had become as real to Suzette as the flesh-and-blood people themselves had been and thickened the black fog that surrounded her in her exhaustion day and night. The Ferrier farm was much smaller than Rosedew, but there was only Ferrier, Oreline, Palmire, Suzette, and Philomene to bring in the crops and keep the household running. Suzette performed mechanically, doing whatever was expected of her, struggling to get up and begin each new day.

Her family had been divided up among seven different plantations along the nineteen-mile length of Cane River, scattered like the fuzzy dandelion wish-weeds she'd dreamed on as a child. When she was young she would close her eyes and make a wish and then bring the flower up to her mouth to blow the seeds away, giving them up to the capricious winds to find their own direction. After two years on Ferrier's farm she trampled the weeds under her feet without even seeing them.

One muggy Wednesday, wash day, Suzette and Philomene were alone at the bend of the creek that twisted behind the farmhouse.

"What's wrong now, *Maman?*" Philomene asked, worry flooding her smooth buttermilk-colored face. She had the washboard pressed firmly between her knees, scrubbing at a dark jam stain on the tiny beige dress that belonged to Oreline's daughter.

How could Suzette tell Philomene that as a grown woman of twenty-eight, what unsettled her most about the shape her life had taken was the absence of the everyday scent of her own mother, the easy knowledge that her family was within her reach? Sometimes, when she was preparing dinner for everyone on the farm, she half expected to look up and see Elisabeth wrist deep in flour, giving form to a pie crust.

"I miss my family around me" was all Suzette could manage.

"I'm right here, and so is Aunt Palmire. Gerant isn't so far away with Papa and Madame Doralise."

Suzette winced, the word like a blow. When the girl first started calling Eugene Daurat "Papa," Suzette had made her go out and pick a peach tree switch from outside the cookhouse on Rosedew. She'd whipped Philomene until her legs bled, but no matter how many times she had tried to teach her, it had no lasting effect.

"What have I told you about that word?" Suzette snapped.

"There's nobody here but us, *Maman,*" Philomene said defiantly.

"You go looking for trouble in the wrong place with that talk and they'll give it to you."

"I *am* Philomene Daurat, and he *is* Papa."

"Hush. I do not have the patience."

Suzette began to hum. When the longing came down on her, like today, she would make up melancholy tunes. The off-pitch notes helped her to stay connected, at least for a while. It was almost like being able to talk to Elisabeth, reaching back along the chain, touching her mother's spirit and the spirits of those she didn't know who had come before.

"We see *Mémère* Elisabeth on Sunday," Philomene offered, as if sensing her thoughts. "And Gerant. That will make you feel better."

"Family is everything, Philomene. Do not ever forget that. A tree without roots cannot survive."

"Can I carry the pass Sunday?"

"Just do your work," Suzette instructed, but the girl wasn't silent for long.

"What is it like in the field?"

"I pray you never know."

"It looks harder than housework."

"That's trying to measure standing against stooping. Both aim to grind you down," Suzette said tiredly.

Suzette had spent her life on Rosedew standing, indoors and outdoors, standing in the presence of white folks, waiting for them to decide what she needed to do for them next. The only time she was permitted off her feet was when she was down on her hands and knees scrubbing or on her back in secret. She was on call to any number of mistresses or masters, snatching a bite to eat whenever she could, waiting for the whim of the next white person of any age who crossed her path.

"See this burn?" Suzette stepped back from the clothes

soaking in the tub and thrust out her left hand. "From pressing damp clothes with the hot irons." She pulled up her sleeve. "This one here? From putting out the grease fire before it could spread. Your *mémère* Elisabeth has a quarter moon burned into her arm from a kitchen scald, just like she had been branded. Sometimes I can barely catch my breath at night after standing over the smoky stove all day. My bad shoulder was sprung from carrying firewood, or toting water, or lugging clothes back to the house. Who knows which? Now each harvest my fingers split from picking, and nothing can take away the headaches and back pains from stooping in the cotton field all day with no shade."

"Clement goes to field and doesn't get a headache," Philomene said.

"Clement again," Suzette said. "How would you know about Clement's head?"

"Madame Doralise. We tell her our messages, and she passes them back and forth between us."

"You need to put that boy out of your mind," Suzette warned.

"When we get older, I'm going to marry Clement," Philomene declared.

"Hush that talk, there is no future there. You're too young, and the brown-skinned boy is all the way over to M'sieu Tessier's plantation."

Philomene tipped the dirty suds water out of the tub and began to refill it with river water from the wooden bucket. She changed the subject. "When I carry water out to M'sieu Ferrier and Palmire, they go down the rows, one after the other, Palmire plowing and M'sieu Ferrier dropping the seed."

"M'sieu Ferrier never owned house or field before,"

Suzette sniffed. "Owner of a farm not even big enough to have a name of its own."

"Is Madame Oreline still quality?"

"She has come down since Rosedew, for a fact, but she is still a Derbanne. At least M'sieu knows better than to let her do her own laundry. And he stays up to the farmhouse at night and leaves us alone. Could be worse."

"*Maman?*"

Suzette looked up, alert. Philomene had slipped into the coldness of her glimpsing voice. "I'm here," Suzette said carefully.

"It will be all right, *Maman*. One day we will all be together again, I see it," Philomene said, her voice flat.

From anyone else, the reassuring words could be dismissed as an idle comment, a hope, or a comforting daydream. Philomene did not deal in any of those realms. Sometimes the girl knew things, with certainty. She had seen the fox get into the henhouse two nights before they lost two of their best pullets. She had pinpointed the exact location where the mudslide would bury an oxcart six months before it happened. Those hard, dry eyes darkened, her mouth would tighten starting at the jaw, and she would announce something whose time was not yet here.

"What do you mean? Who will be together?" Suzette asked softly.

Philomene straightened up from over the washtub as she wiped her hands on her apron, eyes barely closed, concentration etched in her face.

"I can see us inside a house, in a room filled with people," she said. "Like a dining room. Not here. Not Rosedew. Someplace I have never seen before. You are sitting down at the head of a long table, and there are bowls and platters piled high with food. You look old, *Maman,* and your hair is mostly gray. You seem different, happy."

"Who else is there?" Suzette was careful not to disturb the stream of her daughter's glimpsing.

"Every chair around the table is taken, with a smaller table off to the side. A children's table. I see you, Gerant, and me. *Mémère* Elisabeth is at the big table, sitting at the other end. Madame Doralise is there, too, talking to a light-colored man with big teeth and a wide smile. And some other people I do not know. It is mixed up. You and *Mémère* are sitting down, but there is a white man sitting, too, friendly, holding a baby. Gerant is standing, laughing. He is much taller than now. And another baby. No, at least two more babies."

"Is Palmire there?"

"No, *Maman.* I don't see Palmire or *Grandpère* Gerasíme anywhere in the room."

Narcisse Fredieu and his delicate young wife, Tranquillin, came to the farm that evening, as they did one or two times each week, to share supper and evening entertainment with Oreline and Joseph Ferrier.

Suzette cooked a turtle stew, and Philomene helped serve. Clearing away the dishes between the entrée and the dessert, Suzette noticed how prosperous Narcisse looked alongside Ferrier, how smooth and free of calluses his hands were. Narcisse dominated the supper table with his big laugh and self-assured voice.

After supper the two couples retired to the front room, along with the children. Ferrier brought out the tiles, and he and Narcisse began to play *maroc* while Oreline and Tranquillin embroidered by the fireplace, trading Cane River gossip. Tranquillin was a Creole woman of the backcountry with gold-flecked hair and a heart-shaped mouth, good-naturedly quiet. She came from a reasonably good family and was younger than Narcisse by at least ten years.

Suzette put the dishes in to soak and sent Philomene to serve the coffee. No sooner had the girl left the kitchen than she noticed that Philomene had forgotten to put the liqueur on the tray. Suzette grabbed the bottle by its thin neck and hurriedly followed close on the heels of her daughter.

"*Café?*" Philomene said as she entered the front room, hands full. Suzette turned the hallway corner just in time to see Narcisse give Philomene a distinct look of possessiveness. Suzette began silently to count off her blessings. Philomene is with me. Palmire is near. Gerant is not in the field. *Mère* Elisabeth is healthy. She repeated them over and over in her head to keep the threatening black fog at a distance. But as she helped Philomene serve, she couldn't rid herself of the lingering sour taste that lodged itself at the back of her mouth.

On Sunday Suzette, Philomene, and Palmire took the shortcut through the woods instead of the road to Narcisse Fredieu's farm. They could make good time, less than an hour, if they walked briskly. The permission pass for the three of them was well worn, pressed against the flesh under Suzette's blouse.

"Will Papa come with Madame Doralise, *Maman?*" Philomene asked, holding fast to Palmire, swinging their linked hands between them.

"You ask me—you, who looks to the future? All I know is that she said she will bring Gerant." Suzette smiled in anticipation. "Today would be even better if *Père* Gerasíme could come. But we'll see him next month when they bring him to play for the soirée of M'sieu Narcisse."

Gerasíme was four hours north toward Cloutierville by foot. They walked to see him when they could, which wasn't often. The distance was great, and his hip was too damaged for him to walk to them. He had been sold to Hypolite Hertzog, the brother of the man who had bought Rosedew.

"*Maman*, will you tell one of your stories?" Philomene asked.

Suzette hesitated, but only for a moment. Whichever direction they took on their travel Sundays, whether to the Fredieu farm or walking to the Hertzog plantation to visit Gerasíme, Suzette could bring herself alive again.

"Did I ever tell you about the Christmas party on Rosedew?" she began.

Philomene dropped Palmire's hand and ran far enough ahead to face the two sisters. Reverse walking, and deftly dodging pine trees at her back, she pantomimed Gerasíme playing the fiddle, then became Elisabeth picking up her skirts to dance, and back to Gerasíme throwing a broad wink.

Palmire smiled and nodded, and Philomene laughed. It seemed the only time either of them was playful was with each other.

"Tell it again, *Maman*. Don't leave anything out," Philomene pleaded, taking up Palmire's hand again.

When they reached Narcisse Fredieu's farm, they turned south at the clearing around the farmhouse and headed out back. Narcisse owned only six slaves. There were only two cabins, hardly a quarter at all, both rough-and-tumble one-room houses. Elisabeth came out on the stoop of one of them to greet the visitors. Wisps of coarse white hair peeked out from under her *tignon*.

"Rest yourselves on the porch," she said. "I already put some fresh greens from the patch on, and fatback."

Elisabeth looked appraisingly at Philomene. "Go on and get the comb. Let me fix that pretty hair," she said, and Philomene disappeared inside the cabin. Elisabeth sat on the porch chair, and when Philomene came out to sit at her feet, her back to Elisabeth's knees, Elisabeth clamped her thighs on either side of the girl's shoulders. She unbraided Philomene's two plaits, ran the comb through her long chestnut hair from scalp to tip, and began to rebraid, and they all talked of small things.

Midmorning, in a cloud of dust, Doralise and Gerant arrived in Doralise's buggy. Gerant dropped the reins, helped Doralise down, and waited by the buggy until she adjusted her skirts and angled her open umbrella against the sun. They all stood, and it took all of Suzette's willpower not to run to her son and fling her arms around him. Instead she memorized each change since she had last seen him. Gerant had grown almost a foot taller, both his body and face had filled out, and he had the beginnings of a thin mustache. He looked healthy and well fed, a striking, honey-brown boy, quiet, with trouble-avoiding eyes.

Elisabeth offered Doralise the porch chair.

"I brought Gerant to visit," Doralise said, once more arranging her skirts as she sat. "His pass is to stay the night, but he needs to be back before dark tomorrow."

"Can we offer you cool water?" Elisabeth asked.

"*Merci*," Doralise replied. "Let me just find a bit of shade before I am on my way."

Gerant stood by the buggy while Philomene fetched a

gourd full of water and brought it back to the porch. Doralise whispered to Philomene, Philomene whispered back, and Suzette saw a small article exchange hands and disappear into Philomene's apron pocket.

Doralise drained the water and stood. "I will be going now," she said.

"Madame, I want to thank you for bringing Gerant," Suzette told her, hurrying to her side.

"He misses all of you."

"Madame, can I ask what passed between you and Philomene?"

"Just a little rock Clement found and thought she might like."

"He's only a field hand, Madame."

"They seem devoted, Suzette," Doralise replied firmly. "After all this time."

Suzette shrugged.

"I will continue to look after Gerant," Doralise said to Suzette, and Gerant helped her back up into the buggy.

After Doralise had clicked the horse on its way, Gerant joined them on the porch. It took a while before they could stop touching and hugging him.

One raw gray morning in the fall of her third year on Ferrier's farm, Suzette heard her name called from Palmire's cabin. She had spent the night on a chair in the children's room, nursing Oreline's son, waiting for his fever to break.

Ferrier's shout was insistent.

"Suzette!"

Suzette dropped the firewood she was carrying into the kitchen and rushed outside. When she got to the door of the cabin, breathless, Ferrier was pulling on Palmire's arm, trying to get her up from her pallet. His face was knotted with frustration. It was harvest, and he had been coiled tight all week, pushing hard at Suzette and Palmire as well as himself to get the crop in. Palmire was still on her pallet, looking unsteady and dazed, but when she saw Suzette behind Ferrier, she motioned for her to come close. A rank smell overpowered Suzette as she approached her sister.

Palmire brought both of her hands up to her temples and squeezed at her head, twisting her face in pain, and then she put both hands on her stomach as if to vomit again. She reached out to Suzette, her hand so contracted that it looked like a bird's claw, and drew one of Suzette's hands to her chest, guiding it in fast pats. Her eyes were deep in their sockets, and she looked panicky. It was as if the very flesh on her face had shrunk overnight.

Suzette turned to Ferrier, keeping hold of her sister's dry hand.

"I have to take care of her, M'sieu Ferrier. She is sick. Palmire never gets sick," Suzette said, rising.

"I cannot spare anyone today. We have to get the crop in," Ferrier said without hesitation. "Call Madame Oreline."

"Please, M'sieu, no one is like I am with Palmire. Let me stay."

"Go get Madame Oreline," Ferrier repeated.

Suzette let go of Palmire's hand and ran to the house. "Madame, come quick," she called. "Palmire is in a desperate way."

Oreline threw on her wrap over her nightgown without doing her morning toilet and followed Suzette to the cabin. Palmire had already passed into a fitful sleep.

"She is sick right enough," Ferrier said to his wife as she came into the cabin. "You have to spare Philomene from the house today. She comes to the field with us. Can you look after Palmire?"

"Of course," said Oreline, and to Suzette, "I will do what I can for her. Go on now."

In the field, Suzette worried all day. Philomene, unaccustomed to crop labor, stumbled often in the fierce heat between the rows of cotton, and Suzette couldn't erase the image of Palmire's terrified face when she had reached out her hand to her that morning. When at last the sun began to lower in the sky, Ferrier let them come in, hot and sweaty. Suzette rushed to the cabin, and as her eyes became accustomed to the darkness, she saw first Oreline in a chair beside the bed and then the unnatural color of Palmire's face and body. Her sister had turned a leaden blue, dark and mottled. Palmire's skin was wrinkled and folded, as if she were an ancient woman, and her breathing was ragged and uncertain. Palmire turned her head slightly and vomited, but there was no longer any food in her to bring up. What came up was like rice water.

"She just gets worse," Oreline said, looking to Suzette.

Suzette came closer and took a rag to wipe her sister's mouth. When Suzette touched her jaw, Palmire's mouth flew open. Her tongue looked like a dead fish.

Suzette turned to Philomene. "There's *tasso* you can heat up for supper," she instructed, "and make some biscuits with cane syrup. Go."

Philomene ran toward the farmhouse.

"I can take over now, Madame," she said to Oreline.

"I did what I could for her." Looking miserable, Oreline left Suzette and Palmire alone.

Suzette wiped Palmire's forehead, and when her sister's arms and legs began to spasm uncontrollably, she massaged them. She tried to get Palmire to connect with her, to meet her eyes and challenge the sickness, but she was drifting from listless and unaware to coma.

Palmire never regained consciousness and died that night. Fast, from one sundown to the next. It wasn't until the next day they found out that on the Fredieu farm, Narcisse's wife, Tranquillin, had been stricken with the same symptoms as Palmire's, ending in the same abrupt death coma.

Cholera had come to Cane River.

After Palmire died, Suzette was no longer certain she could resist the pull of the black fog.

Philomene found her way to Suzette's side as often as she could, coaxing Suzette to tell her stories, anything to get her talking, but it was all Suzette could do to keep moving and do her work. She tried to hold on for Philomene's sake. She wanted to reach out and stroke the girl's hair, to tell her something important about how to protect herself, but it was too much effort, and she didn't have anything worthwhile to say.

Suzette was vaguely aware that Philomene took on many of her own chores. Philomene got up before dawn, filled the woodboxes with kindling, lit fires in the chilly bedrooms in the morning and evening, washed and ironed the clothes, parched the coffee, and stoked the fires at night while Oreline's family slept. She cooked, fetched water and milk from the springhouse and meat from the smokehouse. She bathed, diapered, dressed, groomed, and entertained Oreline's infant children. She spun thread and picked seeds from the cotton, gathered eggs, plucked chickens, and drove cows to and from the woods. When Suzette went to the field,

Philomene toted water to her and Ferrier before heading back to the house, where she would comb Oreline's hair, lace her corset, and arrange her hoopskirts.

Philomene tried to get Suzette to imagine happier days, off in the future, but when Suzette thought about Philomene's glimpsing, of the long table piled high with food when they were all together again, she remembered who wasn't there. Not Palmire. Not Gerasíme.

Suzette's old dreams of white dresses, St. Augustine, and freedom for her children had proven to be senseless and unreachable.

The future was too heavy for her to carry. It was up to Philomene now.

PART TWO

Philomene

Philomene Daurat and Narcisse Fredieu
Descendants

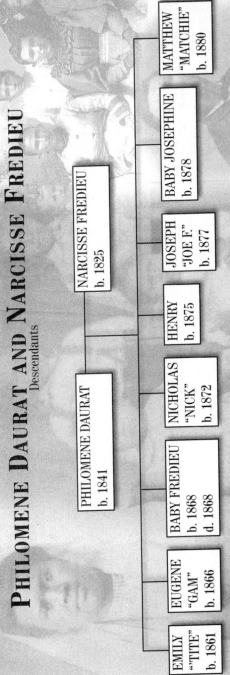

NARCISSE FREDIEU
b. 1825

PHILOMENE DAURAT
b. 1841

EMILY
"TITE"
b. 1861

EUGENE
"GAM"
b. 1866

BABY FREDIEU
b. 1868
d. 1868

NICHOLAS
"NICK"
b. 1872

HENRY
b. 1875

JOSEPH
"JOE F."
b. 1877

BABY JOSEPHINE
b. 1878

MATTHEW
"MATCHIE"
b. 1880

P hilomene Daurat turned the corner of the house on Ferrier's farm with her long-limbed stride, her careless hair flying behind her. The beginning weight of the baby made her body seem different, foreign. Looking down at her fore-arms, exposed below the cuff of her thin gingham blouse, she could see that the Louisiana sun had already turned the ivory yellow color of her winter skin to the deep olive she became in summer. Her arms were muscular and firm from the constant demands of heavy farmwork, and her body was a woman's body, caught up at last to the mind that had always seemed mature.

She was fully aware of the danger that accompanied the emergence of her high breasts and rounded hips, and thanks to her man, Clement, she also understood the pleasures. They were to be married in front of the priest in just five days. She would have jumped the broom, if that was the best she could have made happen, but she wanted something like the real ceremony the white people had. The way her *marraine*, Doralise, had done it.

It was well past first light. Philomene had stuffed her *tignon* in her apron pocket as she'd hurried out of the cabin, intending to capture her hair when she wasn't so behind schedule. She was on her way to the henhouse to collect eggs for preparing breakfast, and her focus was on the task before her, as always. It was the way she had with everything, putting herself into it mind and body, without a spare thought or motion, until she turned herself to the next thing to be done.

She had to blink against the strong sun, still so low in the sky that the side of the house had blocked its glare until she had almost fully passed the front gallery. Before she even saw him there, she could feel his eyes on her.

Narcisse Fredieu.

He had always watched her, for as long as she could remember. She had grown up with those eyes always on her. In the beginning the watching had been just another condition of her existence, like emptying the stinkpots, or obeying Oreline's orders, or the unchangeable fact that Monday was bake day.

At some point, she couldn't recall exactly when, she had begun to sense the singular nature of his watching, and only then had it made her uneasy. Over the years she had added strands of different impressions, until they formed a dense, complicated knot of fear and anger, challenge and loathing, that she carried from place to place deep in the core of her stomach, not unlike the way she carried the baby now.

Narcisse applied different faces to the watching. One day it showed itself as fascination, on another day open desire, on still another domination. No matter the look of the moment, at its base was always a call for submission, so easily recognizable between white and dark.

When submission was demanded, the outward signs of submission were always offered. It was a well-polished survival technique, and Philomene used it especially carefully with Narcisse. Even as she bowed her head or rounded her back or averted her eyes with the watcher, she seethed at his right to invade her in this way, as a dangerous game, as a prelude. Anger had no practical or logical expression against a white man, so she tried to ignore the looks he gave her, his tendency to be in the same places she was, all of a sudden, drinking her in.

She could remember his first wife, dimly, a pasty-faced woman with a soft voice and timid manner. The woman had always looked to Philomene as if the wind could come and blow her to some other place, without the world taking any notice. Mam'zelle Tranquillin, dead of cholera. They didn't talk about her anymore, and Narcisse had started bringing out a new woman when he visited the farm, another of the endless Derbannes sprinkled around the Cane River landscape. The new one's name was Mam'zelle Arsine Derbanne, and she always arrived with a chaperone or two in tow. Narcisse had not brought her along today. He looked to be alone, and early to the farm. He was here too often, as far as Philomene was concerned, but her opinion was neither requested nor expressed.

Philomene hurried her steps toward the henhouse, as if she didn't know Narcisse was watching. She was careful not to glance in his direction.

Narcisse was waiting as she came out of the henhouse with her apron bunched around the still-warm eggs she had gathered to prepare for that morning's breakfast.

"You've tied up your hair already, I see. What a shame," he said, his voice sugary.

Philomene stopped several feet away and assumed her pose, aware of Narcisse's deep-set eyes trying to find an opening.

"Morning, M'sieu Narcisse. I need to get these eggs into the kitchen."

"I understand you want to marry one of Tessier's field boys," he said, brushing aside her remark. "You should have come to me for something so important. You deserve some-one better than a field hand. You could do better. I've known your mother and your grandmother since long before you were born. I could help you do better."

"M'sieu, I could do no better than Clement. It is meant to be."

Philomene stared at an imaginary spot to the left of his elbow as she talked, her head not fully bowed. She kept her voice low but even. It would be easier if she could retreat into her mind and be as unaware as her mother sometimes was, or as patient as her grandmother, but her glimpsings made her promises, set her onto the path of intentions, made her too bold.

"I've heard about your 'gift.' What else can you see? Anything for me?" Narcisse put on a solicitous, playful air, as if he were passing the time with an overindulged child, but his voice betrayed genuine interest and something else, between respect and fear. The Creoles were a superstitious lot.

"No, M'sieu, I am sorry."

"Surely with all of the powers at your command, you can look to wherever you go for your visions and tell me something that could prove useful for me to know."

"Maybe you will have a long and happy life with a new wife," Philomene said.

"You've seen that?"

Philomene could hear the quickening in Narcisse without needing to look into his face. "No, M'sieu. I just hope it for you."

His interest waned, and he came back in a different direction. "What is it that you see in this boy?"

"His name is Clement. We have known each other since we were children on Rosedew."

"You don't need a boy. You need a man. A man who could protect you."

Protect her from what? Philomene thought. From being a slave? No one could protect her from that. "Clement is the only man I need. We will marry, and we will have children. They are already on the way. I saw it, and now it is coming to pass."

Narcisse went on as if she had not spoken at all. "I told Ferrier that he shouldn't let you marry that boy."

Philomene stood immobile, seeming to study the ground at her feet, but she was shaken. Narcisse had influence over Oreline. But she knew what a stubborn man Ferrier was, not one to give in easily to outside influence, and all of the plans were already set.

"M'sieu Ferrier has already given his permission," Philomene said, trying to keep her voice steady. "The wedding is Saturday. M'sieu Daurat is coming, too, to stand up for me."

Philomene included both her owner's and her father's names, as if matching Narcisse's resistance with the mention of two other white men could make him back down, make everything come out all right. She collected herself. She had said too much to Narcisse already. There was no advantage in talking overmuch.

"Will there be anything else, M'sieu Narcisse? They wait on me to prepare breakfast."

"I've known your family for a long time. I want what's best for you."

"*Oui,* M'sieu."

"I will be at the wedding. I have an interest in you. Don't ever forget that."

"*Oui,* M'sieu."

"You have lovely hair, Philomene. I like to see it free of your scarf."

"*Oui,* M'sieu."

"You may go."

Wednesday, wash day, Philomene removed a water-weighted bedsheet from the washtub where they had just boiled it clean. Suzette took one end, Philomene the other, and they stretched the white sheet between them, wringing out the excess water. It took both of them to smooth it out so they could hang it to dry.

"What do you think about Doralise and M'sieu Eugene?" Philomene said in a furtive undertone. They whispered their wash day gossip, even though they were out of earshot of the house.

"It was just a matter of when she moved out of his house," Suzette whispered back.

"Not his house, her house, *Maman,*" Philomene said. "Or at least it was. She got him to sign the house over before she ever moved in. She was shrewd."

"And not such a young woman anymore, either," said Suzette.

Philomene added another bundle of clothes to the steaming water. "*Mémère* Elisabeth says Doralise knows how to turn a situation around to suit her."

"Like a cat, that one lands on her feet," Suzette said. "She got M'sieu Daurat to get her a divorce, and then she takes up with him in his house, in the open. Him so full of her pretty ways that he signs over his house and land to her, with her already having land of her own." She snorted, a flat, humorless sound full of wonder.

Philomene glanced up at the look of concentration on her mother's face as she handled the growing mound of white linen. Suzette always seemed to speak of Eugene Daurat as a distant stranger, without passion or anger.

"*Maman,*" Philomene began cautiously, "you carry no grudge about Doralise going with M'sieu Eugene?"

"That hurt scabbed over almost as long ago as you have been on this earth. Doralise has my regard, coming out on the other side of a tangle with a white man with something in her own pocket to show for it."

"You never talk about you and Papa." What Philomene knew about her father, she had learned from her grandmother. She was surprised when Suzette replied.

"He moved easy from me to Doralise, without ever looking back. I do not care one way or the other about Eugene Daurat except for what he can do for my children. The only thing he gave me was children closer to white. That makes you better than most. Blood counts, but instead you make babies with a brown-skinned boy, when it is on you to carry this family forward now."

"Why do we always go back to that? My light skin and straight hair and fancy speech does not make me free like Madame Doralise, does not get me out from under Madame

Oreline. Every morning, I still wake up a mulatto slave."
Philomene used the word *mulatto* deliberately, although she
hated it. Mules were mixed breeds, too, set apart.

"You better learn how to hold your tongue, gal. Sometimes you seem to forget which of us is the mother and
which is the daughter."

"I am sorry," Philomene said dutifully, eyes cast downward, hidden beneath her dark lashes. "No disrespect
intended, *Maman*." It was an old argument that couldn't be
won. "So is Doralise family?" she prodded.

"*Oui,* she helped when we needed," Suzette said, and
made the sign of the cross. "Doralise did more for you and
Gerant than M'sieu Eugene ever did. He may be through
with her now, but she is still my *marraine*. And yours."

Suzette poked at the laundry with the wooden paddle and
plunged it under the sudsy water. "They hounded them apart,
because he put her up in his own house. Or her house. You
know what I mean. They don't like to see that around here."

"Who is 'they,' *Maman?*"

"White, black, colored, free, slave. Nobody likes it.
M'sieu Eugene was crazy to think he could just move a colored woman, free or not, into his own house in the daylight,
and not pay. And white folks expect land to flow to their
own. They cut him out then, all but a few too fond or too
old to care. The ones who sheltered him in the beginning are
all dead now. Doralise knew from the start, getting him to
give her the house before he got worn down. White men
always choose the same way in the end.

"You ask about grudges," Suzette went on. "What good
are grudges? Doralise went with the man for her own reasons. She is still like family, although there's nothing we can
do for her. She is the one who is free."

Philomene listened politely, showing her mother the silent respect age entitled her to. She didn't agree at all about grudges. It was important to keep an accounting of rights and wrongs, even if there was nothing to be done about them right away. Even if there was nothing that could ever be done.

"Could you have stopped M'sieu Eugene from coming for you?"

"You go too far, girl."

They worked in silence until Suzette broke it.

"What got you asking about Eugene Daurat and me now?"

"I have a white man looking at me." Philomene pushed the words out. "He puts his eyes on me like the next step is his hands. He comes at me out of nowhere, throwing his big shadow and blocking the light."

"Narcisse Fredieu." Suzette pursed her lips and shook her head. "I see him sniffing around. He say anything direct?"

"He said Clement is not good enough for me. That he could help me do better. He said he talked to M'sieu Ferrier about calling off the marriage ceremony."

"I heard them last night while serving. M'sieu is not going to let Narcisse Fredieu or anyone else come on his place and tell him what to do. You and Clement are as good as married."

"It has to be more than 'as good as.' What if that man comes to me in the night? He has it in his mind."

"You stay out of his way as much as you can."

"But what if he forces himself on me? What can I do?"

Suzette averted her eyes from her daughter, and when she finally spoke she was brusque. "You ask the wrong person."

P hilomene heard the whippoorwill call as she patched a frayed shirt collar of Ferrier's in the farmhouse.

She threw aside her mending and hurried into the children's room. Little Josephina was heavy in sleep. Oreline's daughter had settled some in her breathing. The thimbleful of brandy was having an effect. Philomene smoothed the girl's sandy hair from her face, rearranged the blanket, and gave her one last glance. The whippoorwill call sounded again.

She raced to the back door of the farmhouse and saw Clement, tousled and sweaty, waiting for her just beyond the clearing. His shirt had mud splotches down one sleeve, and one leg of his homespun trousers was shorter than the other, but he grinned widely and raised a palm skyward in salute. The upturned palm was an old signal between the two of them from Rosedew. Then it had meant "I'm here, you're there. But we'll manage to be together later." Philomene raised her palm in response and broke into a run to him. She hurled herself into his arms.

"I cannot stay away from the house for long," she said, breathless, looking back anxiously toward the farmhouse. "The girl has a cold and is sleeping. I gave her a little brandy."

"I only have a short while myself. I took a detour in making this delivery to M'sieu Narcisse. I took a chance you'd be here."

"If the little one hadn't gotten sick, that is where I would be now, along with the rest, visiting on M'sieu Narcisse's place," Philomene said, leaning into Clement. "*Maman* went, too. They will not return until after supper."

"I had to see you," Clement said. His arms around her waist, he lifted her until her feet no longer touched the ground.

"Put me down." Philomene backed away from Clement, laughing. "You're wet," she said, looking up from his bare feet to the waterline at the knee on his trousers. The force of a frisson, a small chill, passed through her, and she shivered. "That leaky boat doesn't belong on the river."

"I'm good with the boat," Clement boasted. "As long as I have bailing gourds, I can outsmart the river every time. M'sieu Tessier doesn't trust anyone else with that one, she's tricky. It saves two hours of walking getting to you."

Philomene frowned.

"The river was in a playful mood today," Clement said. "I scooped more than I rowed." He caught Philomene around the middle, pulling her close enough to catch the damp smell of the boat's cypress planks on him. "What mood are you in?"

Philomene couldn't prevent herself from smiling. "Clement, is that all you think about?"

"Close to it," he answered with a slow, lazy smile. "Out in the field when the sun burns, I think of you. In the stable over the red-hot anvil, I think of you. At night on my pallet, I think of you. You and the baby. The rest doesn't mean anything."

"I saw you in a glimpsing last night," Philomene blurted out, "and it made me afraid. The glimpsings do not come as strong as they used to, they are more like feelings than pictures now, but I saw your body cold and still, near a river."

Clement let Philomene go and considered her for a long time. He made a visible effort to shake the mood. "Death by drowning is a better death than most, but I don't plan on going yet," he said simply as he stepped forward and held her again. "At least it won't be smallpox or cholera or yellow jack, or being beaten or starved to death."

"Should I have told you?" Philomene asked.

"Yes. You can always tell me anything," Clement said. "Meanwhile, we're here together. Let's go to the shed. I have something to show you."

He carried a stack of skins by the bundler's knot in one hand, and with the other he pulled Philomene close to him by the waist as they walked to the toolshed. It was a small shed, barely big enough to hold the plow, hoes, pickaxes, and other tools for the farm, but it had a door, and it was out of the weather.

Clement cleared a narrow space on the ground, unknotted the bundle, spread one of the bearskins skin side down on the cold, packed ground, and brought another bearskin and put it skin side up on top of the other.

"Get in between. I want you to feel these skins," he said. "Nothing is too good for you."

"Clement, what if they find out you used the skins?"

"They'll never know. Take off your dress first."

Philomene stepped out of her shift and crawled into the shelter he had made for them, and Clement shed his wet pantaloons and shirt and followed. Under the bearskins he cupped his hands around her bottom and began to move his hands slowly. "What do you have for your brown-skinned boy?"

"Please do not make fun of *Maman*, Clement. I should never have told you she called you that. She's come around," Philomene said. "Listen. *Maman* went to Madame Oreline about you."

She imitated her mother's voice, as if she were talking to Oreline. "'M'sieu Ferrier is looking mighty tired these days, working out in the field like an animal, putting his hands in the dirt. And we should not be doing all this fieldwork, either. None of us was raised this way. M'sieu Ferrier should have some strong boy out helping him, and Clement is just the one. You should get M'sieu Ferrier to buy him in.'"

"What did Madame Oreline say?"

"That M'sieu Ferrier already went to your M'sieu. M'sieu Tessier does not care to sell."

"I thought your mother disapproved of your brown-skinned boy," Clement said, grinning.

"Now what she says is, 'The brown-skinned boy is family.'" Philomene guided his hand to her stomach. "This changed her mind."

Clement left his hand there and massaged her stomach with his fingertips.

"You take too many chances," Philomene said. "What if they miss you, or find out you used the skins?"

"They won't. I made good time on the river coming, I have my pass. I'll head over to M'sieu Narcisse directly and make the delivery, and get back to M'sieu Tessier's without him worrying."

"What would I do without you?"

"Too much talking," Clement said, and moved his hand from where he stroked the high ridge of her rounding belly lower. Philomene smoothed out under his touch.

"You make me feel soft as this fur," she said, sighing. "Like if I lean, you can hold the weight."

The strong smell of the tanning chemicals still clung to the skin side, but the softness of the fur was intoxicating.

"In three days we will be married," Philomene said.

"They put a marrying suit together for me, mostly from M'sieu Tessier's things," Clement said. "I'll do you proud."

"Married by a priest," Philomene said drowsily.

"Maybe M'sieu Eugene got the priest to come, but that doesn't make it any more legal."

"It is as legal as we can get it," Philomene said, her body starting to go tight.

"We can't afford to waste our time arguing. These bearskins need to get where they're going." Clement used his foot to stroke Philomene's leg and gathered the bearskin closer around them. "And we need to get where we're going."

He traced his finger lightly down her cheek, stopping at the corner of her mouth.

"Open the gate, girl."

Philomene relaxed again and smiled wide, revealing the evenly spaced gap between her two front teeth.

"That's my gap," Clement said, and he kissed her.

"Those are my lips," Philomene said, touching his mouth.

He unknotted her *tignon*, threw it to the side, and used his slim fingers to fluff her long, shiny chestnut hair. "Like corn-silk," he said, "but thick and wavy deep. I could get lost in it."

She lifted first her lips and then her body to meet his.

The Saturday afternoon of the wedding, Philomene delivered herself over to Oreline while Suzette kept at the baking. For two days Philomene and her mother had been preparing for the party. Philomene sat stock-still in Oreline's bedroom as the mistress herself stood behind, patiently arranging her hair in complicated basket plaits. The room that Philomene swept, scrubbed down, and aired out every day seemed unfamiliar from the chair where she sat as the center of attention.

Philomene could hear the steady murmur of voices from the front of the house. The wagons had been arriving since early afternoon.

"There," Oreline said, satisfied. "You're ready. Stand up. Let me look at you."

Philomene stood uncertainly. Suzette had taken apart an old white muslin dress of Oreline's and made it over, and the hem floated just above the floor over one of Oreline's double steel hoops. The dress had been left a little loose to accommodate her expanding waistline, and the hoop felt awkward, but Philomene was striking.

Suzette bustled in at that moment, flush, carrying a tangle of wildflowers.

"Oh, Philomene," she said, circling her daughter slowly. "Is that you? You look beautiful, like a lady."

"Merci, Maman."

Suzette turned to Oreline. "They're all out there waiting, Madame. The priest, M'sieu Eugene, M'sieu Narcisse," she said. "M'sieu Ferrier sent me in to say it's time to tend your guests."

Suzette looked down at the flowers she had brought. "These are for Philomene's hair. I could place them."

"Good," said Oreline. "I am finished with the rest. You do look beautiful, Philomene."

"*Merci,* Madame," Philomene said.

"Give me a little time to greet the guests, then come out," Oreline said, and left the room to join the gathering.

Suzette sat Philomene at the dressing table again and began to weave the pale lavender buds and green stems through the thick mass of the basket plaits. Philomene would have been indifferent to her hair were it not for the fact that when people stared at it, they seemed to soften toward her, and Clement seemed mesmerized by it. Philomene's hair was unlike the tight, deep knots and naps of Elisabeth's hair, unlike the springy coils of Suzette's, unlike Gerasíme's snaky twists. It was always a challenge to make it behave, and there was always too much of it pushing onto her face and down her back, but Oreline had tamed it today.

They looked into the mirror, daughter and mother. Both were small boned, but where Suzette's face was round and pleasant, the color of cocoa, Philomene's face was angular, her skin smooth and unblemished, even at fourteen. The eager inquisitiveness that had marked Suzette as a child had been pushed deep inside, far away from view, but a glimmer remained. Philomene was the color of buttermilk biscuits, and the high cheekbones that came down from her grandfather Gerasíme seemed caught in a flight to meet the outer corners of her eyes, giving her entire face a confident and determined air.

"Did they all come, *Maman?*" Philomene asked. "*Mémère* Elisabeth? Gerant?"

"They all wait on you out there, to see you marry this brown-skinned boy."

"Clement, *Maman.*"

"Clement," Suzette repeated. "There will be little sleeping tonight. Everyone got overnight permissions. M'sieu just got back from fetching Gerasíme to play fiddle at the party."

"I wish Aunt Palmire could have been here," Philomene said.

"Yes, I miss her, too." Suzette fussed with the flower arrangement in Philomene's hair. "It would have done her good to see you standing in front of a priest with your man."

"It was meant to be," Philomene said.

Suzette took a step back. "This is a happy day, a day to show off that pretty face. Smile, Philomene."

Philomene obeyed her mother, at first tentatively, but when she caught sight of Suzette's full-to-bursting grin in the mirror, her own smile widened.

"You're mine all right," Suzette said, staring at the telltale gap between their front teeth that made it easy to spot the connection between these generations of women. "But you have it in you to do better, for yourself and the child you carry."

The room became still.

"Come. It is time," Suzette said, and she gave Philomene a small push out the door and down the hallway.

Philomene took a deep breath and stepped into the Ferriers' dining room. Her thick corded hairdo made her feel as if she needed to hold her neck stiffly just to keep in balance. About twenty people were collected in the room, white toward the front and colored farther back, and they all stopped talking when she came in. She saw Eugene and Doralise, Narcisse next to Ferrier, Elisabeth and Gerasíme, and Clement's mother.

Then Philomene saw Clement near the priest from St. Augustine. Clement had on a pair of borrowed black trousers, too long in the leg and patched at the knee. His coat was a heavy formal one of thick worsted wool, with two long tails that fanned out behind him. It could not have been a better fit, but it was more suitable for the dead of winter weather than summer. The stiff white waistcoat and white cravat made him look the man of distinction. Clement clasped his two hands tightly together in front of him, fingers interlocked, as if he didn't know what else to do with them. Just as Philomene entered the room, he brought up his arm and brushed away the sweat running from his forehead with his sleeve, never once unclasping his hands. He had on a pair of oversize gardening gloves, bleached a blinding white. Philomene had to stop herself from giggling. It was her glimpsing come to life. The white hands, the split up the back.

Suzette pushed her from behind toward the priest and Clement.

"Come stand here," the priest said, looking straight at Philomene, and she took her place by Clement's side.

The priest raised his hand for silence and began to recite the special slave ceremony he had prepared. His voice carried to all corners in the small dining room on Ferrier's farm.

"You, Clement, do now, in the presence of God and these witnesses, take Philomene to be your wife;

"Promising that so far as shall be consistent with your relation which you now sustain as servant, you will perform your part of a husband toward her;

"And in particular, as you shall have your opportunity and ability, you will take proper care of her in sickness and in health, in prosperity and adversity; and that you will be true and faithful to her, and will cleave to her only, so long as God shall continue yours and her abode in such places as you can conveniently come together. . . . Do you thus promise?"

Clement said, "*Oui.*"

"You, Philomene, do now, in the presence of God and these witnesses, take Clement to be your husband;

"Promising that so far as your present relation as a servant shall admit, you will perform your part of a wife toward him: and in particular,

"You promise that you will love him; and that as you shall have the opportunity and ability, you will take proper care of him in sickness and in health, in prosperity and adversity; and will cleave to him only, so long as God shall continue his and your abode in such places as you can conveniently come together. . . . Do you thus promise?"

"*Oui,*" said Philomene.

"I then, with the consent of your masters and mistresses, do declare that you have license given you to be familiar together as husband and wife, so long as God shall continue your places of abode as aforesaid; and so long as you shall behave yourselves as it becomes servants to do:

"For you must both of you bear in mind that you remain still, as really and truly as ever, your master's property, and therefore it will be justly expected, both by God and man, that you behave yourselves as obedient and faithful servants toward your respective masters and mistresses for the time being."

The priest took a breath.

"Clement, you may salute the bride," he said.

Clement fidgeted, looking to Philomene to give him some clue as to what to do next. Philomene could only give him a helpless shrug.

"You may kiss the bride now," the priest said.

Clement took Philomene's hand in his and brushed his lips quickly across her cheek, grinning sheepishly as he turned to face the room full of people, waiting for the next instruction.

And so they were bound together in the eyes of all who attended, as they already had been between themselves for some time, and married, after a fashion, as much as they were allowed to be.

Philomene delivered twin girls in the spring, with Oreline attending while Suzette was in the field with Ferrier. The babies were very small, but both seemed healthy. The two girls didn't look alike, except for the similar looks of all newborns, with their jerky movements and changeling features. Clement saw his daughters for the first time on the following Saturday morning, when he rowed down to Ferrier's farm.

It was Philomene's scheme for the naming. The firstborn was named Elisabeth, after her grandmother, and the second twin Bethany, after Clement's grandmother. They all quickly fell into the Creole custom of taking a part of the birth name for the common name, and in short order they could barely remember the christening names. Elisabeth became Bet, and Bethany became Thany.

Old Elisabeth scolded Philomene for changing Elisabeth to Bet, but she was so pleased with her granddaughter and the dramatic leap by two into the next generation of the family tree that everyone could tell her complaints carried no sting.

13

The sky was dark, threatening rain, and Clement was anxious to be off before the storm broke. Dressed in his everyday pantaloons and loose shirt, he carried his only pair of shoes wrapped in his Sunday jacket. He hoisted the heavy packet of bearskins over his shoulder and stopped at Tessier's big house for last-minute instructions.

A full season of planting and harvesting and planting again had passed since he and Philomene had married, and today was his day to present her with a real gift. He had gotten permission from Tessier to work on a rocking chair after his own duties were done, and from Ferrier he had permission to allow Philomene to keep the chair. He and Philomene, who were allowed to own nothing by law, not even themselves, would own this. Clement had taken to calling it "the moonlight chair," since his labors were more by the light of the moon than by daylight.

Tessier, hat pulled low over his head, bushy eyebrows still visible, sat on the front gallery, braiding a horse's leather rein. He bit off a large chaw of rich, dark tobacco and stashed it in his cheek before turning his attention to Clement.

"I'm going to trust you to get my boat back to me, boy," Tessier said, using his tongue to adjust the wad in his cheek. "Narcisse Fredieu is waiting on those skins. Starting this early, you should be able to beat the storm coming. You got the pass?"

"*Oui*, M'sieu Tessier," Clement said in his singsong slave voice, keeping his head bowed. "You can count on me, like always. I'll look after that boat like it was one of my own baby girls. I'll come rowing back on Sunday night, without it being none the worse for wear."

"So, today your woman sees the chair, eh?"

"*Oui*, M'sieu Tessier," Clement said. "I count on her surprise. Thank you for letting me work on it."

"It was your own time, boy, and your money from smithing. Didn't take anything away from me."

For the last two years Clement had been serving as a blacksmith's apprentice. His training came only when he could be spared from the field, but he made good use of what time he had. Mastering the shaping of hot metal in the barn gave him a feeling of working his head as well as his body, and a skilled man was more in keeping with the high-yellow woman he called his wife. He had earned a little money taking on extra tasks for some of the neighboring farmers in the evenings. The serious jobs went to either the *gens de couleur libre* who hired themselves out or to the regular blacksmith, but an occasional small job came his way that allowed him to save four bits here and a few picayunes there. Tessier let him keep half of all he earned and held the money for him.

"You be careful," Tessier said. "The water is rising, and by the look, this one is more than a squall. I don't want to see you lose my boat and get yourself drowned in the bargain. You, the boat, and the furs are worth good money. Get on before the storm takes hold." He let loose a stream of tobacco juice in the dirt.

Clement carried his cargo to the landing and quickly covered the chair, the bearskins, and his extra clothes with an oilskin tarp, lashing them down with a cord around the cypress plank in the back of the dugout. He elevated the packet as high as he could get it away from the water sloshing in the boat bottom, making the narrow dugout harder to balance.

Clement struck off, imagining the look that was sure to come over Philomene's face when he brought her the chair. She was the root of his world.

Clement hummed to himself, an upbeat melody to challenge the darkening of the morning sky. He pulled at the oars, making his way downriver, recognizing plantations and farms on both banks of Cane River. The river had a bite to it today, giving unexpected tugs in first one direction and then another as the currents changed.

He thought about the months it had taken to make the moonlight chair. Finding the oak wood had been easy, since trees and newly felled branches were plentiful in the woods surrounding the quarter on his plantation. The curves of the supports had been the most difficult for him to master, getting them to come out even, and he had redone them several times before he got it right. When he finished the construction he painstakingly carved two images along the wide back of the chair, the full-faced boldness of a brown bear near the top and, directly underneath, the silhouette of a deer in flight. On the front panel Clement carved the likeness of an owl. They were all a little more crude than he would have liked, but he was satisfied they could be recognized as what he had intended, and he was sure Philomene would appreciate the effort. The arms of the chair he studded with melted-down pieces from used horseshoe nails, and he fitted the bottom of the seat with the hide from one of the cows that ran free in the woods, caught and slaughtered at Tessier's order. Tessier kept the meat from the cow and deducted several bits from the money he held for Clement in exchange for a piece of the hide. Clement cured the skin himself, a stinking job that left his hands tender from the salt brine. He worked by the light of the fire in the evening. The others in the quarter teased him about his moonlight chair as they went off to bed, but there was envy in their voices, too.

The dugout lurched. Tessier had been right. The water was rising dangerously, and it was difficult to keep control of the oars. Before he was even halfway down the river, the water started to swirl in strange patterns around him as he paddled. The sky opened suddenly, hurling rain, and the sun vanished behind the clouds at almost the same moment, giving the river a dark and sinister look.

Because he had grown up on the river, Clement respected its moods, but he was also confident of his skill with a boat. He pulled strong against the oars. Normally that would have been enough, but the front of the boat kept getting caught up in furious little circular pockets, carrying him in directions he did not intend. Clement started to sweat through his clothes, even though the weather was cool and damp, and he realized that his body was telling him what his head had not yet registered. He was afraid and was having trouble steering to either shore. Landings dotted the river every hundred yards or so, wherever there was a plantation or farm large enough to need access to the river. Although he was always within sight of land, he couldn't get to it.

The water moved faster beneath him, and sheets of lightning crackled threateningly around him. Clement tried to scoop water out with the bailing gourds, and then his hands, but neither made any difference. He needed to put ashore anywhere he could manage and wait out the passing of the storm. The river slipped from dingy gray to black, now and then becoming so dark that it seemed nighttime, and the storm beat back the sun. At times he could judge his position only during frozen moments when a crack of lightning brightened the sky. By the time the booming echoes followed, Clement was back in the dark. Water began to come rushing at him from every direction, seeping up from below, falling from above, driven from the side by the wind that drove the wet into his face and eyes. Lurching waves brought water in over the low sides of the dugout, as if he were out in open sea rather than on a river.

A strong blast of wind blew off one corner of the tarp, leaving it snapping menacingly in the changeling wind. He could hear the play of tarp against wood, tarp against cargo, and the light rope that had held it in place was a dangerous nipping thing, at the whim of each sharp gust. The only way to save the cargo would be to bring the boat safely to shore without tipping over in the choppy water, a task advancing in hopelessness as the storm wore on and the waterlogged dugout rode lower in the water.

All at once he felt an insistent tug of the water, different from the random tossing he had managed to control so far. Clement looked in front of the boat to his right and saw a suckhole forming, widening in its greed to pull everything it could to its core. He gave up on the idea of being able to save the boat and, in the same instant, yielded to a wink of recognition. It was Philomene's glimpsing of the end for him, by water. The thought did not keep him helpless for long. He had no intention of dying just yet, leaving the wife he had always wanted and two daughters. If it was his time, it would have to fight to take him.

He made his choice, working the chair free from under the tarp by feel, the heavy oilskin and the free end of the rope snapping and lashing at him. It caught him several times on his body, he couldn't distinguish where, but he felt a sharp sting as something caught the soft flesh under his eye, opening him up. It was raw. There was no time to investigate. Standing as high as he dared, and straddling the boat with his feet placed flat against the cypress planks on the side that made up the hull, Clement balanced in the boat the best he could. He threw the chair as far as his strength and equilibrium would allow.

Heart beating wildly, he dove into the cold, rain-pocked river in the same direction as the chair, as far from the drag of the suckhole as he could get. When he broke the water's surface, his lungs pulling in fresh air that came mixed with blinding drops of rain, Clement bumped into something solid. It was the rocking chair, still afloat and bobbing in the roiling river. Clement grabbed hold of the chair with one hand and used the power of his legs and one free arm to swim with all of his capacity, feeling the current massaging his body as if innocent of harmful intent. When he felt he must have swum far enough from the suckhole, he lifted his head to take a quick look around in the water to get his bearings. The rain was varied now, beating down on him hard and soft by intervals, driving into his eyes, and Clement made his plan to swim to the opposite shore, away from the suckhole. His muscles had begun to ache, and a cramp in his left leg formed a hard knot of pain that set his teeth on edge.

When the bank was close the choppy water came to his aid, pushing him this time toward the safety of solid earth. He never let go of the chair, paddling and swimming as best he could, until his toes gripped the slimy mud that let him know he had reached the bank at last.

Clement clawed his way up the slippery slope, aware that he had to keep moving, pulling his knotted, worthless leg behind him. He hung on to the chair, crawling out of the water as if separating himself from the underbelly of the river. He fell back as often as he moved forward, inching his way in stuttering forward progress. He used whatever seemed strong enough to support his weight, cypress knees, branches, palmettos that cut at his hand but propelled him forward, although slowly. He pulled himself closer and closer to safety, away from the reach of the waters that in some spots spilled over the bank completely. At one point he slithered like an alligator on his stomach in the red clay, one hand and arm for pulling, the other for protecting and keeping the chair close to him.

At last he came to rest, when he was sure the wet he felt around him was rain and not the river. He closed his eyes for just a minute, to rest and gather strength, but opened them again with a start as he realized that if he did not keep moving, he would curl himself along the forest floor and drift off to sleep.

Clement knew well the lay of the land along the banks of Cane River from making so many deliveries for Tessier, but he wasn't exactly sure where he was. He was certain that he was on the left bank, instead of the right bank where he needed to be, but it wasn't clear to him how far down he had gone. The sky had ripened into a pale red color, as the sun fought to escape, and he was able to make out shapes better than he had before. He looked back in the direction of where he thought the suckhole should be, but he couldn't see it. It had changed its location or perhaps disappeared entirely. He saw what could have been pieces of smashed wood floating on top of the water near the other bank, but the pouring sheets of rain obscured his view. Even though it was the middle of the day, it was dark and dim, and he wasn't sure of anything. If it was the boat, he thought, he could not have gone back for it anyway.

His muscles complained. The spurt that had allowed him to escape had played out, run its course, and it was all he could do to put one foot in front of the other and move himself forward, he and the chair. Incredibly, the chair looked to be whole, except for gouges in the wood he knew he could fix. It was soaked through, as was he, but of the two of them, the chair was in better shape.

He walked through the woods uncertainly at first, following the line of the bank, until he came to the splayed live oak tree he recognized as marking the Greneaux plantation, on the wrong side of the river. He carried his trophy chair, weary, until he came to Monette's Ferry. The regular boatman sat under the protection of his lean-to wrapped in oilskin, a wiry *gens de couleur libre* who bit off a plug of tobacco as Clement approached.

"I need to get to the other side, M'sieu. I got caught in the storm."

"I can see that myself. You're lucky. It's only habit got me out here today. I can get you across, but you tell Monsieur Tessier that's twelve and a half cents added to his bill."

There was a posted sign, which Clement could not read, but he knew that it advertised the rates for passage across to the other bank of the river. Twenty-five cents for a man and a horse, $1 for any four-wheeled vehicle pulled by two horses, and $1.50 for a loaded wagon or coach with four horses, including the driver and passengers. He had been across many times with Tessier and just as many without him.

"Where you going?" the boatman asked.

"I need to get across to M'sieu Narcisse Fredieu's and then back home. I lost my load to a suckhole, and the boat is gone."

"Only a fool would go out in that storm this morning. By the looks of you, the storm won."

The boatman offered Clement a grimy hand rag, and Clement wiped his face and cleared his eyes. When he pulled back the towel, it was stained with streaks of brownish red, and he cautiously touched the spot at the crest of his cheek where the skin had opened. The gash was tender but not too deep, and still running red. It had missed his eye.

"Well, the river is calm enough now to take you across. Won't charge you extra for the baggage, neither," the boatman said, motioning to the moonlight chair.

Clement stepped forward onto the platform boat, and the boatman pulled him across to the other side of the river by the hand winch and thick rope tied to the sturdiest post on the far shore. As the boatman strained, Clement began to worry about Tessier's reaction to his loss of the boat and Narcisse Fredieu's reaction to the lost bearskins.

It was dawning on Clement that perhaps he had made the wrong choice, between the bearskins and the chair.

Once Clement got to the other bank of the river, he didn't even stop to dry out. He still had a distance to go, and the rain was showing scant signs of letting up. It seemed reckless to him somehow to accept any delay, and it was inevitable that he would get soaked again in a few minutes. Better to keep walking. He walked on along roads and through woods to get to Narcisse Fredieu's farm.

When he reached the familiar markings of the Fredieu plantation, he waited at the back of the house while someone went to fetch Narcisse. He was so tired and so cold that he could hardly tell the difference when the rain stopped its pounding and worked its way into a steady drizzle. Red clay from the river clotted in his hair and, despite the rain, had embedded itself deep into the pores of his skin and his clothes. He was bleeding from cuts he didn't remember, and he concentrated most on swallowing the torment of the random spasms that seized up his right leg, carrying him from numbness to pain and back again. He was shaking uncontrollably as he held the rocking chair to his chest and waited for the white man to come out of the house.

Narcisse came out of the back door, standing dry under the shelter of the eaves overhanging the gallery, dressed carefully in his normal style. "You look a fright. Where are my bearskins?" he said, looking Clement up and down.

"M'sieu Narcisse, something has happened, not my fault," Clement began. "The storm came up so quick and the water had already been rising and M'sieu Tessier's boat was lost. I couldn't save it. I was to deliver the bearskins to you, but they went down the same as the boat. It wasn't my fault. A suckhole tried to drag me down. M'sieu Tessier told me not to let anything happen to the boat or me either, but the river was too strong." Clement waited. There was nothing to do now but wait.

"What are you holding on to there, Clement?"

Clement was bewildered for a moment. The chair was more of a thought to him than a physical presence, and he was almost surprised to look down and see it. He saw his mistake at once, as soon as Narcisse called attention to the chair, but it was too late. He was right in coming to Narcisse Fredieu first, but he should have left the chair in the woods and come back for it later.

"This is a chair I was bringing to my wife on M'sieu Ferrier's farm."

"How is it that you ended up with that chair, and with the same breath you tell me that my skins and Tessier's boat are at the bottom of the river?"

Clement had spent his life tuned to the changing moods of white folks, and the man before him was ready to lash out. Any interchange with him now was like being forced to play with a cottonmouth snake. The outcome was predictable.

"When the boat pulled toward the suckhole, everything spilled out, M'sieu. The chair must have been thrown free of the pull. I just grabbed at whatever I saw when I was swimming away." Clement made his voice contrite. "I could have gone down, too."

"You were afraid for your life, but you just happened to grab for the chair?" Narcisse sneered. "Why not just happen to grab for my skins?"

"It was all so fast, M'sieu. I lost my good clothes and my shoes, too." Clement looked down at the ground as he talked.

"What do I care about your worthless shoes? I needed those skins. I needed them today."

"I'm sorry, M'sieu Narcisse. I was just trying to follow

M'sieu Tessier's orders and save myself." Clement didn't dare look up into Narcisse's face. "I wanted to get here as soon as I could to tell you what happened, so you wouldn't be waiting on me. I should head on back and account to M'sieu Tessier now. He's going to be powerful upset."

Narcisse paused, a long pause full of thought. Clement kept his eyes on Narcisse's boots, but as sure as he was that Narcisse kept his stern, disapproving face, he recognized something different in his voice as soon as he started to speak. Narcisse's voice was peppered with some personal pleasure he could not disguise. It was like the shifting of the river that morning, first sucking him in and then throwing him toward the safety of the shore.

"If it was up to me, you'd pay for the loss in more ways than one. But, unfortunately, you're another man's property, not mine. You make your way on over to Ferrier's farm now, and stay the night, like you always do. Get someone there to dress your cuts. You can't go back to Tessier's looking like that. Go on now."

Clement backed away from the house, slowly at first, not understanding the nature of his good fortune. Narcisse Fredieu was unpredictable, sometimes generous and sometimes harsh; he knew that from quarter's talk. He had expected to bear the brunt of Narcisse's anger, and instead Narcisse had let him go untouched.

He limped on toward Philomene, his moonlight chair cradled in his arms.

Philomene knew the driving rains and the lightning that lit up the inky darkness of the sky would not stop Clement from coming to see her for their permission days. Despite the storm and the warnings from her mother inside their cabin, she went out to check both paths each hour that passed, battling the rain and the winds. The landing was swollen with water. She hoped Clement came on foot.

"You worry those floorboards to death, Philomene," Suzette said. "All you can do is have a warm fire waiting and something ready for him to eat. You cannot get him here faster. Be useful, sit down and work this quilt with me. We will pray for him."

Midmorning the sky had opened of a sudden and poured a dizzying amount of rain. The water came fast and hard, partnering with the wind in first one direction and then another, delivering more than the waiting earth could drink. Exploding light followed by deep thundering booms did not interrupt the flow and the intensity of the rain, and the sky became a mockery of both day and night. Fleeting light produced silhouettes and transient shapes instead of three-dimensional objects with texture and detail. At last the sounds became ordinary, and the rain changed to a steady flow.

In the middle of the afternoon Philomene finally made out Clement's figure coming from out of the woods, hunched and hatless. He moved toward the cabin like a wounded animal, with a slow and dogged determination. He was covered head to toe with red mud, favoring one leg over the other, awkwardly clutching a chair in front of him. Philomene rushed out into the rain to lead him into the cabin, but when she tried to pry the chair from him, he would not let go.

"For you," he kept repeating through chattering teeth.

Clement made puddles on the floor where he half sat, half collapsed, next to the fireplace. Suzette wiped at his face with a washrag while Philomene began to remove his drenched-through clothes. He wouldn't release his hold on the chair.

They toweled him as dry as they could and wrapped him in both of their sleeping blankets before he stopped shaking enough to talk again.

"I had to choose," he said, still clutching the chair.

Slowly he began to tell them what had happened to him. He started with the early-morning warnings from Tessier about taking care of his boat and kept on all the way through to the anger that turned itself into a reprieve from Narcisse Fredieu, with his instruction to come to Ferrier's farm.

"I have to get back to M'sieu Tessier, let him know how it happened," Clement said, and tried to stand. His legs were weak, and he had to sit back down on the pallet.

"Not until the storm passes through," said Suzette. "You are unwell."

"No," Philomene said. "Clement is right. Something is false, M'sieu Narcisse sending Clement here too easy. We cannot leave this to chance." She paced the floor. "We must take the matter to M'sieu Ferrier without further delay. Clement has to convince M'sieu Tessier he did everything he could to save the boat and the bearskins."

Philomene took Clement's cold, clammy hands into her own. "If M'sieu Ferrier takes you back in the wagon today, and renews his offer to buy, you might escape punishment. There is advantage to M'sieu Tessier seeing you as you are now." She held his gaze. "Clement, are you able enough? Two white men bargaining is stronger than any appeal from us."

"I can make it," Clement said.

Philomene turned to Suzette. "*Maman,* you must persuade Madame Oreline to stand up for Clement. Strong enough for her to convince her husband. Do you think you can?"

Suzette looked from Clement, shivering, into Philomene's pinched face. "We will see," she said.

Clement leaned unevenly on Philomene in the slow walk to the farmhouse, while Suzette ran ahead. By the time they reached the back door of the kitchen, Suzette had brought Oreline to the large back room.

"Come in, sit him down," Oreline said.

Clement shook off help and sat heavily on the bench in the kitchen.

"Madame, if you might listen, and report to your husband," Suzette began, and poured out the story.

Within the half hour after Oreline first saw Clement, with his battered face and sickness already coursing through his body, Ferrier had hitched up the wagon.

They watched with both hope and fear as Ferrier urged the horse forward out into the final throes of the storm, taking Clement back to Tessier's plantation.

As soon as Narcisse saw Clement head back to the woods toward Ferrier's farm, still clutching the chair, he called for his horse to be saddled. The boy would make a beeline to Philomene and stay until Sunday dusk before heading back to Tessier's plantation. By the time he gave his account of what happened on the river that morning, Narcisse would have already done what he needed to do.

Narcisse would have preferred to be in front of the warmth of a steady fire with a touch of bourbon, and not out on horseback in this kind of weather, but it was time to pay Jacques Tessier a long overdue visit. If he managed it well, Clement could be visiting Philomene for the last time.

Narcisse rode through the bower of cedars marking the entrance to Tessier's home site, and a young honey-brown man in flapping shoes came running out to take care of his horse. Narcisse took a quick look around as he approached the house. Tessier had done well for himself. His plantation was twice the size of Narcisse's own.

Tessier himself appeared at the front door as Narcisse shook out his dripping coat and knocked the water off his slouch hat under the eaves of the wide gallery.

"Narcisse Fredieu," Tessier greeted him warmly. "This is a pleasant surprise. Come in, get warm. What brings you out in weather like this? I certainly didn't expect any visitors today."

"Too foul a day to be out, that is the truth," Narcisse said as they passed into the front room with the comfort of its blazing fire. "I thought I should get over here as soon as I could about that fool Clement of yours and the damage he's done."

"I sent him out this morning to settle us square on the bearskin business. I've been regretting it since the storm blew in. What's happened?"

"He dragged himself over to my place with some story about losing your boat and not knowing what happened to my skins. You're out a pretty piece of change behind the two of those. But the whole while, he's hugging some chair he claims is his that he managed to save when everything else is lost. The chair looked as good as new. What do you make of that?"

"You say my boat was lost?" Tessier did not look happy. "Is Clement whole?"

"The boy didn't look any the worse for what he claimed he went through. He looked fine to me, just in a hurry to go running off to see Ferrier's girl. He didn't seem to care about your boat or my skins. Just kept talking about how he lost his good clothes and his shoes. Instead of heading back here, he went on to Ferrier's."

"But he did come to you first, to let you know what happened?" Tessier asked.

"Probably just because it was on the way to Ferrier's."

"Why didn't you fetch him back with you?"

"I offered, but he begged off. He had something else on his mind, that was clear to see, on Ferrier's place. I wouldn't be surprised if he isn't sitting in front of a big fire right now, laughing about the whole thing."

Tessier looked doubtful. "That doesn't sound like Clement. If he's hurt, I'd better send someone to bring him back. It's nasty out there. It won't do me much good to have a sick boy on my hands."

"Valuable skins and a boat lost because of Clement's carelessness, and all he thinks about is his own ragged clothes and shoes gone. He's safe over to Ferrier's. When the weekend has passed, he'll come swaggering back at his regular time with some cock-and-bull story of what happened. You shut your eyes to the boy's faults. Tessier, I'm afraid I need to press my claim for those skins. Maybe we can work out some labor arrangement. Clement could come to work the price of the skins off with me. I might even be willing to buy him, minus the price of the skins, of course."

"If you're so down on the boy, why would you want him on your place?"

"I'm just thinking about you and me making the best out of the mess this boy caused today."

Tessier poured more brandy, first for Narcisse and then for himself. "Ferrier has proposed to buy him as well, but I've been sitting the fence because I'm fond of Clement, and he shows promise as a blacksmith. Ferrier wants to expand his farm, and then neither of us has to worry about all this going back and forth so much between our plantations. The truth is, our full-time blacksmith can handle the work fine most of the time by himself, and I could spare the boy. I never much liked these marriages across plantations."

"It seems to me with the bearskins to be worked off, I have the stronger claim."

"The stronger claim rests with how much Clement can bring. I'd want to talk to Ferrier before I finalized an arrangement."

Narcisse kept his face impassive. He decided to let the subject rest for the time being and pursue his advantage later.

The squall ebbed and flowed outside as Narcisse and Tessier talked crops, weather, and the horse race they had both attended the weekend before at Monette's Ferry. The afternoon slipped past effortlessly, the storm beating at the windowpanes and the wind screeching loudly through the trees. It was pleasant to pass the time in front of Tessier's hearth, dry and spared from the excesses of the storm, and they were both surprised to hear a wagon approach around four o'clock as the last of the storm blew itself out.

Both Tessier and Narcisse went to the door to see who would be out in weather like this, as Tessier's mulatto went out in the rain to assist. There were two visitors in the dripping wagon, both with oilskin protective coverings thrown over them.

Ferrier dropped the reins and jumped down as soon as the horse stopped, without the aid of the manservant. The other rider struggled to step down from the high bed of the wagon, moving slowly with clumsy movements, obscured by the oilskin that had been pulled around him.

Slowly the realization came that the man was Clement, clearly battered and moving in halting steps, as if in pain. Narcisse looked at Clement, and ripe bubbles of rage swelled. This good-for-nothing boy had lost his skins and, worse, had captured Philomene. The sniveling brown boy wasn't worth much by what he could see.

Ferrier shook out his oilskin under the eaves of the gallery. As the manservant took the horse and wagon to the protection of the barn, Clement limped to the edge of the gallery, rain streaming from his oilskin onto the cypress planks.

Clement bowed his head and waited.

"What do you have to say for yourself, Clement?" Tessier asked.

"I'm sorry, M'sieu Tessier," Clement said. "I lost the boat and the bearskins to the river. I almost didn't get out myself. I tried to save them. I'm sorry, M'sieu."

Clement's face bore a resemblance to a burlap bag overstuffed with large rocks, lumpy and puffed out in irregular places. One eye was swollen almost shut, and a cut at his temple had reopened during the ride, unleashing a small but stubborn rivulet of blood that crept down his face.

"I have some light to shed on this, Tessier," Ferrier said. "Why don't you send the boy to get dry?"

Tessier's mouth was set. "Go on, Clement. See after yourself. We'll talk about this later."

The three planters walked back toward the warmth of the fire and prepared to sort the situation out.

"I've come to renew my offer for Clement." Ferrier's craggy face looked strained. "His wife and children are on my place. It makes sense."

"Where did that boy get himself off to? We need more glasses." Tessier's annoyance was clear until Ferrier waved away the offer of brandy. "Seems Clement is in high demand. Narcisse just made an offer for him as well, in lieu of lost bearskins."

Ferrier did not try to hide his surprise. "It appears Monsieur Fredieu has a great interest in certain aspects of other people's plantations."

Before Narcisse could respond, Tessier's mulatto entered the room with a show of urgency. "Sorry, M'sieu Tessier, but there's three white boys from downriver come to return your boat. They say it washed up on the bank, and they knew it to be yours by the initials carved on the seat."

"A day not fit for man or beast, and more surprise visitors than I've had in a month of Sundays. Excuse me, gentlemen."

While they waited for Tessier's return, Narcisse and Ferrier talked of the storm. Honor between planters prevented direct words about the events of the day, but Narcisse felt an uncomfortable judgment in Ferrier's eyes on him.

Tessier returned before long, smiling broadly. "It appears everything has righted itself. The boat was found in fairly good condition, considering. The bearskins and Clement's clothes and shoes were soaked through, but still wedged under the corners of the tarp that held."

"I assume that lessens your claim on Clement," Ferrier said to Narcisse. "But my offer still holds if you're willing to sell, Monsieur Tessier."

Narcisse nodded, unwilling to push any further today.

"It's settled, then," Tessier said. "The bearskins go to Narcisse, and Ferrier and I can make arrangements for a loan to be paid off over time."

Before the month was out Clement moved in with Suzette and Philomene and the twins, into the small cabin around the back of the main house on Ferrier's farm.

Stormy March gave way to balmy April and turned to late spring. Clement got up before daybreak each morning except for Sunday and headed off to the field. When Ferrier ordered it, Philomene joined him there.

One early Saturday evening Suzette went to the Fredieu plantation to stay overnight with Elisabeth, and Philomene and Clement had the cabin alone with the twins. It was a rare moment for them to be just the four, and rarer still that both babies were asleep and peaceful at the same time.

Philomene came close to drowsing in the moonlight chair, holding and rocking Bet, letting the motion lull her. The chair produced a flat swishing sound and a slight squeak that Clement had never managed to fix. Philomene looked at Clement across the room from her, holding Thany. The arms of her chair curved around her stiffly, arms that had sustained her until Clement came to live with them on Ferrier's farm. The care he had taken to make the chair, and the risk he had taken to bring it to her, made her love Clement all the more. But there were times, when one of them used the chair to rock the babies to sleep or just to rest at the end of a long day, when she would have to fight off a cruel fluttering in the pit of her stomach, a shadow she could not shake.

An owl's hollow hooting outside the cabin roused Philomene, and she looked across the room at Clement holding Thany.

"This is the picture, Clement. This is what I saw long ago." The trembling in Philomene's hushed voice betrayed her excitement. "I told you then I knew we'd be together, how I saw the wedding first and then the two babies." Her voice rose over the whisper that she intended. "The picture was clear. It was this exact moment, with us starting our own family, you and me together."

She had begun to question the truth of the old unrealized visions, wondering if they would unfold as she had seen them. There had not been a single new glimpsing in over three years.

"Did you believe me then, all those years ago, when I first told you about what I saw?" Philomene asked, admiring the features of Bet's coffee-colored face arranged in sleep. She often asked this question of Clement, whenever she needed to hear the answer he always gave. He didn't disappoint her.

"How could I not believe in something I wanted so much to happen?" he said.

Some weeks the farm was like a remote island, and there seemed to be only the monotony of the work. There were often visitors, but the pace was slow and steady. Narcisse came most frequently, and Philomene was convinced that he was slightly afraid of her, or at least in awe. She was hopeful that his reverence for her glimpsings would continue to keep him at a safe distance. Philomene was of two minds when she heard the Fredieu buggy approach instead of the clipping horse's hooves of Narcisse's mare. The buggy signaled that he came with wife in tow. He had married again, a sharp-faced woman with a tongue to match, not at all tentative the way the first wife had been. Madame Arsine was particularly disdainful with Philomene, ordering her about with a bossy arrogance. Both her mother and Clement slipped deeper into their big house masks when she was around, full of rounded backs and the soft rhythm of slurry Creole words, but Philomene turned sullen and silent.

As much as she disliked Madame Arsine, a part of Philomene was relieved. With his wife present, Narcisse refrained from watching her so boldly.

Even with the onset of the hot, sticky summer, the warmth of Clement's body as he lay beside Philomene in their bed was welcome. They were five in the cabin. Philomene sometimes woke in the night, straining against the darkness long after the banked fire gave off enough light to see, turning toward each distinctive pattern of breathing in the household, and she felt thankful. But she also respected how a jealous God might want to take such fullness away.

Three generations under one roof fortified her. Even Elisabeth was only a short walk through the woods, although her grandmother still grieved openly over the separation from Gerasíme. Philomene did housework, field-work, gardening, whatever needed to be done, in addition to the care of Oreline's children as well as her own twins. The days were hard, repetitive, and never-ending, but they weren't beaten; they had their own cabin, enough to eat, and an ally in Oreline Derbanne.

And she had Clement, whose delicious brown skin seemed actually to crackle whenever it came into contact with her own. She had seen women take up with men, willingly and unwillingly, eagerly and with resignation. She had seen men take up with women, aggressively and passively, with single-minded intent or carelessly. But she didn't believe any to be as matched as she and Clement. They built to a fine luster together, like the silver she polished for first the Derbannes and then the Ferriers, when it was passed down to Oreline.

Clement made Philomene better. She was sure she made him better, too, and together they could produce beautiful babies. She didn't need a glimpsing to tell her that.

17

Mosquitoes and flies invaded Oreline's household at the height of the summer of 1857. The rains came early and overstayed, leaving stilled pools of water everywhere within clear sight of the house. Oreline stayed indoors as much as possible, but the stink of the outside air penetrated the farmhouse. Cane River had been plagued with yellow fever each of the prior two summers, and Ferrier had taken to having Clement burn patches of tar around the house once a week. The smoke rose in thick, noxious clouds, and no matter how many times she had her mulatto girl scrub down the walls, the smell lingered.

Oreline sat quietly in the front room one stifling afternoon, both she and her daughter, Josephina, hunched over their needlework, lost in thought, but she was roused when she heard a loud smack on bare flesh. Across the room at the table where she sat, Philomene slapped again absently at her arm, brushing away the dead insect before she went back to polishing the silver.

There was a commotion outside, someone calling her name, and then the heavy pounding of feet on the wooden gallery of the farmhouse.

"Madame Oreline!"

Philomene jumped up to swing open the front door, and Clement struggled in through the doorway with Ferrier in his arms.

"He just fell down, Madame, in the middle of the corn," Clement said to Oreline, his straw hat sitting crookedly on his head, sweat pouring from him. "One minute we were hoeing and he was complaining of the heat, and the next he couldn't get up. I carried him straight here."

Ferrier let out a small disoriented moan.

"Take him to the bedroom, put him on the bed," Oreline instructed, following closely behind Clement down the hallway. "Philomene, bring some clean rags and get more water."

Clement carried Ferrier to the back of the farmhouse and deposited him on the bed. Ferrier shuddered, big droplets of strange-smelling sweat pouring from his body.

"It is too cold," Ferrier said hoarsely, his teeth chattering so loudly that Oreline could hear the sound from across the room.

Oreline rushed to his side. Her husband threw off enough heat for her to feel the burning intensity before she was even close enough to touch his face. She covered him with a blanket anyway and began to sponge him off with cool water.

"Clement, thank you for bringing him in," Oreline said. "Go on back to the field. Philomene, keep the children out, and send in Suzette."

They nursed him through the night, and by the second day they all knew it was yellow fever. Only Oreline and Suzette were allowed in the back room.

"Let me help you sit up," Oreline said to Ferrier. "You have to try to eat."

"I can't," Ferrier groaned, "it hurts."

"Where? Where does it hurt?"

"Pain in my head, my legs, my back," he said as racking heaves tore through him. "Bring the slop jar, quick."

Oreline and Suzette took turns taking care of Ferrier over the next few days, as they had so often tended to the sick together before.

"I saw it close up last summer," Oreline said to Suzette as Ferrier dozed on the third day. "He has a good chance to recover. I attended a cousin upriver, and he came through it. We have to pray that his skin does not get a yellowish tinge. That would be jaundice. If that happens, later can come the bleeding and, if it turns to the black vomit, death."

"It is good you have experience," Suzette said. "They say up in Natchitoches they counted off over a hundred deaths this summer already. Yellow jack, black vomit, stranger's disease, all the same thing."

Despite Oreline's optimism, Ferrier's fever showed no sign of easing, day after day. They kept him as cool as they could with wet rags, tried to feed him, and gave him quinine. Mostly they waited, and Oreline ordered Clement to keep the tar burning directly outside his sickroom every day until the entire farm had the diseased smell of sulfuric desperation to it. There was nothing more a doctor would have done, even if they had been able to get one, short of letting blood.

By the end of the first week Ferrier's skin sagged all

over his body. He could barely eat, and what he did get down he could not hold on to. He had lost a tremendous amount of fluid. Looking into Ferrier's face was like looking at a dried apple, all of his distinguishing facial features shrunken except for his eyeballs, which were swollen far beyond any natural size and seemed to stare fixedly. The whites of his eyes had turned an antique yellow, moist and glistening. His chin and forehead had turned almost the color of a rotting pumpkin, but the sides of his face were dusky red, as if he were a vain young woman who had pinched her cheeks too vigorously to get the color to bloom.

Oreline was not prepared for the husband of so many unexpected colors decomposing before her eyes. Ferrier was restless and jittery, his motions jerky, and he seemed to speed up the second week, as if he had just remembered that he had somewhere urgent he needed to be. He slipped through the later stages quickly. His skin had become so thin and ghostly that it didn't seem so shocking when the blood began to ooze from his eyes and nose and mouth, as if his skin could no longer prevent the leakage. The black vomit followed, as if on cue, and Oreline knew there was no stopping the march of the disease then. Ferrier began to throw up what looked like black coffee grounds, stinking piles of his own insides.

At the very end, Suzette woke Oreline from where she dozed in her chair beside Ferrier. Ferrier waved his arms frantically, with more energy than he had shown for almost two weeks. His tongue was thick, his yellowed eyes wild, and he thrashed in the bed without logic. Oreline grabbed hold of his hand. His body jerked twice, and he lapsed into a brief coma. He never recovered.

"We've been here together too many times before," Ore-line said to Suzette as they prepared his body for burial. "Together in the death of others."

Ferrier had not reached his thirty-fifth birthday. Oreline missed him desperately, but emotional reflections would have to wait. Practical considerations had to come first. Joseph Ferrier was dead, and the death of a master always triggered some change for both wives and slaves, usually for the worse.

Ferrier's debts were as much of a surprise as his sudden death.

Oreline sent for Narcisse Fredieu, and he came around to the farmhouse immediately.

"Death is no stranger to me, Narcisse," Oreline said, sitting on the gallery while they were served coffee. "I was content with Monsieur Ferrier, but how could he not tell me we were one step removed from being tenants? That this land was not his, but his mother's? He took risks with my money, and they tell me now that there is nothing left. Nothing but debt, for tools and for buying Clement. His mother has told me I must move in ninety days. This land is her only income." Oreline twisted a small embroidered handkerchief in her hands. "I am thirty-two years old with three young children. What am I to do?"

Narcisse looked sympathetic and leaned over to take her hand in his. "You can count on me, cousin. You have two problems, and they can both be solved. On the one hand, you need a husband, and on the other, enough money to relieve your debt."

Narcisse leaned back into his chair and took up his coffee cup. "I know of a man, older, who was also just made a widower by the fever, in need of a wife for his three children. He is a respectable Frenchman who lives upriver, a small farmer and schoolteacher. His name is Valery Houbre. You must know beforehand that he has no land, and very little property, but if you follow my advice, a hasty marriage could benefit you both."

"I do not know him," Oreline said, "but I value your council. And the debt?"

"This is the best course, Cousin Oreline, and the debt is easily discharged. What you no longer need, what you can no longer afford to keep under the circumstances, are all of the slaves."

Oreline began to twist the handkerchief again. "How could I possibly?" she said. "They are like family."

"It must be done," Narcisse insisted. "There is no other way. The creditors will not wait. You must sell while the price is high, and before fever has a chance to strike again. You do this as much for them as for yourself. The first to go must be Clement. I know where a quick and profitable sale can be made. Not here on Cane River, but to a distant relative of mine in Virginia."

"But I cannot sell Suzette and Philomene, or the babies," Oreline said forcefully. "I cannot."

"You must, of course, keep at least one. You are a lady. Philomene can go with you, she and the babies. I can arrange a place for Suzette with my brother, where she will be treated well."

"But Philomene will lose Clement and her mother," Oreline said.

"She won't be alone," Narcisse said. "She still has her girls."

14 February 1855
Natchitoches Parish
Succession of <u>Joseph Ferrier.</u> Petition filed by **Marie Oréline Derbanne,** widow, and tutrix of the minors Florentine, Joseph, and Josephine, issue of her marriage to said Joseph Ferrier. Petitioner respectfully shows that she contemplates contracting marriage with Valery Oubré of Natchitoches Parish and desires to retain tutorship of the said minor children. Whereupon she prays for the convocation of a family meeting to decide upon the question if she shall be retained as tutrix, and that the members of the family meeting and Narcisse Fredieu, the under tutor, be notified to attend, /s/ A. H. Pierson, attorney for petitioner.

Succession of Joseph Ferrier.

Oreline called Suzette and Philomene in to her in the front room of the farmhouse, and when they stood before her she willed herself to speak. "We are forced to make difficult changes now that Monsieur Ferrier is gone."

Philomene slipped her arm through her mother's and held tight. The two women leaned on one another.

"*Oui,* Madame." Philomene talked for both of them. Suzette was clearly dazed, the way she sometimes got, but Philomene was not as easy to read. Oreline had to admit to a trace of fear in what the strong-willed young slave woman was capable of.

"I am to be married again, soon, and must move off this farm. Philomene and the children will come with me."

"What is to become of my mother and husband?"

"Places have been found, good places. Suzette, you will go to Augustine Fredieu, not so far away."

"And Clement, Madame. What becomes of Clement? Back to M'sieu Tessier?" The edgy tremor in Philomene's voice made Oreline uneasy. She wished Narcisse were by her side, but he was on his way to the dock, had left with Clement over an hour before.

"Clement is already gone, on his way to a good home in Virginia."

Oreline expected tears, or pleading, or both, and she had steeled herself for them. But she wasn't prepared for what Philomene did next. Philomene began to scratch at her own face, digging her short fingernails deep enough to draw blood, pulling away strips of raw skin.

"What have you done?" Philomene's voice had become a hiss. The tips of her fingers were slick with crimson. "Where is he? He can't be gone. I have to talk to him."

Oreline was not exactly sure what would have happened if Suzette had not held on to Philomene. Philomene tore at the fabric of her own dress and at her hair while Suzette tried to rock her quiet.

"We had to act quickly, to get him on the last steamer of the month," Oreline said, uncertain whether Philomene even heard her.

Long moments passed before Philomene finally regained herself, but still Suzette did not let her go. "How could you?" Philomene said directly to Oreline, her red-rimmed eyes giving off a frenzied brightness. "My mother, and then my husband?"

"You had better watch your tongue," Oreline said stiffly, trying not to show how much Philomene in this condition frightened her. Suzette's daughter had always been unpredictable. "You have been with me a long time, you and your mother both, but do not forget yourself to me."

Oreline watched the struggle on Philomene's face, and it was with relief that she saw her bow her head slightly at last.

"*Oui*, Madame," Philomene said. "I have no more to say."

Those were the last words Philomene spoke, as far as Oreline could tell, to anyone. She stopped singing to the children, her own or Oreline's. As arranged, Suzette was sold to Augustine Fredieu, and when Suzette left Ferrier's farm for her new home, Philomene hugged her mother but did not utter a sound.

```
One of the Slaves Mented to Marrie Her
[Philomene] But He was sold, Narcease wanted
Her for His Self.
--Cousin Gurtie Fredieu, written family
   history, 1975
```

Oreline was in a sorry mood, uncertain how her future would braid itself together. She found herself short-tempered and angry all of the time and struck the girl several times when she hadn't intended, but she never once withheld visiting from her on Sundays. The Sunday visits and her twins seemed to be the only things that kept Philomene together.

Even though the girl stopped talking, Philomene remained useful to Oreline, taking over all of the household chores on the farm as they waited for Oreline's second wedding day. The cows never missed milking, and the wash was boiled, scrubbed, pounded, hung, dried, ironed, folded, and put away. On her hands and knees, Philomene scrubbed the floors with a bristle brush. The children were tended and the meals cooked and served. But still she never spoke.

Three Sundays after Ferrier died, Philomene came to Oreline. She held two of her fingers upside down and made a walking motion with them.

"Where are you asking to go, Philomene?"

Philomene pointed to the woods, toward her grandmother.

"You can talk, Philomene," Oreline said. "Talk to me instead of this foolishness."

Philomene stood stubbornly in front of her, saying nothing.

"I do not have to allow you to go."

Philomene remained rigid, silent.

"All right," Oreline said, and wrote the pass. "But be back before dark."

18

On a hot, muggy Thursday morning, Philomene struggled to get moving. Bet and Thany had both been fussy for almost the entire week, in spirits as low as Philomene's own, and the girls had cried tiny choking sobs all through the night. Philomene ached everywhere and assumed the twins did, too. Even the touch of their skin hurt her where she held them, and she could not bring comfort to either them or herself.

At first she thought the mix of her own suffering and want of sleep and the dead places in her heart were the reason she had such a hard time getting up before the sun to nurse her babies and light the morning fires on the farm.

Philomene wouldn't allow herself words, even with the babies. There was a freedom in not talking, an extra corner of calm to be gained by not having to participate fully in a world without Clement. If not for the twins, she might have tried to

run off, to get to him somehow, but she didn't know where
Virginia was or where Clement was likely to be held there.
Even if she could manage to find him, she would be sent back
and punished. There was no encouraging course of thought,
no plan she could devise that made any sense. There was no
place to go, except into silence. Philomene wondered if her
aunt Palmire had felt this same fragile, soothing distance.

Ever since they had first told her that Clement was gone,
she had been enveloped by the same heaviness that she recognized in her mother. Then Suzette was gone from her as
well, and the facing of each new day was too much effort.
The farm seemed flat and unfamiliar, absent of all of the
people who had made it home. It had become nothing more
than a discarded, temporary shelter for Oreline and her
three children, and Philomene and the twins, a stopover
until the next place.

If not for my babies, Philomene kept thinking, my mind
would slip away, and my body would follow.

Philomene propped Bet and Thany in the corner where
she could check on them and went about her work. They
were fussy, demanding, and she could barely keep her
thoughts on cleaning out the wall altar in Oreline's bedroom. The day was already blistering, and before the morning had barely started, the rag that she kept in her apron
pocket to wipe the perspiration from her face was as soaked
as her scrub rag.

As the sun blazed higher in the cloudless sky, she felt her
legs melt in the dripping Louisiana heat, felt her cheek slippery and hot against the floor she had just cleaned. Voices
floated like dandelion wish-weeds around her, none of her
concern. River noises had been set loose in her head, drowning out everything else.

She woke up cold and shivering. The noise was louder; fiery water surrounded her. Only her head was above the roaring waves, and she could barely see through the fog that sat on top of the river like soft muslin. The water turned freezing cold and then hot again. She could only make out dim shapes until her eyes got used to the tricks of light and shadow, and then a color, taking on form and getting larger. In the distance she saw a yellow boat coming toward her. In the narrow dugout was Clement, nut brown and strong, his powerful arms straining with each pull of the oars, rowing straight and true toward her through the rising water. Smiling at her, a smile full of certainty and knowing. Without taking his brown eyes from hers across the distance, he scooped up little Thany from the raging water and placed her carefully beside him, safe in the boat. Hadn't she left both girls together somewhere else? Where was Bet?

Philomene lost strength each time her head dipped below the water. She could still make it to the boat, but she refused to go without Bet. If the noise stopped, she could think. There was a stench in the air riding along the surface of the river like a poison cloud, threatening to choke her. It was thick and powerful and carried the harsh sting of burning tar deep inside her chest. The water started to boil and bubble, sending hot blasts of spray at her face and into her eyes. Clement held out his hand to her, palm up, in their old secret code of attachment: "I'm here, you're there. But we'll manage to be together later."

Philomene wanted to go to Clement, so she could cradle her head against his chest, have him soothe the noise away with his fingertips. She wanted to go deep into those brown eyes so that the attacking water could not touch her anymore, but he was telling her to find Bet. As if willed into being, she heard Bet's startled baby cry behind her, weak but certain.

Philomene's head felt fused and stiff against her shoulders, but she forced the muscles in her neck to obey, turning her head. She saw Bet clearly now, off to her right. The little girl was naked and helpless, faceup, looking small against the endless blue water. Philomene managed to grab one of her daughter's chubby arms and pull Bet to her, still breathing. It wasn't too late. If she got Bet to the boat, they could all be together. But as she fought the pounding water with her free hand and turned back with Bet protected in the crook of her arm, Clement and Thany and the yellow boat were gone.

A chill wind was blowing the damp river fog away, and both the noise and the tug of the water were becoming still. There was a faraway sound, but she couldn't make it out, didn't want to make it out. She couldn't bear to leave this place without finding Clement and Thany first. The beckoning sound became louder, and deeper, and broke through to recognition.

"Philomene. Philomene. Come back." It was Narcisse Fredieu's voice, pulling her where she didn't belong. "Philomene?"

Philomene was weak and empty, confused. There was something unfinished, something that nagged at her not to leave the fever dream. Even in the afterlight, as she lay on the narrow cot, fever broken but too worn out to move or feed herself, she knew Clement and Thany had been forever connected, as had she and Bet, but what did it mean?

It took two days before Narcisse and Oreline thought Philomene strong enough to tell her that both her babies had died of yellow fever.

She had no more water for tears.

The beginning of the summer had held such promise, some small measure of fulfillment, even if it was a satisfaction on loan, as it always was for a slave's life. By the end, Philomene was alone, her husband and her children gone forever, a family wiped out as if they had never existed.

Suzette reappeared on the farm, as natural and as foreign as Clement's appearance in her fever dream. Suzette rushed in and out of the cabin as Philomene recuperated, using time stolen from her other chores on the farm. The arrangement was only temporary, orchestrated by Oreline to secure help with both the farm and Philomene. Her mother had come back only on short-term loan. Suzette explained it all to her, but Philomene kept losing track of the thread of her words. She held more surely to the sound of her mother's humming and the familiar hands that held cool rags to her forehead. Time had no anchor for Philomene now, so she wasn't sure how long she had been sick or if she had ever been well. The days drifted, tumbling one into the other, full only of muffled sound, loss, and indifference.

Philomene's only willing thoughts were of her fever dream, its meaning beyond her grasp. Each day that she gathered strength, she tried to puzzle it out, but it wouldn't be solved.

They both nursed her, Suzette and Oreline, taking turns the way they had with Ferrier, and Philomene wasn't sure whether she was supposed to live or die. She didn't care. The quiet she tried to gather around herself didn't stop the others from talking and poking, trying to draw her out, as if her withdrawal were a personal offense to them. They tried halfheartedly to get her to break her long silence, but there was nothing to say that anyone could bear to hear.

A need had begun to take shape in Philomene's mind,

becoming more persistent with each day that passed; but it floated out of reach until almost the end of her convalescence.

She had to see her babies' graves.

Philomene's rocking and digging motions were obvious in meaning. Oreline and Suzette agreed that it was a good strategy for Philomene's recovery to get her up and moving for any reason, even if her shaky steps led her to the quickly dug grave for her children. Together Oreline and Suzette took her out to the grove of fig trees that had become the farm's cemetery when Ferrier died, and Philomene first saw the gentle curve of the freshly turned mound that held her babies, now that she could not. There was only one grave, only one smooth, flat stone from the river that had been placed at the top of the mound to mark the spot. No names adorned the site anywhere. She would not have been able to read them if they had.

One. Only one. Philomene looked at Oreline in disbelief, held up one finger.

"Why is there only one grave for the two of them?" Suzette asked Oreline, becoming Philomene's voice.

"Monsieur Narcisse took care of all of the arrangements. He dug the plot himself, in between nursing you and nursing me, during the worst of the epidemic. If not for him, I don't know how any of us would have fared. We all got at least a touch of the fever, except for him. He said he wanted your two girls to keep each other company, even in death. He has been very concerned."

Philomene saw Oreline's lips moving, heard some of what she said. Bet and Thany, only one grave between them. Maybe this was a blessing. Maybe it was they who had been spared, as she had not.

Philomene missed Clement and the babies as a physical ache. Her breasts were still full of milk that no eager mouths needed. She caught herself expecting to see Clement rounding the bend of the road to come to her for their end-of-the-week time, hot and musky, giving off the sweet sweat of the road and anticipation as he always had when he walked to her. She waited for him to come in from the day's work to the late-evening meal they would share together, he and the girls.

For Philomene there was no more talking, only listening, if not to words, then to the song underneath the words. She knew she should have been grateful to have her mother back close, if only temporarily, but gratitude eluded her. There was nothing that could begin to fill so many empty places inside. They were treacherous, these gaps, and had begun to pulse and echo if she dwelled on them for any amount of time. Her mother talked to her, as she had when she was small, one-sided conversations that demanded little from her, and some-times even the listening seemed too much to give.

"At least you know what it is to want a man, and have him want you back. That's something I never tasted, the choosing of it, the pleasure of it," her mother prattled on one day when she came back from emptying the bedpan. "Your grandmother Elisabeth and grandfather Gerasíme were like that. Your *marraine*, Doralise, and Eugene Daurat had it for a time before the feelings passed. You and Clement had it in your hands for longer than some people get. They can take him away from you, but they can never take that away. You are young, Philomene, and you will fig-ure a way to go on. We need to pray for Clement, that they treat him right in Virginia. We need to pray for Bet and Thany. It must have been their time, and they went on to a better place."

Philomene heard her, and the others, and the pointlessness of the things they said. She watched words float past, plump and ripe, before they burst just outside her line of vision. She was surrounded by those who thought they offered her the comfort of an outreached palm, unaware that they delivered a fist. They were foolish to expect her to talk back to them, to respond to their words.

The long recuperation left her too much time to think. Philomene had begun to play back the glimpsings she had long ago, of the family reunited around a long table. There was some little hope and a great deal of fear in the glimpsings now. The happy picture she had carried for years, of her and Clement and Bet and Thany, had come true but had lasted such a short time. And now they were all gone from her. She wondered if it would be the same with the coming-together glimpsing. A scrap of happiness for an instant, making the ultimate loss a deeper pain. Still, she clutched at the image, trying to believe there could be a life less bruised than the one she was living now. An image with old and young both and promise of future.

There were times that Philomene thought she must have made up the coming-together glimpsing, to calm her mother when she was most skittish, but now she had fallen under its spell as well. The slightest chance of having her mother and grandmother and brother sitting around the same table in a distant future she couldn't even imagine gave her some small measure of hope to weigh against the theft of her husband and daughters.

Philomene was no longer able to live her life in the present, and it was not in her nature to live in the past. She needed to begin again, to create a different future without the old dreams, empty of Clement and that kind of love, but she didn't yet know how.

The first Sunday that she thought she could walk the distance, Philomene made her way to see her grandmother Elisabeth. She had to rest many times along the way, sitting for a few minutes on a tree stump or drinking the water she carried with her in the gourd, but she made it to the Fredieu plantation alone. Her mother had already been sent back to Augustine's, the loan completed. Philomene would be moving soon with Oreline and her new husband, and the journey to see her grandmother would no longer be a short trip through the woods. Oreline had offered to take her in the wagon, but some proud part of Philomene did not want to accept.

She came through the door into the familiar duskiness of the small cabin that Elisabeth shared with three others. Without intending to do so, she flung herself straight into the warmth of Elisabeth's arms.

There was still a dampness to the air, and the warmth of the fireplace with its full kettle, of simmering odors comforted Philomene. It was as if she were a small girl again back on Rosedew, using Elisabeth's strong back to brace up her own.

She had a sudden urge to give in to the liberation of opening her mouth to talk, but nothing would come out. It was as if she had forgotten how, not that she had chosen to keep silent. The words would not come.

"Sssshh, Philomene," Elisabeth said, as if sensing her struggle. "You came to me to rest. You walked a long way for someone who bested yellow jack. You'll talk when you're ready."

Elisabeth rocked her in silence. It was peaceful.

"I heard about Mam'zelle Oreline marrying again," Elisabeth said at last. "You'll be closer to your mother and Gerant now, living up that way. You can visit them. I'll miss you here, child, being able to see you so often, but remember your glimpsing. I believe in it, and you need to hold on to that now, when you can't hold on to me."

Philomene's first labor after she had fully recovered from the aftereffects of the fever was to pack up the place she had called home for the last seven years to move to a new farm, smaller still than the step down to Ferrier's farm from Rosedew. If there had been a courtship between Valery Houbre and Oreline, Philomene in her sickness and recuperation must have missed it. Not even two months after Ferrier died, Philomene found herself in the Houbre house, a spare place full of the habits and children of a recently dead wife.

As they were unused to providing for slaves, there were no cabins on the new place, and Philomene fixed a spot for herself to sleep in the house in a small space that had previously been a storeroom next to the kitchen. The dark, cramped room suited what her world had become. Her moss-filled mattress filled almost the entire space, so she unstitched it and took out half the moss to make more room. Only then was there a place for her rocking chair. There were six children to take care of now, none her own, and she was the only servant.

She adjusted.

Philomene had to rely on the heat from the kitchen fire when the weather turned cold, as she did not have a fireplace of her own for warmth, cooking, or light. Sometimes, instead of sleeping, she would sit in the dark and rock, naming what had been taken away from her. Her aunt Palmire. Her babies. Her man. What had been put out of her reach. Her mother, grandmother, grandfather, and brother. It was a sad list, and with each thrust of the rocker, she would fashion a silent prayer for each of them.

Clement was gone, far away from Cane River in a place so distant that her grandmother had taken days by boat to make the reverse journey from Virginia to Louisiana. It was small comfort to her that he had ended up in the place her grandmother came from, because her grandmother's stories were not generous. She resigned herself never to see him again.

Her pictures were quiet. They had deserted her, and it seemed fitting, a reflection of the emptiness of her future. She wondered if the yellow fever had taken the glimpsing away from her forever, as it had taken everything else.

19

Narcisse came to her instead of sending for her. It was a Sunday, her own day, and Philomene had not gotten out of bed, even though the rooster had announced the day's beginning hours before. Her room off the kitchen smelled of bacon grease and mourning. They all thought she had gone a little crazy, like Doralise's husband, she knew that, but it meant that they left her to herself on Sundays.

His boots sang out on the floorboards, warning his approach. She kept her eyes shut and her face to the wall, but she heard the heavy arrogance of his gait and smelled the cigar smoke he brought with him to the doorway of her room. There was a moment between sounds as he adjusted to the darkness, and she heard him come farther into the room, towering over her, nearby.

"You have a lot of people worried about you," he said almost gently.

Philomene said nothing. She didn't get out of bed. She didn't even roll over.

Narcisse stiffened against this affront. "You hear me talking to you, gal? You better beware, Philomene."

Philomene held the blanket up to her chin, rolled her body into a ball, and leaned back against the wall, still on the pallet. She could smell herself and wondered if he did, too. Her hair bunched in matted clumps against her cheek, unwashed, uncombed, and brittle.

Philomene was seventeen years old, and she felt used up. Wherever she went she could smell the stale breath of bitterness prodding her. Her days were drab and hard, and her nights were full to bursting with the silent grief that her isolation nourished. Loneliness had become an ugly, open sore that festered instead of healing over. She refused to give herself the relief of lingering on what should have been and so drifted on the edge of nothingness from day to day.

Clement was the only man she wanted, but waiting for him was foolish and impractical. He was gone because he had been as powerless as she was. Her glimpsings had tricked her into thinking there could be something more, into desiring, expecting. Losing her children had shown her how futile that was. She was barren and empty, pretending to be human, imitating the things she had done before, long ago. Pretending that it mattered to get up one more day. She was surprised each morning when she woke that she hadn't died of her aloneness the night before. The days were colorless, and there were only fleeting moments of comfort for her at week's end, when she could go to see Suzette, or Elisabeth, or Doralise and Gerant. Occasionally she saw her grandfather Gerasíme, whose hip had gotten much worse.

The weeks had passed with her feeling naked and

exposed, tensing for the next blow, subject to the whims of some force intent on grinding her up until there was nothing left. And when it seemed that she had reached bottom, that the greedy hands could pull her no lower, Narcisse Fredieu appeared in her room. This was the face of slavery. To have nothing, and still have something more to lose.

"Are you listening to me?" Narcisse asked. "Your father asked me to look after you and yours. I told him that I would. That makes three generations of your family under my care. Elisabeth, Suzette, and you and Gerant."

Philomene was afraid of this man in her little corner off the kitchen, whether he had saved her from yellow fever or not. The familiarity in his tone threatened to swallow her up, and she was alone with him, with only the thin blanket and her night shift between them. It was important to concentrate, to listen to him carefully. He was talking about the people left to her, the people she still cared about. She opened her eyes but kept her head down. She refused to let him see her face still raw with the absence of Clement and their babies.

"Your mother and I played together as children. We spent hours in the cookhouse with your *mémère* Elisabeth and in the quarter with Gerasíme. I'm fond of your family and am in a position to make your lives easier. I can protect you. I made that promise to your father. And I'm interested in you. I've told you that before."

Philomene heard Narcisse take in a breath and pause. She waited.

"You have to shake this off, Philomene, you have to get beyond the last few months. You're still young. You've let yourself go down. It's time to think about the future. There can be more children."

Narcisse moved closer, touching her lightly on the shoulder. "We all know you can speak. There's nothing wrong with you."

Philomene tried to identify the tone of voice that the watcher was using with her, the rise and fall of his words as important as the words themselves. His speech was not as gentle as the words buried in them insinuated, an undertow of threat to the calm flow. Narcisse had been circling her for a long time. As long as she had been married to Clement he'd kept his distance. Philomene had gotten to know this man and his crablike moves toward her. Always from the side, seldom forward. How many years had he been watching her, without action or declaration? The fact that he was here now, in her room, with Oreline somewhere in the house, signaled a change in the fragile distance he had kept before.

The puzzling thing was that he was moving toward her with caution, when they both knew he could take her if he wanted, without consequence, especially once her father had left Cane River. Last week Eugene Daurat had come to this very room to announce that he was going back to France. Only then had she realized how much her father's presence had protected her. Without him living on Cane River, she would need to find some other way to defend herself or be prey for any of the men who would come and expect her to service their physical or emotional needs. Narcisse Fredieu was one of those men, but not the only one. She had just known of him longer. She was sure that taking her was precisely what was on his mind, although it made no sense. She disgusted herself, unkempt, dirty, smelling of despair, so dried up that even her milk had been taken from her.

If Narcisse Fredieu was determined to have her, their

long dance could end no other way, unless she was prepared to risk death—his death and then, by definition, her own. Even with all that she had lost, she was not willing to face death. There was more to come for her. She was sure of it. And now with Narcisse Fredieu's hesitation, with his caution, he handed her a shield, however thin. She had to use his lust to her advantage, but her mind was too numb to form a plan.

She could be as outwardly respectful to Narcisse as she needed to be. How long she could hold him at a distance was another matter. The glimpsings had not come to her for some time, and she had never seen Narcisse in any of them. Maybe he wasn't connected to her future. Maybe if she held him back for long enough, his mind would turn in some other direction that didn't include her. Maybe his wife, Arsine, would be able to keep him by her side and away from Philomene's room, although the gossip that traveled the river already had Arsine spending more and more time on extended visits alone outside the parish. Maybe the protection Narcisse talked about was more like the kind Ferrier had provided. The young farmer had never touched her mother or her or Palmire, and she had never heard of him coupling with any slaves. There were no stories, no rolled eyes, no side glances, no café au lait babies attached to his name.

She didn't believe for a moment that that was the kind of protection Narcisse Fredieu was offering.

As if to confirm her thoughts, Narcisse approached her pallet and lifted a handful of Philomene's long dirty hair, stroking it in a grotesque perversion of Clement's touch.

"You need to clean yourself up. I plan to have you, Philomene. It would be better if you came to me willingly.

Better for everyone. I want what's best for you. What's best for all. Think about that. I'll only be so patient."

He left as suddenly as he had come, his retreating footsteps muted by the sound of her own beating heart in her ears.

When Eugene Daurat had told Philomene he was quitting Cane River for good, preparing to vanish as if he had never existed, she'd kept her silence. He'd admitted that he had sold her brother, Gerant. "To a good place," her father had said, "to a neighboring planter who will treat him well." Still no word passed Philomene's lips.

Now one thing had become certain. It was time for her to reclaim her voice, to begin the complicated negotiations for the rest of her life. She needed to turn her thoughts to what she could get in return. Her family needed protection. It was up to her to step up to what needed doing, to use whatever was at hand. She needed to talk to her grandmother, and if she didn't go today, she would have to wait for another week.

Philomene no longer had Clement to safeguard what had been soft in her. She got up from her bed and dressed.

17 January 1858
Natchitoches, Louisiana
Eugene Daurrat, resident of the Parish of Natchitoches, to Henry Hertzog, for $1650: a negro man, age about 20, named <u>Gerand.</u> Hertzog furnished by individual note, payable 1 May next, for value received. Witnesses: G. E. Spilman and Dr. Fleming. Signed E. Daurat and Henry Hertzog. Recorded 2 February 1858. [Natch. Conveyance Book 51: 355–6.]

Sale of Gerant.

It took her thirty minutes to get the pass and then three hours of hard walking. Philomene found her grandmother outside her cabin in the Fredieu quarter, tending her vegetable patch, and Elisabeth held her fast, surprised and excited to see her. Philomene wished she could stay in the comfort of her grandmother's arms, but she gave herself only a moment before she pushed herself away. They sat on the porch of the cabin, out of the sun.

Elisabeth studied her. Philomene knew how she must look. Her grandmother went into the cabin, and Philomene sat on the floorboards at the base of her grandmother's chair on the porch, the way she had as a child. She faced out toward the garden and waited. Elisabeth came back with her comb in her hand, eased herself into her chair, gripping Philomene's shoulders between her knees, and began to use her fingers to unmat Philomene's hair.

"You must get lonesome up to Madame Oreline's by yourself. We all think about you, and pray for you."

Philomene would have liked to cry, to be done with it, but no tears would come. It was time to speak.

"*Mémère,*" she said, her voice raspy and awkward. She had practiced on the walk through the woods, pushing sound out of her mouth again, reopening the gate between thought and word.

Elisabeth's hands froze in her hair, but for only a moment. "You've come back to us," she said, squeezing her hands around Philomene's shoulders. Elisabeth continued to untangle Philomene's hair and began to work the snarls with the comb.

"I've lost everything." Philomene's stored-up voice had a hard edge.

"No. Not everything."

"*Mémère,* I came to tell you about what I saw."

Elisabeth turned Philomene's face toward her, looking at her granddaughter sharply.

"A glimpsing? It's been a long time."

Philomene shook her head. "In the fever."

Elisabeth kept at the combing as Philomene talked.

Philomene told her grandmother all of the details she could remember about the fever dream, the bubbling water, Clement's appearance and rescue of Thany in the yellow boat, cradling Bet in the crook of her arm.

"There was something to the dream, like a message from a glimpsing, but . . ."

Philomene let her voice trail away, taken with another thought. "You have to believe in the last glimpsing, *Mémère.* It is important." It hurt her throat to talk, but she didn't want to stop. "You will sit at one end of the table, and *Maman* will sit at the other. You wait and see. It will be our own food and our own house, and we will be together again."

"God will provide."

"I believe God will provide, too, *Mémère.* Just that sometimes He needs help to remember who to provide to."

"I have always believed in your glimpsing, child."

"I am going to make it come true," Philomene said.

"What can you do?"

"M'sieu Narcisse has come to me. I must use that."

Elisabeth's thighs pressed hard into Philomene's shoulders. "Lord, how many times?" she said, her voice a strangle. "Can you go to Mam'zelle Oreline?"

"Madame Oreline was the one who sold Clement," Philomene said bitterly. "She makes menu choices, and sets up social affairs. She can appeal to a husband, but she is in the spider's web along with the rest of us, like you always say. Waiting for the spider to get home."

"There's no keeping out of his way?"

"Things have gone too far in M'sieu Narcisse's mind for him to stop now. I want something in return. Not a trinket now and then. I want big things. Freedom. Land. Money. Protection. For all of us."

"You play with fire, child."

"M'sieu Narcisse has two farms already, and big desires. And he is smitten, like a boy in short pants. With no doing on my part, he has watched me for years. If I put some work into it, he is my best chance at a protector. Like Madame Doralise would do. Now that Papa is leaving, it will be somebody. At least with M'sieu Narcisse, he has a fascination with me he cannot let go. He could have taken me long ago, but he didn't. He has fear and superstition alongside the fascination."

"Don't be so reckless to think you can win Narcisse Fredieu's heart," Elisabeth said.

"What am I to do with a white man's heart?" Philomene's response was icy. "I want his head, his mind. I am not helpless, *Mémère*. I can watch people, too, look into their souls, know them. He wants me to know him, but he will never know me. I will use the glimpsings."

"You haven't had a glimpsing for years. You may never have another one."

"If I made up a picture now and then, he would never know," Philomene said. "The glimpsings could keep him afraid."

"What about children sure to come?" Elisabeth asked. "You are fertile, Philomene, and you don't know which kind of white man he is. The sneaking kind sprinkling seed from one quarter to the next, never looking back, or the kind to keep his own flesh and blood off to the side, hidden, slipping them something now and again. Not many are the third kind, a man who comes out to his children in the daylight."

"I've seen him with children, white and colored. He has a true fondness," Philomene said. "He might buy the children in. I want my children to be free. He could buy me, so that any children would belong to him, by law as well as blood." The thought made Philomene shudder. Narcisse was a complicated man with complicated moods and complicated motivations. It was impossible to know what he would do, how he would react.

"Nobody who wasn't born free is getting free these days," Elisabeth said. "When you finally open your mouth to talk again, child, everything that comes out frightens me."

"Clement and the babies are gone," Philomene said. "They were yesterday. Today is Narcisse Fredieu. Tomorrow will be the children."

It didn't take long for Narcisse to come to her again, and this time Philomene was ready.

"I had a glimpsing, M'sieu. About you and me."

"So, you choose to talk again, after all this time. That is progress." Narcisse sat alert in the moonlight chair in Philomene's room. "Tell me about this glimpsing."

"I saw you come to me for the first time, but it wasn't off the kitchen, not inside this house. It was a cabin of my own. You had just picked a ripe persimmon with its green stem still attached, and you gave it to me to eat."

"Persimmons are not ripe for months," Narcisse said, his dark eyebrows knit.

"I do not control the glimpsings, M'sieu. I only tell you what I saw."

Philomene stole a glance at Narcisse. He was hanging on her every word. She was not sure Narcisse would believe her lies, but his long-standing belief in her powers allowed her to hope. She concealed the outward signs of her relief when he stood up to go.

"You will be mine, Philomene. If it makes it easier, it may as well be the way you saw it."

Narcisse had Philomene moved from the dark, airless room off the kitchen. One of his slaves built a small cabin on Oreline's property, behind the farmhouse. It had its own fireplace and was for Philomene only, a foolish expense on someone else's rented land. And he waited until the fall, when the persimmon trees bore fruit and he could bring one to her, stem intact, before he claimed the prize.

Through it all, the betterment of her living quarters, the feverish return visits to her cabin by Narcisse Fredieu, Philomene grew in strength. She had found at last a useful direction for her bitterness.

20

"I saw something important, M'sieu Narcisse," Philomene said to him as soon as he entered her cabin door. Even in the dimness of the small room, Narcisse could see how she held herself erect, away from him.

"You don't even give me time to take off my hat, or stop to pour me coffee?" Narcisse groused, weary from a long day.

"It is a glimpsing," Philomene said, standing ground where she was.

Narcisse placed his hat on the table. "What did you see?" he asked. His tiredness was gone.

"There is going to be a child, and you must give it protection," she said.

Narcisse's mind raced. A child. His child. "Protection?"

"I am with child. You must provide," Philomene repeated.

Narcisse rushed toward her, barely registering the momentary confusion on her face. He gripped her arm roughly, wild hope and pride edging him forward.

"Do not toy with me, Philomene," Narcisse demanded. "What about the child? Will it be a boy, a girl? What will it look like? What kind of glimpsing is this?"

Philomene shrank back from him, as if in fear. But that frozen moment was all there was, and then her face closed again into composure.

"A lady," she said. "A fine lady, beautiful, fair in face and figure. I see our daughter grown, standing in a dark silk dress of the best material, and a feathered hat. She is quality. And you stand next to her, holding her by the arm for all the world to see."

Philomene looked radiant, triumphant. Narcisse collapsed gently into the hand-carved rocking chair, his eyes moist.

"I am pleased," he said.

His yearnings were beginning to bear fruit in ways that finally quieted the worsening dread that had gnawed at him each successive year of his two marriages. Philomene was carrying his first child.

The year 1861 started badly. Louisiana seceded from the Union at the end of January, and Narcisse was unable to find a buyer for his cotton, already bagged and baled. Not only had his New Orleans factor refused him, he was unwilling to extend credit for next year's crop, either.

Abraham Lincoln had come to office the prior November, such an obvious declaration of hostility toward the South that Narcisse was forced to side with more extreme voices in the cause to beat back Northern aggression. By the time the Confederacy fired the first shot at Fort Sumter in April, all hope for a compromise between North and South was gone.

Both Narcisse's brother, Augustine, and Oreline's oldest son, Florentine, went in the first wave of volunteers. They joined an unruly but enthusiastic outfit tagged the Natchitoches Rebels, including men and boys from all over the parish. It took over a month for the volunteers to be mustered in by the state, longer still by the Confederate government. Filling up companies took time, so the volunteers drilled, attended endless rounds of barbecues along the length of Cane River held in their honor, and waited.

At last, in the middle of May, the outfit was ready to leave by steamer for New Orleans. The turnout at the dock was overwhelming. It seemed that all of the white planter families from Cane River had some brave boy to see off. A makeshift podium had been set up just to the side of the landing, draped with bunting and streamers. Several eloquent and not-so-eloquent Cane River citizens had already spoken that morning.

The volunteers being honored were bunched together beside the podium, of a certain look regardless of age. Their outfits had been stitched up by the hastily formed Cane River Women's Society, as soon as it became clear the Confederate government was not yet in a position to issue uniforms. Augustine's and Florentine's coats were identical, except in size, long double-breasted tunics of cadet gray, fronted with two rows of buttons with blue trim at the edges, stand-up collar, and cuff, to denote infantry. Their trousers had been cut loose in the leg and fanned lightly over the Jefferson-type boots that both Augustine and Florentine sported. The men's pants should have been sky blue, but the ladies had been unable to procure so much dyed material on short notice and instead used the same gray they had on hand. The volunteers' provisions were ready to be loaded on the steamboat as soon as the send-off ceremony concluded, stacked in careful heaps at the far end of the landing.

Narcisse stood with Lersena, Augustine's wife, and their three children on one side, and Oreline and Valery Houbre and their children on the other.

After a heartfelt prayer by Dr. Danglais, Lersena pushed her daughter Augustina forward. "Do as we practiced," she whispered a little too loudly. "Make your father proud."

Shyly, starched dress flowing over her hoop skirt, Augustina stepped in front of the podium.

"On this great day," Narcisse heard his niece begin, "we send our men off, brothers, fathers, sweethearts, friends, to protect us against the Yankees. But we want them to remember us when they are far from home, and know that our hearts are with them." Augustina took a deep breath. "And so we present our Natchitoches Rebels with this homemade battle flag."

Augustina turned proudly to Augustine and handed him the folded flag. Without shame, Augustine wiped a tear from his eye and kissed his daughter on the cheek. Father and daughter each took an end, and together held up the red-and-white flag for everyone to see. The crowd cheered.

This was the last of the formalities, and the volunteers began to move toward their belongings, making their last-minute good-byes.

"Let me help you load your things," Narcisse said to Augustine, and the two brothers walked toward the provision area.

"A moving ceremony. Augustina was splendid," Narcisse said to Augustine. "Let's hope this war doesn't last long."

"We take the steamer to New Orleans, and then by train to Virginia or Kentucky. A few battles will give the yellow-hearted invaders a taste of what we're made of, and they'll run back to their own soil," Augustine said to Narcisse. "If you don't join up now, you'll miss the whole thing."

At thirty-eight, two years older than Narcisse, Augustine was more eager than the younger men, impatient to be off in the thick of the fighting. Narcisse recognized the excitement of the hunt in his brother's voice.

"I'm needed here, Augustine," he said. "I'm going to join the Home Guard." He looked over to Oreline's son. Florentine appeared young, even for fifteen, his face pale but resolute. He was going off against his mother's wishes.

"Cousin Oreline is worried over Florentine," Narcisse said. "You will look after him?"

"Of course," said Augustine. "He may be your godson, but he is my cousin as well."

"Have you given further consideration to the matter regarding Augustina?" Narcisse asked.

"When is the baby due?" Augustine asked.

"They say any time now," Narcisse replied.

"Brother, I know how important the child and the woman are to you, but I hope you will be discreet," Augustine said. "Yes, Augustina can stand up and be *marraine*."

Several Negroes had already begun to load the volunteers' gear onto the steamboat, and Narcisse motioned to one, pointing to Augustine's provisions. The man immediately came over and gathered up the pile.

"You go well prepared," Narcisse said to Augustine.

"Lersena would have nothing less," Augustine answered.

Augustine's wife had packed shirts, trousers, socks, drawers, an extra jacket, and mud boots, along with twenty pounds of ham, two hundred biscuits, coffee, sugar, and pound cake. Augustine also carried blankets, a coffeepot, a frying pan, rope, and the battle flag. Most of the other men were similarly encumbered.

"I'll look after Lersena and the children," Narcisse promised Augustine, "and your farm."

Behind them, Oreline was weeping, giving Florentine final hugs.

"It is time for the boy to go, Cousin Oreline," Narcisse said, approaching the group. He turned to Florentine. "Stay close to your cousin Augustine," he said to the young boy, thinking that would ease Oreline's mind a little. "We will hold things together here until your safe return."

Many of the volunteers had already boarded the steamer when Narcisse saw Henry and Hypolite Hertzog push their way through the crowd toward the group where Narcisse stood. It was easy to tell they were brothers, both blond, squat, and ruddy. Trailing behind them was Gerant, freckles already prominent from the spring sun.

"We bring news, Madame Oreline," Henry said, twirling his hat in his hand. "When we went round to fetch my brother, Hypolite, for the send-off, he told us Gerasíme died this morning. I know how fond you were of the old man, and sent Gerant over to your place to let you know as soon as it happened."

Henry jerked his head toward Gerant, lingering in the background. "You had already left, and the boy went to check on his sister." He lowered his voice. "Her baby is coming."

"There is no one to assist," Oreline said. "I must go back, quickly."

She gave a final hug to Florentine. "Come back to us safely. Monsieur Valery will wait until the steamer sails, until it is out of sight. Write. I will think of you each day." She dabbed at her eyes with a handkerchief.

"Cousin Narcisse, will you take me back to the farm? The children can come back later with Monsieur Valery."

Narcisse hurriedly pulled the buggy around, and although he drove the horse hard, the ride back to Houbre's farm seemed to Narcisse to last forever. All he could think about was that his child was on the way.

"A shame about Gerasíme," he said to Oreline, searching for conversation. He had always been partial to the wild-haired old man whose eyes blazed when he played the fiddle, whose cabin he had frequented so often with Suzette and Oreline when they were small, and he was genuinely sorry at his passing.

"Suzette will be brokenhearted," Oreline said. "And you must tell Elisabeth."

"Yes, of course." Narcisse cracked the whip lightly over the horse's ear, urging him on. "Augustine has agreed for Augustina to act as *marraine*."

"We consider Philomene part of our family, cousin. That is why Monsieur Valery will stand as *parrain*. No ill will come to her while she is under our care."

"I mean to do right by the child, cousin."

Narcisse drove the buggy straight to Philomene's cabin and helped Oreline down, but when he tried to follow her through the doorway, Oreline blocked his path. The tension of the day showed clearly in her face.

"Philomene is indisposed, cousin. Go up to the house and wait. I will let you know when the baby comes."

Narcisse did not argue; this was women's domain. When Valery and the children returned from the celebration, he was still in the front room, waiting anxiously.

"The boat got off," Valery said. "They looked so young."

"Thank you for agreeing to stand godfather," Narcisse said.

"All of God's children need protection," Valery said.

Narcisse and Valery Houbre made small talk for hours. It was late evening when Oreline entered the house, flushed and dangling her bonnet by the tie string. Narcisse couldn't help but notice the dark circles under her eyes, her drawn face, the sleeves of her best dress rolled up, and a large damp stain on her bodice.

"It is a healthy baby girl," Oreline said. "Philomene has already done the naming. She asks that she be called Emily."

"Emily," Narcisse repeated. "It is a fine name."

"I told Philomene about Gerasíme, cousin," Oreline said to Narcisse. "She became quite upset when she heard of the death of her grandfather and insisted on seeing you as soon as possible. She was very . . . forward."

"I'll go now," Narcisse said.

Philomene's cabin seemed different to Narcisse. He had spent countless hours there, but this time when he entered there was a weight, a significance about the place, that he had never experienced before. Inside this room was his daughter, flesh of his flesh, a miracle he had almost given up on. Philomene's tiredness showed plainly in her face; her usually stern expression had relaxed somewhat, loosened by her ordeal. She held the small bundle that was his daughter close to her breast, and she was hidden by the blanket.

"Your daughter is here." Philomene held her up to him.

Narcisse came closer to the bed and took the child from Philomene, settling the baby awkwardly in his arms. Nothing had prepared him for this, Emily's warmth and fragility, and especially not the fierce rush of protectiveness that took hold of him.

"Her name is Emily Fredieu," Philomene said. "She must never work in the field."

Narcisse didn't trust himself to speak, barely touching the soft hair like peach fuzz on her head, looking for family features in her face. She was as white as any of the babies he had ever seen. She was beautiful. When Philomene reached out to take her back, he didn't want to let her go. Narcisse could still feel the heat from Emily's small body on his arms, even when she was back at her mother's side.

"My *grandpère* Gerasíme died today, the same day Emily was born. We need to have a ceremony for him, with all my people there. Will you arrange it, M'sieu?"

Philomene was working herself into one of her strange states. Narcisse didn't want anything to spoil this day. "Yes, there are many on Cane River who would want to honor Gerasíme."

"But it must be delayed until the baby and I can travel. This is important, M'sieu Narcisse. Emily's life depends on it."

"The baby is in danger?"

"Not if we hold the ceremony. Do you promise to arrange everything? It is for the sake of the child."

Narcisse touched Emily's cheek. She was asleep, unconnected to her mother's growing distress. "I promise," he said.

2 September 1862
Baptism of Emelie, born 19 May 1861 to **Philomene,**
slave of Valere [? Valsin] [—?—]. Godparents: [—?—]
Pinson [?] and Augustina Fredieu. ["Baptisms of Slaves
1847–1865 and Baptism of Negroes 1865–1871," St.
John the Baptist Church, Cloutierville; no page number;
see attached photocopy.]

Baptism of Emily.

*C*ivility had lost much of its hold in the general relations among white, Negro, and colored along Cane River in the years leading up to the war, diminished further in the paranoia of the secessionist spring of 1861, and stretched to snapping after the firing on Fort Sumter. The snake-quick volatility of moods and random anger along Cane River made the community raw, edgy, and suspicious.

But Gerasíme, in death, cleared the way for a brief truce. They buried him in the hard earth at the same time they were breaking ground for new planting. Two days after the old man died, Hypolite Hertzog announced that a ceremony would be scheduled for a time after the urgency of plowing for this year's crop eased.

The funeral was held on a bright, warming late-spring Sunday five weeks later, on an afternoon full of the promise of overdue renewal. Narcisse came to Houbre's farm to col-

lect Philomene and Emily just after noon dinner, Elisabeth
sitting beside him in the wagon on the broad wooden seat.
She had abandoned her everyday madras *tignon* and wore
her best white scarf around her head.

Narcisse swung down from the wagon and spoke
quickly to Philomene in passing where she waited on the
farmhouse gallery, holding Emily. "I'll be back directly, and
we'll get on our way," he said, and disappeared inside.

Philomene gave him a tight-lipped nod. Despite the
unrelenting demands of the newborn, she had grown
increasingly optimistic about the future, and the recovery
from this childbirth had been swift. Her body seemed to be
well engineered for the business of producing babies.

Philomene carried the baby over to her grandmother
and handed her up to Elisabeth's reaching arms. Emily did-
n't wake.

"That's a fine-looking child," Elisabeth said, her blunt
hand smoothing back Emily's hair. "Like cornsilk. No telling
what color it will end up, though." She took measure of
Philomene. "You look well, granddaughter."

"I am so sorry about *Grandpère* Gerasíme, *Mémère*,"
Philomene said.

"The Lord brought him back to His side. He's past suffering now."

Philomene missed her baby from her own arms already.
"I wish Emily could have known him."

"I hope the funeral works out how you want," Elisabeth
said, fingers still on Emily's hair. "Some say Gerasíme is
beyond feeling, and Emily before remembering, but you do
what you think is right. You always had a power." She nodded toward the farmhouse to indicate Narcisse. "You talked
him into arranging this last time for us with Gerasíme."

"Emily's life depends on it, *Mémère*," Philomene said.

Elisabeth nodded and studied Emily's sleeping face. "Let me hold the baby up here with me the rest of the way," she said.

Philomene hesitated.

"We all want to keep our babies close," Elisabeth said, "for as long as we have them. Today I bury my husband, and I see my children, the ones left. And their children. Today let me hold my great-granddaughter for the first time. You have tomorrow."

There was no arguing. Philomene climbed empty-armed into the back of the wagon, just as Narcisse came from the farmhouse, followed by Oreline and Valery.

"My thoughts are with you at the service, Elisabeth," Oreline said, leaning close to the wagon, her eyes moist. "Gerasíme was a fine man, much loved. He will be missed."

Philomene's mouth grew tight watching Oreline and Valery get smaller as Narcisse drove the wagon to the main road. When they came to the dirt path turnoff for Augustine's farm, Suzette was waiting at the gate.

She wore her black cotton Sunday dress, and her *tignon* sat high on her head. She looked older than Philomene remembered, creases playing at the corners of her eyes. Philomene had seen her six weeks before and hadn't noticed.

"Morning, M'sieu Narcisse. We appreciate you taking us to the service," Suzette said. "*Mère.*" Her gaze lingered hungrily on Elisabeth and Emily, but she lifted her skirts and climbed into the back of the buckboard wagon with Philomene.

They braced and bounced for some time, Suzette and Philomene talking softly.

"Madame Oreline came to the farm to pay her respects," Suzette told Philomene. "She had M'sieu Valery carry her over first to Elisabeth and then to me, within the nine days, just like we were white folks. She brought little Valery and Valerianne, and she cried over Gerasíme."

Philomene leaned close to Suzette, her voice barely a murmur. "Her tears come quick since Florentine went off to war."

"A mother's tears are deepest," Suzette said firmly. "Madame Oreline has always been on our side."

"Not always," Philomene said, and let a moment pass. "She could have paid her respects by attending the funeral."

"What has come over you?" Suzette whispered nervously, glancing toward Narcisse's back. "A proper Creole lady would never attend a public funeral, and certainly not a Negro service."

The wheel hit a deep rut, and Philomene held herself steady by the side of the wagon.

"We need to be grateful M'sieu Narcisse saw fit to arrange today," Suzette said loudly. "Imagine, the first time in ten years, since Rosedew, for all of us to be in one place."

Narcisse made no sign that he heard over the clatter of the horses and wagon.

"Almost everyone managed to get brought, by begging or bargaining," Suzette said, her voice low again.

Finally they rolled through the open double gate of Hypolite Hertzog's plantation and continued on foot to the cleared copse that served as the Negro cemetery. The five of them started up the small hill, Narcisse in the lead, Elisabeth with Emily in her arms, Suzette, and then Philomene.

The turnout to honor Gerasíme's passing was relatively large, an increasingly rare excuse for the gathering of such a mixed crowd. Narcisse went off in one direction to join the Hertzog brothers. Elisabeth picked her way through the crowd to get close to the actual grave site, cradling Emily, her solemn brown face closed like stone and glistening in the heat, her children fanned around her in loose circles of family. They crowded around for a look at the new baby.

Philomene stared directly at her people, memorizing the little evidences that bound them together. Gerasíme and Elisabeth's three surviving children stood close together, and such was the power of the day that Philomene included the mute presence of Palmire, more real to her in some ways than the aunt and uncle she barely knew. Apphia, short and muscular, yet with a maternal softness to her features. Small, pleasant-faced Suzette, bearing her usual air of distracted acceptance. Lean, hard-bodied Solataire, his face ripe with fresh purpled bruises and one misshapen eye that drooped almost shut.

Gerant found his way to Philomene's side. Short, wiry, and brown eyed, her brother favored the elders, but thinned lips, a narrow nose, and freckles across his pale butternut skin more resembled Philomene's own features.

Philomene heard a blend of voices around her, mostly in quarter gombo, stray fragments of too many conversations in which everyone tried to catch up at once.

"Sweet young thing, white as new cotton and hair like cornsilk."

"The white man said I didn't get off the road fast enough when he passed yesterday," Solataire explained. "The Widow almost refused to allow her son to bring me today."

"Young Henry going off to join LeCompte Guards. Madame is beside herself."

"I remember you when you were no bigger than a June bug, sitting on his lap when he went to fiddling."

"Euger run off. They haven't caught him yet. Pray for him that he made it out."

Philomene watched the crowd, a mix of white, *gens de couleur libre,* and slave, and took note of how many Cane River farms and plantations had sent mourners to pay tribute to her grandfather. She lost her count at fifteen when she heard the baby begin to cry.

Transferring Emily from Elisabeth's arms to her own made Philomene almost whole again. She looked down at the cool paleness of her daughter's face and the fine sandy blond wisps of hair that jutted from her head, all that was visible from the folds of the wrapping blanket Oreline had given on the day Emily was born. Philomene positioned the girl at her right breast, fussing with the covers and her dress to hide her nursing.

Hypolite Hertzog began the service, but there was little room for his dry words in Philomene's head. Visits to her grandfather had been few, but she recalled vividly the magnificent wildness of Gerasíme's hair and the feverlike brightness in his eyes, like a flame the wind could not blow out.

After Rosedew, the crippling in his hip forced Gerasíme backward, from a full hand, to a half hand, and finally to an assortment of odd jobs. Seldom put to field unless they were in the middle of full harvest, he swept up the yard's cow paddies with an old crude broom alongside the children too young to go to field and too old to be allowed to play all day. He shucked corn and tended other slaves' gardens for them. Occasionally he drove the Hertzog family in their buggy.

But when he was called to play his fiddle, it was difficult to imagine that this could be the same old man who moved in such an awkward shuffle with a hoe or broom. He played standing upright, the position that least aggravated his hip, and he called out the figures for dances with such authority and enthusiasm, it was impossible for dancers and onlookers to prevent themselves from being similarly infected. Gerasíme had been rented out for parties on Cane River up until the month before he died.

It was Gerasíme's ability to find enjoyment out of life under the most unreasonable of circumstances that Philomene wanted for Emily. Gerasíme harvested joy in the same barren patch that for others bore only a bitter fruit. Philomene could teach Emily to cook, sew, farm, and take care of herself enough to survive. And if Philomene managed to keep her hold on Narcisse Fredieu, Emily would have more comforts than most, and her family around her as she grew up, no matter the outcome of the war. But if freedom materialized, Philomene reasoned, the slippery secret of joy, passed from old to young through fragile baby bones, could assure her daughter a different kind of life.

One by one they threw handfuls of dirt on Gerasíme's grave. When it was Philomene's turn, she came forward with Emily, and as she stooped and closed her hand around the reddish Louisiana soil, she spoke her words softly, indistinct to anyone else.

"Stay with her," Philomene petitioned humbly to the grave site. "Take her beyond survival.

"Bloom where you're planted," she whispered into Emily's tiny sleeping ear.

22

In June Confederate notes began to circulate, and Narcisse began to hoard both food and money. It was the same month that his first letter from Augustine arrived.

May 28, 1861

Brother,

We went east from New Orleans by train, stopping many times along the way. We get free meals from cheering locals wherever we go, city or town. There is little to do except drill, and we are all at loose ends waiting for the regiment to fill up. Men and boys from all over the South are here, and we pass the time at gambling, mostly chuck-a-luck. They are fine fellows for the most part. You would have trouble believing how officers try to force senseless rules, having to go on guard duty when everyone knows there are no Yankees for two hundred miles. Both Florentine and I are in good spirits. He is a good boy, and writes to Cousin Oreline as I write to you. He misses

*his mama. Other than too much English has to be spoken, we
are having a grand adventure.*

Augustine

By November another year of cotton with little prospect
of purchase was being picked in the field, and the tone of
Augustine's letters had changed.

November 17, 1861

Brother,

*I miss Cane River more than I can say. Are you looking after
Persena and the children? Letters often do not reach us. We
spend the days marching and moving from place to place. Our
shoes have worn out. Food is very poor, always the same thing,
and being a man from the country, tent living with so many
always right up under you is disagreeable. We have gone to winter quarters. Who knew it could be so cold in Arkansas? There is
snow on the ground. Give my love to all there. I wish I was home.
Florentine is heartsick. I try to cheer him up when I can.*

Augustine

By the second year of the war they all understood the
long-term nature of the path the South had chosen.

March 28, 1862

Brother,

*By now you must know that young Florentine died of
typhoid fever at Maysville, Arkansas. They say they will send
the body back. He acquitted himself well at the Battle of Oak
Hill. I wrote Cousin Oreline about it. I know this was difficult
to hear about your godson. Comfort her the best you can.*

This is going to be a long war. Most of the time we march

and wait. I do not wish to describe the battles. There is little glory in them. I trust you are taking care at home. Please send food if you are able, although if you are short there, you may want to keep it for yourself. The provisions here are not sufficient, and more than almost anything else, contribute to the low spirits. The clothes I gambled away so as not to have to carry them in the beginning would be welcome now. Could you see your way clear to send a pair of trousers? Mine are so worn in the seat, they are an embarrassment. Any color will do.

Augustine

In April of 1862, even though food was in short supply, Narcisse had an afternoon coming-together at his plantation. He invited Oreline and Valery Houbre and their children, Augustine's wife, Lersena, with their children, and the Hertzog brothers. Henry and Hypolite were among those men along Cane River who stayed behind that first year of the war, following the cause of the South through newspapers and letters.

"Have you heard? New Orleans has fallen," said Henry as they sat down to the table, "occupied now by Federals. Yankee soldiers walk the streets as if they own them."

"And us sitting on so much cotton, caught between the Federal blockade of the ports, and the Confederate government embargo," Narcisse said. "I've given up on selling my cotton quickly."

"Once Europe is starved for cotton, they'll come to our aid and force the North to reason," Hypolite said.

"With the new harvest so soon to come behind the old, I already had my Negroes store my bales farther north on my wife's property in Campti. Augustine's, too," Narcisse said. "I'd rather wait it out than engage a speculator, purchasing for pennies on the dollar."

Elisabeth served supper, such as it was. They had corn pone, corn fritters, and corn-parched coffee.

"Excuse the poor fare," Narcisse said as a matter of courtesy.

"Confederate money buys so little," Henry said, "and food supplies have dwindled."

"As if the Yankees aren't bad enough, our own government squeezes us," Narcisse said, warming to the subject. "Just last week I had to turn two of my hands over to a Confederate impressment agent, to work on the defenses of the Red River. There was no refusing. I can only hope that when I get them back, they don't have Yankee fever, spreading foolish ideas and dangerous habits they've picked up to the others."

"Monsieur Greneaux reported two runaways last week," Henry said.

"We keep ours close to home. No more passes," said Hypolite.

"Even the soirées have no life," Augustina complained, "with all the young men gone. All anyone wants to talk about is the 1860 crop. Papa said the war would be over by now. When will he come back?"

Conversation stopped.

"The war has affected her manners," Lersena said apologetically to the table at large. "Hush," she said to Augustina sternly. "Let the men talk."

Narcisse threw a disapproving look toward Augustina in her faded day dress, but even so, looking at his daughter's godmother reminded him of how impatient he was to visit Philomene's cabin later, to hold Emily.

"The longer the war goes on, the slower mine work," said Hypolite.

"I see it on my own farms and Augustine's, too," Narcisse agreed. "The Negroes in the field and the house are skating along the ragged edge of disobedience."

"This is going to be a long war," Valery said, a new voice around the table. "Too many lives will be lost to defend the right of a few to own slaves."

"You are a slaveholder, too, Valery," Narcisse said. "There's no pretending you are not one of us."

"I am a schoolteacher, and a farmer," Valery said, "and only own the one my wife brought with her. We treat her and the child fairly."

No one spoke for a few moments. "Were you speaking against the government, Monsieur Narcisse?" Hypolite asked, taking the conversation back to the host.

"No. I've done everything requested," said Narcisse. "I already reversed my crops, from staple to provision. I planted only one hundred acres in cotton, and three hundred in corn, food we can all eat. Not many have complied."

Oreline surprised the men, breaking in to speak with ferocity. "You can keep your Confederate government," she declared. "This war will not get my other two sons."

In the fall of 1862 Narcisse received another letter from Augustine.

October 12, 1862

Brother,

Narcisse, don't come if you can find some means around it. It is too hard a life for you. We eat only cornmeal mixed with water and tough beef three times a day, and watch more men die from disease than battle. They have rejected my request for furlough, but I will try to come home as soon as I can manage. I am sick of soldiering.

Augustine

Immediately after receiving Augustine's letter, Narcisse went to A. B. Pierson in Natchitoches. His attorney had proven helpful in the past, and he hoped he could be equally helpful now.

"Is there any way for me to stay on Cane River?" Narcisse asked.

"The new conscription laws are plain," Pierson said. "All men under the age of forty-five are to serve the Confederacy. I am myself forty-eight, past the age of going by force, and too sensible to go by honor. How old are you, Monsieur Narcisse?"

"Thirty-seven."

Narcisse Fredieu.

"And how many slaves have you?" Pierson asked.

"Twenty," Narcisse said, puzzled.

"Then there is no problem, if you have five hundred dollars," Pierson said. "That is my fee. Not payable in Confederate money, if you please."

"I have the money, if you can keep me home," Narcisse said.

"The Confederate Congress says one man can be exempted for every twenty Negroes on a plantation. I can draw up a petition for your exemption on the basis of the twenty-Negro law."

"How soon?"

"Consider it done," said Pierson.

Narcisse was granted his exemption. Three days later he received an anonymous package of tattered white petticoats left on the front gallery of his house. The note attached, in a neat hand, read "Rich Man's War, Poor Man's Fight."

He burned the note in the fireplace and had Elisabeth dispose of the petticoats.

23

If 1861 was a year for righteous idealism and hopes for a swift conclusion to the war, and 1862 was the year of dislocation and disarray, 1863 was the time for facing the sobering reality of permanent adjustment. Most of the men were gone, even those safely past the age of conscription, like Valery Houbre.

"You're fifty, Valery, surely you can stay and watch over us here," Philomene had heard Oreline plead. "I've lost Florentine already."

But he had gone anyway, on foot so they could keep the mule, marching off in the direction of Cloutierville, leaving a house full of women and children to do the best they could with the farm.

"At least young Joseph and little Valery are too young," Oreline said bitterly to Philomene one evening in the farmhouse common room, as she took apart an old dress Valerianne had outgrown to refashion into a skirt for Mina.

With Valery gone, Oreline was undisputed head and Philomene anchor of the farmhouse, all of the children theirs jointly to protect. The household was a hodgepodge of parentage. Oreline's two children by Joseph Ferrier, Josephine, thirteen, and young Joseph, ten, grew up along-side Mina, twelve, the youngest of Valery's children by his prior wife. Valerianne, eight, and little Valery, four, were Oreline and Valery's together. And Emily, two, was the youngest, the child of Philomene by Narcisse Fredieu.

Oreline took care of the children during the day while Philomene worked the seasonal crops. They had given up on cotton altogether, bothering only with food crops, corn, sweet potatoes, and beans, and by 1863 the barn stuffed to the rafters with unsold bales of cotton seemed to belong to a distant, faraway life.

Their remoteness from town, their distance from both the main road to Natchitoches and the banks of Cane River, made their lives harder, but it also made them more self-sufficient, with fewer expectations. On Houbre's mean little farm, they were better off than many of their neighbors, still in possession of a few chickens, a hog, a mule, a lean cow running free in the woods, their crops, and the vegetable garden that Oreline kept.

Narcisse never came empty-handed. Circumstances turned him into a manager and benefactor, overseeing the affairs of his own plantation, his widowed mother's plantation, his absent brother's farm, his wife's farm in Campti, and guiding Houbre's farm. Like a hen spreading warmth to all of the eggs in the nest, Narcisse took from one to give something to the other. At each of his stops he was received with profound gratitude. Others along Cane River saw only an able-bodied man under forty-five still safe at home.

"Cousin, wherever did you get your hands on salt?" Oreline stared with an open mouth at the supplies Narcisse unloaded. "Next time we have fresh meat, we'll make *tasso*. But tonight you must stay to supper, share what we have. Mina has made a vegetable stew."

On a blistering day in the middle of summer, so hot that even the squirrels sprawled low on their bellies in the oak trees, the mule kicked over Philomene's pail of water in the cornfield. She put off the trip to the river for refilling, bargaining with herself to finish just one more row, and then another, until she found herself so dizzy that she was forced to break plowing early. Light-headed and weak, she managed to get herself to the house, where they had just sat down for their noonday meal. By normal routine, one of the children would have brought her portion to her later in the field. Oreline took one look at Philomene, jumped up, and helped her to a chair at the large pine table where they took their meals.

"Get her water, Valerianne, and a wet rag for her forehead," Oreline ordered. "Mina, fix up her dinner plate. Hurry."

Oreline gave Philomene sips of water and mopped her forehead until she showed signs of returning strength.

"Everyone get back to eating," Oreline said. "Can you keep food down, Philomene?"

Philomene forced herself to nibble at a biscuit, until the dizziness passed, and then she began to eat ravenously. Feeling seven pairs of curious eyes on her, she pushed herself up from the table. Oreline waved her back down.

"You might as well stay where you are," she said. "You need to let some of this heat pass before you go back out. There's plenty to do inside for a while."

And so it began that Philomene and Emily ate at table with everyone else whenever there were no visitors. So many of the old rules had already been bent. Now Philomene would come in from the hot sun at midday, her muscles aching, her clothes stained with sweat, and dinner would be ready. Oreline, Josephine, or Mina could all squeeze out a passable meal in the kitchen.

They endured during the war years. Everyone had chores beyond their age and upbringing, except for Emily, who was too small to be responsible, but even she did her part by giving little trouble. There were only two things that Oreline steadfastly refused to do. One was fieldwork, and the other was washing the clothes, both of which fell to Philomene. The children gathered fruit and berries and put them up into preserves, and Narcisse would take some away and come back with a hind of bacon, or seedlings for the vegetable garden, or a partly full barrel of thick, sweet cane syrup.

Emily was brought up by all of them, not just Philomene. She cut her teeth, began to walk, and called almost everyone *Maman* when she was first learning to talk. Emily was just another child in a struggling house full of children during the war, a youngster of charm and spirit, smaller than all, lighter in color than several, petted, ignored, disciplined, and teased by turns.

* * *

Outside the cabin on Houbre's farm, Narcisse gave a full-bellied laugh at the spectacle his daughter made, lifting her feet and dancing, keeping time to the beat he clapped out for her. She was nearly three, an open, trusting child. For her the war had no meaning. They had made it almost to the winter of 1863.

"Come, Emily, enough, you wear me out just watching," he finally said. He took her on his lap, smoothed her dress. "You show promise to be an accomplished dancer, mademoiselle."

Emily beamed, turning her dimpled face up to Narcisse to be kissed.

"Now run along up to the main house, Emily. I have to talk to your mother."

Emily pouted for just a minute but did as she was told, off on a skip.

Narcisse turned serious. "I'm thinking you and Oreline should take the children up north to my place in Campti after I'm gone. It might be safer above Red River."

"I cannot see that it would be safer for me and Emily to be in your wife's house."

"Perhaps not," he conceded.

"Why go? You stayed until now."

"So you'll miss me, then?" Narcisse said with a grin.

"We've done better under your protection," Philomene said.

His grin faded. "It's my duty to go," Narcisse said. "We can still win."

Philomene thought it more likely his change of heart was due to the growing resentment aimed toward him by the countless women without their sons, husbands, brothers, and sweethearts, to the snubs he endured. She judged the time to be right. "Best to tell you now, then. I've had a glimpsing."

Philomene looked him directly in the face, the candle-light flickering across his features. She detected his willingness to believe, mixed with his usual fear.

"Do I come back?"

"You come back here, safe," Philomene replied carefully. They had seen men and boys return for a time, weary, disillusioned, only to be sent back again, missing fingers, teeth, arms, and legs. They had seen Florentine return, three months after receiving word of his death, in a white pine box. "But the glimpsing is about both you and Emily. She's a proper young girl, maybe ten or eleven. Her hair is long, sandy colored, almost to her waist, and you've given her a flower to wear in it. Magnolia, maybe. She's reading to you out of a book."

Narcisse looked doubtful. "Reading?"

"Madame Oreline would teach her when the time comes, if you asked. You could talk to her about how you want Emily raised, before you go. Emily is destined to be quality."

"She is a special child," Narcisse mused, "but what does the girl need with reading? Was that all there was to the glimpsing?"

"That's all I could see."

"You must take good care of Emily while I'm gone," Narcisse said.

"You must take good care of Emily when you get back," Philomene answered.

Narcisse moved toward Philomene, the craving look in his eyes.

"Will you talk to Madame?" Philomene asked.

He didn't answer.

"You won't forget?" Philomene pushed.

"I'll talk to Oreline before I leave," Narcisse said, removing his coat. "You're a striking woman, Philomene. Take down your hair."

Philomene couldn't understand her staying power for

Narcisse. She was twenty-two, her skin coarse and darkened by the sun, angry red blisters her bonnet couldn't block at the back of her neck, her hands callused. But he was still drawn to her, he still listened, guided by her glimpsings.

She unwrapped the scarf from around her head and shook her hair free.

Weeks after Narcisse finally rode away from Cane River to fight in a war over cotton and slavery, Philomene discovered she was pregnant. She had not known about the coming child in time to weave a protective glimpsing around it.

*   *   *

The war came into Cane River's backyard in the spring of 1864.

Food was scarce, but they had learned to make do on Houbre's farm despite dwindling supplies, the drought, boredom, isolation, and uncertainty. They counted totally on themselves, Oreline, Philomene, and the children, growing their own food, hunting, foraging, and stretching what they still had, mostly corn, beans, and the remains of a side of bacon in the smokehouse. Corn, which in different times had been grown mostly to fatten hogs and feed slaves, had become the mainstay of everyone's diet. Philomene trapped what she could, and they sometimes had fresh meat, but not often.

They had long since grown used to having no money, and even if they had, the price of everything was so high that they could have bought little anyway. With Narcisse no longer bringing either necessities or luxuries, and the Confederate soldiers who now occupied the valley appearing at random intervals on their doorstep to cart away corn or fodder as provisions for their units, the women hid the least replaceable of their foodstuffs. The troops drew most heavily from the plantations, but even the smallest farms were not immune. The single, scrawny spike-horned cow with the Houbre brand on its ear had disappeared before they'd had a chance to slaughter it for themselves. Foraging for nuts, fruits, and berries had become a competition among children, soldiers, runaways, deserters, and farmers.

In the spring the invading Union army pushed its way up from New Orleans through Natchitoches Parish, following the course of first the Red River and then the Cane River. It was the driest spring in twenty years, the river falling to barely three feet.

The morning was gray, the air cold and smelling of smoke. Philomene and young Joseph had been pulling up spent cornstalks since daybreak to get them ready for burning when four Confederate soldiers in ill-fitting mismatched gray uniforms rode their horses onto the farm, heading straight for the house. Philomene wondered how much of their food would be taken this time. There was little enough to spare, and although her appetite hadn't increased as much as when she'd carried the twins, or even Emily, cutting down on portions again would be difficult.

"Let's get to the house, M'sieu Joseph," Philomene said, throwing down the hoe. "Better they see all the mouths needing to be fed."

By the time she and young Joseph got close, Oreline was facing down the four men on the gallery.

"But how will we get back on our feet again?" Philomene heard Oreline say to one of the soldiers as he set out in the direction of the barn.

Oreline carried Emily in her arms, struggling to catch up to the soldiers. Josephine, Mina, Valerianne, and Valery followed close behind her, their faces full of fear by the panic in Oreline's voice.

"They're going to burn the cotton," Oreline blurted out to Philomene as soon as she caught sight of her.

The fourth soldier lagged behind. He was a nervous boy whose pale eyes darted. He glanced at Philomene with suspicion and then said to Oreline apologetically, "It might be best for you to stay here, ma'am. We're burning all the cotton so the Yankees don't get it."

Philomene stayed behind Oreline and kept young Joseph close. She could see how young the soldier was, his eyes a mottled gray blue that didn't fit his face.

"You're even younger than Florentine was when he left," Oreline said in wonder to the boy. "How old are you?"

"Twelve, ma'am."

Oreline glanced back to where Philomene stood with her arms draped over young Joseph's thin shoulders, his back leaning into the roundness of her belly. Oreline pulled her eyes away from her son and turned back to the young soldier.

"You mustn't burn our cotton," she said, trying to reason with the boy. "You're on our side."

"Those are our orders, ma'am. The Yankees have already been through here once on the way up to Mansfield on the Red River campaign. You were lucky they missed you. They're following the river. But they'll be back through, this time for the cotton. We have to torch it."

"What about the barn?" Philomene whispered to Oreline.

Oreline, eyes grown dark, ran ahead to one of the older men, a coarse-looking soldier with both teeth missing in front. He appeared to be the leader.

"Wait," she said. "What about the mule, the plow? You can't burn down our barn."

"We have a job, and not much time. Anything you want from the barn that's not cotton, you better clear it out in the next few minutes."

"Will you help?" Oreline pleaded.

"I'm giving you time," the soldier said, wiping at his forehead. He stopped and took a long look at Oreline, hesitating. "I have a farm, and a wife alone. Her hair is the same color as yours. We'll just take the chickens, not the mule or the hog. You better hurry."

Oreline ran back to where they all stood. "We have to get everything we can out of the barn," she ordered, hastily handing little Emily off to Valery. "You two stay put. Everyone else to the barn. Hurry. Hurry."

Valery started to hiccup, but the little boy stayed put, clutching Emily so tightly that she started to cry. The rest followed Oreline.

Inside the barn, Oreline grabbed Philomene's arm. "What should be saved?"

"Get out the mule and plow and as much of the fodder as you can," Philomene said. "And the grain and seed stored in the corner. The children can carry the tools out. Make sure of the harness and reins. And sacks. I'll get the hog away."

Philomene opened the gate and drove the hog with a peach tree switch as far from the barn as she could, the heavy porker grunting and squealing. When she got back to the barn, Oreline was still struggling with the mule, which refused to budge.

"Madame, move the seeds," Philomene said. "I'll see to the mule."

Philomene pulled at the length of rope Oreline had fashioned around the mule's neck, but the animal brayed and sat on its hindquarters, determined not to move. She picked up a buggy whip and struck at the mule until her arms ached, and at last the beast got up onto all fours. Philomene ran around to the back of the mule and gave him a savage lash to get him moving. She never really saw his hind leg kick out, but suddenly she was down on the ground, the wind totally gone from her, a deep pain in her stomach. She looked up to see the mule bucking and braying, moving away from where she lay sprawled in the dirt, starting at last toward the sunshine.

The farm was in turmoil, dust flying, sounds louder than she could bear. She picked herself up unsteadily amid the squealing, braying, and crowing. She heard Emily's cry, mixed with other shouting voices, and saw the young soldier with the gray-blue eyes helping young Joseph drag a bag of grain through the barn doors. She grabbed a harness and took it out to the growing pile outside the barn.

"No more time. Everybody clear out," pronounced the soldier with the missing teeth. He took a large can from his horse's saddle and splashed the bound bales of cotton with the liquid contents. Flames flashed upward as soon as he struck the match. It took some time for the fire to engulf the stacks of cotton, giving out a dark, suffocating, dense smoke, but then the flames grew bolder and more greedy, ripening until they were as high as the beams of the barn.

When the Confederate soldiers were satisfied that the cotton was beyond reclaiming, they mounted their horses and rode away. Neither the boy with the gray-blue eyes nor the man with the missing front teeth looked back to where the women and children huddled together, watching the flames.

Philomene took Emily from little Valery and held on to her, in the same way that Oreline drew young Joseph close to stand next to her. It was all they could do, watch helplessly as the barn and everything inside burned, hoping the wind wouldn't shift and carry the sparks to the house, henhouse, corncrib, or smokehouse, or Philomene's cabin.

"What will Monsieur Valery say when he comes back?" Oreline said.

Philomene watched the flames curl.

Philomene lost the baby the next morning, her stomach cramped so hard in on itself that she couldn't get up, but she could stand again by the afternoon and joined in with the salvaging of Houbre's farm. Four babies and only one safe, she thought.

The barn still glowed in spots into the next night, and they went on as best they could, making a new sty for the hog, gathering the last two scattered chickens the soldiers had not caught, pulling the spent cornstalks, reburying the precious sack of salt behind the smokehouse.

From their farm they could see the ribbons of flame fan out for miles as lifetimes went up in smoke. They ate plentifully for the next few weeks, less willing to hoard what they assumed would be confiscated by one army or the other coming through. For two days they heard volleys of gunfire, most of the time distant but sometimes so close that they huddled inside the house together, terrified, and the sound of explosions came from the direction of the river. They cooked only during the day, when the smoke would not be as visible, their only defense their remoteness, their invisibility, and they didn't venture off the farm.

"If Yankees come, they'll burn whatever we have left," Oreline said.

Philomene thought of the moonlight chair in her cabin, the only thing she owned. "Maybe they'll stick to the river," she said.

When gunfire became random and sporadic, young Joseph Ferrier ventured out alone one morning, beyond the closed-in island they had made of Houbre's farm. He did not return until late afternoon, dragging the carcass of a small shoat. His face was charred, and there was animal blood on his clothes.

Oreline fell on the boy at once, hugging him and crying. Philomene began to butcher the pig as young Joseph told them how he had come into possession of it.

"I cut through the woods, hiding behind trees at any sound, and followed the line of the river," he said. "All the

General Banks's army crosses Cane River, 1864.

fence posts and ties within sight of the river were gone. There were several people moving about.

"When I came to Monsieur Tessier's plantation, it had been torched. Only the stone chimney was left. Tessier sat in the dirt, surrounded by charred lumps at his feet. I came closer and saw they were dead pigs. He told me to go back home, that it wasn't safe to be out, that there were still Yankee stragglers."

Oreline kept touching the boy, even as he talked.

"He had sent his family away, up to Campti to stay with relations, and stayed behind to protect the place. The Yankees burned every plantation for ten miles, from Rachal's to Monette's Ferry. At Tessier's they slaughtered all the hogs, but they carried off only the fat ones and left the others to spoil. They even burned the chicken houses. They took the last ears of corn and the last pound of bacon. What they didn't carry or burn, they smashed or scattered.

"And then his Negroes stole his mules and followed off behind the Yankee troops.

"He told me there were two fights, one on the river and one on land. The explosions were from the Union boats, trapped in the low tide. They must have run out of coal, and they were trapped until Union soldiers slipped ashore and stripped the land of all the fence posts, carrying the wood back as fuel. They fired up their boilers and got out.

"Monsieur Tessier told me to take one of the small pigs, and I dragged the rotting carcass the whole way. I heard Negro singing from the other side of the river, some verses plain. 'When de Linkum Gunboats Come' was one. 'The Day of Jubilation Is Near' was another."

The invasive smell of burned cotton choked the air, and the women and children on Houbre's farm went on day by day, salvaging, repairing, and surviving. The war was not over, but there was an inevitability that settled over the farm like a heavy fog. Even after several months, when the wind blew in a certain way, Philomene still breathed in the smothering odor of flaming raw cotton.

It smelled to her like freedom. Freedom for herself, and for Emily.

It was a confusing time after the war was officially over, masters without slaves and slaves without masters.

Oreline Derbanne looked sour, the features of her face wavering between disbelief and anger. "How can you think to leave me now? After all I've done for you and your family? I looked after you more times than you could know, ever since you were a baby. I was the one who took you, Suzette, and Palmire in together against the best judgment of my first husband. Your life could have been very cruel indeed if not for me." Her unsheathed fury snaked across the room.

Philomene shrugged, detached, momentarily distracted by the uncontrolled fluttering of Oreline's hands. They stood facing one another in the common room of Houbre's farmhouse, the same room where they had spent so many evenings banded together, getting their children through the war.

"You've never been whipped," Oreline persisted. "Balance the scales, give us time to get past the ruin. It's not too much to ask that you stay here, instead of going off on your own just now, stay to help with the land and the children. Not forever, but until Monsieur Houbre gets his health back and can work again."

Philomene had been free since spring, and most of the white men had made their way to Cane River by now. Narcisse had returned three months ago, long enough to give Emily his last name, long enough to plant another baby. Already the days were getting shorter. It was August, and Philomene had stayed to strip the leaves from the cornstalks and lay them out to dry to use as animal fodder. It was the last of the fieldwork she intended to do on Houbre's farm.

"Speak up, Philomene. Will you stay?"

"We've stayed longer than we had to," Philomene said calmly. "It's time for us to move on, Madame. You never whipped me, true enough. If you had enough to eat, we had enough to eat. I can't complain about our clothes, same as that mule over there wouldn't complain about having to go without shoes. But these are freedom times now, and the account between us is closed and paid up in full."

Philomene's belly would soon be large again, noticeable, and she was anxious for this confrontation to be over. She wanted to be settled in her new home before the baby made her movements more difficult.

"If it hadn't been for the wretched war," Oreline said, "I was prepared to see after you forever, put food into your mouth, and that of your children, put clothes on your back, nurse you if you got sick, the way I did when you got the yellow fever. I treated Emily as if she were one of my own, and I was prepared to keep on taking care of you, even after you were too old to do for yourself. Are you saying that's not worth something?"

"We made the arrangement work, Madame, and there's no need for harsh words now that things have changed." Oreline kept saying *forever,* Philomene thought. She isn't asking us to stay *forever,* she would have done for us *forever.* The only "forever" for a slave was more work at someone else's bidding and an uncertain future left in others' hands. "My body will wear out soon enough, Madame. I want to have something of my own before that happens. Something I can leave to my own children, the same way you want me to stay and do for you and your children, and your farm. I've been taking care of you and yours my whole life. I have to put my own children in the first place now."

Philomene rested her hands on her belly, finished, and then decided to try once more, picking her words carefully.

"I won't let freedom for Emily and me go to seed for lack of nurturing." She thought of her unspoken bargain with Narcisse Fredieu, both all that she had lost and what she stood to gain. "My Emily will have a different kind of life from mine. I can't do that on this farm."

"Just stay the year," Oreline negotiated, "and then you can go off on your own. That's what a lot of your people are doing. Just work out the year for a part of the crops."

It would have been easier to follow the path Philomene knew so many others had taken. Just pack up and leave without the weight of words or explanation, but she wanted the break to be civil and clean. The law declared her free, but the desperate woman standing in front of her was still white, and the need for caution was just as strong as it had always been.

"I am sorry, Madame. I do not have an extra year to spare," Philomene said. "It is a late start for me already."

266 of Lalita Tademy

"Six months, then. You owe me that."

"And what do you owe me for selling my Clement to Virginia?"

The idea of freedom had made her so heady that the words were out before Philomene thought them through. Unmistakably accusing words that couldn't be recalled. It would have been an unforgivable exchange between slave and mistress. In these shifting times they were disconcerting words between a freed woman and a landless farm wife. The previously unspoken took solid form and drew in breath of its own, putting the two women out of easy reach of one another.

"You ungrateful girl," Oreline said, her face twisted and ugly. "Standing there talking to me that way, carrying another bastard child. Those were difficult times. I did what I had to in order to save us all." Oreline panted softly, as if her breath were being stolen away. The air was too thick with bared truth to go forward safely.

Philomene drew back and reconsidered. There was nothing to gain by revisiting what could not be undone. Freedom or no freedom, there was everything to lose by setting up a backcurrent of ill will from her former mistress. Philomene no longer hated Oreline for selling Clement. That had become too heavy a beast to drag day after day, and she had deliberately forced herself to give up the hatred. She had long since shut out everything about Oreline except for whether she was useful or not useful, and she had bided her time. It was the way of things that Narcisse could be more advantageous to her now, and this was the right moment to move on. Antagonizing Oreline was foolhardy and counterproductive, and Philomene regretted pursuing that course.

"*Oui*, Madame. Forgive me. You are right. I overspoke."

She drew in her voice, making it soft and humble, conciliatory. "You've been a good mistress, to my mother and to me and to Emily. I am grateful. It's just that now is the time to go off and build up something for my own children. You are a mother. You must understand."

"Your mother would never do such a thing, running off at the first opportunity."

"I am not my mother, Madame."

"I see that now," Oreline said. "Go, then. Leave me alone."

Philomene was glad to go. She never again wanted to work a farm on which she had no chance of earning a stake. She was aching to tackle fresh land. From the first news that the Yankees occupied New Orleans three long years before, she had played with the idea of staying on to work the land on Houbre's farm as a free person. The teasing specter of freedom sharpened with each whispered report of Southern battles lost, and her dreams got bolder each passing year of the war. The more trampled and hopeless the Southern cause became, the more she allowed herself to envision her own land, and the Houbre farm became a hope too small, outgrown.

But Philomene was not one for idle dreams and wishful thinking. She had learned the hard lesson about land ownership from watching the chain of events after Ferrier died from yellow fever. You could be forced off land you didn't own, in the same way that if you didn't own yourself, you or yours could be sold at any moment, on someone else's whim. Neither Oreline nor Valery actually owned the land they were working for someone else, hoping for a good crop to split a small profit. If Philomene stayed with them, she was that much further from her goal.

Freedom changed everything.

Land was what burned at Philomene now. Her own land. With Narcisse's sponsorship, if she worked hard enough, she could save to buy land herself. It was possible. She was sure this was the path for gathering her family back to where they belonged, together.

Narcisse never answered her repeated requests for a piece of his own lands, ignoring her completely or clearing his throat and bringing up the subject of long-term debts and back taxes, but he arranged for Philomene to work part of his neighbor's property. Narcisse agreed to move the cabin she had on Houbre's farm to its new location, at the south-west corner of Richard Grant's old plantation.

Philomene didn't care that Grant wasn't French, wasn't considered quality. There were more ruined quality folks than could be counted in Natchitoches Parish these days. Philomene cared only that she was free, and her children would be free. She was going to be a sharecropper.

Narcisse came back from the war changed. He wasn't a broken man, but he moved more slowly, as if some of the air had been let out. Many of the men who came back were already reliving the battles, full of talk and opinions on the war and the insulting absurdity of the new government. Narcisse refused to say anything about where he had been, what he had seen, and he seemed relieved that Philomene didn't probe. He was more content than ever to sit with Emily on his knee, letting his little daughter amuse him with her bright ways for hours at a time, playing in his beard, digging in his pockets, singing him her special made-up songs. There was little need to prod him in his duty to Emily. His daughter delighted him, and when he first returned he was incautious in his love for her, carrying her everywhere.

Narcisse's wife, Arsine, had died just before war's end. His mourning seemed genuine to Philomene, even though he had never been that fond of her while she lived, as if he were uncomfortable at the thought of being without a wife. Many of his friends and neighbors were crushed or ruined by the war, financially and emotionally, but Narcisse came back whole, gone only a year and with the means to start over. Almost no one had managed to keep hold of their cotton along Cane River, but neither the Yankees nor the Confederates had uncovered the cotton stored on his wife's farm in Campti. When Southern ports were thrown open, Narcisse recovered some of his wealth, at least enough to settle unpaid back taxes, debts, and interest.

He held on to most of his lands, even as he allowed his world to narrow, letting things happen around him of their own accord, no longer hard-charging at life. He returned to Philomene's cabin with a new hunger, as if the thought had entered his mind for the first time that she didn't have to accept him there and that Emily was his only flesh-and-blood legacy.

Philomene, determined to be settled into a new life by the time of the new baby's coming, asked Suzette, Elisabeth, and her brother, Gerant, to move in with her on Richard Grant's plantation, the first step in her plan to restore the family. It was to be the beginning of the realization of her true glimpsing. Elisabeth nodded, deciding immediately, eager for the chance to have her grandchildren and great-grandchildren around her, but Suzette was vague and non-committal, no matter how hard Philomene pressed her. Gerant agreed, willing to do any kind of labor himself. Gerant had married, and as long as his wife, Melantine, would not be expected to go to the field, he was eager to move onto the land. They put that behind them, he said, and they wouldn't go back.

Philomene gambled with another false glimpsing, the first she had spun for Narcisse in more than a year. She found that his blind belief had gotten even stronger.

"We'll have a son, a younger brother for Emily," she said to Narcisse, and he was as receptive as always, his desperate wanting blocking all else.

She knew how to play the trick now. If the baby turned out to be a girl, she would say that the glimpsing must have been of a future son they would soon have. It would work out either way. "I see Emily and your son together, and he has the Fredieu look. Both he and Emily carry your name. The brother and sister play together, in front of a house. It isn't this house we have here, it's bigger, and there's a wide door leading inside, on our own land. Elisabeth and Gerant are close by."

Narcisse stroked his dark beard down to its wavy point, considering.

Every day Philomene prayed to herself. "Just get the child born. Let him grow up free and strong, and don't let him be taken away from me."

The responsibility for the new life inside her thrilled and terrified Philomene, her first child to be born free. She woke sometimes in the middle of the night soaking in her own sweat, the details of her dreams scattered, recalling only vague uncertainties.

What if Clement came back? Before freedom, she had never allowed herself to believe that she would ever see Clement again. Now he could come back to her with the same determination he had shown in the storm. She couldn't feel him alive, try as she might, and without Clement

Narcisse was her best bet for the life she envisioned. But what if she was wrong about Clement? What if he made his way to her? She had been living as if man-woman love were dead, substituting man-woman practicality, and she wasn't sure what would happen if Clement found her now, hard and used. What would he do? What would she do? How far had she bound herself to Narcisse Fredieu for the sake of her family and her children?

What if her glimpsings couldn't protect this child, as they had protected Emily? What if Emily was all she was allowed?

There were too many questions, and too few answers.

25

Elisabeth sat alone on the front gallery with a wide-mouthed bowl squeezed tight between her knees, shelling peas. A figure approached in the distance, his gait slow but steady. When he turned off the wider dirt road toward the farmhouse Elisabeth shared with Philomene and her two children, she paid closer attention.

He was a colored man of middle age, and too much exposure to the sun had given his light honey-colored face the appearance of a golden-baked crust. His skin was pulled smooth and tight, most likely from hunger, Elisabeth supposed. One of the hordes of the displaced that flowed in or ebbed out like the tides since the war ended. As he came closer something tugged at her about the purse of his lips, the set of his eyes. This one was a high-yellow man, with a wide mouth, dirty reddish brown curls, and clothes that gave away that he was from somewhere else. That, and the soft slanting of his words as he came up to stand before the gallery and address her.

"Good afternoon, Madame," the stranger said. His French was halting and stiff, but he could be understood. "Is this Elisabeth's house?"

"This is my granddaughter's house." Curious, Elisabeth thought. Slave Creole in words, but foreign in dress and manner. "You look like it's been a while since you rested. Help yourself to a little water from the dipper."

"I have been on the move for some time. I appreciate it. Thank you, Madame."

Elisabeth went back to her peas as he drank. She sized up this stranger asking about her. He seemed soft to her.

"You're not from around here," Elisabeth said. "Where you come from?"

"I'm from Virginia, Madame."

"Have you eaten?"

"Not in quite a while, Madame."

"Come on inside with me while I dish you up something. We have the leavings of the stew from supper."

Elisabeth rose stiffly and carried the half-full tin of peas with her. The man followed her into the dark house, through the front room, and into the kitchen. Elisabeth waved him to sit at the pine table. She scraped out all that was left of the stew from the kettle into a wood bowl and handed him a spoon, and then she cut a quarter round of yesterday's cornbread. She poured him some buttermilk and lowered herself into the chair across from where he sat.

He hunkered over the bowl like a ravenous dog, barely taking the time to chew the small bits of meat in the stew. Mostly it was vegetables blended beyond recognition in the long cooking. The man crumbled what was left of the cornbread into his buttermilk and drank it down in gulping swallows. Only when he was finished did he look up, embarrassed.

"I'm sorry. Like I said, it's been some time since I last ate. That was very good."

"Sorry there's not more." The stranger seemed harmless enough, but he was fidgety, rubbing his fingers together nervously. "What are you doing looking for Elisabeth?"

"No disrespect intended, but that's something best taken up with her. I mean her no harm. They say she came through the war all right, and she lives here on this farm, but I might have gotten turned around on the road a little."

The man was trying to study her when he thought she wasn't looking.

"Lots of women called Elisabeth in these parts."

"The Elisabeth I'm looking for comes from Virginia. She was sold away from there almost fifty years ago to a man called Pierre Derbanne, and ended up on his son's place called Rosedew. She has a granddaughter, Philomene."

Elisabeth's old memories began to stir, and she looked carefully at the man's face for clues. She had liked this soft-spoken stranger who came out of nowhere, but now she was uneasy, unwilling to believe that she could make it all the way into her sixties, through slavery and freedom, and still feel the lurch of life shifting and becoming unsteady beneath her. "Who are you?"

"Again, no disrespect, but I've already been to Natchitoches, Cloutierville, Isle Brevelle, and Monette's Ferry tracking this farm down. Please, is it you?"

"I'm Elisabeth. What do you have to do with me?"

"You left Virginia nigh on fifty years ago? From Lost Oak Plantation?"

"Yes, that's me. What's your business?"

"You had two sons, John and Jacob?"

Elisabeth's throat seemed to dry up, sealing off the escape of her words. The longer she took to respond, the more uncertain the man became, until he looked like a frightened little boy forced to drop his pants as he waited for a whipping. "You better tell me what you came to tell me, stirring up old sadness like yesterday's soup."

The man spoke quickly then, but he tripped over his words, as if his courage had wound down. "They call me Yellow John. I think I'm your son. I came from Virginia to find you."

Off in the distance a jay screeched, and another of his kind answered the call. Elisabeth leaned back in her chair and closed her eyes. When she opened them again, he was still sitting there in front of her. She half expected him to disappear, carried away by the same play of mind that summoned him in the first place.

"My John? What trick is this?"

"No trick, Madame. I'm sorry. I've had more time to get ready for this than you."

Elisabeth began to cry softly where she sat, her head in her big hands. "Praise be," she said finally. "Come help me up."

Yellow John pulled her up from the chair, slowly, a bit awkwardly, as if he were afraid to touch her. Elisabeth used her hands to try to find herself in his face, and then she folded him in her arms. They stayed that way until she let him go.

"How could you find me, all the way from Virginia?"

"It's a story that bears telling, Madame, but first, could I bother you for a little more to eat? I haven't eaten for several days."

Elisabeth gave him the rest of the cornbread and fried four eggs in the skillet, turning back to look at the man sitting at her table. Yellow John was more controlled in his eating this time, rationing his bread and eggs carefully to make sure he didn't run out of one before the other, using the bread to sop up every bit of the runny yellow yolks. The plate he left behind looked as clean as if he had washed it.

"Thank you kindly." He pushed himself back from the table.

"Who told you about me?"

"Old Marse Robert. He didn't hide from Jacob or me that our mother's name was Elisabeth, and she'd been sold to a place called Cane River in Louisiana. He used us to get back at his wife, I think, never denying we had his blood, bringing us up to the big house under her nose, even teaching us to read a little."

Yellow John stole glances at Elisabeth as he talked, as if judging whether or not he was holding on to her attention.

"I grew up, and got me a wife from there on the place, and we tried to have children, but we kept losing them before they were born. The third time, my wife made it through to the end, but the little one tried to come out feet first. They couldn't save mother or child. I lost them both on the same day. It doesn't seem I was meant to have children of my own." Yellow John hesitated, as if he weren't sure what to say next.

"Go on," Elisabeth prodded, but she was careful not to spook him.

"One day, I overheard young Marse talking about a slave they just bought, sight unseen from some distant relation from Cane River, Louisiana. I made my way down to the quarters to see this new boy as soon as I could manage. He was a barrel-chested fellow, quiet, had the slow look of someone fresh sold. He couldn't speak one word of English. He was young, and still shy of coming into his full force, but he knew his way around hot metal and horses."

"Clement?" Elisabeth had trouble keeping up with so much news, so many twists and turns.

"Yes, Clement. We went fishing together almost every Sunday, and we fashioned a language together while he taught me his French and I taught him my English. He had a quick mind, but it took some doing to draw him out. He was about the age my dead boy would have been had he lived, and I came to think on him as a son."

"And Clement told you about us?" It was more statement than question.

Yellow John nodded. "It was slow going at first, but he understood more, bit by bit. I was hungry for news of Cane River, and after a time, it became clear that his Elisabeth and my Elisabeth were the same. His Elisabeth hadn't been born to French by the speaking of it, and she came to Louisiana from Virginia, with a sad tale of children left behind, and being sold to a family named Derbanne. Philomene had told him the story before he got sold to old Marse Robert.

"He described Cane River as the most beautiful place on earth. Virginia is pretty country, too, but his mind was on his old river home. He talked of you, and his own mother, Eliza, and your daughter Suzette, but mostly he talked about Philomene and their two baby girls, Thany and Bet. I've never seen a man so set on one woman. There's no shame in marrying again when you have to leave someone behind, especially so young, and there were plenty of girls ready on our place, but he never committed to just one."

"Where is he? Where is Clement?"

"When the whisper talk of freedom started, we decided that on the very day of jubilee, we would set out walking to Cane River together. Clement never got to put one foot on the path back here. He died after the men of the place went away to fight in the war." Yellow John's voice became soft. "His was a stupid death, with no meaning at all in it. A water moccasin must have bitten him first, his leg was so swollen with poison, but he fell into the river and drowned. I decided to come on to Cane River by myself anyway. I know Clement would want me to tell Philomene that he didn't ever let go of her."

As she tended the blood-filled blisters on John's feet, Elisabeth didn't know whom to cry for first. Clement, who had died away from his home, so close to being able to come back to Philomene? Philomene, who had yet to hear about Clement and had already traded love for protection? Yellow John, whose torn and bloody feet would heal, but who had spent an entire lifetime nursing an empty hole where his mother was supposed to be? Or herself, looking at this stranger calling himself her son, unable to replace the sweet little baby in her mind's eye with the weary man in front of her now? Instead of the joy of reunion, she felt the theft of the past years that had taken so much from both of them. Her pain was mixed with anger at the waste.

Her son was no longer a young man. She had missed it all. First steps, favorite foods, selection of a wife. His dark, curly hair was uneven and touched with gray, untended. She knew nothing about him other than the fact that he craved her so much, he had come all the way from Virginia to see her.

"And Jacob. What happened to my Jacob?"

"Jacob is a shoemaker in Richmond, with a wife and four grown children. He was lucky. After we were free, he knew where all his children were." The lids of Yellow John's eyes drooped almost shut for a moment, and he fought back a yawn. "We agreed if I couldn't find you, I'd go back to Virginia to live out my days with them."

"You've walked a long way, and you need sleep. There's fresh hay in the barn, and I'll get a blanket. When you wake up, we can talk more. You're home now."

Elisabeth was tired, too, more than the usual dip at the tail of the afternoon. Seeing Yellow John had worn her out, and she was uncertain whether her dreams would be restful when she closed her eyes. She would tell Yellow John later about his half sisters and half brother, and about his great-niece Emily, five years old and down for her afternoon nap on Philomene's bed.

There was too much to tell. He didn't know that Philomene was the strong one who planned the next step. That when a lifetime of being a slave made it hard to make decisions, Philomene did the thinking for all of them, and they let her. That the young guided the old.

Elisabeth had a son who was healthy and could even read, and the Lord had led him back to her only through the bad business of Clement being sold. Sometimes good came out of hurt, compensation came out of pain. He gave with one hand, and He took with the other.

Her son was with her now, but it would fall to Elisabeth to tell Philomene that Clement was dead.

It was almost dusk by the time Philomene and Gerant came in together from the field. Elisabeth came outside and waved them aside before they could go into the barn to bed the mule. They left the animal outside and went into the house instead.

"There's someone sleeping in the barn," Elisabeth said. "Someone important to this family."

Her grand-daughter's work dress was ringed with sweat stains, and a rag tied around a burst blister on one hand had dried stiff. "Who is it, *Mémère?*" Suspicion clouded Philomene's face, her body newly tensed as if ready to do battle, her tiredness pushed aside.

"My son, lost once, but found again." Elisabeth felt sapped of her energy, but she pushed herself forward. "I had to leave him behind in Virginia."

"We have an uncle?" It was as if Philomene had to play with the idea in her mind for a few moments before she could accept Elisabeth's word as fact. "Are you sure he's who he says he is?"

"A mother knows her child."

"How did he find us?" Philomene was beginning to warm to the notion of an unknown family member presenting himself. "Is he by himself? Weren't there two boys?"

"This one is Yellow John. Jacob has a family in Virginia."

"Has he come to stay?" Gerant asked.

"My boy walked here all the way from Virginia. I hope so."

Elisabeth wanted to tell Philomene about Clement before Yellow John woke. She took Philomene's hand. "Sit down, child. There is something to be said."

Philomene obeyed, growing solemn at Elisabeth's manner. Gerant pulled up a chair too and sat next to his sister.

"Philomene, there's no way to say this but straight and fast. Yellow John is from the same place they sent Clement. Baby girl, Clement is dead."

It was as if Philomene hadn't heard. "I'm not the same

girl as when Clement left," she said. Her back was stiff and her eyes dry. "He'll be disappointed."

Elisabeth and Gerant exchanged a quick glance in an attempt to make sense of Philomene's response. Elisabeth tried again. "Clement has gone on beyond this world, to a better place. Do you understand what I'm telling you?"

Philomene just sat. Elisabeth thought she might scream or cry or fly apart, as she had when Clement was sold away. Or retreat into silence. She tightened her grip on Philomene's hand, but it was limp inside her own.

"Was it by water?" Philomene's tone was as flat as her eyes.

"Yellow John said Clement drowned, but he was planning to come back to you."

"After a while, I couldn't feel him anymore."

Philomene stood and walked toward the kitchen to dish up the supper Elisabeth had prepared.

"At least he never knew about Bet and Thany and the yellow fever," Philomene said, as much to herself as anyone in the room. "At least Clement never knew about Narcisse Fredieu."

26

A neatly dressed, fresh-cheeked young man the color of oatmeal pulled up in a buggy alongside Suzette's cabin in the quarter and brought the horse to a halt. With the quickness of youth he jumped down and was by her side, helping her up into the seat beside his.

"Good afternoon, Madame Jackson," he said.

"Good afternoon, Monsieur Valsin," she replied in her best voice, savoring the exchange. Suzette had been ready since noon. After she'd fixed Saturday dinner for Augustine Fredieu's family, the rest of week's end was her own. She had changed into her good dress, a shabby calico but freshly ironed, and carefully rewrapped a spotless bleached *tignon* around her head. Then she'd waited for Doralise's grandson to come for her, watching out for the buggy the way a child waits for a promised candy. But she was nervous, too. To be invited to Doralise's home with a gathering of *gens de couleur libre,* to ride in the front seat of a buggy like a grand lady all the way to Cloutierville, to be addressed with such respect by her new last name. Cane River was topsy-turvy.

She had to keep reminding herself that the *gens de couleur libre* were no more. They were all free now, although Doralise's house was one of the few places former slaves mingled regularly with former Cane River colored royalty. Most of the *gens de couleur libre* refused to mix with any but their own, but Doralise pulled in a stream of visitors and went out of her way to make Suzette welcome. Especially since Yellow John had come to Cane River.

In the first few months after the war, little seemed to change for Suzette, but in important ways everything changed. She worked hard as ever in Augustine Fredieu's kitchen, living in the same cabin she had shared for the last few years with another family. When Augustine Fredieu came back to his farm, he asked each of his former slaves left on the property to sign up to stay for a year. The contracts called for a small bit of money to change hands at the end of the season. Augustine explained that there wasn't much money to be had until the farm was built back up.

"My daughter wants me to move in to sharecrop with her on Richard Grant's plantation down near the lower part of Natchitoches Parish," Suzette told him. "And Madame Oreline has asked me to move to her farm, too." Like the *gens de couleur libre,* Augustine wrapped himself in old habits, still expecting to be treated in the same way he had before the war. Suzette didn't care one way or the other, willing to do whatever would make things smooth. "You and I don't need a paper, M'sieu Augustine," she had said. "We can keep on like we always have until I finish my planning. I'm not ready to put my X on anything yet."

Madame Jackson. Suzette silently rolled the words over her tongue again.

When for the first time they were allowed to create a last name for themselves, it was her mother, Elisabeth, and not Suzette who decided that the name would be Jackson. There was no hidden meaning to the choice, no long association with some significant event or person. Elisabeth merely said that she liked the clean sound of Jackson, that it didn't sound so French, the way everything along Cane River had her whole life. If she got to choose her own last name, she wanted it simple, a new beginning.

For a time Suzette tried to persuade Elisabeth to consider DeNegre, a last name she had invented as far back as Rosedew, but her arguments were of no use.

"My name is Jackson," Elisabeth had said. "I hope you see your way to carry the same name."

Suzette wanted that tie, a thread between her mother and herself that everyone could see, so she became Suzette Jackson, finally one of the Ones with Last Names.

Suzette took pleasure in the taste of freedom, wanted to savor it without committing to anyone, at least for a while. Philomene had managed to collect eleven of the family close together in bordering sharecropper cabins: Philomene, little Emily, and Philomene's youngest, Eugene, born right before Easter; Elisabeth and Yellow John; and Gerant, Melantine, and their children. It comforted Suzette to know they were all so close, but as powerful as the temptation to drift back into the comfort of family was, Suzette hesitated, at a crossroads.

Stay on Augustine Fredieu's farm, go to her daughter, or go to Oreline. There was something so delicious about having choices that she found she couldn't let go just yet.

Suzette preferred to remain where she was, making plans, weighing her options, humming her way through work that demanded more of her hands than her mind.

Madame Jackson.

By the time they reached Cloutierville, Suzette's excitement had turned to quiet reflection. By the time they came to Doralise's house, it had turned to dread.

Her godmother's house was plain, not unlike the other houses in the town, but well kept up. Clumps of jasmine were planted beside the front steps leading up to the gallery, and bright scarlet tufts of early-bloom azaleas poked up from window boxes on either side of the front door.

Suzette and her young escort entered Doralise's front room. Six or eight people were there already, some seated, some standing, talking among themselves. It was a blur to Suzette, but she immediately noted everyone in the room had lighter skin than she. The darkest before she walked into the room was the color of honey.

"Suzette." Doralise called to her, waving her over to where she sat in her favorite chair, an overstuffed plush green. She was flanked on one side by a man of middle age and on the other by Yellow John. Since Yellow John had come to Cane River, he and Doralise had become as comfortable with each other as a pair of old slippers. The sight of her half brother gave Suzette more confidence, and he greeted her warmly, but she knew she wasn't the match of the people in this room. They had lived a different life, had a different future in store. The only one she saw who didn't carry the shame of slavery was Yellow John, and even he could read.

Then she recognized him. The man sitting calmly on

Doralise's other side. He was older, more heavyset than she recalled, his short-cut graying hair receded and thinning at the top of his head, but he had the same sleepy-eyed kindness to his face. Nicolas. Nicolas Mulon. She still owned the old strip of cowhide he had given her when she was a girl. It was a miserable, shapeless piece now, worn beyond any possible use. The stubborn stiffness of the scrap reassured her each time she rubbed it for luck. He had been staring at her, she realized, since she'd walked into the room. Suzette knew how much she had changed and chafed at how disappointed he must be to see her here. She wanted to turn tail and run, spare them both the embarrassment.

"Suzette, you're here at last," Doralise said. "Monsieur Mulon has asked about you often. I thought to invite you both so you could become reacquainted."

The room grew small for Suzette, devoid of air, until Nicolas Mulon gave Suzette the shy smile she remembered from so long ago.

Sunday was reserved for church and Philomene's farm.

"I don't understand why you won't move in with us, *Maman*."

The supper dishes were cleared away, and Suzette, Philomene, and Elisabeth sat talking on the front porch, which was cooler than indoors. Gerant and Melantine had gone for a walk, and the children were off getting into their own mischief. Suzette came to Philomene's house as she did every week, continuing to resist the invitations to move in, nursing her joyous secret. Surrounded by most of the people she loved best in the world, she smiled to herself. One was noticeably absent, she thought.

"It is comfortable enough where I am, for now," Suzette

told Philomene. "I'll decide where to go when I finish my planning."

"I'm going to pull us all back together again," Philomene said. "On our own land. I don't know how long it will take, but we can work our own place better than we can someone else's."

"How are you going to get your own land?" Suzette asked. "There's no money. Everyone around here is scratching just to get from one day to the next. Be grateful for what you have."

"Sharecropping is slavery with a different name." Philomene looked combative. "Even when money changes hands, it goes back to settle debts."

"Not even Madame Oreline has land anymore," Suzette said.

"We're family, and we'll find a way to take care of our own. What Madame has or doesn't have isn't our worry. We can all take in washing, ironing, and sewing while we share-crop. We can save. I'll put myself behind a plow again if it means that girl over there will never have to," Philomene said, nodding in Emily's direction.

Little Emily sat cross-legged on the far side of the porch, absorbed, dangling a twisting slip of green ribbon between her small, thin fingers in front of a tomcat that batted at the moving target with his paw.

"Keep her out of the sun," Suzette scolded. "You know what it will do to her skin. That's her future. She's meant for better."

Philomene nodded in agreement and kept at her mend-ing. "We can grow most of our food, fish and trap the rest. We'll make out."

"I have a different plan for what comes next." Suzette

sat back in her chair, enjoying the look of bewilderment that crossed Philomene's face.

"What plan is that, *Maman?*"

Suzette sported a slow grin, the gap between her front teeth prominent. "I have a gentleman who wants to marry me. In the church. A real marriage they put down in a book, not one of those slavey things."

Philomene's face seemed to go slack for a moment, and Suzette's smile withered as she realized what she had said. "I'm so sorry, Philomene. You had as real a marriage as there could be. This old woman has gotten foolish and hurtful. That's what happens when God hands you a gift long after you stop hoping."

Philomene gave Suzette a careful, appraising look. The same long look Suzette had given her own mother after Yellow John had arrived in Cane River and she'd realized Elisabeth had a life she knew nothing about. "*Maman,* what gift?"

The timid smile crept back into Suzette's voice. "Before you were born, a boy lived next door to us on Rosedew." She turned to Elisabeth. "You remember him, *Mère*. Nicolas Mulon. Now he's a colored shoemaker set up in Cloutierville. We were confirmed at the same time and took first communion together."

Elisabeth nodded.

Suzette turned back to Philomene. "When I was a girl, I wished so hard that Nicolas and I would grow up and get married that sometimes I actually thought it was true. It was not possible then. He was *gens de couleur libre.* Later, Nicolas married a free woman of color, just the way *Mère* always said he would."

"Go on, *Maman*," Philomene said.

"The war brought some down, and raised others up. Most of the *gens de couleur libre* still play at being grand after losing everything, because they were free before the rest of us. *Marraine* Doralise was never like that. Or Nicolas. I saw him again for the first time in over twenty years when I visited Doralise. His wife died this year, leaving him with three children to take care of, one still in breechcloth. Nicolas . . . remembered me."

Suzette turned shy, all at once hot, using her embroidery hoop as a fan. "And I remembered him. He has a little piece of land near Cloutierville, and we've been talking about me living with him on it, becoming stepmother to those children."

"I never thought of you living with a man, *Maman*," Philomene said. She paused, carefully unwrapping the unexpected turn of events, examining each fold. "Do you love him?"

"I never had a man for more than an hour at a time all my days on this earth," Suzette said. "I wouldn't mind somebody to make a life with, without what you call love. But yes, I love Nicolas. I want to be with him, and do for him, and I want him to do for me. I knew the first evening over at Madame Doralise's, and so did he, like time skipped back and we got a second try."

Philomene didn't hide her puzzlement, her thick eyebrows knotted in concentration, her lips pressed almost to a grimace. "Did you love my papa at all?"

Suzette shifted uncomfortably. The mood had turned strained, with too much talk. Three generations of women out on the front porch, four counting little Emily, trying to put words around a past and a future that could never be explained. But the rawness in Philomene's face persuaded Suzette to make the attempt.

"No. There were no parts of love there, except you and Gerant that came out of it. That was a different time. Philomene, I saw how you were with Clement. That was young love. *Mère,* you and Gerasíme, that was love, too. Gerant and Melantine, still more love. I've been surrounded by it, but never thought I'd get a taste myself. Eugene Daurat and me, there was no choice. Love is pull. That was all push."

The light outside was beginning to fail. They would need to call the children in soon.

"So you're going to marry Nicolas Mulon?" Elisabeth asked.

"As soon as we get enough money saved," Suzette answered. "Others have the same idea. Folks already living as man and wife can make it proper now. Doralise and Yellow John will marry when we do, and we thought we would share a party together after. Gerant and Melantine may want to consider coming forward, too."

Suzette sat back in her chair, enjoying the surprise around her. There was nothing more satisfying than having plans.

27

Even with both the front and back doors open to encourage a breeze, the air barely stirred at all in the sweltering heat of Philomene's four-room cabin. She turned the heavy pressing iron on end to cool, brushing the sweat from her eyes with the back of her sleeve. It wouldn't do to scorch the starched, delicate lacework she needed to deliver to Widow Greneaux by afternoon. Fancy ironing generated more money than flatwork and required full attention. With two children and a grandmother depending on her, and two years of freedom gone, Philomene had learned to navigate the world of money paid for service. She glanced outside to check on the children.

"Emily Fredieu, how many times do I have to tell you not to let the sun get to your skin?" she called through the window. "March yourself and your brother inside. That sun will make you common."

"Aunt Melantine lets Cousin Alice and Cousin Adolph play in the sun," Emily said.

"I know I don't hear sass in your voice," Philomene said. At six Emily was old enough to know the consequences of talking back.

"No, *Maman*." The girl brushed dust from her shiny black shoes with one hand and took Eugene by the other to lead him into the house.

"You're meant for better, Emily Fredieu. Just stay where I can see you."

"Yes, *Maman*."

"Your papa comes this afternoon to carry you visiting. Take Eugene Fredieu to *Mémère* to clean him up."

"Bring the baby to me, Emily." Elisabeth took off the girl's bonnet and hung it on the peg by the front door and had Eugene lift up his arms to slip off his soiled undershirt. "You're as color-struck as Suzette," she said to Philomene.

"Fair skin will give them advantage," Philomene said. She looked at her children. Their sandy brown hair was straight, and all their features were French, not African. "Either could pass."

Elisabeth grunted. "That kind of thinking breaks up families."

Philomene knew she would be an immediate giveaway if she ever tried to lead her children into that kind of life. The olive in her skin darkened with the slightest exposure to the sun.

"Emily and Eugene do fine right here," Elisabeth went on. "Even M'sieu Narcisse doesn't fuss when you call them Fredieu to his face."

"Emily Fredieu and Eugene Fredieu will have choices," Philomene said to her grandmother, carefully folding the frilled collar piece, still warm, and adding it to the pile.

The evening cooled down almost enough to be pleasant, with an occasional short-lived breeze. Philomene and Narcisse stayed out on the porch of the cabin after everyone else had gone to bed. Smoke curled around the tip of Narcisse's fat cigar, and Philomene embroidered by the unsteady light of the oil lamp.

"Is that from the general store?" Narcisse used the cigar's smoldering tip to point to the cloth in Philomene's lap.

Philomene held up the small blue garment for Narcisse to admire. "A new visiting dress for Emily Fredieu," she said.

"On last month's bill, you spent almost as much on material and sundries as flour, sugar, salt, and seed combined."

"They need proper clothes."

"I have never scrimped with either Emily or Eugene," Narcisse said, taking offense. "The girl does not need another new dress. They remarked on it today at Augustine's. Emily has more dresses than his girls, twice her age. You spoil her overmuch."

"You spoil her as well, Monsieur Narcisse."

"I mean it, Philomene. No more. Don't make me close off the account to you."

They sat on the porch, sewing and smoking in silence.

"I have seen your future," Philomene said after a time.

Narcisse got up and moved his chair to face Philomene, slowly, as if he were an ox being led to field, pacing himself for the full day's work ahead. "A glimpsing?"

Philomene heard the same strange blend of dread and excitement that always preceded these particular conversations, a drooping and quickening, one on top of the other. In their eight years together she had created five false glimpsings for Narcisse, including this last. She allowed a moment to pass, and then another.

"You can go out and find wives to marry, but I'm the only one who can give you babies."

Narcisse blinked away a bewildered look, then grabbed Philomene roughly by the arm. "Why do you say that?" A small damp piece of brown tobacco clung to the corner of his mouth.

Philomene shifted the weight out of her shoulders and farther down into her back, steadying her hand to continue her embroidery. She forced herself to calm, taking her time, speech measured and deliberate.

"I see you, an old man, visiting graves of two women you married. When you are through, you come back to me. There are many children surrounding you, from big to little, a mix of boys and girls. Our children. They have been brought up quality, never hungry, and they wear new clothes and soft leather shoes fit to their feet. We live in a house big enough to hold all the children, not this cabin. They call you Papa."

Philomene paused, trying to read his mood.

"What else?" Narcisse stared sharply at Philomene, as if by so doing he could decipher some word or gesture she had purposely left unspoken. His intensity threatened to unnerve her.

"I can only tell you what the glimpsing shows," Philomene said.

Narcisse leaned back again in his chair, as if dismissing her. "I come and go as I please," he said.

"You try to skip from this too lightly, Monsieur Narcisse." It was Philomene now who brought her face closer to his, but she lowered her voice to barely a whisper. She wanted him to have to strain to hear. "First one wife could not give you a child, and then another with the same result.

Even your rutting with trash from the hills came to nothing. Forget about a white child. I am the only one who can ever give you offspring, but you must take care. Treat them well."

Philomene put aside her sewing, stood, and took up the lamp to go into the cabin.

"Mark my words, Narcisse Fredieu. For you, there is only one way to have children, and that is through me."

In 1872, just months after baby Nick was born, Emily stood before Philomene and Narcisse in the common room of Philomene's cabin. The old green sofa Narcisse had brought from one of his other houses sagged in the middle under his weight, the cushions almost flattened by his bulk, but he sat with great authority, a pose he didn't take often with his daughter. Philomene rocked the baby in the moon-light chair.

Emily waited dutifully for Narcisse to let her know why he had called her. At eleven she was soft-spoken but not quiet. Philomene could imagine that her daughter thought she had been summoned to entertain, for which she needed little encouragement. Narcisse loved to watch Emily dance or listen to her sing. Her girlish voice was high and sweet, with a slight unexpected trill she added to the words, and she sang constantly to her brother Eugene, who followed her everywhere. She sang to the chickens as she scattered their feed, she sang to the baby, and she sang for her father when-ever he visited. Amusing people was natural to her.

A responsible girl, especially with Eugene and baby Nick, Emily went a step beyond, making everything she touched special. She was partial to colors, brought fresh, vibrant wildflowers into the house in spring and summer, and placed green potted plants in the corners in winter. She convinced her uncle Gerant to make her a small table and shelf but insisted that the carved shapes on them be a design of her own making. Emily could always talk Philomene into another new scarf or lace collar or special embroidery to freshen up an old garment.

But for all the style and charm that drew people to her daughter, Philomene was most proud that Emily could read. For a time she had studied under a tutor, the old schoolteacher Valery Houbre, widowed since the death of his wife, Oreline. Philomene thought it fitting that their old master be the one to give Emily advantage. Monsieur Houbre was now frail and in ill health, but he had always been a friend to the family. He had taken Emily as far as she needed to go in French, but Philomene and Narcisse had been discussing for some time how English had begun to intrude on their world.

"Emily," Narcisse announced, "we're sending you to New Orleans. You'll learn to read and write in English and make your first communion there."

Narcisse seemed pleased with the proclamation, but Emily grew flush. She always blushed easily. "Papa, I don't want to leave Cane River."

"This is for your future, Emily Fredieu," Philomene said. "An opportunity not many receive."

Philomene had never been apart from any of her children. Already she missed Emily, but the promise of her daughter continuing her studies was worth almost anything. Philomene planned for Emily to be in a position to teach her brothers when the time came. No one would ever be able to set aside the learning once taught.

The color rose higher on Emily's cheeks, the youthful bloom highlighted in her distress. "Please don't send me away," she said in a small voice.

"You must do as I say, Emily," Narcisse said.

"I'm scared, Papa," Emily said, her eyes filling with tears. "I'll be so lonely."

"There will be other girls, quality girls," Narcisse said. "You deserve better than you can get here. One year, and then you'll be back."

Philomene could see the struggle in Narcisse, even though he sounded decisive and unwavering. He had never been a match for Emily's tears.

"I'll take you down on the steamboat myself to New Orleans, and visit often. I've written a friend who will look after you there. The year will be up before you know it." A fine sheen of sweat had broken out across Narcisse's forehead. "Now go help your mother get you ready. We leave at the end of the week."

28

Narcisse paid extra for the hired carriage and coachman to wait for him outside the convent gate. It took better than an hour and a quarter to arrange the unloading of Emily's trunk and to enroll her with the nuns. Only then could he take the next step of his journey. The steamboat trip had been fatiguing, from Cane River to the New Orleans dock, but father and daughter were more emotionally spent than physically tired. Narcisse made the trip once or twice a year, but he had never had to release his only daughter into the hands of strangers.

"I'll be back to visit tomorrow," he told Emily. There had already been tears the week before leaving, and more tears on the boat. Narcisse felt that if he didn't leave immediately, he was likely to shed a few himself.

Narcisse usually stayed at the St. Charles Hotel, but Joseph Billes, a distant connection from his mother's side of the family, had insisted in their correspondence that Narcisse accept his hospitality. He set out for the French Quarter without quite knowing where he was going. The coachman had little trouble finding the house on a narrow side street, away from the water. It was a modest-looking building set far back behind a stunted four-foot-high iron fence, but there was handsome grillwork around each of the second-story balconies. A pleasant woman introducing herself as Joseph Billes's sister answered the front door and took him out to a lovely interior courtyard while the coachman unloaded his valises and brought them in. There he met Joseph Billes face-to-face for the first time. Joseph had a wiry, French look to him, but cheerful, and was at least fifteen years his junior.

"Welcome to my home." Joseph embraced Narcisse as if they had known each other a lifetime. "I take it you have already settled your daughter into the convent? Once we establish you upstairs, you can decide how best to shake off the dust. Certainly the completion of such a difficult task begins with brandy."

Narcisse had looked forward to an early night and a firm bed, but he got his second wind. On that first evening they talked and played cards after supper, Joseph, several cousins, and other guests who stopped by. Joseph entertained them all with stories, then brought out a handsome mandolin, a magnificent instrument with an all French polished orange front, ebony fingerboard, and rosewood-and-mahogany ribs. He accompanied himself as he sang and had a surprisingly rich, deep voice for such a thin man. Narcisse liked Joseph immediately. He laughed at Joseph's unflattering stories of his dealings with Americans and his more forgiving tales of dealing with the French-at-heart, and Narcisse recited his own reports of the planter's life along the Cane and Red Rivers. Both men embellished for effect.

Fatigue finally forced Narcisse to excuse himself. He retired to the guest room, but before drifting off to sleep, he itemized those things he needed to accomplish in New Orleans on this trip. He had his cotton to sell, his promise to Emily that he would visit her every day until he went back home, and two weeks to amuse himself while waiting for the return boat back to Cane River.

The next day proved to be overcast and drizzly, and after attending early-morning mass, Narcisse took Joseph with him when he visited Emily at the convent. Narcisse was taken aback when he saw her in her new austere setting. She seemed lost inside a coarse gray dress that swallowed her. Not even the drabness of her new uniform in the convent, however, so unlike the way Philomene would have dressed the girl, could rob Emily of her prettiness. Again Emily looked close to tears.

The three met in the convent parlor, then went outside in the courtyard to find a seat on a wood bench in the shade of a large magnolia tree, under the watchful eyes of the patrolling nuns.

"So you are Mademoiselle Emily," Joseph said before he sat. "Such a small thing." He leaned down to kiss Emily lightly on both cheeks. "I am Joseph Billes, and once your father returns home, child, it will be up to me to bring you some fun from outside these convent walls to keep you from melancholy." He had a mischievous glint in his eye, as if he and Emily were planning an exotic journey together, but Emily looked more dejected than ever.

"I see I haven't said the right thing." Joseph made his face serious. "We must work very hard at being friends, you and

I. Your father will have my head if I don't honor my promise to cheer you up while you are in New Orleans. You don't want me to lose my head?"

Emily tried to smile.

"Can you guess where I'm from?"

Emily looked at her father's friend shyly. "France, but you don't sound like any of the Frenchmen I've heard."

"What a good ear you have. I am here only two years from France, but I am told that since I grew up so close to the border with Spain, my French is not so pure. But then, neither is the Creole French most speak here."

"I like the way you sound."

Narcisse watched the two of them, relieved to see a little of Emily's spirit returning, grateful she was warming up to Joseph.

"Already I can see that we must call you by a very special nickname, and it has just come to me what the name should be."

"A name for me?" Emily was clearly drawn in, had seemed to forget for a moment how miserable she was.

"You are so dainty, I must call you Mademoiselle Petite."

This time Emily managed a full smile. Joseph had won her over.

Over the next two weeks Narcisse and Joseph discovered how alike they were in their love of fun, drink, and parties. An ambitious man, Joseph seemed full to overflowing with ideas and short-term schemes. Narcisse envied Joseph his independence and wandering, his nose for risk and opportunity, and the intensity and stamina of youth, and Joseph was clearly intrigued by Narcisse's descriptions of life in the countryside of central Louisiana.

They both visited Emily for the permitted hour each remaining day Narcisse stayed in New Orleans. Narcisse couldn't help but swell at the beauty Emily radiated. While he was a substantial man, so fond of food and drink that he found it increasingly difficult to button his vests, everything about Emily was small and delicate, from her tiny feet to her slim waist, but she was neither frail nor fragile.

At the end of the two weeks Narcisse had to admit that the results of his trip to New Orleans were mixed. Although he had safely established Emily at the convent, his business dealings had been far less satisfactory. The most he'd been able to arrange was just over eight cents a pound for his meager cotton crop. When he boarded the steamship *Danube* for the trip back to Cane River, he left New Orleans leaden with the absence of his daughter, already missing his new friend, and pessimistic about the dismal financial prospects of yet another planting season.

Narcisse and Joseph began to exchange visits back and forth throughout the year Emily stayed in New Orleans. In April Joseph came for the first time to Cane River to visit, and Narcisse introduced him into both his white and his colored life. They went together to soirées, they joined several hunting parties, and they fished. Narcisse was full of pride at being able to show off the splendor of the Cane River countryside. At Philomene's, Joseph dined on crawfish stew, pig's knuckles, and black-bottom pie, and he met Eugene and Nick, Emily's younger brothers. Joseph became a favored guest in Narcisse's circle, carrying his mandolin with him everywhere and winning over audiences with his music.

But on each of Narcisse's return visits down the Mississippi River to New Orleans, he confronted the march of

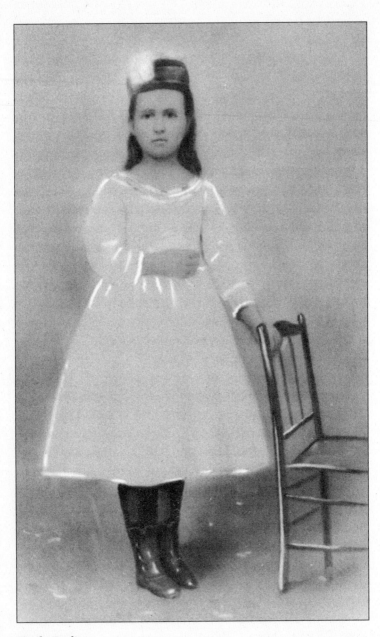

Emily Fredieu.

time. Emily was fast slipping past girlhood, more noticeable because he saw her with a fresh eye every few months. It started out as a small idea, on the porch of Philomene's cabin one evening as they talked of how much they missed Emily, but by the next day Narcisse had become determined to capture his daughter's image before she crossed over into womanhood. At his request, Joseph located a painter in New Orleans who did inexpensive oil portraits, and he secured permission from the sisters for Emily to leave the convent for the three required sittings at the artist's studio.

Emily wore her intended communion dress. Joseph's sister had sent a sketch of the current style to Cane River, along with yards of fluffy white organdy material, and Philomene spent two weeks sewing to match the picture. The dress was simple, emphasizing the quality of the material. Intricate lace decorated the scooped neck, matched by the same lace around the tips of the sleeves, and the bodice was unadorned. It was designed to fall from the cinched waist to the middle of Emily's calf.

The artist managed to capture Emily's bearing on his

Receipt for "Jerome Rachal" (Gerant)
from Narcisse Fredieu, 6¢ per hour.

canvas. She appeared both serene and lively, from her long exposed neck to her tiny boot-clad feet. Her left hand skimmed the bowed crown of a small straight-backed chair, and her right was held palm inward, primly, in front at her waist. Sandy light hair fell behind her ears and down her back in ringlets, and as Narcisse had requested, she wore her new cone-shaped hat plumed with an ostrich feather.

Narcisse was pleased with the portrait, as was Emily. He personally oversaw the packing for shipment and took the painting back with him to Cane River. Keeping the portrait near softened the ache of not having his daughter by his side.

After Emily's year of study at the convent ended and she took her first communion, Narcisse went down to New Orleans to collect her and bring her home. Another bad crop year had forced him to concede that his holdings were not going well. Something had to be done soon, something bold. Both the War Between the States and Reconstruction had taken their toll, and there appeared to be no way to restore his personal fortunes of earlier, better times. He had already sold some of his land to keep things going, but the buyers had the advantage, and he didn't have much more land to sell. The condition of his homeplace and even his farm animals was deteriorating alarmingly.

An opportunity finally presented itself that could turn his fortune in a positive direction, although Narcisse had to admit he had neither the financial wherewithal nor the appetite for personal labor required to make his scheme work. He needed a partner.

There was land to be gotten cheaply on the other side of Red River in Grant Parish, not far from his homeplace as the crow flew. It was thick with virgin pine trees that could be used for timber and turpentine and, after it was cleared, for farming. But the real advantage was its location. The land bordered huge expanses of protected government property, and for a man willing to take the risk, substantial money could be made. While the owner of the property cleared and cultivated the rightfully purchased land, he could poach the inexhaustible trees on the adjacent government land at the same time, sending them upriver to hidden sawmills. Narcisse knew he could easily find the labor. Plenty of freed men scratching out a living would be happy for the work and could be trusted not to share the details of their illegal doings. Philomene's brother, Gerant, had worked for him before on a smaller scale, for six cents an hour, and there were others who would do the same. The profit potential was enormous.

Joseph Billes would fit the bill perfectly. Joseph was anxious to put down roots in a French-speaking community, ambitious enough to bend as necessary, smart enough to keep the undertaking going, and willing to work hard to make the project successful, and he came with money in his pocket to fund the venture up front. And he knew how to have a good time in the bargain.

Narcisse sent a letter off to New Orleans, expecting an answer by return post.

Cane River, December 22nd, 1874

Dear Monsieur Joseph,

I hope this letter finds you well and preparing for the joy of the holidays. We expect to spend a traditional Christmas and New Year's here, and would welcome a visit from you if you are not otherwise engaged. Your mandolin would certainly be appreciated for the festivities, as would, of course, your splendid company.

There is another motive for this letter and invitation. We have talked in the past about your growing fondness for this beautiful country, away from the turmoil of New Orleans. I have an excellent proposal to discuss with you that could be of benefit to both of us. I dare not entrust it to a letter. This demands a frank discussion between two friends, and I am sure a man of your talents and ambitions will grasp the unlimited opportunity this partnership could bring. We need to act quickly, before others understand the possibilities. This could be the beginning of a solid partnership in addition to our friendship.

Say hello to your sister and your cousins for me.

Looking forward to hearing from you soon. Your committed friend.

Narcisse Fredieu

Christmas and New Year's came and went with no word, as Narcisse's creditors became increasingly impatient.

Finally, near the end of January, a posting came, not from New Orleans, but from Pointe Coupée. Narcisse recognized Joseph's neat hand on the envelope.

Point Coupée, January 27th, 1875

Dear Monsieur Narcisse,

I make haste to answer your letter, dated December 22nd, from last month. You will excuse me for not having written back sooner. I was gone into the countryside here with friends who had come to town. And they insisted very strongly that I come with them. I have therefore been working until now. And every Saturday, we played music at local dances. I am quite happy with the friends here. My uncle had your letter sent to me, by an opportunity, the other day. But since you are telling

Pointe Coupée le 27 Jeanvier 1875.

Cher Monsieur Narcisse
Et Ami.

Je m'empresse de vous faire répons, à
votre lettre daté de 22 Décembre de moi passé
Vous m'excuserez si je vous et pas plutot.
J'étais parti pour la campagne ici. avec des ami
qui sont venu En ville. Et il ont voulu que je monte
à toute force avec eux sa fait que j'ai travaillé jusqu'a
Présant. Et tous les Samedi nous feuisons de la musique
On feusait des bals. je me trouve très bien avec les amis
D'ici. Mon oncle ma fait parvenir votre lettre par une Occasion quel autre jour.
Mais puisque vous me dite que vous avez une excellante
Place pour moi Et que je vienne, je l'Accepte avec plaisir
Pour me rapprochez de vous. Comme je vous Et marqué dans
les lettres que je vous Et écrites. que j'annuie votre compagnie
Cher Ami Narcisse, Vous en verjé les preuves, je quitte tout
Pour venir auprès de vous. je prendré le Barthebel, pour
monté de Samedi En huit. Venir vous Donné une poigné
De main D'Amitié. A vous. ainsi que Madame Sophaisye
Et Mlle Litte Et le petit gaim. Et à tous les Amis.
Bien des Compliments pour moi à tout la femmille. pour moi Sans Oublié
tous les Amis.
Plus rien pour le présant. En attendant De vous revoir bientot
Je suis en vous quittant votre tout Dévoué Ami Pour la vie
Joseph Prilli

Joseph's letter to Narcisse, 1875.

me you have an excellent place for me, and that I should come,
I gladly accept in order to be closer to you. As I have noted in
letters I have written to you, I appreciate your company. Dear
Friend Narcisse, you will see the proof of it. I will take the
steamboat <u>Bart Able</u> on its way north from New Orleans to
come next Saturday to give you a friendly handshake, to you,
and also to Madame Philomene and to Mademoiselle Petite, and
to the little boys, and to all the friends. Nothing more for the
present.

    While waiting to see you soon, I am, as I take leave of
you, your fully devoted friend for life.

Joseph Billes

In less than two months Joseph moved part-time to Red
River and began to demonstrate that he had a gift of sweeping land and money to him like a broom.

29

I wonder what Monsieur Joseph will do with the land he bought over in Grant Parish?" Emily began at dinner one rainy afternoon in June. There was hardly space enough at the table in the common room to move without having to slide a chair forward or bump elbows with someone, but they gathered here every Sunday for family dinner. There seemed to be more family to squeeze into the cramped cabin every month.

"Unless he was the one to put the food on this table, we are not talking about Joseph Billes again today," Philomene said.

"A man, after just the one thing," Suzette mumbled, and quickly lowered her eyes.

Emily felt herself blush furiously, but it was to Nicolas that her grandmother Suzette sent an apologetic look when she lifted her head again. Since she had married and moved in with Nicolas Mulon, Suzette had become looser in her speech when the pair came to Sunday dinner. Nicolas gave Suzette an indulgent return look. An easygoing husband, he fit in well, and it had sealed the collective family opinion unanimously in his favor when he'd crafted each of them a pair of custom shoes from his cobbler's bench.

"The Frenchman is older than I am," Philomene said. "I have no intention of allowing any more child mothers in this family."

"Let the girl be," Elisabeth brokered, but then turned to Emily. "You might want to talk about something else until you have some fresh news. It has been almost two months since any of us even saw the man."

Emily had been overjoyed to come back home to Cane River. She hadn't really seen too much of the city of New Orleans, tucked away as she had been most of the time behind convent walls, and what she had seen had made her miss her home even more. Too many harsh sounds, vendors yelling along the street, people close together and in a hurry, not enough soil where things could grow. The other girls were nice enough, but it was temporary, and she had missed her own people more than she'd thought possible, even her younger brothers. But being delivered back safely into the arms of family meant she saw less of Joseph, and she could hardly bear it.

Emily had been intrigued with Joseph Billes from the moment he'd appeared alongside her father in the New Orleans convent parlor. He carried more of France than Louisiana in speech, outlook, and bearing, clearly a newcomer to a foreign land. His visits to the convent helped ease that lonely year in New Orleans, even though she knew his attentions were at her father's request, merely looking after a friend's daughter. He had a side-by-side shyness and self-confidence in his manner, and even though he was a white man, he conducted himself toward her with unaffected acceptance. Emily found it dizzying.

At the New Orleans convent Joseph had been polite yet playful, treating her in the affectionate but offhand way an adult treats a child. The first time he called her Mademoiselle Petite, his eyes danced. From his eyes to her heart. By the time she left the convent a year later, each breath she drew, every thought she held, took Joseph Billes into consideration. She was almost fourteen, a woman now. Joseph Billes just didn't realize it yet.

Emily's high spirits and optimism could turn in a moment to an irritable restlessness, and she seemed powerless to stop it. She lashed out at her younger brothers then, the way she would not dare with the old women. Emily could see how baffled her brothers were, no longer as eager to be around the moody, sullen girl. She was sulky when Joseph was gone away from Cane River and snappish when he returned but didn't come to visit. Sometimes she spilled over, stalking off, furious at how tightly everyone hung on to her. She got into the habit of taking long walks by herself, staying away for an hour or more with no explanation, and because she came back in a quieter mood, the household tolerated her disappearances. Emily was the first generation they could afford to pamper.

Most times Joseph came around to pay his respects to Philomene's family, he did so with Narcisse. Whenever he came alone, Emily was assigned chaperones. As if she could get Joseph to think of her in that way, Emily thought. She glowed in his presence and wasn't coy about showing her delight with his company. She wore only her best dresses, pinched her cheeks to redden them, and spent hours practicing in the mirror, piling sandy brown hair on top of her head in styles that made her look older. But someone—siblings, uncles, aunts, mother, grandmother, or great-grandmother—always had a vigilant eye out. If Emily retrieved her long-billed bonnet so she and Joseph could take a walk, Philomene or Elisabeth would call, "Eugene, Nick, go with them." Henry, the latest baby brother, was too small, or he would have been assigned to watch, too. It seemed that everyone except Joseph thought she was in danger of his advances.

On Emily's sixteenth birthday the old women invited Joseph and Narcisse to a celebration in her honor. Joseph had just returned from New Orleans, and in a particularly good mood. He brought all of them gifts, not just Emily. He gave Elisabeth a black-and-red fan that opened and closed with an impressive snap. For Suzette he brought a tatted lace handkerchief, so snowy white and fine that she kept it folded in her drawer, taking it out only to run her fingers gently over the fabric or stare at it in wonder. He presented four tins of high-quality snuff to Philomene. The boys got spurs, a slingshot, and a harmonica, according to age.

Joseph saved Emily's present for last, pulling a flat wrapped package out of his storage sack. He handed it to her without any of his usual joking. He simply said, "For you, mademoiselle." Emily felt him watching her, as did everyone else in the room. She happily unfolded the brown paper and lifted the top from the slim box. Inside was a pair of fine black lace gloves, not the usual peppermint candy he always brought. She knew it was a signal that she had grown up in his eyes at last.

From that day forward Joseph's visits to Philomene's house took on a different tone, and he came more often alone. Joseph seemed hard-pressed to pull his eyes away from Emily's dimples or the fluttering of her hands. In those early days of their start-and-stop courtship, Joseph spent half his time in New Orleans and half at the store he had opened in Grant Parish. Whenever he returned he came calling to Philomene's cabin, bringing fresh stories of a world beyond Cane River.

As far as her mother knew, Emily and Joseph were never alone. Philomene doubled her chaperone efforts when Joseph officially came calling, but Emily became especially clever at taking her alone walks, out of the sight of nosy younger brothers and prying women. A tangle of sparse woods dotted the path to a small abandoned cotton house a brisk twenty-minute walk from the cabin, and whenever they could arrange it, Emily slipped away to meet Joseph alone there. By then his pet name for her was Mademoiselle 'Tite. Their talking quickly gave way to touching.

Everything about Joseph, his wiry build and careless walk, the sharpness of his nose, the thick flow of his hair, thrilled Emily, but his ears were her weakness. Joseph told her once that he had gotten into fistfights as a boy in France, defending the size and shape of his ears, unwilling to take the teasing. They stood out from his face at an assertive angle, brash and uncompromising in the same way Joseph was. Emily liked to trace the bold sweep of those ears with the tip of her finger, making him laugh, and then he would follow the small arc of hers with his blunt hand, his hazel eyes and spare lips working together to produce a devilish smile.

Bringing that smile into being was Emily's yardstick of her own happiness. His thick mustache was like a waterfall, covering his top lip completely, and the stiff hairs prickled when they kissed. Joseph showed her the special comb he had purchased for his whiskers, an indulgence for such a frugal man. He spent more time combing, cutting, and shaping that mustache than he did the sandy hair he kept trimmed short on the top of his head. The rest of his face he kept clean-shaven. His cheeks were full for such a thin man, and because the underlying bone structure was high, a deep shadow played constantly between his ear and his mouth. An inner amusement crackled in his deep-set eyes, almost overshadowed by thick, wayward eyebrows that would have startled and overwhelmed his face had they not been muted by their sandy brown paleness.

Emily's skin was smoother and more fair than Joseph's, because she always took such care to cover herself against the danger of the darkening rays of the sun, and he was an outdoorsman. Her hair was as straight, her nose as thin, her penmanship hand straighter and stronger. Everyone told her she was beautiful, had been telling her that since before she could understand their words. They also told her she was better, meant for better things. But she was colored and Joseph was white, and to most those were the defining facts that mattered. In the cotton house there were no such discussions, no such limitations.

After the initial upheaval, those ancient women Emily came from took the news of her impending motherhood in stride. Their presence had cocooned her for as long as she could remember, and although their disappointment at the beginning stung, they helped her without blame in every way they knew how through the carrying and delivery. By the time little Angelite arrived, the baby was absorbed seamlessly into the cabin as if she belonged to all of them.

Each of the elders was eager to demonstrate her mother cures. When a wasp stung Angelite, Philomene applied tobacco juice and the swelling went down. When Suzette visited, she would hold the baby and rock for hours, using her finger to rub Angelite's gums, giving the little girl some relief from the violation of her emerging teeth. Once, as Emily helplessly watched Angelite struggle for air, her great-grandmother Elisabeth fried down a piece of mutton, added turpentine and salve to the suet, soaked a piece of flannel in the fat, and put the warm concoction on the baby's chest until her breathing eased. Occasionally the women disagreed among themselves about the most effective remedy for this cough or that fever, and Emily would just wait for the winning strategy to emerge. As if she had not helped to move four younger brothers from diapers to long pants, or had not taken care of the little sister who struggled to live in that first year of her life before giving up the fight.

It was comforting to have so much knowledge at her disposal, always an extra set of hands when needed, especially with Joseph gone so often.

Joseph still lived across the river in the back of his store, and Emily's place was on Philomene's farm, even after Angelite was born. She rose before dawn every morning, sometimes leaving the baby with Elisabeth, sometimes carrying Angelite with her for the day, and crossed the river to help Joseph. She felt daring, adventurous, venturing out beyond Cane River and across the Red River into an entirely different parish.

Emily carried herself above the side glances and the sly whispers. Insatiable tongues told stories about the Frenchman and the quadroon, endlessly cataloging what was wrong, what was unnatural, about the two of them being together. It wasn't the appearance of the child that sparked such heated interest from the people in the woods and in the town; it was Joseph's dogged insistence on including both Emily and Angelite in his talk, in his thinking, in his plans.

30

hese children are yours," Philomene said, the flushed skin of her face stretched taut and her eyes narrowed. Narcisse had reached a dangerous age, an age when men's thoughts turned to their own mortality, when they examined all they had managed to build in a lifetime of work and could feel only the urgency of where it would go when they were dead. By law he needed legitimate children to pass his inheritance to. If his children had been white, he could adopt them. If Philomene had been white, he could have married her. It was an impossible situation for a man obsessed with heirs. Philomene had seen his mind working the problem for some time, even as he supported and defended his colored family. "You may be getting yourself ready to walk on to something new, but that doesn't change you being the father."

Philomene and Narcisse sized each other up, like a pair

of old fighting cocks preparing to spar one last time. They were especially careful, either capable of drawing first blood, each searching for the best possible opening.

Philomene looked with uncompromising eyes at the man grown soft around the middle, deep lines etching his forehead. Getting ready to leave her after twenty years and seven children, two lost in infancy. Philomene had to give him due credit. He still kept himself clean and neat, and his beard was recently trimmed with a precision and patience reserved for the very rich or the very vain. The truth of the matter was that he had really left her the year before. They had just not spoken of it.

The power she exercised over him for years had diminished, until what they held between them now was mostly habit and old scars. And their children.

As soon as Philomene heard he was to have a child by Clemmie Larioux, she knew her time had run out, the spell broken. It hadn't taken long for the news to travel the byways of Cane River that Narcisse had gone back to white. Clemmie had been safely delivered of his white child, a girl. By all accounts Clemmie was poor white trash living in the piney woods hill country, probably another shadow union for Narcisse. Philomene was sure he would marry again, if he proved to himself he could produce a legitimate male heir by a more respectable woman.

It always seemed to come to this. No matter what happened early in their lives, whatever choices these Frenchmen made in their youth, in the end the need for a legitimate heir reasserted itself, all the stronger for being ignored. The need became as singular and focused as their original lust had been. There was no way around it. The best Philomene could hope to do now was protect her children from indifference and desertion.

Narcisse squared off. "I know they're my children," he said. "When have I ever turned my back? You've lived a good life from it, too. Both Emily and Eugene can read. I didn't have to do that. Nick, Henry, and Joseph will get their turn. Not one has ever gone hungry. They hold their heads up, dress better than most. You've lived in the same house for over ten years, your only task to raise them. I saw to that."

"My only task?" Philomene's tone was strained, but she kept her voice steady and didn't allow him to bait her. She had to think clearly. There was much more at stake than her pride. Her family depended on her to manage the situation. "You think I don't know you're ready to go?" she said. "That I don't know about Clemmie?"

"Mademoiselle Clemensieu to you," Narcisse snapped. "She's a white lady. You show her respect." He eased back immediately, seeming to think better of attack. "All these years gone, years with you saying I could only have children by you. I love each of my children, and I'll do right by them. I need an heir. It's time to take care of my line, get back to my own kind."

"You will do whatever pleases you," Philomene said. "But you still have these five children, and a grandchild. They are your line, too. Some of them barely out of short pants, some not walking yet. They have needs." She paused and her eyes narrowed, judging the timing. "And another on the way."

Narcisse hit her, a sudden blow to her face with his closed fist. She hadn't seen it coming. It happened so swiftly that Philomene registered the flat, hollow sound before the pain. She stayed where she was, staring at him, not even bringing hand to face to touch her swelling jaw. No more glimpsings could protect her now. They stood facing one another, both breathing hard.

"You'll say anything now to keep me from going," Narcisse said. "How do I know there really is another child? It won't change my plans."

Philomene stood erect, saying nothing, and a long moment passed.

Narcisse broke the silence first, a compromising quality to his softened tone. "I'll still give you something from time to time."

"Something and time to time are not what I'm looking for," Philomene said. "You have plenty of land, and we deserve some of it to build our own place. And a stake to get us started. A cow, a horse, and some chickens. We can work the place ourselves, while you move on to your legitimate heirs." She spat out the last as if it were blood collecting in her mouth.

In spite of the growing redness, she kept her face steady and unyielding, and she stared directly into Narcisse's eyes. He glared back at her, a look mixed with anger and contempt. This was her last stand with him. They both knew it.

"I'll give you whatever I have a mind to give you, and nothing more," Narcisse said. "You'd better keep a civil tongue. I don't know who you think you are, making demands, hanging on beyond your time. You think you can steal all of these years from me without consequence, making me believe I could never have white children, and then try to tell me what I have to do for you?" His face had turned a dark, mottled color, and there was an angry twitch to his mouth as he talked. "You think you are so high and mighty that you can make up anything else, and I'll believe what you say? I gave you a decent life. A slave, and I treated you better than you had any right to expect."

Philomene silently stood her ground. She knew this

man, and if anything could influence him, it would be the dawning acceptance that there would be another child. The last few months had not all been tight silences, absences, or arguments, especially after the death of their little Josephina.

"I should have known all along you didn't have the power to see into the future," Narcisse said. "All these years thinking you could find out about Bet through glimpsing, and you're as blind to that as anything else that hasn't happened yet."

"Bet?" Philomene's voice faltered. She had no idea where they were headed as the familiar direction of their confrontation lurched off course. Narcisse never talked about Bet and Thany, and she never talked about Clement. It was one of their wordless agreements. Her daughters had been dead for almost twenty years. She still sometimes went alone to visit the site where Bet and Thany had been buried in their single grave. A stunted willow tree grew over the lonely spot on what used to be Ferrier's farm.

"You hold yourself above other people with your glimpsings," Narcisse went on. "You tricked me, but the whole time you had no idea that your daughter was just a few miles away. You're not as clever as you think."

"What are you saying, Narcisse?" There was no bite left in Philomene's words, no strategy, no calculation, no demand.

Narcisse hesitated. "Bet is alive," he said. "She didn't die in the yellow fever epidemic. Thany couldn't recover after the fever, but Bet was stronger, and she fought harder."

Philomene backed away from Narcisse, one wobbly step and then two.

"Oreline had just taken sick and couldn't leave her bed. I was the only healthy one still able to move around on Ferrier's farm by then. A boy came from my plantation, just minutes after I watched Thany die. I had been gone for two days, and they sent him because they were worried. Bet was sick, but still fighting, so I sent her away with the boy to one of my farms downriver. There was a slave woman there, Aunt Sarah, a good nurse. I was so tired already, and I hadn't been able to save Thany. I thought she could look after the baby better than I could, while I stayed on with you and Oreline. It seemed the best course at the time."

Narcisse spoke in a monotone, as if the too long hoarding of the story had ground down all of the contours. "After a few days, Oreline was getting better. She only had a mild case, and even you were starting to come around a little, but it was clear you couldn't take care of a baby in your condition. You could barely lift your head. Even after your delirium passed, you were so weak that you didn't have any idea what was going on around you. I just left things the way they were, and said both babies had died. I'm not sure why. Oreline wasn't part of it."

Narcisse found his way to the moonlight chair and slumped into it.

"I thought it was better to wait and see whether Bet recovered before telling you any different. A family down on my place raised her as Elisabeth, without knowing any of this. She didn't move after freedom. She married a boy down there."

Philomene barely breathed. All she could think of was the terrible loneliness she had felt after the yellow fever, when she woke up to find everyone in her world gone, a loneliness so deep that she thought she would die from it. Even the attentions of Narcisse Fredieu seemed preferable to that. Bet, alive? She heard a raw, low guttural sound that seemed to have neither beginning nor end, but when she looked past Narcisse to find the source, she found it came from her. She couldn't stop.

Narcisse stared at her uncertainly. He looked as if he were waiting for something more. She had seen the expression before, whenever they talked of the glimpsings. Narcisse seemed almost contrite to Philomene, his face a curious mass of slits and folds and whiskers. He struck her as odd and ridiculous, and she started to laugh, great gulping laughs, so deep that she could hardly catch her breath. The longer she laughed, the more alarmed Narcisse looked, but he kept his distance across the room. At some point she couldn't remember why she was laughing, and she stopped. Silence hugged each corner of the room like a shroud.

"Philomene, listen to me. I have land near where Bet is living, down at the mouth of Cane River, near the Grant-Natchitoches Parish border. I've always intended to deed you that piece of land, and you can raise the children there. Bet will be just a few minutes away. It's not too late to get to know her."

Philomene didn't respond, pacing absently.

"Get out of my chair," she said finally.

"Philomene, let's talk."

She turned her back, unable to look at him. "Get out of my chair," she said again, to the wall.

She heard scraping noises that let her know he was standing. Philomene turned and crossed the room, passed in front of Narcisse but was careful not to touch him. She curled herself into her chair, pulling her knees into her chest.

Narcisse walked out of the room then. Through the open bedroom door she saw him stop to say something to Emily in the common room. Emily gathered the family to her as Narcisse disappeared, and they gave Philomene worried glances.

Philomene rocked, stroking the smooth arms of the moonlight chair under her fingertips, embraced by the chair that had cost Clement his life. She was dimly aware of Emily coaxing her to come to their bed, but Philomene couldn't leave the chair, not until she had a sense of what direction her life should take. At some point she dozed, and when her eyes opened again it was still dark outside. She was covered with a quilt someone must have put over her as she slept. Philomene thought of Emily, the daughter she knew so well, and now Bet, the daughter she had not been allowed to know at all. Half sisters.

Slowly in the night a plan began to take shape. Philomene beat back the temptation to let herself drift into the comfort of hating Narcisse. It would only get in the way, and she didn't have the time. She had to make sure she settled on the land he promised, quickly, and that it was legal. She would move and take her family with her. All of them.

By first light Philomene was ready to go find Bet.

Philomene saddled their horse and set off downriver with little Joseph, missing close to a day's work around the farm. She got back shortly before nightfall and called everyone into the kitchen, putting Joseph down in the crib. Her children gathered around her, Emily holding Angelite, and Eugene, Nick, and Henry.

When Philomene spoke, her voice was level. "You all have an older sister now. Soon we will move near her to a new place. Your sister's name is Bet. She's nineteen, older than Emily, and already married. Next Sunday she'll join us for dinner. You'll treat her like our own."

She ignored the bald look of surprise from her sons and the darting flash of something she couldn't quite identify that distorted Emily's features for a moment. Reproach, jealousy, anger?

Philomene's tone precluded questions.

After Narcease Fredieu had used up most of
her [Philomene's] life he bought much land
and moved Her and the children on it.
--Cousin Gurtie Fredieu, written family
  history, 1975

Each Sunday was set aside for family on the new place. Short of fever or flood, everyone was expected for Sunday dinner at Philomene's. There was no great distance to travel. By 1880 they all lived on her property.

Philomene asked them one by one to live with her. "One hundred and sixty-three acres, signed over legal," she told them.

"I always knew you had it in you," said Elisabeth.

"We need more room, with all these families and children. If you get the materials, I can build the houses," Gerant offered.

"Yellow John and I would like nothing better than to be a part of your family," said Doralise.

"Isaac is strong, and we can both help," said Bet in the quiet, generous way Philomene was coming to understand. "Anything to be close to you."

The houses and the land belonged to Philomene, but she took the third position behind Suzette and Elisabeth in Sunday's kitchen. Her grandmother presided over dinner preparations from her chair by the rough-hewn kitchen table, passing judgment on the dishes as they were being prepared. She gave advice on coaxing the lumps out of gravy, whipping the butter and sugar together to get the fluffiness for sweet-potato pie, and heating the grease exactly hot enough, the secret to frying the best chicken. No one dared say to Elisabeth that they considered themselves accomplished cooks, taught at her own knee.

At eighty-one Elisabeth conserved her movements, navigating slowly from chair to couch to bed after so many years spent standing. Her eyesight frequently failed her, especially for close work, and at night, no matter how bright Philomene turned the light up for her, Elisabeth had to give up her needlework. Even stitching quilts was more than her stiff fingers could manage. But she continued doing what she could and oversaw everything. She could still pluck a chicken clean by feel, and she gave counsel to her children, her grandchildren, and her great-grandchildren. From her central spot in the kitchen, Elisabeth was as much a part of Sunday dinners as the heaping bowls and platters of food that made their way to the table in the chipped and mismatched containers. Elisabeth always had her big wide-mouthed tin bowl near, handy for shelling peas or washing greens or a hundred other uses, and it was she who officially started Sunday dinner each week while everyone else went to early-morning Sunday mass. Elisabeth celebrated God in her own way.

If Elisabeth was the guiding mind in the kitchen, Suzette provided the hands. Philomene had finally gotten her mother to move in with her after the death of Nicolas Mulon in the late spring flood of 1880.

Suzette was Madame Mulon, and Philomene hoped she never saw herself through the eyes of some along Cane River who talked of her as if she had been a second-class keeper for someone else's children, now grown and on their own. Philomene had watched her mother make the long leap from no last name at all to Jackson and then Mulon. Suzette embraced Jackson, as if it could erase the indignities of the past and make her whole. After she and Nicolas married, she had been just as fervent about becoming Suzette Mulon.

Nicolas's people still looked down on Suzette. The old, deep ruts of class temporarily dislocated by emancipation reasserted themselves, but Nicolas had been clear in his choice. A more stable time would have rejected the match outright as crossing too many lines of color and class, but the years after the war were no such time, and the circumstances called for compromise. Philomene was grateful at how peaceful her mother seemed to be now, how sure she had been of Nicolas.

They gathered around the Sunday dinner table. Elisabeth, an old woman stooped and marked with life, had an active face, a participating face that made itself felt. She lived with Philomene in the main house, and they all took care of her in tribute to the way she had taken care of each of them, the oldest of the old generation. Next to her at the table were Doralise and Yellow John, beyond the age of parenthood but content in a quiet and comfortable marriage. Gerant and his wife, Melantine, lived in one of the outer houses, had five children already, and never came empty-handed, bringing a jar of preserves or a three-layer jelly cake as their offering. And Philomene's own children, ranging in age from twenty to not quite three: Emily with her own daughter, Angelite, and Eugene, Nick, Henry, and Joseph. And Bet.

Bet was a miracle, a piece of Clement. Philomene could see him in Bet's face, in the slope of her forehead, the way it swept out and up. Fresh faced at twenty-two, she was already married to a serious boy named Isaac Purnell. Bet was larger, darker, more accepting, and without Emily's fire or charm, but she also had a quiet gentleness that sought out only the best in everyone and put them at ease. Philomene regretted that Emily and Bet didn't get along better than they did, but she could recognize Emily's resentment at having to give up her cherished spot as the only daughter, her bewilderment at Bet's late-coming challenge. Philomene was just beginning to know the shy young woman who was her other daughter. Bet and Isaac lived with her in the main house.

Philomene was glad to sit. She was almost to term carrying her tenth child, including the one buried under the willow on Ferrier's farm and two buried at Marco cemetery. It wasn't difficult to see herself through her people's eyes, the huge swelling of her belly straining against the material of her dress, again, the tired circles under her eyes, the downward pull that time demanded of most of her body. Her face was even beginning to take on a roundness like Suzette's, a wild departure from the haughty look of the sharp-faced young woman she had been.

It felt like a time of triumph. Noisy chatter and full-throated laughter rang out at the big table. At the children's table there was so much youthful energy between her children and their cousins that she had to fix her eye on them to make sure they behaved.

Joseph Billes, Emily's Frenchman, had taken it upon himself to entertain, telling noisy stories at the dinner table. This was the serious occasion of his first Sunday dinner at Philomene's, and he was trying hard to be accepted, as if he fully understood the significance of the invitation. The women of the house debated for some time how best to handle the Frenchman who always went away and always came back to Emily and baby Angelite when he returned. Joseph and Emily were like magnets, a union not of convenience or opportunity, but of the most central necessity, a union that threatened such permanence that the household had to make special arrangements to accommodate it.

The familiarity of the scene teased at Philomene's mind as they passed the food around the table, filling up their plates. They were all here together: Elisabeth, Suzette, Doralise, Gerant, Emily, Bet.

Philomene leaned forward to take the large blue-banded bowl of creamed corn from Bet's hands when her fingers seized up with the sudden recognition. The bowl dropped, breaking into several large, jagged pieces, and too many smaller shards to count, the yellow juice leaking into the floorboards. As both Bet and Emily jumped to their feet to clean up the mess, Philomene laughed aloud.

Everyone around the table stared at her in surprise, but there was too much joy in the moment for her to try to contain her gladness. The final glimpsing had come to pass. The one that had brought hope to Elisabeth, Suzette, and herself when it seemed the world had taken a perverse personal interest in making sure that their family would be torn apart.

They were all together again, and there were seeds of new beginnings.

PART THREE

Emily

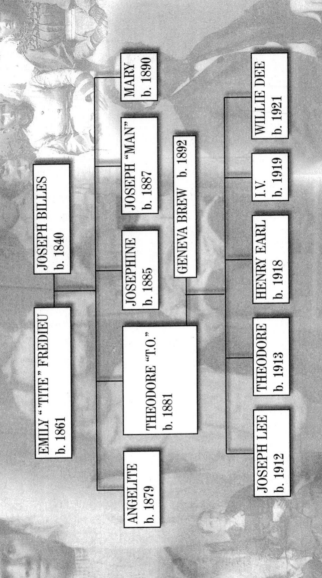

EMILY FREDIEU AND JOSEPH BILLES
Descendants

JOSEPH BILLES
b. 1840

EMILY "TITE" FREDIEU
b. 1861

MARY
b. 1890

JOSEPH "MAN"
b. 1887

JOSEPHINE
b. 1885

GENEVA BREW b. 1892

THEODORE "T.O."
b. 1881

ANGELITE
b. 1879

WILLIE DEE
b. 1921

I.V.
b. 1919

HENRY EARL
b. 1918

THEODORE
b. 1913

JOSEPH LEE
b. 1912

31

If Emily hadn't been so nervous about how Joseph would react to this thinly disguised Sunday appraisal, it would have been almost entertaining to watch her women swarm him without ever leaving their seats around the dining room table. They probed him with veiled eyes and unasked questions, all moving inexorably toward the same challenges. *Will you be good for our Emily? When will you get tired enough to pick up and leave? Will you take care of the children? How long?*

This Sunday dinner was an acknowledgment of the seriousness of their liaison, a public act as momentous as the arrival of Angelite. Today was Joseph's first official family function.

The new house near the meeting point of Cane River and Red River seemed to Emily to be shrinking, so many relatives had been taken in. With Joseph's frequent absences, the company was welcome, but the house, although much bigger than their old cabin, was already bursting at the seams, too small for so many generations of women. And it was difficult to watch her mother moon over Bet under the same roof.

Emily could see the snaking of each of their thoughts as they inched toward Joseph. Elisabeth had taken to him as soon as she saw how he held Angelite with fondness and protection. Suzette, always a changeling in the presence of white folks, was wary. She fussed and flitted, smiled wide enough to reveal the gap between her front teeth, and pressed food and drink on him, all the while listening over the noisy conversations of Sunday dinner for evidence of the timing of Joseph's inevitable departure from her granddaughter.

But it was her mother's opinion that worried Emily most. Philomene tolerated Joseph and was civil to a fault, but Emily knew her mother was waiting for Joseph to somehow prove himself further, this Sunday dinner invitation notwithstanding.

Emily was proud to bring Joseph into this den of women and young boys, a man of her own who was making something of himself. A man who came willingly into her mother's house and sat to table under the critical eye of three generations of women.

They fawned over Emily's chosen, but that didn't mean they were accepting, that they weren't watching for signs, unwilling to forget they had been property of the likes of him a dozen years before. Emily didn't remember the twisted life they hinted at, the slavery times, and each of the women hid the memory of those days as if there were shame in them, seldom talking particulars, at least when she was within earshot. They talked obliquely, as if it were an affliction she had escaped, a void of understanding that made her fortunate.

Emily and Joseph had no part of those long-ago days. Her only memory was of dancing for her father in the woods before he went off to war, with her mother looking on. Joseph had still been in France, undergoing his own struggle, trying to overcome the bitterness of being cheated of his inheritance by his older brothers, working his way toward the idea of opportunity in America. Neither of them was so tied to a past that they couldn't see a future stretched out before them like a twisting stream they could ford together. Joseph was full of infectious ideas of land and money, and when he was in a good mood, he talked to Emily for hours about his plans. He burned as hot with proving to his brothers back in France that he could acquire a fortune as he did for the company of Emily and their child.

It had taken six months after the baby was born for her wardens to finally invite Joseph to Sunday dinner, the time reserved for family. The table was full, piled high with food, every chair in the house pulled into the dining room to accommodate the guests. They were all here: Elisabeth, Suzette, Doralise and Yellow John, Gerant and Melantine, Bet and Isaac, and the small ones at the children's table. And Philomene, heavy with her tenth child, who would be uncle or aunt to Emily's little Angelite, although Angelite would be a year older. Broad and full around the middle, Philomene carried this baby low and was so big that she had to slowly ease herself into the chair at the dining room table.

Emily thought about how different she was from each of them sitting around Sunday's table, marveling that she could have come from them at all. The old ones had not shaken the submissive ways of their years as slaves. Even her mother was scarred, incapable of looking for the joy Emily intended to claim as her due. Her half sister, Bet, was more like them, tame and too easily content.

Suddenly a blue-banded bowl went crashing to the floor, spilling the creamed corn. Philomene stared around the table, looking in wonderment from face to face, as if the gummy yellow mixture had not splattered on her shoe or the sharp splintering of the bowl had not set Angelite to crying. Philomene settled her hands high across her stomach, fingers laced one over the other, and began to laugh.

"We got them this far," Philomene said, exchanging a satisfied look with Elisabeth and Suzette. "We can ease up just a little. My two girls can handle it now."

Side by side, light and dark, Emily joined Bet in cleaning up the mess.

32

Narcisse removed Emily's portrait from the wall opposite his bedroom door. The room was to be repainted a cool cream color before Liza moved in on Saturday.

He studied the picture as he had done so many times before. Emily stared back at him, chin tilted just so, the jaunty hat atop her head. He would give up the painting tomorrow, but it was still his to enjoy today. Her grace and dignity disarmed him as always, reached out to him, making him both sad and proud. He had protected her as best he could.

Narcisse had been without a wife for twelve years, drifting too long without a legitimate heir. Circumstances were no longer as rosy as they had been in the full bloom of his youth, back when he still counted upon the earth to deliver its bounty to him and fortune always smiled. The time had come to get his tangled affairs in order, to make right what had somehow gone so wrong. Within a few days he would marry again for the third time, and there were still the legal matters to finish off first.

So much time wasted, and misspent energy. How long ago could he have produced an heir if he hadn't been fooled? It had turned out to be the women's fault after all, not destiny, not some curse. Once the white children started coming, his manhood reasserted itself vigorously, building to a potency that produced five children in the last four years and another on the way. Whether they came from the former slave woman who had managed to twist his thinking for so many years, the hill woman who had broken the former's hold, or the respectable Natchitoches woman who was to become his wife, Narcisse loved each of his children. They were his own blood after all, but his dreams were fastened on Edd, the youngest, the son he would legitimize in just a few days.

Just yesterday he stood up in the courthouse to formally adopt his two daughters by Clemmie Larioux, and he would continue to care for them as he would his colored children. Of course, he couldn't adopt his children by Philomene, but they all carried his last name, even the two little ones dead in the ground. One had come out blue, a son, the cord wrapped around his neck, never taking a breath, and another, tiny Josephine, wasn't strong enough to reach her first birthday, but they were christened Fredieus just the same.

Ten years of barren wives, fifteen more tricked into believing he couldn't sire a white child, four more before he had the inescapable proof of a white son who could live. The evidence swept away the last of his superstitions planted by Philomene and allowed him with a clear heart to bring the mother of his heir into the light and make her his wife. His heir, Edd, named after his own father, Eduord. There was peace in knowing that when his life was done, his lands, everything he was, would pass to his son.

Narcisse planned to teach him to hunt, fish, farm, and dance, how to live life with gusto. He could carry him into town openly, starting him out early with a private tutor to open up the world of possibilities for the boy. Narcisse didn't hold to the notion the carpetbagger government pushed, that all children should attend a public school set up in the parish, regardless of their color, race, or previous condition of servitude, mixing indiscriminately. No good could come from that. It was wrongheaded to expect his taxes to pay for children he didn't know and had no responsibility for, whose own parents couldn't pay for their education. Everyone should take care of their own. He had engaged tutors for all of his children, white or colored. Those who couldn't afford to do similarly would have to fall by the wayside.

The wedding would be simple, small, with Joseph Billes as his best man and witness. Narcisse was very fond of Joseph, had been drawn to him from their first meeting in New Orleans almost a decade before, but he was beginning to pose a real dilemma. Already a few of the local men from town had come to him, speaking against Joseph. It was awkward, intercepting warnings about Emily and the man who was like a son.

Just a few weeks ago Narcisse had counseled Joseph about being so open about Emily. It wasn't the way things were done. Joseph listened politely, leaned forward, spat out his tobacco, and changed the subject. It wasn't that Narcisse didn't understand. He had gone down a similar path not so many years before. The difference was that Narcisse had the good sense to know how far he could go. Joseph flaunted.

Emily was as precious to Narcisse as his right arm, but his daughter was as headstrong in her own way as Joseph. She would be forgiven some things as Narcisse Fredieu's daughter, but she would never be forgiven forgetting her place.

At the end of the week Narcisse would marry. It was time to put certain things behind him. When his wife-to-be told him pointedly that the portrait made her uncomfortable, he knew what he had to do. She knew about his past, all of the wives, all of the children, many of the alliances, but there was no need to exhibit them.

Tomorrow he would give the painting to Emily. He hated to part with it after all this time, but a new chapter in his life was beginning.

33

Behind Billes General Store in Aloha, Emily heard the sharp, shrill whistle of the steamboat *Danube* in its steady advance upriver, announcing its intended stop at Billes Landing to deliver supplies. One long, two short, and another long. Rivulets of sweat ran down her face from the steady fire under the kettle, and when she wiped at her eyes, stubborn bits of lukewarm wax still clung to her hands from her candle making. She had hoped for the warm, rich signal of the *Bart Able,* whose captain, like the full-throated whistle of his steamboat, seemed much more respectful toward her. Although Joseph had told both Captain Montgomery of the *Danube* and Captain Meecham of the *Bart Able* that Emily acted on his behalf for deliveries, this captain did everything he could to put Emily in her place. He looked her up and down as if she were his for the taking whenever Joseph wasn't there, or spat in her direction and refused to allow his stevedores to load supplies into her wagon, even when she waited on the dock.

She locked up the store, hitched the horse to the wagon, loaded her basket of boiled eggs, and got down to the landing just in time to watch the broad stern of the steamboat pull away from the Billes Landing dock. The need to hurry gone, she eased her grip on the reins and slowed the horse's pace. They had already unloaded the delivery and moved on. The sharp, rich odor from the sacks of coffee reached her even before she got down from the wagon, mixed in with the sweetness of the oranges in their wooden crates. Sacks of cotton seed, two barrels of flour, two of beer, and several of sugar also lay heaped on the pier.

The captain, well aware that the steamboat's passing was an opportunity for her to sell her eggs for five cents a dozen to the passengers and crew aboard, hadn't waited for her, again. Captain Meecham would have waited.

The two cords of oak wood her uncle Gerant left were gone, and the landing was messy with the hasty leavings of the pine knots and pine kindling the stevedores loaded for use under their boilers. Joseph had a contract with the steamship line to leave timber for them weekly, and he employed Gerant to cut it. The landing needed sweeping after she got the supplies to the store. Yet another task added to the day.

There had been a time when Emily found each steamboat's unique whistle romantic, an intimate invitation from some mysterious place. Lately they all just signaled more backbreaking work, and she found herself relieved whenever she heard the one long blast that meant there was no delivery today, that the ship was just passing through.

Joseph was due back in town tomorrow, Saturday afternoon, and on Sunday she looked forward to him crossing the river for dinner at her mother's. Emily pulled on her heavy gloves, retied the fastening on her long-billed bonnet, and adjusted the sleeves of her shirtwaist so the sun couldn't get to her skin. Gerant was off working somewhere in the woods this week, and the other hired man was running errands, so it was up to her to get the provisions from the landing to the store. At least this was a small shipment. The sacks weighed almost as much as Emily, but she pulled and tugged, inching the bags forward bit by bit until she got each into a position where she could pull it up into the bed of the wagon. No matter how she maneuvered, she couldn't lift the barrels, and she dared not leave them on the landing for too long. She would have to take the wagon home and come back on foot for the barrels, turning them on their side and rolling them the mile to the store, pushing them up the gentle rolls of the forest bottom, and making sure they didn't gather too much speed on the declines. Her back ached just thinking about it.

Most days the full burden of the store fell to her. She and Joseph had built up their merchandise until it included almost anything a family needed that they couldn't make or grow for themselves. They kept a regular stock of staples, brown and white sugar, flour, salt, coffee beans, vanilla beans, cream of tartar, and the like, but they often laid in raisins on the stems, figs, and dates. The local women chose from the bolt of gingham and two of calico for making their shirts and dresses, cottonade for bedsheets, and lowells for cotton sacks. The assortment of ribbons, buttons, thread, needles, scissors, sunhats, stockings, and shoes was small, but so was the town. They even carried a few pots and skillets, smoothing irons, stovepipes, ax handles, and axle grease. The section nearest the front of the store was for medicine, castor oil, calomel, quinine, liniment, snake oil, iodine, and laudanum. Peppermint and licorice in sticks or blocks were favorites, but by far the biggest sellers were the whiskey and chewing tobacco Emily kept behind the counter. Most of her day was spent in the store, checking the shelves, stocking and restocking, waiting on customers, writing down deliveries and purchases in the big book. Cash was preferred, but usually they tallied their neighbors' purchases as credit until the crops were in and sold and they could afford to settle up their bills.

For months after little T.O. was born, the store suffered. There were many days Emily couldn't break free to cross the river, and if Joseph was gone, the store stayed closed, supplies sometimes disappearing from the dock. When Joseph handled the store alone, his memory never failed about who bought what, but Emily often found that he had not written down the transaction, and she would have to double back and reconstruct the lost day. Now that Angelite and T.O. were older, she could leave them with the Grands or bring them with her during the day, but Emily still dreaded the deliveries if she was alone. She could barely straighten up after rolling the barrels. Her hundred pounds were no match for a barrel filled with flour.

But she didn't complain.

*   *   *

"We need to talk about Emily."

Philomene spoke directly to Joseph, her face arranged into its most severe expression, and although she never raised her voice, everyone in the dining room grew silent.

"Go on, then, Madame," Joseph said. He stroked the stiff hairs of his mustache between forefinger and thumb in an absent gesture Emily knew well. The Sunday dinner had been heavy, and he had overeaten.

"You're going to suck the life right out of her, loading her up with babies and still expecting her to run the store," Philomene said.

Emily was horrified. She tried to catch Joseph's eye to let him know she had nothing to do with her mother's outrageous behavior, but Joseph and Philomene were locked in to one another as if they were the only ones in the room.

"Emily would follow you to the bottom of the swamp if you led her there," Philomene went on. "Since she doesn't have good sense when it comes to pleasing you, you need to be the one to look after her, better than you've been doing. Are you paying any attention to how run-down she's gotten, or are your eyes only for that store of yours?"

Emily reached out for Joseph's arm to give him a reassuring touch, but he had already pushed away from the table, storming out of the house without a word. She ran after him into the full heat of the day. Emily caught up to him as he put boot to stirrup and swung up onto his horse. The bright sun blazed yellow orange from behind his head, and she had to use her hand to shield her eyes as she looked up at him.

"You know how my mother is, Joseph," Emily said quickly. "I'm just tired with the children, that's all. I want to help out."

He scanned her face, and she knew he took notice then of what they had all been telling her, the dark circles that had become a permanent fixture under her eyes, the edgy exhaustion in her voice.

"Don't come to the store tomorrow," Joseph said. "I can work something else out."

"Are you coming back?" Emily's voice was small.

"She's right, 'Tite," Joseph said. "Don't tell her I said so. We have to do this another way." His voice softened. "Of course I'll be back."

*   *   *

Joseph began to clear a spot on his land to build a new house a mile inland from Billes Landing on Red River. Within a few weeks he had raised the barn and moved into it until the house could be finished. Emily prepared his old room behind the store for the arrival of his relatives from New Orleans.

"These are my people, 'Tite, to help you in the store," Joseph said. Emily knew that for them to refuse him would have been difficult; they still owed him their passage money from France.

Within six weeks of Philomene's scolding, the cousins arrived in Aloha, five of them in all. Joseph's young cousin and her husband, both in their twenties, slightly older than Emily, with their three small children.

The arrangement did not go well from the start. Joseph set his cousin and her husband to work alongside Emily, and even so there were tasks that went undone every day. The cousins complained bitterly about the isolation, the tightness of their living quarters, Joseph's stinginess, the heat, the inadequate help, Joseph's absences, and the monotony of country life. Their children were constantly underfoot. It was true that Emily no longer had to cross the river so early to open up the store, but if Joseph was not present, the cousins would follow neither her suggestions nor her requests.

Over the weeks, and then months, an uneasy truce developed between Emily and the cousins, a truce that held only because they treated her as if she were their servant, no different from Joseph's other hired hands. Even the little cousins came to the practice.

"My mama says fetch me lunch," the youngest girl would say, and not wanting to upset the order of things, Emily did, but she stopped bringing her own children to the other side of the river each day. T.O. was too young to know the difference, but she didn't want Angelite to see how they treated her. As time went on, Emily began to make excuses for why she couldn't go in to the store at all. She squeezed an extra day or two to stay away if the baby fell sick, or the water had risen too high to cross safely, or Elisabeth needed tending. Anything to avoid the cousins.

When the house on Billes Landing was finally finished, the cousins claimed two of the rooms in the new house as their own, relieved and pleased to be able to spread out. For a time everyone was in a better humor, and even the tension in the store eased.

"At least we will be able to entertain again," said the cousin.

Joseph came hat in hand to Philomene's farm. Late rains had resulted in extraordinary fruit harvests, and the kitchen reeked with the rummy odor of the overripe mayhews the women boiled down into preserves for the season. Joseph paid his respects to all of them, Elisabeth, Suzette, Bet, Emily, but it was to Philomene that he eventually turned.

"This concerns Emily." Joseph used the same serious voice as when he conducted his business.

Emily stayed seated at the kitchen table with her head down, as if she were studying the glass jar that threatened to shake out of her trembling grip.

"Madame Philomene, you suggested that I was not taking proper care of Emily," Joseph said. His thin lips were taut, and his deep-set eyes had turned dark. It was a look Emily recognized, a look that said he had thought the matter through, had made a decision, and would not be denied. "I am requesting that she and the children move with me into my new house on Billes Landing. There are no other claims for my affection, and as you know, I have the means."

"There will be trouble," Philomene said without hesitation. "It is dangerous for Emily to be caught in the middle."

"I have friends in Aloha," Joseph said. "Most owe their livelihood to me, one way or the other. We'll see to it she is all right. Monsieur Narcisse will help."

"The girl is better off here, with you gone so often," Philomene said.

"They belong with me," Joseph said.

Emily stole a look at Joseph's face in the long, quiet moment that passed. The uncompromising set of his jaw matched her mother's own.

Philomene appraised Joseph carefully before she spoke again. "She was raised quality. Emily can go with you if that's her mind, but we'll be watching." As if an afterthought, she said, "There is something to be said for a father who wants to take care of his woman and his children."

The tautness in the muscles of Joseph's face relaxed. "That's done, then," he said. "There is one thing more. If you could bring yourself to part with the oil painting, I would like to hang it in the new house. I propose an exchange. The painting for the new potbellied stove I just got into the store."

Philomene leaned back into her chair and took a moment to consider. "Her papa gave that painting to Emily.

It's hers to take where she pleases. Looks like she settled on you, and you on her. No one is going to make it easy for the two of you, but it won't be me blocking your path, as long as you treat her decent."

"I will," Joseph said.

Philomene checked the consistency of the simmering fruit in the kettle. "We need to get back to the canning."

"I'd like Emily to go for a walk with me," Joseph said to Philomene, and she nodded.

Emily followed Joseph outside, and as they walked he put his arm around her waist. "Now you're free to move to Billes Landing," he said.

Emily hesitated. "Your cousins won't like it, Joseph."

"The cousins live in my house, not the other way around. That's my responsibility to handle them. I want you there, 'Tite. The house will be ours. We'll put your picture in the front room over the fireplace for everyone to see. We have nothing to hide."

"My people are all here."

"And they'll still be right across the river. You can come back to visit anytime."

"I'm afraid."

"A woman's place is with her man," Joseph said.

Emily agreed then, quietly.

"Emily and the children will be moving into the house in a few weeks," Joseph announced to his cousin and her husband as they closed up the store the next evening.

The cousin's face grew flushed, shock mixing with outrage. "How could you think to bring such shame into your house?" Her mouth twisted to show her contempt. "It is pure evil."

"You betray your race, cousin," her husband said. "She has put some spell on you. We hear of such things with those people down in New Orleans."

Unblinking, barely breathing, Emily waited for Joseph's response.

"Enough," Joseph said, holding up his hand, his thin nostrils flaring. "You will not talk to me like that in my own house. It's natural for me to want Emily and the children near, and that is the way of it. There need be no further discussion."

From that moment the cousins whispered among themselves and did as little as they could in the store. Debt or no debt, they packed themselves up and moved back to New Orleans within the week rather than continue to live side by side with evil.

Joseph arrived early to Philomene's farm and loaded up the wagon with Emily's belongings for the long overland trip to the other side of the river. Philomene came outside to say her good-byes, fussing over the children in the wagon.

"Replant the rosebush as soon as you get to the other side," she said to Emily, checking the tightly drawn rope that anchored the burlapped rootball of one of her best bushes to the wagon. "Dig the hole wide and deep. It will take some care and patience, but you can get it blooming again."

"Yes, *Maman*." Emily felt Joseph's unease beside her on the buckboard, as if something remained undone, when normally he would be anxious to get under way.

Joseph coughed into his hand, and Emily held her breath. "I do have eyes for other than the store," he announced to Philomene. "I understand my responsibilities, and intend to protect Emily. Angelite and T.O. are dearer to me than my own life."

Philomene flicked the back of her hand twice, as if shooing chickens away, but she nodded in acknowledgment. Joseph tipped his hat to Philomene, then snapped the reins for the horse.

*   *   *

Joseph accumulated more land beyond the Natchitoches Parish borders. Common wisdom held that the land was too thick with trees, the farming inferior to that of Cane River's rich bottomlands. Emily did not know exactly where the money came from, but he bought a parcel here and a foreclosure there, always in cash. First sixty or one hundred acres at a time, and then two to three hundred. Joseph managed to follow behind other people's financial failures and profit. He worked hard and spent little, and he expected Emily to do the same, and for many years they lived a life they both understood. They hired a man to help with the store even though it was an added expense. Without the cousins underfoot, the work itself lost its sourness, and except for Joseph's absences, Emily considered herself happy.

With the cousins gone and Joseph so often away, Emily had a house bigger than her mother's almost to herself. It felt empty in comparison, and late at night after the children were asleep, she roamed the rooms in awe of the stillness she would find in unoccupied corners. Her brothers got in the habit of riding out to check on her often, especially when Joseph was out of town, and she packed up the children and went back across the river every Sunday for the dinners at Philomene's, appreciating the adult contact.

When she couldn't sleep, in the pause when demands were gathering their strength for tomorrow's chores, when fugitive thought threatened to rob her of her sense of herself, Emily would slip out of bed, light the lamp, and go to the front room. She considered the girl in the painting over the fireplace, remembering the confidence that allowed her to gaze not back or down or up, but straight ahead to a future she believed was waiting for her. Joseph had picked out the spot for the painting and hung it himself, in a place of honor. It reminded her that this was her house, too.

Bet stepped tentatively through the entrance of Billes General Store, holding the door ajar. "You sounded a little melancholy last Sunday, and *Mère* Philomene thought you might want some company." She nodded toward Isaac in the wagon outside, the reins still loose in his hands. "She sent Isaac to tend to patching the chicken coop while Joseph is away."

Bet's brown-skinned face glistened in the heat, drops of sweat sliding down her cheek from hairline to chin, and she took off her small brown hat to fan herself with it. Her hands were rough and chapped from taking in other people's washing. Emily was glad of company, even Bet's.

Emily made a quick decision. "It's such a slow morning, and so hot, I think I'll close up the store for a few hours. We can go up to the house. It will be a pleasure to visit." She gathered up Angelite and T.O. and locked the door behind her, and Isaac drove them the short trip to the house on Billes Landing.

After gathering his tools from the wagon, Isaac set off in the direction of the chicken coop, Angelite and T.O. trailing behind to watch. Bet and Emily were left alone.

Emily made small talk, leading Bet through the front room and back to the kitchen. "You've never been to the house before."

"You never asked me to come," said Bet, quiet as always.

Emily put the water on to boil and ground beans for coffee. Although they sat in the kitchen, she passed over the everyday mugs and brought out the good cups to serve the coffee, pleased to be able to show them off.

Bet looked around the room, at everything in its proper place. "You have so many nice things." She sipped the chicory-laced coffee. "These are pretty little cups. So dainty."

"Monsieur Narcisse gave us the entire coffee service," Emily said.

Bet paused midsip and deliberately replaced the cup in the raised hollow of the saucer.

"I am sorry," said Emily. "I know you have no fondness for Monsieur Narcisse."

Bet's soft voice was firm. "He stole both my mother and my father from me. Maybe he sent you to New Orleans to learn fancy ways and fancy talk, but he kept me from my own people."

Emily didn't know what to say. Bet stared down at her hands, as if she were surprised at her own words. "How is *Maman?*" Emily said at last.

Bet relaxed a little. "*Mère* Philomene still misses you under her roof, after all this time and you coming every Sunday."

Curiosity overcame Emily's good manners. "Why don't you call her *Maman?*" she asked.

Bet looked ill at ease. "I came so late to the family, *Mère* Philomene seems to suit us better."

There was an awkward silence. Emily rose and arranged tea cakes on a plate, setting them in the center of the table between them, then sat back down. "I was jealous of you, in the beginning," Emily said.

"I know."

Another moment of stillness passed.

"*Mère* Suzette would be pleased to see your roses bloom scarlet here," Bet said. "Bad luck follows yellow roses, but red brings good."

Emily laughed. "Who told you that?"

Bet did not join in the laughter. "*Mère* Suzette believes in the color of roses, the same way *Mère* Philomene's lucky fruit is persimmon and *Mère* Elisabeth buries a hair from a horse's tail beside the front door each April to protect the house and honor Gerasíme."

"They never told me those things," said Emily.

"They don't tell me," said Bet. "I listen hard."

Emily became serious again. "Sometimes, the way you sit with *Maman* and the Grands, sewing or shelling, plucking or picking, or just quiet, I envy you. I need to move, dance, ride my horse, not sit still. You seem more able to be like one of them."

Bet thought this over, took her time. "We understand one another, *Mère* Philomene, the Grands, and me."

"I grew up a little scared of the Grands," Emily confided. "Especially *Mémère* Elisabeth."

"But they spoiled you, all of them, gave you everything they could."

"You think I don't know what people say, how they talk about me?" Emily said. "The quadroon, the uppity one, the temptress, the one who doesn't know her place."

"Not your family."

"No, not the family."

Bet picked up her coffee cup again, shyness creeping back into the features of her face. "You must be lonely when Joseph is gone. I could no more bear Isaac going off and leaving me alone for weeks at a time than he would think to pick up and go. We like things steady, him and me."

Emily searched for signs that Bet was trying to mock her but found none. Her brother Eugene suddenly came to her mind. He had left Cane River for Texas the previous spring, determined to pass for white, maybe lost to them forever. She thought of being separated from her people by the river, and of Joseph's frequent absences.

"I do get lonely," she admitted. "Joseph used to be more interested in the store, but now I am the one to keep it going, managing this big house, raising the children. People expect too much, and I am by myself."

"By yourself?" Bet drew her cheeks in tight as if to stop herself from speaking, then released the air in a measured breath. "You grew up knowing a mother and a father. You can read and write. A man with influence takes care of you. One word from you, and they drop everything on the other side of the river and come running, send all of us running. How can you call that by yourself?" The faint edge in Bet's voice dissolved. "I used to wake up every day wondering who my mother and father were, whether they were sold or dead, looking into every face to find a likeness."

"I am sorry, Bet."

"No. Don't be sorry. *Mère* Philomene searching me out was the best thing that ever happened to me. That and Isaac. There is no place I'd rather be than with them."

"It is just that none of this is mine. Not the store, not the house. If anything happened to Joseph, I would have nothing."

"We have the Grands and *Mère* Philomene," Bet said. "Look to our mother. She says there are always choices. If you want something enough, you keep working toward it." She looked around the kitchen again, and Emily saw her take in the polished table, the store-bought stove, the indoor plants placed perfectly in their bright ceramic pots. "There's no telling what important things Monsieur Joseph would be willing to do for you if you asked."

Emily stopped to reconsider her half sister. Maybe Bet had fire after all.

34

On the front gallery of Philomene's house, Elisabeth's great-great-grandchildren whipped small piles of cotton with peach tree switches.

"You've beat it enough," she said hoarsely. "Bring it here. It should be plenty fluffy by now."

Angelite and T.O. threw down their sticks and scooped up the cotton, carefully carrying the fleecy mounds over to where Elisabeth supervised the others in the making of the patchwork quilt. The circle of women took the cotton and pressed it between layers of material, stitching the insulation inside.

Working the quilt gave Elisabeth time to think in the way she liked best. She could let the thoughts take shape and reveal themselves in between the steady progress of the stitches, even as she brought forward the creation of a new thing. She would gather together slighted and separate scraps, forgotten leavings from some other project, and piece them together, using tricks of eye or material or craft to form a handsome design that held at the center and became more than any of the fragments. Her fingers could barely hold a needle, and her eyes were no longer keen with patterns, but the young ones asked her advice every so often, and most times they seemed sincere.

She was almost through with this life, having put in over eighty-five years, weathering all the changes that came her way, good and bad. Tossed about from here to there, and still she kept going, waiting for the spider to come home. There had been two things that sustained her along the way and made the letting go bearable. One was her God, and the other was her family.

Five years before, her family pride had blossomed to bursting. Getting up after her afternoon nap, she'd known by the hush to the house that everyone else was gone, taken with chores or off playing. She had the house to herself. She had just set the coffee to drip when the dogs set up a racket outside. Even with her dimmed eyesight she could make out the caller coming up the front steps as one of the Prud-homme boys, grown up. She knew their family well, had done some washing and ironing for them years back. The children had all come out dark haired and oversize, awk-ward but powerful, built for the backcountry. They all had that same ruddy look to their face, boys and girls alike.

She shouted at the dogs to cut the racket and answered the knock on the door. He introduced himself, backwoods courteous, and asked her to come out to answer a few ques-tions, but at that time of day it was cooler in the house than in the oven of the Louisiana summer. Elisabeth knew that she had to get off her feet soon before they swelled up and invited him inside instead, offering him fresh-brewed coffee. She put a few tea cakes on one of their good plates and brought the coffee out in the cups with the bird patterns, all the while studying the man sitting in her granddaughter's front room. He seemed a pleasant enough white man, unlikely to do immediate harm, although with his red leather-bound recording book and pen, he came ready to poke into their business as though it belonged to him and he had a right to it. For the government, he said, for the 1880 census.

She could tell he was playing it over in his mind whether she could be trusted to recall each member of the household. That was foolishness. Of all of the ways that time had reduced her, remembering family and who belonged where and when and to whom remained firm.

She was living with her granddaughter Philomene then, same as now, the girl whose visions dried up in her when she forced them to come true. Back then they all lived on Philomene's land. Her daughter Suzette, Bet and her family, her son Yellow John and Doralise, Emily and baby Angelite. That was before T.O. was born, before Emily moved off to the other side of the river to live with the Frenchman, and when they still took Sunday dinner together every week, no excuses. They were more scattered now.

The first thing the census man wanted to know was who headed the household. That was easy. It was Philomene. Elisabeth kept repeating "Philomene Daurat" slow and clear for the census man, because he was an English speaker. He kept asking her to say the name until they both got tired. She told him she couldn't help him out on the spelling of the names, he had to puzzle that out for himself. They didn't get to reading, writing, and spelling until Emily.

The census man finally scratched something down in the book. Elisabeth wasn't sure whether he got it right or not, but they went on. He didn't have so much trouble with any of the other names that came after, or he didn't want to take so much time on them, she didn't know which. He asked about each person who lived in the house and what their relationship was to Philomene. He didn't seem interested in what they were good at doing or what kind of people they were, so she didn't offer. He only wanted to know what they did to make ends meet, farmer, laborer, or housekeeper, like that. She gave names and ages, as best she knew. He even asked where each was born and where their mothers and fathers were born. When he asked about marital status, married or single, that really wasn't any of his business. If the father of the children was living, she said married, and if he was dead, she said widowed. That satisfied him, and it satisfied her.

She answered all the questions the census man asked, and he recorded her answers, and then he got up, thanked her for the tea cakes, and went away down the road to the next house. She watched the dogs sniff after him as they followed him partway down the road, more forgiving because he was on his way off their property.

Elisabeth did some hard thinking for the rest of the afternoon, into the time when the house filled again for three o'clock coffee and throughout preparation for supper. She deliberated on the census taker's visit into the next day, but still the troublesome notion refused to declare itself. It was not until the full family had gathered in all of its breadth that Sunday that she finally could see what had been in front of her all along.

Five generations under one roof, all women, in an

unbroken sequence, starting with her and descending down to Angelite. From coffee, to cocoa, to cream, to milk, to lily. A conscious and not-so-conscious bleaching of the line.

Each held a place of honor in her mind, no one any better than the other or less valuable in the inevitable formation of the chain. Where would any of them be without Philomene's determined and clever ways, her clarity, her austerity, her singular focus? Where would Philomene be if not for Suzette's way of bending in a storm, her ability to pull into herself that brought her safely to the dawning of another day to begin again? Could Emily be the joyous one, petted and adored, refusing to allow sadness around her, taking the step beyond survival, without the halo of the others as both a beacon and a shield? They were handing down the birthright, one after the other. Her birthright.

Back then, on the Sunday of Elisabeth's insight, there had been only the one great-granddaughter. Now Emily had a boy-child, too. Theodore was his christening name, but he was known as T.O., a quiet and watchful boy with a quenchless thirst for all things family. Elisabeth felt a special relationship with him that crossed generations, the way it sometimes happened. Physically he took after his father, not just about the ears, which made the connection so easy to spot. T.O. had the same nervous air, the same tendency to withdraw and pull away from the crowd when things became difficult. He was a center of attention among the women in Philomene's house. They cherished him for his maleness, even at the tender age of four, as if he were a precious creature delivered to them from some other sensibility, some other place. He seemed to always be right up under one of them, silent, eyes darting, drinking in the stability, breathing in the attachment.

It heartened Elisabeth to see how generous Joseph was
with Emily and his children, in material matters and affection. He doted on all of them, his little family, indulging and
coddling them. Angelite had stolen his heart, Theodore had
turned his thoughts to legacy, and now Emily was carrying
their third child. Elisabeth knew they played with fire. She
was no stranger to a white father taking pride in his side
family; she had seen just about everything in her time. But
Joseph refused to pretend that Emily and the children were
on the side, publicly declaring them the only family he
intended. Flaunting the forbidden invited danger, and Emily
was just as headstrong as Joseph in her circumspect way.

There were two years between T.O. and Angelite. The
two children weren't allowed to play with others outside of
the family, and they had to find ways to amuse themselves. As
the oldest, Angelite took the lead. Elisabeth watched them
with worry and amusement both. Theodore followed
Angelite around, trying to imitate whatever she did, sticking
as close as he could before she shooed him away.

There had been the time of being worked and sold, like
an ox, with nothing to hold on to except each other over
increasing distances. They bided their time and collected
themselves back together again as they were able, from up
and down Cane River and as far away as Virginia, because in
family there was strength that couldn't be drawn from anywhere else.

When the census taker looked at them, he saw colored
first, asking questions like single or married, trying to intro-
duce shame where there was none. He took what he saw and
foolishly put those things down on a list for others to study.
Could he even understand the pride in being able to say that
Emily could read and write? They could ask whatever they

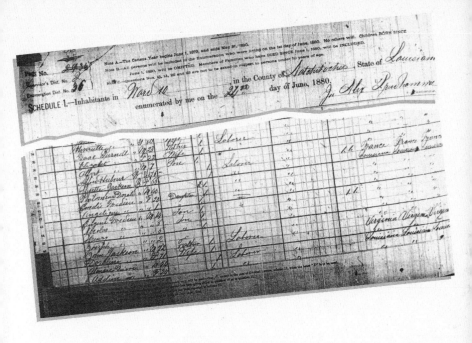

1880 Federal Population Schedule
Natchitoches Parish, Louisiana

p.691-A (s.d.2, e.d.36, p.35)
Ward 10, 23 June

Isaac Purnell	B	M	23	father	married	laborer	LA	LA	LA
Elizabeth	B	F	22	wife	married	laborer	LA	LA	LA
Albert	B	M	7	son	single		LA	LA	LA
Alfred Hubner	W	M	76	—	widowed	laborer	FR	FR	FR
Suzette Jackson	B	F	66		widowed	laborer	LA	LA	LA
Philomene Dorald	B	F	40		married	laborer	LA	LA	LA
Emelie Fredieu	B	F	20	dtr		laborer	LA	LA	LA
Angelique	B	F	1	dtr	single		LA	LA	LA
Eugene Fredieu	B	M	14	son	single	laborer	LA	LA	LA
Nicolas	B	M	8	son	single		LA	LA	LA
Henry	B	M	5	son	single		LA	LA	LA
Joseph	B	M	2	son	single		LA	LA	LA
John Jackson	B	M	72	father	married	laborer	VA	VA	VA
Doralise	B	F	71	wife	married		LA	LA	LA

1880 Natchitoches, Louisiana, Federal Census.

wanted, but what he should have been marking in the book was family, and landholder, and educated, each generation gathering momentum, adding something special to the brew.

Now that she was old and had the time, Elisabeth was proud of each one of them for how they had come through. They would continue to find their own way, as she had found hers. And the ones who came after would build from that.

35

Shortly after dusk, Joseph walked into the kitchen of the house on Billes Landing, his work clothes and hair filthy with sap and pine chips. Emily knew how it must look to him, the disorder of the kitchen, her unkempt appearance, the dimness of the room. She hadn't yet lit the lamps. A ball of biscuit dough and the rolling pin lay abandoned on the counter, and Angelite's dark eyes darted from Emily to Joseph and back again as she attempted to put supper together. At eight she was overmatched. Josephine played on the floor at Emily's feet, disconnected to the gloom laying claim to the house. She smiled and clapped when she saw Joseph, holding out her arms to be picked up. Alongside, T.O. sucked his thumb, a habit he had given up the year before, his brown eyes moist, wide, and questioning, his face streaked with the residue of old tears. Joe slept in the crib.

Joseph scooped up Josephine, and she began to play with his mustache. "What has happened, 'Tite?" Anxiety gripped his voice.

Emily was powerless to halt another round of tears rising from deep in her chest. "Great-Grand Elisabeth died today," she said.

"I am so sorry," Joseph said, touching Emily's shoulder, the contact comforting and familiar. "She was old. It was her time."

Emily nodded tiredly, pushed herself up from the table, and wiped her face with her apron. It didn't take long to rescue Angelite's efforts and turn out a supper of biscuits, cane syrup, and fried ham. She remained silent preparing the meal and silent as they ate. Joseph kept his head down, his movements small and cautious. Emily wasn't hungry but watched the others eat. She set the dishes in the tin washtub to soak, put the children to bed, and sat down again opposite Joseph at the table.

"*Maman* sent Uncle Gerant over by boat to fetch us early this morning, not long after you left." Emily's voice labored, stopping and starting with difficulty. "There were as many horses and wagons outside as on a Sunday. We went directly back into Great-Grand Elisabeth's bedroom. She looked so small."

Emily sorted through a jumble of images. The stark white of the often washed sheets on the bed, the closeness of the room that had gone unaired for too long, the wooden tray in the corner with a bowl of forgotten broth, the chamber pot half-visible under the bed.

"She judged me harshly at the end. I know it. I stood in that room with the rest of the family, but I couldn't look in her eyes."

"She thought the world of you, 'Tite."

"Her arms were so thin that the skin sagged, but she had a perfect quarter moon just below her elbow. The tips curved around and came to points at the top and bottom. *Mémère* Suzette and Great-Uncle Yellow John were in the room. It was like going into church, each generation marching in front of her. Great-Uncle never had children, so next it was Uncle Gerant and *Maman*'s turn. Gerant was oldest, so he went first. He and Melantine took their children forward. One by one she laid her hands on them. I saw how it was to be done."

Joseph put his hand on top of hers. Emily took a deep breath to allow her voice to regain some of its steadiness.

"*Maman* pushed Bet and her children toward the bed, and then me, as if I wouldn't know what to do on my own."

Emily drew her shoulders back and mimicked Philomene's voice. "Emily is here, *Mémère* Elisabeth, and her children by the Frenchman."

Shamefaced, Emily abruptly stopped the imitation of her mother. "That was just how she said it," she went on. "Great-Grand Elisabeth reached out and touched me on the arm, her hand drawn up into itself with almost no weight to it, like being pecked by a bird's beak. She was under the covers to her neck, only her head and arms showing, and all I could think was how big she always looked, and how small she really was."

Carrying a marker, a burned image of the moon on her arm, Emily thought. The unfinished circle of the moon.

"I had to get in close for her to tell me she wanted to give me the quilt from the bed. Angelite was trembling, but I brought her forward and the old woman touched her.

When it was T.O.'s turn, he walked up to the bed on his own and took her hand. She stroked his hair, and he stood straight, looking right at her. We had to pull him away from her side so the others could take their turn."

Her family, Emily thought, paraded past the dimming eyes of the oldest of them, shouting their summarized stories out loud. Children of the Frenchman. Eight-year-old Angelite, the china doll beauty. T.O., the devoted six-year-old. Josephine, the toddler, a throwback, who faintly carried a traceable stain of color. Joe, still a babe in arms. Elisabeth touched her own children, and their children, and their children's children, one by one, all the way down the line.

Emily sobbed briefly, a tired strangle of a cry. Joseph scraped back his chair, patted her on the shoulder, and went out to the barn to feed the horses.

Joseph Billes.

Emily sought Bet out a few weeks later and found her hanging clothes on the line behind Philomene's farmhouse. A small, unsatisfactory breeze kicked up briefly, with barely enough authority to make itself felt, nudging stale pockets of hot air a small distance before dying out. Emily selected a pillowcase from the wet wash basket and, standing on tiptoe, pushed home the wooden clothespin to attach it to the line.

"The middle of the week and you here again," Bet said. "Who's watching the store?"

"Joseph," Emily said indifferently. "Or the hired man."

They worked side by side, the two sisters, smoothing oversize sheets between them before hanging, the small items such as handkerchiefs and rags seeming to dry almost as soon as they were fastened to the line.

"I miss her, Bet."

"We all miss her," Bet said. "*Mémère* Elisabeth connected us."

Emily agreed. "It's been months, and the old woman has a hold on me, stronger in death than in life. I wish I had thought to ask her about herself when she was alive, that I had been ready to listen, the way you did."

"She didn't answer questions. It wasn't her way."

"Tell me about her."

"I don't know much more than you. Why not ask *Mère* Philomene?"

"She won't talk about their before-life with me."

"Joseph is worried about you. He's even come to talk to *Mère* Philomene about how you've changed."

"I love Joseph dearly, there can be no other man for me, but this has nothing to do with him. He wants to be a man and rule in his own house, but I am not sure I can be my old self."

"Is that why you've been spending so much time here, away from Billes Landing?"

"I need this side of the river. To spend more time with *Maman* and *Mémère* Suzette. And you."

"We're always here," Bet said.

"I was ashamed of her, you know, of her dark skin and nappy hair and broken speech."

There was a long moment when pure hurt darted across Bet's face. "Like me? Someone who takes in other people's washing and ironing?"

Emily regretted her words at once. "Don't be cross with me, Bet. I couldn't bear it." She wanted to explain herself. "It's just that I have more advantage because of how I look. My children will have a better life because of how they look."

A large white sheet separated them, droplets slowly splattering at their feet from the hemmed bottom edge, Bet on one side and Emily on the other. Emily could not see Bet's face, and when her sister spoke, her voice seemed slightly disconnected. "She talked to me while we worked a quilt once. She called it the bleaching of the line, and I think she was puzzled by it. It wasn't about color for her. Not good. Not bad. Just a stubborn course our family seems to keep following."

"I want my children to become more than anything she could even dream of," said Emily. "I want her to be proud of how far we can go."

"That would surely please her," said Bet.

Joseph and Emily's house on Billes Landing saw a fair amount of traffic, despite its remoteness in the backwoods. Emily thrived on company. Many of their neighbors were friendly enough, woodsmen and their families. The old women, Bet and the brothers, cousins, and uncles all stopped by as often as they could. But there were others who came to their home to see only Joseph, and Emily faded into the workings of the house until they were finished with their men's business.

She saw after the babies, and the cooking, and the cleaning while Joseph sat on the gallery, drinking home-made wine and chewing tobacco with these men. She could always figure out later what sort of visit it had been, either by his words or by his mood. Some things Joseph talked about with her, and some he did not. Often when he came in, he would announce that he was going to the courthouse in the morning to buy up a piece of land.

One evening, late in the summer of 1888, a knock at the door interrupted the silence as Emily washed supper dishes. Joseph sat at the table, making an elaborate ceremony of shelling, picking, and eating the pecans her uncle Gerant had brought them earlier that day. Emily answered, drying her wet hands on her apron. She recognized all three men at their door, although two of them stood back in the shadows, partially hidden by the half-light on the gallery. Each had frequented her dinner table before. Narcisse was in front, and behind him she recognized the broad, smooth face of Joseph's cousin and business partner, Antoine Morat, and Joseph Ferrier, a man her mother helped raise, son of Oreline Derbanne and her first husband.

"Come in," Emily said, holding the screen door open. "I have tea cakes."

The three men fidgeted but didn't make a move to come inside. "We've come to speak to Joseph," Narcisse said, his eyes shifting away from hers.

Joseph got up and went outside then, and as the men settled themselves on the front gallery, little T.O. came barreling straight out the front door barefoot, his nighttime shirt flapping.

"*Grandpère*," he whooped, trying to scramble onto Narcisse's lap, Emily directly behind him.

Narcisse didn't smile and blocked his grandson's path.

"Go to your mother, T.O.," Narcisse said, the look on his face grim. "We have serious business to discuss tonight."

T.O. made a small questioning sound, sat down hard on his bottom at Narcisse's feet on the gallery, and then began to wail. Emily soothed T.O. the best she could, bringing him inside and putting him back to bed. Her stomach churned.

The men sat out on the gallery and talked in low tones, too low for Emily to make out. Long after she heard the creaking of the gallery chairs and the sounds of retreating horses, Joseph stayed outside. When he finally came into the house, his eyes had receded deeper into his face, and they glided past her own, as if unwilling to make the connection.

Joseph slumped wearily in his chair, and Emily stood behind him, massaging his temples, careful to keep the circular pressure even.

"Joseph, what is it?"

Joseph shifted uneasily, taking a long time to respond. "I need to go away, for longer than usual, to New Orleans."

"I don't understand."

"The folks in town have gotten themselves worked up about us living out here together. Someone had hard feelings about property that came my way instead of his, and he's been stirring the pot. You'll be safer with me gone than with me here. It'll take the steam out."

"How can we be safer without you here?"

"You can always get to me through Narcisse. Use the money from the store for whatever you need." Joseph seemed numb, as if he had been turned to stone. "I'll be back, 'Tite, as soon as I can, and in the meantime, count on the three that came tonight to look after you and the children."

And so, in 1888, with hardly any warning, Joseph moved away from the house on Billes Landing and took up permanent residence in New Orleans.

36

J oseph could not imagine life with any woman other than Emily at his side, but in the year he had been away from Aloha she had changed. Not in drastic or obvious ways, but something had shifted between them. Emily's devotion to the children was never in question, and she was as beautiful to his eye as ever. Her skin was creamy smooth, her long chestnut hair soft and inviting, her long neck gave her a bright elegance he couldn't quite define, and she still had the gift of finding delight in everything she touched. Emily sang in her high, sweet voice as she fed the chickens or slopped the hogs, and she smiled at him the way she used to, coaxing him toward happiness. But now that he was back from his extended stay in New Orleans, Emily had become increasingly bold in asking for money of her own. As if she didn't trust him to take care of the household. It offended his masculine pride that she could doubt his commitment in this manner.

"Joseph," she had said just today, "when our customers settle their accounts after the crops come in, I would like to keep a little of the cash from the store. For myself." As if that were the most simple of requests.

By then the store had been enlarged to accommodate the Mexican workers pouring into the parish with the coming of the railroad, the hill workers flush with the novelty of cash money in their pockets from the sawmill, and the Negroes who scratched out a living from the soil.

He should have paid more attention to the beginnings of change in those difficult few months after her Grand Elisabeth died. Emily had become distant from him, aloof, spending so much of her time across the river with kin that he feared he had lost her. Before then she had always seen to him as her first priority, making him laugh, calming him, igniting his passion. He came and went as needed, without burden of the silliness he saw in other women who looked pretty without real benefit or who were helpful to their men but too severe to enjoy.

Not long after Elisabeth died, Joseph had awoken one night and discovered Emily's side of the bed empty and cold to the touch. He'd found her in the common room on the settee, hugging her knees to her chest, a small figure in her nightgown. "Joseph," she'd said, the urgency in her pleading eyes almost breaking his heart, "I need something for my own, whatever you can spare. An allowance."

She had seemed so fragile to him at that moment, suffering, her pain within his power to ease. Against his better judgment he had indulged her, to help her through her grief. He'd faithfully handed over two dollars in coin each month, even though he knew she simply hoarded it, hid it, even from him. Joseph had been relieved when Emily finally seemed to find herself again, thought of his needs again. He intended to put a stop to the payments, but before he could do so he was forced away to New Orleans. Now she asked outright for more.

"If you aren't here, I need to be able to take care of all of us." Joseph noticed the hard little points behind Emily's eyes. It was becoming an old argument, repeated often. "Our children need a future."

Joseph bristled. He considered himself a good provider. "I will always make sure you're taken care of, 'Tite. We've talked about this before. I had to stay in New Orleans last year to keep us safe."

Emily gave no quarter. "We have no rights in the eyes of the law, not me, and not the four children I brought into the world. If you love the children, protect us now, with land and money."

Joseph went outside to sit on the gallery, refusing to argue. More than anything, he just wanted his old Emily back.

Joseph and Emily had one last child, Mary, their fifth. Mary grew from babe in arms to a stubborn-minded three-year-old, strong and healthy, suffering only the normal childhood ailments.

On Billes Landing, the store and the family prospered. Back in the Aloha woods, where poor families white and black were dependent on his largesse, Joseph and his family were left mostly unchallenged, the level of interest in Joseph's affairs leaning more toward how much liquor and tobacco he had on hand and less toward his living arrangements. But in town, in the parish seat of Colfax, people who used to smile at Joseph or at least leave him alone grew cold and turned away. Even when his acquaintances seemed polite, Joseph read judgment in their posture, their forced tip of a hat.

"Leave that colored woman alone," they began to urge

Circa 1895. L–R. Mary Billes, Emily Fredieu, Josephine Billes, Angelite Billes, Theodore (T.O.) Billes, Joe Billes Jr.

him. "Take care of the children, if you must. But come back to your own kind before it's too late."

One balmy Tuesday, after a brief afternoon shower cleared the air and brought relief from the late-summer heat, Joseph set out the nine miles to the Colfax courthouse to register a mundane land transfer. He thought nothing of the two ragged youngsters with the look of underfed farmboys who trailed behind him on the wide, dusty thoroughfare of the main street once he got to town. It flashed through his mind that they seemed misplaced, at loose ends, maybe too old for the schoolhouse and too young for the mill. He tethered his horse and went inside the courthouse, and when he came out, his business done, the boys were still idling near the hitching post in front of the notary's office. As Joseph turned to mount his horse, he felt the dull burst of an egg gone bad against his cheek and its long, gooey slide from the fleshy part of his ear to his chin.

"Nigger lover," he heard, but by the time he collected himself and looked around, the boys had run. There were few others out in the heat, two old men on the bench in front of the courthouse, a woman strolling on the wooden sidewalk with an umbrella open against the sun, but no one moved to help or raise their voice in either outrage or sympathy. Riding out of town toward the Colfax border, Joseph used his crisp, freshly ironed pocket handkerchief to wipe at the sticky mess. He didn't share the incident with Emily when he got back to Billes Landing, but the next week he moved a majority of his business to his New Orleans bank rather than use the local bank in Colfax. The climate in town had changed, and it was getting more difficult to know whom to trust.

In early spring of 1894 Joseph rode out to check on Narcisse Fredieu. Liza, Narcisse's wife, brought the two men coffee and left them to talk on the front gallery. Scanning the homestead, Joseph took in the decline in the state of the property.

"You look well, my friend," he said to Narcisse. Narcisse's long white beard had thinned, and the milky clouding of his eyes had robbed them of color.

"I'm almost seventy, slow and tired, and most of my friends are already dead," Narcisse said with a forced chuckle. "But I do appreciate the thought." He lit his cigar. "How is Emily? She hasn't been by for weeks."

"'Tite is fine. The younger children and the store keep her busy."

"Every one of my children still visits the old man," Narcisse bragged.

Joseph knew how much time Joe F. and Matchie, Narcisse's two youngest boys by Philomene, put into his farm, providing their labor, helping the old man out. Even Narcisse's wife didn't complain about his colored children being so visible, they were of such benefit.

"The boys brought Angelite over Tuesday. They heard I was feeling a little poorly, and Angelite made a Sarah Bernhardt. Thoughtful girl. She knows my favorite cake, and stuffed it with double helpings of ollenberry jam." Narcisse gave a fond pat to the broad mound that had become his midsection. "She has her mother's beauty and spirit, that one does, and I detect a mischievous streak from you. Did she tell you she met Jacques Andrieu here last Tuesday? We had a little party for him, as welcome to the community. A delightful fellow, fresh off the boat this month from Perpignan. Jacques has interest in Angelite. She dazzled him. He hasn't stopped talking about her yet."

"Angelite is only fifteen," Joseph said.

"And how old was Emily when the two of you came together?"

This wasn't a conversation Joseph wanted to pursue. He changed the subject. "Are you prepared to part with that little piece of land we talked about near Monette's Ferry?" Joseph asked. "I am ready to buy."

"I hear you struck a deal with Louisiana Railway and Navigation for your own switch off the main track, that you have a flagstop named after you now."

Joseph enjoyed the easy camaraderie of men, sliding effortlessly between business and social matters. "The steamboats haul in the materials to build the railroads that will put them out of business. The flagstop makes it easier to ship my timber away. We have to change with the times."

"The times seem to have left me behind," said Narcisse. "I know you buy my land out of loyalty, not need, and I appreciate it, my young friend."

Joseph laughed. "Young indeed. Fifty-four this summer." He turned sober. "Don't be absurd about the land, Narcisse. It is located perfectly for my needs."

"Not a promising beginning to a conversation where we need to talk truth, Joseph."

"Monsieur, not again."

"Yes, again. You'll always be my dear friend, like a son, but face facts. You cannot hold back every hothead in Grant Parish. You have enemies, Joseph, and they grow in strength and number. This is not only about you. Emily is my daughter. Those are my grandchildren. You cannot go on under the same roof. I am not so influential as I once was. There's a new crop of men around here now, and the talk is ugly. Local and statewide petitions are being circulated to get cohabitation between the races declared a felony. Not that the locals need law on their side. If you care about Emily and the children, you have to protect them. Provide, yes. Love them, yes. Joseph, you need to move them somewhere safer."

Joseph's face was hard. "That I will not do."

"Keep them close, but marry white," Narcisse said. "It is the way of things."

"My position in Aloha is stronger now than in '88 when you convinced me to run," Joseph said. "We keep to ourselves, we don't go together to town, we don't provoke. We just want to be left alone."

For his fifty-fifth birthday Joseph gave himself a small party, bringing out his mandolin for the first time in months. They laid

Old man Narcisse Fredieu and white family.

in large quantities of food and liquor and invited only his closest friends, the ones who accepted him and Emily together. It
was a small and lively group, old women, young men, children,
white, Negro, colored. Emily enlisted the help of Philomene
and Suzette in the kitchen, and Gerant came, too; and Joseph
invited Narcisse Fredieu, Joseph Ferrier, Antoine Morat, and
Jacques Andrieu, Angelite's beau. The children were allowed to
stay up late, even Mary, and everyone danced while Joseph

played. Emily and Joseph sang several songs together, their high and low voices complementing each other well.

"More, more," called Narcisse, clearly enjoying both the homemade wine and the singing, and Joseph began to play "Danse aux Ma Mamselle."

The music and voices were so loud at first that Joseph did not hear the horses outside. Jacques, who stood closest to the window, began to quiet everyone and motioned for Joseph to stop playing.

"Come on out of there, Joseph Billes."

The gay mood of the evening evaporated at the sound of the deep voice.

"Take everyone to the back," Joseph whispered to Emily, and handed her his mandolin. Emily, Philomene, Suzette, Gerant, Angelite, T.O., Josephine, Joseph, and Mary all slipped quickly into the kitchen, near the rear door.

Joseph picked up his Winchester. He strode boldly out the front door beyond the gallery, and Narcisse and the other white men from inside the house followed.

"What do you want? What are you doing on my land?" Joseph said loudly to the men on horseback. There were three of them. "Alphonse, is that you?"

"Joseph, we came to talk to you quietly, no need for the gun. We didn't know you were entertaining."

"Then go on now and we'll talk over any business later in town," Joseph said.

"This is personal," the lead man said. "What's going on here isn't right. It would be best for us to get down and discuss this calmly now."

"Just stay on your horses." Joseph walked toward the men, his rifle in view. "Your boy enjoying the clerkship I arranged, Alphonse?"

"You've been good to this town, Joseph, but you can't expect us to stand for this abomination before God any longer. You have to quit it, or we can't be responsible. The others wanted to make a different kind of visit here tonight. I'm here instead because of what you did for my boy."

"This is my home, and my land, and you have no part of that," Joseph said angrily. "I say what happens here. Get off my property."

"It'll go down hard on you, Joseph. See reason."

Narcisse walked closer to the horsemen and stood directly beside Joseph. "We go back a long way, Alphonse," he said.

"Evening to you, Narcisse."

"Go on and leave now," Narcisse said. "Your message has been delivered."

The lead man stared down at Narcisse and then Joseph and turned his horse around, heading toward town. The others followed. Narcisse put his arm around Joseph's shoulder, and they walked back to the house.

The party was over.

One week later a fire broke out in the barn, and they barely managed to get the animals out before dousing the flames. Within a month of the fire Emily came out one early morning and found five of their chickens thrown onto the front gallery. Their throats were slit.

37

In 1896 Narcisse Fredieu died of pneumonia, leaving behind a small estate laden with debt, one legal widow, sixteen surviving children, and eight grandchildren. His widow was forced to sell off his possessions to pay the debts, and no one expected much left over. The value of his estate was reflected in the old age and condition of his oxen and the barely usable old tools he gave to his sons Nick and Matchie before he died. The inheritance he had hoped to leave behind eluded him.

For Emily, her father's presence had always meant a certain kind of immunity. As long as he was just across the river, she believed she could rise above common opinion, could confound the law. She was Joseph Billes's woman and Narcisse Fredieu's daughter, an implicit warning to others to think twice, to keep their hands to themselves. It had always meant a pass, the benefit of the doubt. Narcisse claimed race

and for Grant Parish Louisiana
duly Commissioned and sworn
proceeded to take an inventory
and cause an Appraisement
to be made of all the property pointed out to me as belonging to the Succession of Narcisse
Fredieu deceased, situated in
the State said Parish and State
being assisted therein by H C
Rogers and by O B Brett
good and competent ap-
praisers, and in the presence
of attesting witnesses, all of
the Parish of Grant La. Which
Inventory and appraisement
are as follows:
Real Estate +
S½ of N E¼ & N½ of S E¼
Sec 15 Tp 7 N R 4 West
160 acres with improvements
valued at four hundred
Dollars   4400.00
Of W½ of N W¼ Sec 15
Tp 7 N R 4 West — forty
acres — valued at fifty
Dollars   50.00
Personal property
Three head mules

valued at — being old and
worn out — valued $60.00
Four horses small and
very old Stock — valued $60.00
Twelve head Cattle, Cows &
Calves — valued at $100.00
Two Yoke Oxen — valued
in very bad Condition — $40.00
Twenty head hogs in
the woods — valued $30.00
Ten head Sheep valued $10.00
One old wagon valued $15.00
One Sot house hold
furniture consisting of
2 Bedsteads, 2 Armoirs
1 Bureau, 6 chairs, one
rocker, 2 tables, 2 clocks
1 Stove, 1 safe, wash
bowl, 1 Sot bedding, 1 Sot Crockeryware
1 Sot Cutlery and Cooking
utensils, Brooms $6.00 $205.00

One lot tools farm — value — $5.00
(3) Three Bales of Cotton
valued at 7¢ 500 lbs $105.00
Fifty Bushels Coon @40 $20.00
One plantation Bell on
River place — valued — $7.50
+   +

Also 640 acres land being
All of Section 16 Tp 7 N R
4 West — valued at
30 acres in Cultivation —
About 150 acres in River — $500.00

Recapitulation
Real Estate   950.00
Personal Property —   469.00
Recapitulation   1,419.00

There being no other pro
perty pointed out to us
as belonging to said
Succession we hereby close
this Inventory and ap —
praisement amounting to
Four teen hundred & nineteen — Dollars
This done and signed
at the residence of Narcisse
Fredieu decd on this 21 December
21th 1895 — Grant Pl La.
H C Rogers
O B Brett
Witnesses
Eugene Dubien
Nick La Fredieu
mark
W L Shackelford
Clerk & Ex Officio
Notary Public

mixing as an individual right, an old-school throwback, but his death coincided with a moral hardening of the times against such a minority view.

His children paid him the purest homage. From oldest to youngest, colored to white, from Emily to Edd, they grieved his passing and took care of his grave. Week after week following Narcisse's burial, Emily asked her mother to visit the grave site with her, but Philomene always refused.

Finally Philomene bent in the face of Emily's persistent appeals and consented, and Suzette went with them. Narcisse Fredieu's presence had always been an unbroken force, snaking back and forth through all their lives, master, consort, father, tormentor, protector. It took some adjustment to conceive of a world in which he played no part.

The three women traveled together by buggy to the Cloutierville cemetery, a long and dusty ride. When Emily identified Narcisse's burial spot for them, Philomene stood motionless at the foot of his grave, studying the inscription on the cool, polished marker.

"What does it say?" she asked.

Emily read the chiseled message. "It says 'Narcisse Fredieu, 1824 to 1896, Beloved husband and father.'"

The granite, ordered and paid for by Joseph Billes, gave off a mottled gray sheen of pedigree and respectability. Philomene ran her fingers across the slab. Then, with slow deliberation, she hitched back her shoulders, drew deep down into her throat, and spat on Narcisse's grave, putting her full weight into it. Calmly she wiped her mouth with the handkerchief she kept in her dress pocket. Emily kept surprise from her face, thinking how little she knew of these women she came from, trying to do as Bet would and listen. She studied the set to her mother's jaw, the stiff back, and saw a small flicker of confusion, an involuntary knitting of Philomene's dark eyebrows.

"He was a thief." Stone-faced, Philomene paced at the foot of the plot. "He stole my youth, he stole my man, and he stole one of my children for twenty years. He made me hard. I want satisfaction."

Suzette didn't move from where she stood, the high sun full on her, no shade to be had. She shielded her eyes from the bright light with one hand and talked quietly to Philomene. "Daughter, you always were smart, and you had the glimpsings," she said. "But you got powerful in yourself. Narcisse Fredieu forced some of that on you."

"Are you defending him?" Philomene said, eyes darkening against her mother.

"I do not excuse one thing the man did, but he is part of the children you're so proud of. Maybe not the best part." Suzette tried to break the tension with a throaty chuckle. Philomene did not soften. "You and Gerant were the only children of mixed blood not sold away early on Rosedew. Privileged among the scorned. To free you were slave, to field you were house, to whites colored, and look at you now. You made a place for yourself and family. Your own land, children who can read and write. Narcisse Fredieu is six feet under the ground and you're here standing on top."

It was only four years until the turn of the century, and groups of night riders haunted the backwoods of central Louisiana. They were small in number, informal and inconsistent, and drew their ranks from across culture and class, from hill men to businessmen. Most of their work was under cover of darkness, terrorizing Negroes they decided had overstepped in some way, had forgotten their place. They randomly burned, maimed, even killed, and were seldom challenged. Such was the force of their mission for racial purity that they served up reminders to white men as well.

Jacques Andrieu received a visit from three men he did not know late one night in 1896. Rousted from a sound sleep, Jacques found himself jostled outdoors in his night-clothes. Two of the night riders forced him down, his back to his woodchopping stump near the house. The third man poured gasoline around his barn and set the match. Jacques helplessly watched the flames consume his property as the man who lit the match strode back casually.

Jacques Andrieu.

"Hold his hand out flat," he barked. On the block, wedged blade down, was Jacques's hatchet. The leader shimmied it free.

"That the hand you use to touch the nigger gal?" Without waiting for a response, he brought the cold, sharp edge down on Jacques's little finger, below the knuckle, a clean slice. The stroke seemed almost effortless.

"We don't need your kind here," he said. "We mean to keep this land pure."

Angelite came to Emily as she tied back the grapevines in the small vineyard behind the house on Billes Landing.

"*Maman,* Jacques is leaving to go back to France," Angelite said.

"Alone?" asked Emily. Angelite looked tired, her eyes rimmed red, her cool, pale skin drained of color beneath her sunbonnet.

"I do not want to go with him."

"He would marry you in France," Emily said. "Jacques came to Joseph to plead his case. He wants the baby born in Perpignan."

"Do you want me to go?" Angelite asked.

"I want you to think about the child. If you stay, we'll take care of both of you, but Jacques asks you to be his wife once you get to France, the way he cannot here."

"He's asking me to turn my back on family. He says to remain here punishes the child for what he calls an accident of birth. Jacques wants to bring our children up white. I won't pretend to be white, here or in France. I will not pass."

"Your uncle Eugene took that road," Emily said with sadness. She hadn't heard from her brother since he'd left Cane River for Texas.

"I want to stay near you and the Grands," Angelite said.

"Remember *Grandmémère* Elisabeth?" Emily asked. "The touching before she died ten years ago?"

"Of course," Angelite said.

"For months after I was starved for family, and *Mémère* never left my thoughts. I struggled with where I belonged. On one day I would see myself as weak and alone, and the next as the sum of everyone who had come before and everyone who would come after. Joseph tried to be helpful, but somehow I knew my comfort lay on the other side of the river, with Bet and the Grands. *Mémère* Elisabeth touched each of us, Angelite, and when I understood that she was with me, in me, forever, that became my inheritance, not the quilt she left to me. Whatever you decide, to follow Jacques or stay here, you already have that inheritance, too."

"Jacques is not like Papa," Angelite said. "He will not stay to fight."

"The night riders have become more bold, striking white men. Jacques is right to be afraid. His little finger was a warning. Only his white blood kept him from death that night. And now that the baby is obvious . . ."

"Papa stood up to them." For a moment Emily clearly saw herself in her daughter. The blind desire for a strong man to keep her safe from the reality of the times.

"Joseph has a stronger place in the community, and he and your grandfather stood up together. Narcisse Fredieu is gone now."

"I told Jacques I would give him my answer by the end of the month."

Emily nodded, unsure of what Angelite would choose.

Jacques returned to France exactly six months after Narcisse died, leaving Angelite behind. When the child was born Angelite christened him Joseph, after her father, the same as her brother, but they called him Buck.

It was a blow to the whole family, not just Emily, when Joseph Billes married Lola Grandchamp.

A settled and mature woman in her late forties, Lola was from a marginal but old-line Natchitoches family. Never married and understandably closemouthed about her age, she subtracted several birthdays in her own mind over the years and still lived with her father on a small farm near Cloutierville. Lola was of unspectacular but sufficient lineage to blot some of the stain of Joseph's scandalous behavior for the last twenty years. She was neither worldly nor clever, but she was unimpeachably white. Lola was as old-fashioned as her age implied, slightly stout in the Creole tradition, and a devout Catholic, with more pretensions to society than success in that arena. She would do for Joseph's purposes.

There was speculation on both sides of the river why Lola would settle for a self-made Frenchman with such a conspicuous and dark past. Some thought it romantic that a woman her age could find true love, but they were very few. Most attributed her decision to marry Joseph to a quiet but desperate desire to change the contours of her days at home with an overbearing father and his third wife rather than enchantment with Joseph himself, not to mention his money. Lola carried herself with a superior bearing, and her scowl in even the most joyous of times betrayed her closely held belief in the inescapable disappointments of life. She vigorously disapproved of the life Joseph Billes had lived before approaching her and had been heard by those on the Natchitoches side of the river emphatically condemning any mixture of the races. But she also went on to defend her fiancé, and the salvation that awaited him, now that he had chosen to denounce his sins and rejoin the white community. He was, after all, a man of some means and, she assumed, eager to change.

Emily kept up with all of this from the house on Billes Landing. Information traveled along strange roads in the backcountry. Joseph never talked to her directly about his plans to marry, only about the need for Emily to move from their house, but stories of Joseph's whereabouts reached her, and she was able to follow each stage of Joseph's parallel life as he created it. The proposal. The acceptance. The setting of the wedding date. The donation in good faith to Lola Grandchamp of 850 acres of land, including the house on Billes Landing.

Emily no longer worked in the store, one more public display Joseph felt the town would not tolerate. He hired a full-time man to clerk and stock, replacing her there as he prepared to replace her elsewhere. Two miles away, at a bend along Cornfine Bayou, Joseph built Emily a house in the middle of seventy-four acres he deeded to the children.

"I built the house big enough to hold Suzette and Philomene, too. They could move in with you."

"This is my house," Emily said to Joseph, waving her hand broadly to indicate the front room where they stood. "Four of my five children were born here. Mary is not yet seven, Angelite eighteen."

"The new house is not far," Joseph reasoned. "I will visit often, and the children can come back here anytime."

Emily did not answer Joseph, busying herself elsewhere.

As Joseph's wedding date approached, their conversations became more strained, with no new arguments to offer. The larger unspoken issue overwhelmed them both, exhausted them both, and by comparison the details of day-to-day living seemed too trivial to share. The silences grew between them like the lilies that skimmed the surface of the swamp, spreading wider and faster in the summer heat. The new house was finished, had been finished for over two months, empty and in waiting for Emily to accept her part with her usual dignity.

Two days before the scheduled wedding date, Joseph came in from the woods just before nightfall. He had cut timber that day and was spotted with the sticky amber resin from the trees, the smell of pine sap clinging stubbornly to his clothes.

"Emily, we have to move you to the other house," Joseph said. "Tomorrow."

"You better take off those overalls so I can wash them out," Emily said. "Otherwise you'll get that sap all over my good things."

"There's no more time, 'Tite. I called a few of the boys to come and help get you settled in the new place tomorrow. They'll be here directly after sunup."

Emily sat down hard on the settee and cast an accusing eye on Joseph. "How can you look at these children and toss me away? How can you look at the store? You weren't here, always in New Orleans or off on some trip. It was me that built the store. It was me who rolled those barrels of flour until I could hardly stand up straight. It was me they held in contempt, doing the work, while they smiled in your face. Part of this is mine. Now you expect me to pick up my things and go so you can move that sour-faced white woman in here? These are my things."

"We can move all your personals with you, anything you want," Joseph said. "I have to do this, Emily. None of you are safe here. I'm not safe. You never have to worry. I'll take care of you and the children for the rest of your life, but there's no other way. They'll hurt us all if we go on as we've been. I'll come see you in the new house."

Joseph took a breath. He was still standing just inside the doorway, circling his floppy sunhat around and around in his blunt-tipped hands. His movements were slow and heavy, and he had been drinking more than usual.

"She's not coming here to replace you, 'Tite. That's not the purpose of this. I've told her about the children, she knows how I feel about them, and they can visit. I've talked to Angelite and T.O. They're old enough to understand, especially Angelite. She and Jacques already had to make their choice." He advanced farther into the room, until he was close enough to reach out and touch Emily, but he kept both hands on his hat. "The little ones need to realize their father isn't abandoning them. They're what I'm proudest of in my life. We can't marry, we always knew that, and we can't live under the same roof now, either. Even your father knew, and tried to warn me when he was alive. They'll come for us, by fire or bullet or rope, and we won't even know who did it. It is already hard for me to do business in town. This is the way it has to be."

Emily lifted her chin. "You do this thing and I can't be held to loving you again." Even as she spoke the words, she recognized the falsity in them.

Joseph sat warily in the straight-backed chair, as if he were a stranger in his own house. He pulled out the pint bottle of whiskey he carried during the day and lifted it to his lips. It was almost empty. Emily watched the last of the dark brown liquid disappear.

"At least you'll be alive," he finally said, wiping the wet from his mustache. "At least we'll all be alive."

He stood, slightly unsteady, and disappeared through the front door.

The evening light faded, and later that night Joseph still hadn't returned. Emily started her nighttime preparations, making the rounds in the house, checking each of her children. She spent a moment looking at her portrait over the fireplace before retiring to the bedroom, where she turned down the wick on the lamp to begin her wait for Joseph to come to the bed they had shared the entirety of her adult life.

He never came.

*   *   *

The next morning broke clear and dry, a perfect May Louisiana day. Emily had Angelite bring her a fresh washbasin of water, then sent her out to see to the children's breakfast and dress. Emily had washed, starched, and ironed everything two days before and instructed them all to wear their Sunday clothes. She settled herself in front of the dressing table in her bedroom and spent a good portion of the early morning there. Joseph could milk the cow himself. Her movements were exact, with no joy to the preening. Today she had to look her best. She was determined that the inevitable move be civil and orderly. She piled her hair high on top of her head in a loose topknot, designed to look more effortless than it really was, working faithfully to catch each stray strand that misbehaved.

Laboring in front of her dressing table mirror, she heard masculine voices outside, but she did not break her morning preparations to investigate. When she was satisfied that she smelled fresh and that her hair was perfect, she called for Angelite to help pull her corset tight. She picked her best dress from the armoire, a long, dark gray frock that fell to the ground in three layers, cinched tight at the waist and accented by a jewel-buckled belt that emphasized the petiteness of her figure. The sleeves were massive and tulip puffed at the top, in the fashion of the day, and narrowed as the material traveled the length of her arm, ending with six round buttons that sparkled if the light caught them the right way. There was delicate black lace at the cuffs and matching black lace at the collar. It was Joseph's favorite dress. She removed her hat from its hatbox and set it on the bed. Emily drew on her delicate black transparent gloves with the intricate spidery pattern. They were cut off below the knuckles and left her long, elegant fingers exposed. The gloves were the first grown-up gift Joseph had ever given to her.

By the sounds, the men were gathering outside. Emily gave herself one last look into the mirror, took a deep, steadying breath, and entered the front room, where she inspected her children, each outfitted in their best visiting attire. Angelite held Buck in her arms, and from T.O. all the way down to Mary, they stared at her anxious and wide-eyed, stiff in their Sunday finery, but they did not speak. Only when she satisfied herself that they looked their best did she pull back the curtains and peer into the front yard.

There were three buckboard wagons and several restless horses already harnessed out front. Three white men loitered around them, looking aimless and slightly chagrined. That didn't include Joseph, who stood off to the side, alone. He still wore his workclothes from the day before.

Emily recognized each of the men. Antoine Morat, Joseph Ferrier, and John Fletcher. Joseph's friends, lowly placed on society's ladder, the best he could do as long as he was with her. This had to be one of their more unpleasant chores on Joseph's behalf. These men performed his odds and ends without questions. They had come to the house in more settled days, and she'd served them dinner and wine at her table or provided a cool drink after they'd witnessed a business transaction or moved oxen from one pen to another. Often they came just to drink and tell lies to pass an evening. Today they waited for Joseph's command to move her away.

She gathered up the smallest ones, Mary and Little Joseph and Josephine. Emily wanted her family above reproach. "Keep a close eye on them, Angelite."

"I'll take care of you, *Mère*." T.O. stepped forward, serious, in his black suit, starched white shirt, and floppy black tie. "I'll find a way to take care of all of us." His eyes were like coal, blazing from his ashen face with the bravado of a frightened man-boy of fifteen. A lock of his sandy hair had defied the comb. She licked her fingers and smoothed it back.

"You are the man of the family now, but today we do this my way," Emily answered. "Help Angelite mind after your sisters and brother. I don't want any talking or crying in front of those men, not by any of us. Keep everyone in the house and keep them quiet. Will you do that for me, T.O.?"

"*Oui, Maman.*"

"Thank you."

Emily smoothed her dress one more time. She tilted up her chin, pushed back her shoulders, and slowly stepped outside onto the front gallery.

"Monsieur Joseph, these are my rosebushes. How will you give them to me?" She kept her voice strong, as if she were exchanging pleasantries with a shopkeeper.

They all turned to look, six pairs of eyes from inside the house and four from outside.

"Come now, Emily," Joseph said. "We're going to move whatever you want. You just take these boys in the house with you and point out what you need. We have plenty of space in the wagons."

"The horse in the barn is mine, given to me by my father. And I'm not going anywhere without my rosebushes."

"We can dig up some of the bushes so you can replant them at the new house."

"It has to be before three o'clock," Emily said.

"What?" Joseph said.

"You know it's bad luck to touch the roses after three o'clock," Emily said. "The roses are your responsibility."

"Emily, don't do this." Joseph shifted his weight forward

and looked directly at her. His tone turned hard and dangerous, caught between his two audiences.

Without further word, Emily went back into the house, leaving the door open behind her. There seemed to be no motion anywhere, inside or out, except for hers. Her children watched her carefully, waiting. The oil painting mocked her from its position of honor over the fireplace in the front room. She allowed herself only an instant to wonder at the strange, overconfident girl captured on canvas, hand resting lightly on the chair, staring out at a future full of promise. Emily moved quickly. She had to drag a chair over and stand on tiptoe, working at the hook and wire to get the portrait down. She didn't call on anyone to help her, and each was hesitant to come to her aid unasked. The painting had never been removed before, and the rectangular patch of wallpaper underneath looked fresh and new compared with the familiar pattern exposed to the air and sun. Emily gently placed the painting next to her rocking chair and sat down calmly.

"Come," she said to her children, trying to give a reassuring smile, motioning to the couch and chairs.

They followed suit and sat down tentatively, alternating between keeping their eyes down and glancing apprehensively at this tiny woman who was their mother.

As if a signal had been given, the men moved inside. It was Joseph who decided what went to the new house. Emily asked for nothing other than the rosebushes, her horse, and the painting. She was unresponsive to questions the men put to her, and they stopped asking. She rocked. The men edged around them reluctantly, throwing guarded glances toward her and the silent children, loading those things that Joseph pointed out. Except for Antoine Morat. He caught Emily's eye once when Joseph was in another room, and Emily was sure she saw a slight gloat to his smile.

The men loaded up all of the children's beds, miscellaneous furniture, lanterns, and most of the kitchenware. One of the wagons was for livestock, hogs, and chickens, and they tied a milking cow behind it. Last, Joseph loaded up her dressing table and the rocking chair she had been sitting in, both gifts he had given in happier days.

They used the lead wagon for the human cargo. Joseph Billes's family, Emily, children, and grandchild, were helped into the buckboard and began the journey to their new home two miles away. Joseph himself drove the horses forward, in silence, and the other wagons followed. The strange caravan made its way from the river side of Aloha over to the wooded side on Cornfine Bayou where the new house waited.

When they arrived the men began to unload and carry the heaviest furniture into the house.

"Come to the barn, 'Tite. This is important," Joseph said. He untethered Emily's dapple gray horse from the back of the wagon and led him to the barn.

Emily left the children in the wagon and followed. Out of sight and earshot of the others, Joseph pulled a package from the saddlebag and handed Emily a small canvas bag.

"There's five hundred dollars in cash here, 'Tite. Don't let anyone know you have it, and hide it well. If there's anything you need, just send T.O. over. He can come for me anytime, to the house or the store or the mill."

"It appears that suddenly you see the wisdom in me having money of my own," Emily said, but there was no satisfaction in it.

She stuffed the sack between two piles of hay and collected her children out of the hot sun. T.O. drew up water from the well, and they waited in the barn until the men left. Before going into the new house for the first time, Emily dampened the roots of the rosebushes the men had left leaning against the gallery.

"We will replant them along the side of the house first thing in the morning," Emily said to her children. "There is never any excuse for a bare-dirt yard."

Joseph Billes married Lola Grandchamp the next day in a small, private ceremony in Cloutierville and brought his bride back to his house on Billes Landing.

To the townspeople, Joseph Billes had mended his ways and married white, a signal that it was safe to return to the substance of their own pursuits.

```
Joe Billis was very fond of His Children
but all his friends demanded Him to a
White Girl He did.
--Cousin Gurtie Fredieu, written family
   history, 1975
```

Two weeks after the incident at Billes Landing, on a muggy midsummer day, T.O. came to Philomene's farm. Suzette sat on the front gallery, snapping beans for supper, and she could feel her great-grandson's misery even before he got off his horse. T.O. dismounted, respected her politely by tipping his hat, and went straightaway to the side garden where Philomene tended the tomatoes.

"It's *Maman*," Suzette overheard T.O. say. "She will not get up from her bed. She won't eat."

"Does she have fever?" Philomene asked. Alarm made her voice rise.

T.O. reddened. "It isn't urgent. She is not that kind of sick."

Philomene brushed past T.O. without stopping to take off her work gloves or change her bonnet. Harnessing the mare, she called to Suzette, "I will be back when I get to the bottom of this." Philomene rode straight-saddle in the direction of Emily's new house on Cornfine Bayou, T.O. straining to keep up on his horse beside her.

Night had fallen and the full moon was high when Philomene returned alone, worry chiseled across her forehead. "We must act quickly, *Maman*," she said to Suzette. "The girl is hurt, she needs us near. Emily doesn't know what it is to be without a man, crying all day for what is already gone."

"Emily could move back here," Suzette said. "We can make room."

"No," said Philomene. "Joseph put the land in the name of the children. If she leaves the property, even for a short while, there could be trouble later. We must move there."

Suzette knew Philomene well enough to know she had already decided on some course of action and would be almost impossible to sway. She protested anyway. "There are twelve years of sweat, prayers, and Sunday dinners put into this house."

Philomene untied and removed her bonnet, and Suzette noticed for the first time a lone gray strand in her daughter's hair.

"I made the arrangement already with Monsieur Billes," said Philomene, putting aside the sweat-stained hat, her face hard. "That was the reason for my delay. I agreed to sell him this property, minus a piece for Bet to stay on as her own. In exchange, we get land on the other side of the river next to Emily's." She struck a more conciliatory tone. "We earned every acre here, *Maman,* and it served us well, but this parcel was the poorest of Narcisse's land, ringed by swamps. It gave our family a start, but most have gone on to their own lives now, or died, and the farm is getting to be too much for us alone. We'll have less land, but the soil around Emily's new place is richer, the house bigger and already built."

"I am old, almost at the end of life, and you would uproot me again?" Suzette heard the whine in her own voice. Although she spoke the words, and her mind could reach back over seven decades, it was almost impossible for Suzette to accept herself as an old woman. Time had forced her to create a special place in her mind for death, a place already packed to overflowing, so many of the people who shaped her already gathered there. Elisabeth, her sister Palmire, Gerasíme, Nicolas Mulon, *Marraine* Doralise, Oreline Derbanne, Narcisse Fredieu. She had outlived them all.

"We can bear the move across the river to Cornfine Bayou, for Emily." Philomene stood unwavering in the face of Suzette's resistance. "Family does for family, and young life around will do us both good."

*   *   *

The night before the move, Suzette rummaged in her private storage, a cigar box where she kept her special things. Inside was a broken string of white rosary beads, an old oak figurine Gerant had carved, and her tatted lace handkerchief. She removed the shabby cowhide strip Nicolas had given her and rubbed it for luck. Memories of long-ago days broke free. She felt her whole life had been spent traveling from one cramped space to another. Always there seemed to be a next place.

As Philomene checked the house before turning in to bed, she came upon Suzette, reflecting. "You seem lost in thought," she said, entering the room.

"I've been thinking about a last name," Suzette said.

"You have a last name, *Maman*. Madame Mulon."

"If I can pack up and start fresh at my age," Suzette said,

"I can change my last name." One of the few advantages of growing old, she decided, was the freedom hidden in it. People seemed to relax their expectations, suddenly allowing so much more, word or deed. "*Mère* Elisabeth is gone, bless her soul, and Nicolas's people never did want me to be one of them. There's no need to hang on to Jackson or Mulon. From now on, everyone is to call me Suzette DeNegre."

It amused Suzette to take a new name, especially one of her own making, insisting they all call her by something entirely different. If she felt like it, she might even change her last name again. If she felt like it.

At Emily's new house Suzette took as a personal campaign the effort to save the transplanted rosebushes, whose flowers were wilted and drooping since the short journey from Billes Landing to Cornfine Bayou. She pruned back stems to the five-leaf, slow-soaked the bushes to encourage deep rooting, and set traps for beetles. Already she saw improvement.

All of the women shared chores, helped tend Emily's children, looked after the chickens and livestock, put in a vegetable garden. Family Sunday dinners moved with Philomene and Suzette to the other side of the Red River, to Cornfine Bayou.

In the beginning the house was unfamiliar, and Suzette had great difficulty keeping still in bed. From her room she listened to the night's quiet sounds or pushed her feet into slippers to walk the house before returning to bed. One night, prowling noiselessly down the narrow hallway toward the kitchen, she heard the subdued hum of conversation. Philomene's reassuring voice played counterpoint to Emily's hollow-toned dejection. Not wanting to disturb their intimacy, Suzette stayed silent, listening.

"It is difficult for you to believe at this moment, but you can survive this," Philomene said.

Emily's voice sounded limp. "I know you mean well, *Maman*, but you can't understand. There is no happiness left for me. Surviving isn't enough."

"You have never allowed sadness around you, child. It will be that way again."

"Why, *Maman*?" Emily asked. "Why would you give up your farm to move here?"

"A family belongs together."

"Bet is on the other side of the river."

"Bet doesn't have the same kind of pain." Philomene sighed heavily. "Emily, I understand the suckhole loneliness makes after love disappoints. *Mémère* Suzette and I can help."

"This is nothing you can mend. Joseph has left me, humiliated me." Emily's voice threatened to break. "Even so, I still want him."

"That will play out in its own way, in its own time. For now, it's you and the children that matter." There was a long pause, and Suzette heard the pouring of coffee, the soft scraping of a cup replaced on the table. "Emily, there is one thing you must never forget. You do not come from fragile stock."

Suzette thought then of her own mother, how her death left an emptiness even now but had brought young Emily closer. Maybe this was the lesson each generation had to learn, over and over again. Where the strength began, and how it kept itself alive.

Philomene's voice was low and soothing, almost crooning. "I am the rock in your garden, Emily, and you are the bloom in mine. Count on me."

Angelite Billes and husband Dennis Coutee.

Suzette quietly retraced her steps down the hall to her room, leaving mother and daughter alone in the kitchen.

Life went on, for all of them.

It took time, but the flush came back to Emily's cheeks, and the Sunday came when she sang and danced for them again. Joseph reappeared in their lives. The first reasons given for his visits were to make repairs to the house on Cornfine Bayou or to bring gifts for the grandchild, but finally the detailed excuse making fell away, and his appearances became frequent and accepted.

As a new bride still in the habit of trying to please her husband, Lola Grandchamp reluctantly permitted the children to visit their father at Billes Landing three or four times a year, at Joseph's insistence, but even then they couldn't enter the house. Before allowing them to go, Emily examined each of them, inspecting their freshly washed hair, the press of their Sunday-best clothes, the polish to their shoes.

L–R. Mary Billes, Angelite Billes holding Buck Andrieu, Emily Fredieu, Josephine Billes.

Only then could they leave their house on Cornfine Bayou, the six of them together, Angelite, T.O., Josephine, Joe, and Mary, with Buck in Angelite's arms, eagerly setting off for Billes Landing, a family adventure. As Buck got older he walked alongside them through the woods. The house on Cornfine Bayou emptied out by six, leaving behind three older generations of women, Suzette, Philomene, and Emily.

T.O. brought back reports of Lola sitting off to one side

in the deepest shade of the gallery, while Joseph basked in the center of the circle of his children. It was an uneasy truce for all of them, but they managed. For years they all managed.

Angelite entertained the attentions of several suitors. She settled on Dennis Coutee, a tall, lanky colored farmer with an even disposition, as fair of skin as she. He was a neighbor, a sharecropper, and wanted from the first to make her his wife. Angelite broke new ground in the family by marrying Dennis and soon afterward becoming pregnant, in that order. She lived with her new husband on his plot and was close enough to walk to Emily's house every day. The couple often took supper there.

T.O. worked in the sawmill, with no greater ambition than a little money in his pocket, but he had a restless disposition like his father. He passed all the way into his late teens committed to no one thing in particular and often went off by himself, appearing and disappearing at will. He was a polite and self-effacing young man, handsome in a gentle way, but he kept his own counsel. T.O. was never quite the same after the move from Billes Landing, except with Angelite. Only his sister seemed to coax him toward liveliness, keep him from brooding, from going into himself too deeply. With Angelite he laughed and even joked.

Josephine and Mary, young women five years apart, were so compatible that it became difficult to think of them separately. They preferred their own company to any other; both were shy with outsiders. The girls seemed content around the farm.

Joe Jr. grew tall, so confident in himself that they began to call him "Man." The most forward of the colored girls in the small community competed for his notice, and he

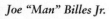

Joe "Man" Billes Jr.

encouraged the attention, unable to resist a pretty face, but he never allowed himself to become entirely distracted from learning all he could to be able to follow in his father's footsteps. Joe had Joseph Billes's drive, did well in school, and worked hard at his lessons.

The turn of the century came and went, and they set up their own routines on Cornfine Bayou, mixing in the past and the future. The young outnumbered the old, and they all prepared for the imminent arrival of Angelite's second child.

Angelite delivered a small, weak son, but they lost her in childbirth. After a long and difficult birth, passing from one day into the next, life and death made an unbearable trade.

It was then that Suzette began to feel she had spent enough time with both the living and the dead, that to outlive a great-granddaughter meant she had surely gone on for too long. The death place in her mind was overfull.

They mourned on Cornfine Bayou, a deep and profound grief, but the demands of the living trumped the call of the dead. Emily plunged headlong into the raising of her two orphaned grandsons, a woman's concession to the caprices of life. Philomene spent extra hours in the kitchen preparing food, forcing everyone to eat. Little Buck wrapped his bony arms around their necks, and they consoled him in turns.

The old women had children to raise, food to put on the table, the farm to run, and each other. Josephine and Mary grew more inseparable every day. Joe, the clever son, was smart and popular, surrounded always by friends as well as family, and found his solace there. Everyone else had someone, but T.O. and Angelite had been the natural pairing in the family while she lived, his confidante, and after she died T.O.'s absences from the house became longer and more frequent.

Angelite Billes Coutee gravestone.

Joseph Billes started to come apart, an alarmingly rapid deterioration. Overnight he took on an old man's shuffle, halting, tentative, losing a full inch of his height. Weight vanished from his too thin frame, the flesh covering his gaunt cheeks pulled overly tight across his face, his brooding eyes pronounced and watery.

With Angelite gone, a neediness opened in Joseph so profound that it seemed to push aside caution. He couldn't get enough of his remaining children and summoned them more often to the house on Billes Landing. The unbearable tension there between Joseph and Lola grew tauter than a hangman's noose, with Joseph seemingly oblivious of the hostility Lola directed toward the six of them in their Sunday finery when they marched en masse through the gate. They went whenever summoned, still six, with Angelite gone and little Ernest added.

39

Joseph sent word to Cornfine Bayou that he requested the presence of his children on the upcoming Saturday at Billes Landing, the first anniversary of Angelite's death. They were their customary six, outfitted in Sunday best, dresses and shirts starched and ironed, shoes polished, backs stiff even in the heat. They sat on the edges of their chairs along the cramped gallery, and Joseph held Ernest on his lap. T.O., the oldest of the Billes children now, was twenty-four, Mary at fifteen was the youngest, and Angelite's baby, Ernest, celebrated his one-year birthday.

Joseph made idle conversation while Lola fanned herself on the far side of the gallery. When he cleared his throat and coughed grandly, a staged sound meant to signal an announcement, T.O. put down his coffee cup.

"As my natural children and grandchildren," Joseph said, "this land is to be yours when I die."

Lola let out a small, surprised gasp and quickly pulled her lace handkerchief to her mouth, as if by so doing she could swallow Joseph's offending words and make them disappear. She stood, all eyes now on her, and after an awkward moment of apparent disorientation fled into the house, the petticoats under her cotton dress rustling violently.

The next time the six came to Billes Landing, instead of her regular spot at the far end of the gallery, Lola refused to appear. But she was a presence just the same, perched inside the front room with the front door ajar and the outer screen door latched shut, a pair of listening ears and a voice that could lash out at them whenever she chose.

"Mongrels," Lola said midway through the visit. Her voice was distinct, the word clear to everyone on the gallery.

"Mongrels," she repeated, more loudly this time. "More of that trashy life you led before me. I won't be a party to it. I don't want them on my property."

"Woman, shut that noise," Joseph said as if to the air. He had been drinking, and there was a slight slurring to his words. "You know whose property this is, and I'll have anyone I please here. These are my children."

He made a show of bouncing Ernest on his knee until the toddler, too young to understand the mood, grinned his delight.

After that day the invitations to the house on Billes Landing were withdrawn. No more summons, no need for T.O. to slick back his hair or polish his shoes. Joseph asked them to stop coming to the house, showing up instead more often on Cornfine Bayou.

The rains were heavy, and it was a nasty wintry day at the tail end of January. T.O. was grateful for the protection of his everyday fedora. As a boy he had run these same woods, but the groves were thicker then, the trees so close together that they kept out the light and either dampened some of summer's oppressive heat or provided shelter from the worst of winter's downpours. The pines had been thinned since those days.

His pace was unhurried but deliberate, and he sorted through plausible explanations for why he was in this part of the woods at this time of the afternoon. He could say he was taking a shortcut to his mother's or uncle's

Theodore (T.O.) Billes.

house for early supper, or running an errand to borrow a blade for Mr. Ephrom over to the sawmill, or on his way to pick up a sack of salt. Now and then on his visits he came across men on foot or on horseback, usually his father's renters or men otherwise in Joseph Billes's employ. Some were friendly enough, stopping to make small talk, happy to run into another soul in the backcountry, and some just passed without speaking. It was a small community, and most knew who he was, as he knew them. There were times when he heard someone approach and hid until they passed, but more often than not he didn't see anyone, coming or going.

When he had first started the visits, his fear of discovery had been strong. Now T.O. didn't worry about this part of the journey. He knew these woods as well as he knew the habits of the catfish in the river. Still, it wouldn't do to be caught this far into Joseph Billes's property without a reason ready to his tongue.

The rhythm of the visits had settled into a familiar pattern, always starting with a vague feeling of restlessness, just beyond his grasp, as if something deep inside were fighting to be given its due. As though he were trying to remember some important promise made to a friend that kept sliding away because the doing had been left off for too long. That feeling could last for hours or it could last for days, until the sharp jolt of anxiety and panic gripped him and would not allow him to sit still. The need to take action pained him in a physical way, in the twisting of his stomach or the pounding of his head. When the pattern first started, he hadn't known how to help himself. By now he understood that whatever else he had been doing would have to wait, no matter whether it was day or night, storm or clear, winter or summer, convenient or no.

He needed to start on the path out to his father's house for the visit.

As soon as he rounded the last bend and saw the roof of the house, his heart sped. The house had power over him, fear, anger, and anticipation all balled up in a knot with each breath he took. His reaction was the same every time, as if it were the first.

T.O. tasted that knot as it rose from deep in his belly up into his throat and threatened to choke him. What kind of life was this for a twenty-six-year-old man? For two years now he had spied on his father and his father's wife. The urgency started from the first week Joseph had told him not to come to his house on Billes Landing anymore, that he and the others were no longer welcome there.

Ten years had come and gone since Joseph had brought his wife from St. John the Baptist Catholic Church in Cloutierville across the river to the house on Billes Landing. Direct from the wedding ceremony to the house that had been T.O.'s home just the day before.

T.O. decided to take his position behind the chicken house, his favorite site when the weather was wet. He could use the eaves to keep the rain off and still have an unobstructed view of the screen-enclosed gallery. T.O. knew all of the comfortable places to hide around the perimeter of the house on Billes Landing, each giving him a different vantage point of the grounds.

When he had first been pulled to Billes Landing, T.O. sometimes kept to his position for almost an entire day, just for the possibility of a momentary glance of Joseph or Lola. Now it was enough to know that the house entwined them both in unhappiness with each other. Their sorrow was his tonic. Sometimes it took only a few minutes for the weight of the house to take hold, for him to feel soothed and strong enough to take his life back, and he could head back home without so much as shifting out of his original crouchlike stance. He never stayed more than a few hours anymore.

Joseph often left early in the morning and stayed away late into the night. Sometimes he came home for dinner or supper, but many times he did not, and they had few visitors. In the last two years, since the banishment, Lola had also made clear that Joseph's society-marginal friends were no longer welcome in the house. When his old acquaintances needed work, gossip, or favors, they intercepted Joseph elsewhere or called out from the gate to see if anybody was home without entering the front yard or climbing the steps.

Even as T.O. approached the chicken house, he heard voices from the gallery. It was Antoine and Joseph, arguing. T.O. quickly hid himself deeper in the shadows, but he could still hear.

"Be reasonable." Antoine's voice was honey. "I am your closest relative here. Two thousand acres cannot fall into hands incapable of overseeing it properly."

"My children are my closest relatives," Joseph said.

"They cannot inherit."

"How is it you have come to be so familiar with the law?"

"It is common knowledge, your foolishness about the inheritance." Antoine did not keep the disapproval from his voice. "I would administer it on their behalf."

T.O. lost a few words when Joseph lowered his voice, but he picked up the thread again.

"We won't do any more business together, Antoine. There's no use working with a man you can't trust. I was the one who made it possible for you and your family to come to this country, and this is how you repay me?"

"Some would say it was money owing," Antoine said, but now his voice was strained and harsh. "You talk trust? People in town want to do business with me now, it's me they trust. You insist on turning your back on your own kind, even now. It's not decent."

"Do not ever dare come back to my house," Joseph said.

T.O. heard Antoine mount his horse and ride away to the east and then the bang of the screened door as Joseph retreated into the house.

T.O. thought about Antoine Morat for most of his walk back to Cornfine Bayou. Since he was a small boy, whenever white men frightened him, it was Antoine Morat's face attached to the menace. Antoine was part of a blurry memory T.O. carried of his grandfather Narcisse pushing him out of his lap in the cool of an evening long ago, before his father went away to New Orleans. Antoine was one of the men who had moved them out of the house on Billes Landing twelve years before. All of the colored in the area knew Antoine could be mean and high-handed, and he was one of the white men in town calling for a cleaner separation between Joseph and Emily.

But it was A. J. Morat, Antoine's son, whom T.O. hated. Five years younger than T.O. and born to a life of white privilege T.O. could only dream of, A.J. was away at medical school while T.O. picked up odd jobs at the sawmill. Joseph had always been conspicuous in his affection and admiration for the boy and lavish in his desire to provide him opportunities in life.

T.O. sometimes felt as if his very life were being stolen away. As if every time he tried to draw fresh air into his lungs, something tightened its grip around his body, like a snake slowly crushing its prey. They took their toll, the menial tasks at the sawmill, the spying that only confirmed the contempt people harbored for his family, his corrosive longing for other people's lives, the unquenchable need for his father. And he was drawn to the same cycle again and again. The jitteriness, the pull, the walk, the pounding heart, bitterness confronted, the numbing calm, and the long walk home.

He remembered happier times, when they all lived in their house together and his mother would laugh and clap and dance to the tunes his father played on his mandolin.

How they would all sing together. But he also remembered his father's absences and his mother taking on the back-breaking work. It was like hitching up a butterfly to pull a plow.

By the time T.O. reached halfway between the house on Billes Landing and Cornfine Bayou, he was calm enough to think about how to break the cycle of the visits. Joseph and Lola were still miserable together, and Antoine had been dismissed from his father's business. The next time the nervousness beckoned he would fight the urge and get on with his life, the way other people managed to do. He would find a good woman and marry. They would settle down and have children. There were jobs at the sawmill or the railroad, enough to support a family. He would begin his life again on his own terms. It all seemed possible.

There was almost a lightness in his step by the time he set foot on Cornfine Bayou. Maybe he had taken his last visit. The pressure in his stomach was relieved, and his head was full of the possibility that evil could be punished, that good things could unfold for him, too.

```
Soon after He [Narcisse] and others
incourged Joe Billis to Marrie awhite
Woman, they wasn't as happy as they all
thought they would be.
--Cousin Gurtie Fredieu, written family
   history, 1975
```

Two weeks later T.O. was pulled back to Billes Landing, the cycle unbroken. From his position behind the chicken house he had a partial view when Joseph appeared at the front door of the main house midmorning, walking his old-man shuffle. He made for the barn, saddled his horse, and rode off in the direction of the sawmill. Only minutes later, as if they were waiting, Antoine Morat rode onto the property with another man T.O. didn't recognize. The unknown man had a professional air about him. When he took off his hat, a great shock of black hair curled around his face, thick as a horse's mane, setting off little gold-framed glasses that perched at the bridge of his thin nose. He had on a dark jacket and matching trousers, a suit that looked as if it couldn't carry the weight of an honest day's work, and thin-soled shoes. With a confident gesture the man pulled a sheaf of papers from his jacket pocket and tapped them against Antoine's sleeve before Lola let them inside.

Something was seriously wrong. Wrong enough that he needed to tell someone what he had seen. T.O. was sure these men were up to no good.

Emily was the last awake, the last one up for the night, in a slow, restless prowl around the house when she heard the disturbance from the front gallery. It was no doubt Joseph, his high-strung disposition stretched to breaking. He drank too much of late, she thought, the liquor making him absent and vague, but it took him beyond the sting his life had become. He often didn't come into the house, just sitting out on her gallery into the night, and she usually let him be; his behavior was so erratic that even she couldn't calm him some of the time.

The screen door creaked in protest as she went outside. Joseph was sprawled in the rocking chair, his hand tightened around a piece of paper. He slept heavily, the sleep of the willfully numbed, or he had passed out. She would find out soon enough. Emily assumed he had suffered another disappointing trip to the lawyer.

She gently shimmied the creased page from his grip, a note written in his own cramped hand. The moonlight was too dim, so she left Joseph where he was and went back inside to light the kerosene lamp, letting the wick up high to make out the script on the page. The writing was alternately pinched and sprawling.

Billes Landing
January 29, 1907

If I kill myself it will be for the trouble that my wife has given me for 10 years. Bury me in my garden near the asparagus plants. I am tired of hearing her quarrels and abuses of me. I have worked hard and deprived myself to gain what I have, and today see that it has all become misfortune. I cannot understand for what reason she does not want my children to be around me, or come to see me. I have no more life nor hope, so I might as well die or take my life. Without the children, I have nothing left in this world— not relatives nor friends. Those who I thought were friends have turned against me. Those who I thought would help me for my children's sake have banded together to refuse my wishes.

My wife has been lost to me for several years. She has treated me lower than a Negro, which has caused my trouble until today, all because my children were colored, but I hope that the law will give them justice notwithstanding their color. I have not been able so far to guarantee their future as I had hoped. My wife knew that I had these children before I married her. She does not eat with me at the table, and does not show any affection or understanding. She always has some excuse to give, and it is for this reason that I give up the fight, to end this life. It is better to have it end.

Joseph Billes

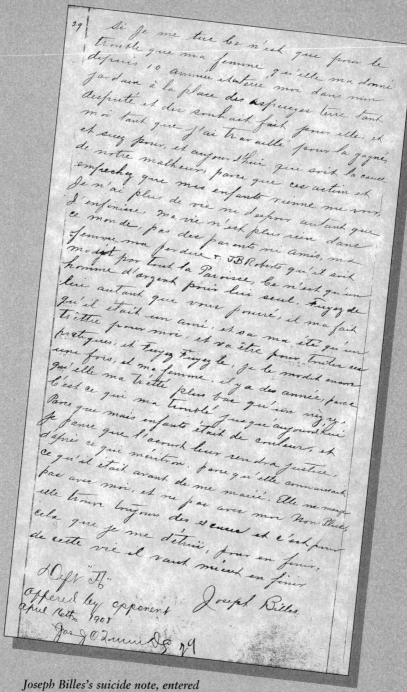

Joseph Billes's suicide note, entered
into evidence, Louisiana Supreme Court records.

Emily exhaled softly. Once more, to this.

She went to the kitchen and set a pot of strong coffee to drip, and while waiting for the coffee to brew, she checked to make sure everyone else in the house was asleep, looking into their rooms as if they were still her little children to watch over. Mary, the youngest at seventeen, shared the bed with Josephine, twenty-two, like two parts of a whole, even in sleep. T.O. and Joe had both spent a full day at the sawmill and slept the deep sleep of exhaustion at the back of the house, on the closed-in porch that served as their room. Her mother and grandmother shared the back bedroom, both snoring, one a soft whistle, the other a train straining uphill. Her family. The aroma of the coffee pulled her back to the kitchen. Emily tasted the hot, bitter brew, satisfied it was strong enough.

She poured the coffee in two oversize mugs, sweetened them heavily with sugar, and took them out to the gallery. She set down the mugs, brought another chair from the house, and pushed at Joseph until he crossed to wakefulness. She stroked his grayed hair where it was thinnest. He leaned in to her touch, as grateful as one of her cats. Finally he opened his eyes, and they sat and drank the strong brew in silence for a time.

"I saw the letter," Emily said gently.

"It's just my first copy," Joseph said, swirling the coffee slowly in the mug. "I'm really going to do it this time, 'Tite, but I couldn't without telling you first. I brought you more money." He pulled a thick packet wrapped in canvas from inside his jacket and handed it to her. His skin gave off a combination of stale tobacco, coffee, and liquor.

"This is from my account in New Orleans," he continued. "No one here has any idea of how much I keep down there. I opened it separate from the business. I don't trust the Colfax bank. They've shown they're against me. And you."

Emily took the package, setting the bundle in her lap as Joseph leaned back in the chair, closing his eyes against the dark. "Joseph, what possible good comes from the things you talk about in this letter?"

"They can make me marry, but they can't make me live," Joseph said, eyes still closed. "It all turns to dust anyway."

"Your children still need you here."

"The children are grown, there's nothing more I can do for them. They won't let me."

"No one ever let you do anything, Joseph. Why grow faint now?"

Joseph was quiet for a moment. "You remember Frank Rigsby, scratching out a living on his farm?"

Emily felt a knot grow hard and cold deep in her stomach. "Of course. He took up with Sarah."

"They burned his house to the ground last night, and now he's disappeared. That wasn't an accident."

"Is Sarah all right?" Emily was more frightened than she wanted to show. She knew there would be trouble the moment Rigsby moved Sarah in with him, a penniless white farmer and a Negro woman without standing. "You said it yourself, Rigsby was poor, without connection. He didn't have anything to fight back with, not like you."

"Sarah is safe for now, back with her people, but you can't afford to put a good face on this, 'Tite. You have more to lose than anybody. How many times did they come to me to say leave that colored woman alone? Rigsby was a fool for not listening, and Sarah is lucky she didn't go down in the fire. It could have gone much worse. It's impossible to fight them all, 'Tite. It's not just one or two. They drove Rigsby out, and nobody knows whether he's dead or alive, except that he's gone. That could have been us, ten years ago."

The two of them sat, nursing their cold coffee.

"I went to the lawyer again today," Joseph said. "He said I don't have much of a chance, that I have to give it up."

"Give what up?" Emily asked.

"Trying to pass my land to the children. He says it can't be done inside the law. That even if it was legal, the town wouldn't stand for it. He says only so much can be given because they're illegitimate, but it's really because of color. He won't help."

"We couldn't marry, and now they say the children are illegitimate." Emily shook her head wearily. "Joseph, my mother would say, 'That's the way of it, now what do we do about it?' Threatening to kill yourself again isn't any answer. This is all the more reason for you to stay around and take care of them. You left me a long time ago for that woman. Packed me up and carted me out of my own house. That is for you and me to carry between us. But who will be the children's father if you do this?"

"I'm tired, 'Tite. It's too hard."

Emily sat upright in her chair, her back no longer touching the supports. Her voice was even, but her coffee spilled as she set the mug down too hard on the small table between the two chairs.

"You're tired? You're the one who's tired?" She brought her face up close to Joseph's. "You don't have the right. You're the one in the big house on the Landing, stealing down here when you have a need. The girls wait for you to come around as if you're a beau instead of their father. They're of the age when they should be finding men of their own, but they're too good for the Negroes and not up to the standards of the whites. T.O. and Joe Jr. come home at night with 'Papa did this, Papa did that,' full of dreams. They need you to clear a way for them through the banks and the railroads, the sawmill and the courts. You have a duty to your children."

Joseph ran his fingers through his thinning hair. "Listen, 'Tite, there's no more to be done. I tried. You have this land and the house. No one can take that away. I've made out a will leaving everything to my nephew. He'll make sure you all are taken care of. Lola won't get anything, and my brothers won't, either."

"Do you think I care who *won't* get something? All I care about is giving your own flesh and blood a better chance. We need you here. You're quick to trust Antoine's son, when Antoine has been so set against us all along. I know you love the children, Joseph, and you have to help them now, even if that makes it harder for you."

"They've been to see me, the night riders." Joseph gave a helpless shrug. "You'll be safer if I'm not here."

"Are you thinking of me now?" Emily's eyes flashed hot, and the money bag slipped from her lap. Stacks of paper money spilled out on the cypress boards of the gallery. She left it there. "You write a fool note saying you're going to kill yourself, and I'm not even in it. All you talk about is your precious white wife, and how she treats you. Was I just a servant to you all those years? Bearing your children, running the store, making a home? You loved me once. When did that play out?"

Joseph placed his hand on Emily's, but she batted it away and used it to gather the money back into the canvas bag.

"That's one thing that will never change," Joseph said. "You know that, 'Tite. I was stronger once, but they've threatened all of you unless I let the will go."

"Think, really think about your children. In my family, we don't share all of our stories, but it's easy enough to fill in the gaps, full of white men who left and the colored women who took over the children. Left for France, left for marriage. Angelite was the last to act it out." Emily set the canvas bag on the gallery planks and took one of Joseph's hands in hers. "After Jacques left, Angelite turned it inside out and married colored. The first in our family to have a marriage and a baby both, one before the other. Maybe that's enough of an example to shape a change for the rest, but I don't think so. You left to marry someone else, Joseph, but you never left your children behind. Don't leave them now."

She poured more coffee from the pot for both of them, the dark liquid barely warm now. "I'm worried about T.O.," she said, shifting her tone. "There's something you should know. You told me that you broke with Antoine, but your wife still meets him at the house. Antoine and somebody else T.O. didn't recognize."

"How could T.O. know that?"

"That's why I'm worried," Emily said. "He's been hanging around that house without you knowing for years. You need to help the boy get on with his own life."

"He's hardly a boy," Joseph said. "He's twenty-six years old, and you tell me he spies on me? How long have you known this?"

"I didn't until he told me today, but I can't say I'm entirely surprised. Your leaving hit him harder than any of the others. He worshiped you."

"I know." Joseph held his head in his hands. "Lola never said a word about seeing Antoine. He has no business at the house anymore."

"I thought it might be important." Emily pulled her shawl tighter around her shoulders. "Joseph, about the will. If you made one, you can make another. Go see some other lawyer outside the parish, but don't tell anyone here you're still trying to leave the land to the children. I know how fond you are of Antoine's son, but I don't trust that family."

"I should be able to do as I please with my own money," Joseph said.

"That's not the world we live in."

"Bring me some paper, 'Tite," he said finally.

Emily went into the house and returned with the lamp, a page of Billes Lumber Company stationery, and a pen.

"You can take back anything you said before and put this one in its place," she said as she handed the paper and pen to Joseph. She looked over his shoulder as he drafted a new document.

Billes Landing
February 22, 1907

Today I make my testament in my own hand, and I leave all that I have to my children and Antoine Morat, my nephew, in equal parts. My children are all recognized in the records of the courthouse that they were my children, and I gave to them 74 acres of land that day at the same time. I give them my money that they will find in the bank and elsewhere, and the property to be divided in equal parts.

Joseph Billes

This will is in French. It reads textually as follows:

Billis Landing
February 22th, 1907
Aujourd'hui je fait mon testament de ma propre main, que je laisse tour ce que j'ai à mais enfants et à Antoine Morat mon neveu, à part egale, Mais enfants sont tous reconnue dans le recorde de court house que c'était mais enfants et je leurs ai donné 74 acres of land en même temps, Je leur donne mon argent qui trouveront en Banque et ailleur, et les propriétés à partage egalle.
Signed.   *Joseph Billes*

Joseph Billes's will, entered into evidence with Louisiana Supreme Court.

They both read the note over, and Emily nodded. "Go on home now, Joseph. Sleep in your own bed. No use making things any worse than they already are. If you start to lose your nerve, remember the ones you'll leave behind. T.O., Joseph, Josephine, Mary. You can find another lawyer tomorrow when you feel stronger and have him hold the note for safekeeping."

"You have to believe me, 'Tite," Joseph said, squeezing her hand so tightly that it began to hurt. "I'm willing to lose the last drop of blood I have for my children."

41

A cold, steady rain fell, and from the look of the dark clouds across the night sky and the smell of the woods, it could keep up until morning. T.O. pulled his jacket tighter across his slender shoulders. The grayness of February had pressed in from early morning, and the night added its own oppressive dimension. Although the route was familiar through the dripping piney woods to his father's house, a tightness deep in his chest convinced T.O. something terrible was in the making.

Even after the shameful confession to his mother, after his promise that he would stop the visits, here he was again, after only one day. But he was the eyes and ears for his family, and trouble was closing in from every direction.

Joseph Billes was the center of a storm brewing. His threats to find a way to leave his money to his children had caused the resistance to him to grow more forceful, whispers and grumblings yielding to open discussions about moral depravity infecting the community. White people were angry, speaking openly to protest, and it didn't seem possible things could go on at the same pitch much longer.

The changes in tone started back when the evenings were still warm and the collected heat of the day turned sunbaked houses into ovens. Folks kept to their galleries late, sitting, talking, occupying themselves the best they could. The warm night air easily lifted their words and carried them to T.O. Now, in the cold, damp fogs of an extended winter, he had to prowl ever closer.

T.O. circled around the back of the house on Billes Landing, and as he approached, angry, insistent voices pressed past the drizzle and hung on the windless air. Since last summer, through fall, and into winter's cool grip, Lola and Joseph argued all of the time, without caution or reserve. Every word they exchanged was charged, and between them there seemed to be only silence or explosive irritation. Whatever truce they had fashioned over the years had unraveled, beyond repair.

T.O. crept even closer, crouching on the sodden ground just under the window at the side of the house, his boots caked with sticky, rust-colored mud.

Lola's voice was raised, wounded but crystal clear. "I may have been deceived in the beginning by your assurances of reform, but you are utterly incapable and indisposed to make a change in the manner of life you led before. It is only in the presence of your mulatto children and their shameless mother that you are civil, or so I hear. Is that where you were last night?"

"You never tried to understand me, making only the most feeble of attempts to live with me as a wife." Joseph's voice was distracted, almost offhand, as if this were an old dance and he was duty-bound to perform the obligatory steps. T.O. heard the drink behind the words.

"The only reason you married me," Lola said, control gone from her voice, "was to protect yourself from the townspeople. You courted me, and married me just to better your position in a community that had rejected you for your wickedness."

"It was my money you were after," Joseph said. "No other man would have you."

"What good is the money to me? You are so stingy I never benefit. I don't even have servants."

"You have no call for complaint. You don't sit to table with me, you have run off my friends with your airs, you never made me welcome in the bedroom."

"Coward." Lola dangled the word, thick and accusing, her voice slightly unsteady, and T.O. realized she too had been drinking. "Using me because you are afraid for your own personal safety. You never meant to put aside your colored family."

"You knew about the children from the beginning," Joseph said tiredly. "You pretended to take me, children and all."

"How often do you sneak over to Cornfine Bayou to see that mulatto woman and her mongrels? Do you suppose you can use your money to place those children somehow into decent society? I married a fool. It can never happen."

"I want them to inherit what it took my whole life to earn, the way any father would." There was passion building in Joseph's voice now. "You are cold and uncharitable, unable to grasp flesh-and-blood needs."

"Fidelity and support is your obligation under the law, and you have given me neither. Ten years as your wife means it is I who should inherit. You forced me to sign back the land donation you gave before we married, and I did so because you were my husband, entitled to obedience. No one explained my rights to me then. But your shameful conduct now forfeits all such respect."

"You were never forced," Joseph said quietly. "You gave back the land donation in front of witnesses. It is far too late to change that now."

Lola began to cry. "I am alone and friendless in the middle of nowhere," she said between sobs. "I want to move into town. I cannot go on living in this house."

"I built this house and made too many sacrifices to tolerate this contempt of your life in it. It wouldn't be proper for you to live alone in town, and I have no intention of moving."

"There are people willing to help me," Lola said thinly, tears gone. "I am not as defenseless as you imagine."

"Have you been putting our business before strangers, Lola?"

"The whole town talks about us, and what to do about the evil you have brought in their midst. I am a churchgoing Catholic woman, virtuous and honest, and I am tired of being exposed to the lowest creatures on this earth. I have been too shamed and too humiliated before now to publish to the world my unhappiness, and unwilling to give up my profound religious duty as a wife."

"Other wives take care of their men. You could learn a lesson from that."

"I performed for years as best I could under the circumstances, but the good people of the community are not going to stand by quietly any longer."

"I will leave the land to my children, the only ones who bring me happiness."

Lola's voice firmed. "You seek happiness no place else, preferring the company of Negroes over decent people, trying to pull me down, too, but I will not let you do it."

"You mean less than nothing to me."

There was a pause between the two of them, as if the exhalation of the one's vicious breath needed time to provide fuel for the other's response.

"The children you set such store by are an abomination before God," Lola said. "The oldest girl, just like her mother, taking up with any Frenchman she could entice with her free and easy ways, producing babies without a husband, without decency. Too bad the little nigger bastard survived. And the oldest boy, timid, afraid of his own shadow, hanging off your every word. No wonder you are so fond of them all. They are the only ones who look up to you."

Lola's words entered T.O. like poison, contempt and loathing so strong and thick that it passed through the walls of the house on Billes Landing and directly under his skin, full strength. T.O. turned away from the house. Their fighting filled him with dread instead of soothing him. Soaked through, he retraced his steps toward Cornfine Bayou, stumbling repeatedly on the tangled undergrowth that pulled from below.

Distracted, he almost didn't hear the approach of horsemen coming through the woods at first, until they were almost on him. There were at least two riders, and he heard the nearby snort of a hard-ridden horse as one of the riders stopped in the path he had been getting ready to take. T.O. eased himself behind the base of a wide oak tree, pressing his back into the damp trunk, closing his eyes against the rain.

"Hold up. I don't want to go any farther. Can't we do

this another way?" It was Antoine Morat. T.O. recognized the voice at once. He was careful not to move, willing himself invisible, slowing his breathing to drive the pounding from his ears.

"You've waited a little late to go soft."

T.O. didn't recognize the voice of the other man.

"I tell you I can't do it," Antoine said.

"What happened to your big talk? The old Frenchman brought it on himself, carrying on the way he has. That land rightly belongs in your hands, the right hands. Have you forgotten your own son's needs so quickly?"

"But Lola wasn't supposed to be part of this," Antoine said.

"There's no other way, otherwise it all reverts to her. Do I have to remind you how much you need the money? And now, him making all this trouble about the inheritance, cutting you out entirely. He's laughing at us. There isn't a respectable man anywhere in these parts who would excuse his behavior with the colored woman."

"I tell you I just can't do it. He's my cousin."

"By the time you get your nerve up, there won't be anything left to fight for. I can't hold him off forever from finding a means to pass the land the way he wants. Meanwhile he's selling off bits and pieces of the property to the railroad, and Lola and the rest of the Grandchamps have their hands out, too, expecting a share."

"Lola thinks she's in with us."

"There's no helping that now."

"I won't do it. We'll go and talk to him. Make him see reason."

"The old fool is too bullheaded to reason, or we wouldn't have had to come this far. We're beyond talk. Let's go. We need to get it done."

T.O. caught the sour odor of his own fear leaking out in his sweat. They were headed out to his father's place. He should follow them. And do what? This was a matter for the law, so only white could help. He couldn't get tangled up in white business without hanging himself somehow. He would have to explain why he was out in the woods, how he happened to overhear the conversation. He wouldn't be believed and would end up being blamed for something.

T.O. shook, wet and weak against the tree, caught in indecision long after the riders had gone.

At last he straightened up and began to move with as much of a sense of purpose as his legs would allow.

T.O. was so jittery that he made Emily nervous as they worked side by side in the garden, tying back the string bean vines. High-strung, like his father. When T.O. had refused to go to the sawmill this morning with his brother, Joe, for the second day in a row, Emily put him to work around the farm, thankful he wasn't out snooping around Billes Landing. She was convinced he was keeping something from her.

The weekend had come and gone, she hadn't heard yet from Joseph, and she was worried. She had lived through Joseph's black moods before, and the sooner he found a new lawyer and proved to himself he was in control of his own affairs, the sooner he would break out of the grip of despair that held him fast.

Emily heard the horses before she saw them and was surprised to see her son Joe riding with the sheriff and several other men toward the house. Something was very wrong.

They must have gone by the sawmill first to get Joe and bring him back to Cornfine Bayou. The men tethered their horses at the side of the house and dismounted. Emily threw Joe a questioning look, and Joe lifted his shoulders slightly, signaling that he didn't know what this was about, either.

"We're here on official business," the sheriff said to Emily, "here to talk to everyone in your house."

"Go collect the girls and *Maman* Philomene," Emily said to T.O. To the men she said, "Let's go inside."

The sheriff, a heavyset man with a doughy face and stubborn stubble, followed Emily to the front room, sitting on the far end of the same couch where Suzette half lay, half sat, a quilt tucked neatly around the lower half of her body. This was Suzette's regular day place, surrounded by a small pile of socks and other garments waiting to be darned or patched. The sheriff's circle of men continued to stand. Although it was only midmorning, the sheriff looked as if he were at the end of a particularly long day. As they waited he glanced at the oil painting hanging over the mantel. A flickering question registered briefly in his eyes and disappeared again.

Philomene and the girls entered the house quietly, stray bits of hay still clinging to their clothes. T.O. followed. Barely subdued panic flooded the faces of both girls. They stood along the wall in a tight clump, and Mary took Josephine's hand.

There wasn't a single rustle or cough, and the sheriff seemed to wait overlong for a silence already descended in the room. Finally he turned to Emily.

"There's been an occurrence out on Billes Landing," he said, speaking in English. "Joseph Billes and Lola Grandchamp are dead."

There was a collective gasp that met in the middle of the room, impossible to separate into individual sound, belonging to each of them. The sheriff paused, judging reactions to the news, looking boldly from one face to another, making no attempt to disguise his scrutiny.

"On Saturday night or Sunday morning, Joseph Billes killed his wife by shooting her in the back, and then turned a gun on himself," the sheriff said. "I have a list of questions, the same questions we're asking all his neighbors and relevant acquaintances."

Emily had trouble keeping up, already a beat behind trying to translate the sheriff's English words to French. She had just seen Joseph, touched the warmth of his cheek, stroked his hair. Joseph dead? It couldn't be true. She exchanged the briefest of glances with Philomene; her mother's face was impassive, but her gaze reached across to steady Emily. Joseph wouldn't have murdered Lola. Or turned the gun on himself. But if Joseph and Lola were dead, someone would have to pay. Was it someone in this house they had chosen? Emily steeled herself against the endless possibilities of what could turn dangerous because of these white men in her house.

"Joseph is dead?" she couldn't stop herself from asking, although it was as much a statement as question.

The sheriff nodded, then made a small beckoning motion with his hands. One of his other men brought forward a sloppily wrapped bundle and handed it to the sheriff.

"Evidence, collected at the scene of the crime," he said.

He unfolded the cloth to reveal an old-style French pistol, a Winchester rifle with a dark walnut stock, and a large pocketknife. Why were there so many different weapons?

Emily had to pull her eyes away from the objects in front of her. The French pistol was Joseph's. The rifle and knife were not.

The sheriff addressed himself to the Billes men. "Do you recognize this pistol as belonging to Joseph Billes?" he asked.

The brothers looked from one to the other.

"Just answer the questions, boys."

Emily saw T.O.'s eyes go soft and silently willed him to stay strong.

"No, sir, I never saw that gun before." T.O.'s voice had fled to a whisper.

"I don't recognize it either, sir," Joe said.

Then the questions came in rapid succession: How about the rifle? Have you seen the knife before? How often did Joseph Billes drink whiskey? How much? Would you consider him a drunk? When did you see him last? Did he seem troubled or bothered? Did he seem a rational man or a desperate one?

"I haven't seen my father since Christmas," T.O. said. "He seemed fine then."

"I saw him last Wednesday," Joe admitted. "I borrowed a team of his oxen to do some hauling, but we didn't talk long. There was nothing different than usual."

The sheriff turned to Emily and repeated the same questions, as if he were already bored with them. In spite of the swift deadening of her mind and the clawing beast housed in her chest, she gave the same answers as her sons. She moved through her exchanges with the law as if they were dancing a slow waltz.

"Yes, I used to live on the Billes place and was moved away by Joseph Billes.

"Yes, I was a neighbor and friendly as such with both Mr. and Mrs. Billes.

"No, I don't know whether he was in any way troubled.

"No, I can't remember ever seeing this pistol or that rifle or a knife.

"No, I don't know what went on between Joseph and his wife, Lola."

As she spoke, conscious of Philomene's steady gaze, Emily felt the force of her mother's voice deep inside her brain. *Deny.* There were real questions, and the men in her front room didn't seem interested in asking them. Who could have really done this thing? *Caution.* What ugly repayment was this for the choices she and Joseph had made? *Calm.* She wanted to defend Joseph, defend herself, convince these men how impossible it was to think Joseph shot Lola in the back or himself. *Grief has to wait.*

The white men in her front room seemed easily satisfied with the answers and began to shift restlessly, impatient to get away. Even the sheriff's heart wasn't in it. His eyes kept drifting back to the oil painting.

At last the sheriff rose. "We don't require any more answers at this time, but we might have to come back later," he said.

It didn't seem as though they were on a search to lay blame at Cornfine Bayou, and they didn't bother to question the girls or Suzette and Philomene.

The men mounted their horses and left. Only when the pine trees canceled the sight and sounds of their visitation completely did Emily sit down to cry.

Soon He [Joseph] drew much Money carried it
to Emily, devided so much each child, and
so much for Buck and Earnest, He went back
home and killed His bride made meny tracks
of blood over the floor and wrote on the
wall with Blood YOU MADE ME MARRIE BUT YOU
CANT MAKE ME LIVE, then shot hisself, in
1905.
--Cousin Gurtie Fredieu, written family
   history, 1975

The news traveled like wildfire, from the bottoms to the
hills, in the towns and back in the country, even into the
most remote recesses of the piney woods, but it was Edd
Fredieu who brought the first newspaper article out to
Cornfine Bayou. Narcisse's white son often came to visit, a
part of the mélange of extended kinfolk, black and white,
that collected under Emily's roof each Sunday. He pulled the
newspaper out of his saddlebag and folded it under his coat
jacket as soon as he got off his horse. The house was bustling
and full, as it was every Sunday, and he waited for an opportunity to pull Emily aside.

"I brought the newspaper for you," Edd said in low
tones. "I wasn't sure whether you wanted to be alone with
the news or not."

Emily studied her half brother, full of good intentions.
"Just wait long enough for everyone to get here, and then
read it out loud for all to hear," she said.

They gathered in the front room before Sunday dinner,

cousins, sister, nieces, nephews, aunts, uncles, grandparents, grandchildren. In a shamed voice Edd read the newspaper account of the murder-suicide described to Emily by the sheriff four days before.

Edd finished reading and gingerly laid the newspaper on the small table in the front room, as if it were a breakable thing. There was silence.

Emily knew then there was no use fighting, what with a newspaper article shamelessly making the claim that Joseph had shot himself in the head with a pistol, cut his own throat, and then come back to shoot himself in the face with a rifle. There would be no true investigation. The town was invested in the sheriff's account, and to seek a different explanation for the events on Billes Landing would undermine the collective relief that justice had at last been done.

Joseph was dead. There was nothing more to do about that. It almost didn't matter which one pulled back on the trigger or applied pressure to the blade; it was the acting out of the town's desire, finally snaring Joseph when his offense was over a decade gone. Caught because he tried to leave his children money and land.

Emily felt a hand pushing at the small of her back, moving her, and she found herself no longer in the front room but seated at the dining table, looking up at Philomene.

"We are not bringing this mess to our table," Philomene said, taking hold of the room's quiet gloom. "They print up anything that comes into their heads. Dinner is ready, and we aren't going to let good food go to waste. T.O., we're short a seat. Bring up another chair and put it at the children's table."

The next Sunday T.O. read aloud from a soiled, torn-out

The Colfax Chronicle

Official Organ of Grant Parish

Official Organ of Grant Parish School Board and Town of Colfax

Subscription $1.00, in advance

SATURDAY, MARCH 2, 1907

A Horrible Tragedy

Joseph Billes and Wife Found Dead

Billes Is Supposed to Have Killed His Wife and Then Committed Suicide

One of the most terrible double tragedies that ever occurred in Grant Parish was discovered at the home of Mr. Joseph Billes last Tuesday morning. The discovery was made by Mr. Adolph Dubois, who rode up to the gate for the purpose of getting permission to pen some oxen in Mr. Billes' pasture. He discovered the body of Mrs. Billes lying in the yard, and called for help, but receiving no answer he rode over to a neighbor's house and gave the alarm. Mrs. Billes was found in her nightclothes with a pistol bullet through her body. A posse of citizens broke open the house, which they found securely locked and barred from the inside, and discovered the body of Mr. Joseph Billes lying on the bed, his throat cut and two gunshot wounds in his head.

Sheriff Swafford and several citizens of Colfax went to the scene of the tragedy, which is on Red River twelve miles north of this place, at what is known as Billes Landing. A coroner's jury was impaneled by Magistrate L. G. O'Neal, assisted by Dr. J.L. Woodall, and sat into the night making investigations. Being unable to arrive at a satisfactory verdict the jury adjourned over until Thursday.

Mr. Billes, who was a native of France, was about 65 years of age, and his wife was about 60. She was a Miss Lola Grandchamp, and they were married at Cloutierville, Natchitoches Parish, six or seven years ago. Billes conducted a store about one mile south of the mouth of Bayou Nantachie for about twenty years, and had accumulated a good deal of property. He quit merchandising several years ago, and has been giving his attention mainly to his landed interests, having lately sold his timber lands for a large sum of money. He had raised a Negro family in that locality by a mulatto woman, and as he and his wife did not get along peaceably, it is thought they were a matter of rupture between Billes and his wife, leading possibly to the terrible tragedy.

The mulatto woman and her several children were moved to another house, and Billes and his wife lived at his old home by themselves, not even having any servants. They had no children, and the nearest neighbors are said to have lived a quarter or possibly a half mile away.

The coroner's jury was composed of the following citizens: I. McCain, L. Calhoun, C. G. Guin, W.L. Dowty, and B. E. Woods. At their sitting on Thursday they decided that Mrs. Billes came to her death from a rifle bullet fired into her back by her husband and that Joseph Billes killed himself.

The dead man's watch and pocketbook with a small amount of money in it were found undisturbed. He had been drinking a good deal of late to the point of delirium. The theory is that Mrs. Billes was killed Saturday night or Sunday, and that after killing her Billes locked himself in the house and decided to kill himself; that he first shot himself with his pistol, the ball passing under his jaw and out near his temple without reaching a vital spot, and lodging in the ceiling overhead; that he afterward tried to cut his throat, severing his windpipe half in two, but being unable on account of the dullness of his knife or his weakness and nervousness to cut the jugular veins; and that he then seized his Winchester and placing it under his chin fired a ball through his head, managing in his death struggle to fall across the bed before life left his body. Mrs. Billes must have laid out in the yard during the rain of Sunday evening and night.

The bloody finger marks and footprints about the room, and the streams and pools of blood, and the weapons with their crimson ghastly stains are said to sustain the theory of the jury's finding.

The remarkable thing that these two bodies should have lain for three or four days without discovery is hard to comprehend. Also the uncertainty as to the motive for the crime leaves a murky mystery; and there are lingering suspicions that after all it may be a horrible double murder, carefully planned and concealed by some fiend incarnate bent on robbing the old man of his coveted wealth.

Colfax Chronicle, *March 2, 1907.*

strip of newsprint. He said he'd found it in the New Orleans paper.

> A statement found today in the effects of Joseph Billes, the wealthy old Frenchman who last week shot and killed his wife and suicided at their home in Billes Landing, near here, indicates that the double tragedy was deliberately planned. The statement, which is signed by Billes, relates that should he be found dead at any time the end was to be attributed to an unhappy life with his wife. Billes also censured a prominent attorney of this section. The statement was written in French and dated Jan. 29th, of this year.

New Orleans Times–Picayune, *March 4, 1907.*

Emily's carefully hoarded reserve of energy drained away. Joseph had never destroyed his supposed suicide note, as she had done with so many others over the years. Now they used it as evidence that he'd planned to kill himself and Lola all along.

"I don't know where you got that paper," Emily said to T.O., "but I hope you have the good sense to keep to yourself and not provoke anyone. We all have to be especially cautious now."

"When the time comes, *Maman,* I'll get us our inheritance." There was a fever glint to his eyes that made Emily fearful of how indiscreet her son could allow himself to be.

That evening Emily brought hot sassafras tea to Philomene and Suzette. Suzette was fighting her third infection of the winter, confined to her bed, and Philomene sat with her.

"You look tired, daughter. Come sit with us." Philomene smoothed a place on the bed near her chair.

"I think I will sit for a few minutes," Emily said. "I seem always so close to exhaustion or weeping these days." As if to prove the point, her eyes moistened, but she closed them for a long moment to hold back the tears.

Philomene sweetened the tea for all three of them. "Is it that article in the newspaper?"

"I suppose." Emily's thoughts were sluggish. "There's no talking back to the page. People can present truth however they like. That article today makes clear that they found two documents. It wasn't until the second note that he censured the attorney. But they didn't mention one word of his wishes to leave half of his estate to the children. Only the suicide note."

"Someone still walking among us killed Joseph and Lola both, I am just thankful you were not a part of it," Philomene said. "That's the truth that matters. The only thing to do now is stay out of the way until the blood appetite passes. We have everything we need right here on the farm."

Emily shrugged. "It seems so hopeless. Joseph dead and T.O. with his manhood wrapped so tight to an inheritance he'll never see."

Suzette suddenly grew frantic, gesturing Emily closer. "You have family to look after," she whispered. "Throw down pride and go to the white man. It's the only way."

"To ask for what, *Mémère?*" asked Emily.

"Freedom."

It took several moments for Emily to understand that Suzette had gone back in her mind to the past. Emily nodded weakly, patting Suzette's hand reassuringly as again she fought back tears. Philomene was tight-lipped. They both stayed with Suzette until she fell into a ragged sleep.

"Keep T.O. from going into Colfax," Philomene said to

Emily as they got up to go to bed. "He's asking for trouble. His is the same talk that got Joseph dead."

They couldn't get enough of the story in town. Each day brought some new speculation, some new piece of evidence that proved once and for all that Joseph Billes had gotten exactly what he deserved. They were divided down the middle on whether he killed himself or not, whether he murdered his wife. For each fact that supported one side, there seemed to be another that fed the arguments of the opposing camp. The first doctor on the scene had written a report stating that no man, drunk or sober, could have sustained so many wounds by his own hand and still have the strength to cut his own throat.

The suicide note that his lawyer produced two days after the discovery of the bodies was indisputably in Joseph's own hand. Those who knew him and those who didn't debated whether Joseph was a drunk, whether he was a violent bully or a fun-loving man, a devilish fellow full of high spirits or just a devil.

There was, however, little disagreement that whatever the instrument, he had reaped what he had sown.

There was little talk of Lola. She had come too late to the margins of the town to hold as a centerpiece for the tragedy. Her family had no strong ties this side of Red River, and she was more a curiosity, a fuzzy detail, an unwitting accomplice in her own dark fate. The most popular of all the stories going the rounds was of the wailing, ragtag mulatto family being dragged out of Joseph's home and loaded into wagons so the new wife could move into the same house the next day. With each telling the family got larger, the confrontation between white and colored more

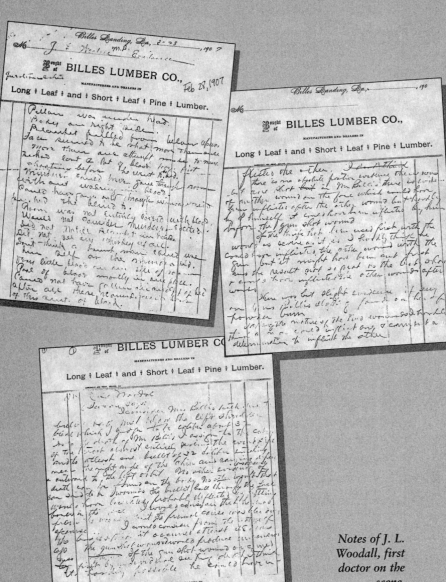

Notes of J. L. Woodall, first doctor on the scene.

violent, the more eyewitnesses who had always known what Joseph Billes was capable of. Lola seemed to have faded from view, eclipsed by the magnitude of the lesson still to be taught, a backdrop for the real story of moral decay and depravity.

By the second week the murder had been replaced as the front-page story of the *Colfax Chronicle*, but within the inner sections of the thin tabloid, beside the main advertisements and land sale notifications, T.O. found an editorial and brought it back to Cornfine Bayou. He read aloud to the family.

"According to this paper, Joseph's crime wasn't in having a colored family, it was in raising them," Philomene said when T.O. finished reading. There was more disgust and acknowledgment than anger in her voice. Her eyes darted from face to face. "We put this behind us today. We keep to ourselves, hold on to the land we have, and go about our business."

"He wanted us to have his property," T.O. shouted, almost a pure bellow of pain at the end. He slapped his open hand on the table so hard that the newspaper slid to the floor. "It says so right here. They admitted it."

"T.O., let it go," Emily said gently.

T.O. faced his mother directly, breathing hard. "You said to let it go when he moved us out of our house. You said there was plenty of time for me to be a man. That time is now. We can't just let him go like this."

"Don't be foolish," Emily said harshly. "Why do you think Joseph is lying in the cold ground? As soon as he started the talk about inheritance, it was set. This isn't over yet. The white folks will fight over that land, but there won't be anything more for us. You want to do something, T.O., find out Antoine Morat's plans. He's the one speaking for the estate."

T.O. quickly drew his hand to his face, but not before Emily saw the muscle below her son's left eye begin to twitch uncontrollably.

The Colfax Chronicle

Official Organ of Grant Parish

Official Organ of Grant Parish School Board and Town of Colfax

Subscription $1.00, in advance

SATURDAY, MARCH 9, 1907

The Sin of Miscegenation

The "Race Question," which has agitated the United States, and especially the Southern States, has lately been shown up with the distinctness of an awful tragedy in Grant Parish. We refer to the death of the Frenchman Joseph Billes and his wife, an account of which was published in the Chronicle last week.

It develops from a letter or statement found among the effects of Billes, written in French, that he killed his wife and then committed suicide. This is the tragic end of a white man who committed the crime against his race of raising a family of mixed Negro blood.

Joseph Billes was the last remaining representative of five white men, who fifteen and twenty years ago lived within a few miles of Colfax in open concubinage with Negro women or their quadroon offspring. His consort or paramour was the daughter of Narcisse Fredieu by a mulatto woman. Billes "took up" with her, and the couple lived together as man and wife, raising a family of several children. In the course of time Billes, by the help of this woman, who was frugal and helpful, and was really of comely appearance, amassed a pretty fair fortune.

Finding that his mongrel family was a matter of reproach to him among the white people, and prevented his mingling among them upon terms of social equality, Billes decided it was best for him to get himself a pure-blooded Caucasian wife.

Some eight or ten years ago he was legally married to Miss Lola Grandchamp, a spinster maid of about fifty years, and his concubine and her children had to be forcibly removed from the house before his legal white wife could take possession. The wife proved exacting, and objected to the constant exhibitions of affection which Billes manifested for his offspring and their mother who lived near by, and were maintained by the bounty of the father. No children blessed his legal wife, and the illegitimate children were a constant cause of strife. And so the matter grew from bad to worse.

His affection for the offspring of his youth and their mother grew upon him, and he wanted them to have his property. He consulted his attorney, and was told his illegitimate children could not inherit his estate; that only a portion of it could be devised them by will, and that only in a particular way.

He brooded over the matter, and in the French writing left by him, said it seemed that he had descended so low as to be no better than a Negro. This sheds a glare of light on the tragedy, and shows the frenzy into which he had worked himself to commit the terrible deed, by which he seems to have vainly imagined he could atone for the wrong done his innocent offspring, and palliate the crime against the white race.

In letters of blood he has left written the inexorable law of this Southland, that the taint of the inferior race forever debars admission into the social precincts of the Caucasian home. Let us hope and pray that poor Billes is to be the last in this path that will ever follow in this footpath of evil.

Colfax Chronicle, *March 9, 1907.*

T.O. was the protector of his family now, and it was his place to go. He found Antoine at the mill.

"Can I speak to you, Monsieur Antoine?" T.O. asked above the noise of the grinder.

"Not now, boy," Antoine yelled back. His bland face was composed, as if there were no surprise in the request. "Come around to my house after supper this evening."

T.O. waited for over an hour in Antoine's backyard before he heard the approaching crunch of boots on soil.

"That's too bad about your papa," Antoine said. "What is it you want to talk to me about, boy?"

T.O. backed away a small step and took a deep breath. "Joseph Billes wanted us to have the land, Monsieur Antoine. He told us it was our inheritance. They say you're the one looking over it. That's all we want."

Antoine laughed, a long, loud laugh. "That's all you

want? Two thousand acres of timberland, or what's left, that's all you want? Your papa was a murderer, and your mama raised a fool who doesn't know his place."

"He didn't kill anyone," T.O. said. "They can say whatever they want, but somebody else was there that night."

Antoine's smile faded. "You can be a smart boy, and turn around and go on back home to your mama, or you can end up like Joseph Billes. It isn't in you to be brave, boy. I'll see to it you come out of this just fine, you and your family. Hell, I'm godfather to your brother. I have your best interests at heart. It's what Joseph would have wanted." Antoine spat a stream of tobacco juice into the dirt at his feet. "You'll never go hungry. But you put aside this loose talk about inheritance and land. You don't know what you're up against, boy. Nobody wants to see you or your family hurt. It's over now. Closed."

"I saw you," T.O. said.

Antoine didn't change expression but turned to face T.O. squarely. "Just what is it you think you saw, boy?"

"I saw you going up to Billes Landing that night." The admission tasted strange on T.O.'s tongue. He had told no one about what he had seen in the woods before now.

"Nobody is interested in what you think you saw, boy."

"I heard you with another man," T.O. said, light-headed.

Antoine considered T.O. carefully. "Let's say you did see me that night. What of it? If you're trying to say I'm the one who killed Joseph Billes and his wife, you're crazy. A white man could testify against me in court, even though he would be mistaken. But now, that's not you, is it?" He sounded almost curious. "What has gotten into you?"

T.O.'s stomach burned. He knew the smart thing to do but couldn't make himself retreat. "He wanted the land to go to us."

Antoine didn't try to hide his disbelief or his anger. "It's your choice now. You repeat what you just said to anyone else, and I promise the whole lot of you will go. That's a promise. From the old lady to the baby. Fire burns hot and hides everything. I don't want to hear one more word about where I was that night. You don't have any rights, boy. I'm all that's standing between you and sure disaster. Now I'm tired of this. I'll tell you what you're going to do. You're going to go back to your mama, and you're going to praise me for not taking away the little bit you already have. I still have to straighten out Joseph's affairs in court. I'll do right by you, and you'll do right by me. You will never talk about that night again to anyone, including me. Is that what you plan to do next?"

T.O. felt hollow. "*Oui,* Monsieur Morat."

"I didn't hear you, boy."

"*Oui,* Monsieur Morat."

"That's better. Go on, get on off my property, while I'm still feeling generous."

Although Emily seldom left Cornfine Bayou, visitors brought word of the strange unfolding of testimony as one court proceeding followed another for months. Witnesses swore to Joseph Billes's temperament, his drinking, his intentions, his treatment of Lola, his colored family, and an earnest parade of supporters and detractors canceled each other out. As far as Emily was concerned, it was only the land they fought over. The two challengers in the courtroom were Antoine Morat on one side and Lola Grandchamp's heirs on the other.

In recent memory, from Montgomery to Colfax, there had been no story this exciting, no events firing so much speculation. Most had heard of the old Frenchman back in the woods who for so many years lived openly with his mulatto family, bringing them under his own roof, in the end coming to his senses to marry white. As the trials wore on,

Joseph Billes became an object lesson, useful when parents lectured their children about the consequences of race mixing or the inevitable aftermath of giving in to temptation. He became the topic of sermons on reaping and sowing and the subject of a series of editorials in the *Colfax Chronicle* on the evils of miscegenation.

Eventually on Cornfine Bayou they lost touch with the daily proceedings from the courthouse and settled back into farm life. Everyday issues crowded out the unreality and distance of the trials in Colfax. Suzette fell into ill health again in the worst of the season's heat and developed a deep cough that wouldn't ease. She hovered between sickness and recovery all summer, and they all did their best to make her comfortable.

Six months after Joseph was killed, late one muggy evening, Emily dragged her rocking chair out to the front gallery to join Philomene. They sat and rocked to the hypnotic clicking of crickets' music carried on the still air.

"I loved him, *Maman,*" Emily said out of nowhere.

"I know," said Philomene. She crocheted a white lace doily for the whatnot table, looping thread around her hooked needle and pulling it through itself in quick, expert motions. "He was all you ever knew."

"If they had just left us alone," Emily said. "We weren't hurting anyone. First they killed the us in him and me and then they killed him to make a lesson of it. All he wanted was to settle into old age surrounded by his children. He never would have left them, no matter how much he threatened, no matter if he wrote a thousand notes." The weight of the ongoing trials had exhausted Emily, although she'd played no part. "They took him away twice."

Philomene stilled the rocking of her moonlight chair and lowered her crochet needle to her lap. "Daughter, flesh-and-blood men killed Joseph, not 'they.' It gets too hard to figure out what you need to do next unless you bring it back around to particulars." She took up her crocheting again. "No one was ever strong enough to kill what the two of you shared."

Emily nodded, but the shadows of the night wouldn't release her thoughts of Joseph and all they had lost. "What people say about him at the trials, that he was fun or nervous or devilish or stingy, each one got it right and got it wrong, too. They saw him from the outside and offered up one piece of the man at a time, like it was the whole cloth. He was more than that."

"We need to get this family pointed to the future," Philomene said. "There's no bringing Joseph back. You're still here, safe, and that's a blessing."

The lone screeching of a hoot owl filled the night and then fell quiet.

"I can't speak of him anymore," Emily whispered, and the admission hurt her. "I can't speak his name out loud."

"Whatever allows you to get up and go on another day. You were left with more than you think. The children have his name, and that matters," Philomene said. "And there's the money."

Emily collected herself. "Almost two thousand dollars in cash, hidden safe around the house and yard. The Colfax bank refused Joe's petition for a loan to expand his lumber operations, and I've been thinking about backing him, but by rights, T.O. as the oldest should come first."

Philomene stopped the motion of her rocker again. "We have to be careful how we spend the money. Joe has a gift with timber, men, and numbers, same as Joseph, and big dreams. Six men already and more work than he can handle. Use a piece of the money for him now, and in due time it will come back to us. As for T.O., money isn't what he needs."

Emily sighed. "These trials are eating him up, following each detail night and day like a man possessed. He's lost so much weight that his clothes hang on him. I want to help him past this, but T.O.'s hiding something. And the truth is, I can't bear to hear any more about the proceedings."

"T.O. will find his way in time," Philomene said. "But he can't put himself into anything now but the idea of bringing back a lost inheritance."

"I'll give Joe the money tomorrow," said Emily.

"It can't seem to come from us," said Philomene. "We have to make it look like he gets his backing from outside the parish. Joe can go to New Orleans and open a bank account with the cash, and then come back talking about a white partner from down there."

"I get so tired of fighting," Emily said.

Philomene clucked her tongue softly. "You fight just by drawing breath and sitting on your own property on Cornfine Bayou. The important thing now is the battles you choose. The one that makes a difference is keeping the family together and giving the children a better chance." She pulled a plug of tobacco from her apron pocket and shook her head thoughtfully. "Once, I thought I was bringing you into an easier time."

"You did fine, *Maman*." Emily smiled a tight smile. One of their farm cats jumped into her lap and she stroked its short, sleek fur.

"I bore ten children, and you had five," Philomene said, lightening her tone. "Bet has given me eleven grandchildren already, and from you only Angelite's two. What are your children waiting for? All of them should have settled down to start their own families by now." She leaned back and closed her eyes. "Josephine came crying to me about you running off that dark-skinned boy from Aloha trying to court her."

"Josephine understood her responsibility," Emily said primly. "His people had no standing. It is better to take these things in hand before they have a chance to go too far."

"Sometimes while you wait for what you think is better," Philomene said, "what is good enough slips away."

Summer gave way to fall, and Antoine Morat was named administrator for Joseph's estate while the case dragged on. He came one windy Saturday afternoon to Cornfine Bayou to give them fresh news of the trial, pulling a small sack of salt out of his saddlebag as a gift. They were all home and assembled in the front room. Only Suzette was absent, napping.

As Josephine served tea cakes and coffee, Antoine began to complain. "The Grandchamps have the money from the estate tied up. Madame Lola's relations have more interest in her dead than when she was alive, fighting us every step of the way, but I'm looking out for you." A small martyr's smile played at Antoine's lips, and Emily waited for the real purpose of his call. "There are many hardships in the duties of administrator, but justice triumphs in the end."

Suddenly Antoine slapped both palms flat on the table, rattling the teacups. The sound made Emily start. "We found Joseph's last will and testament," he said, grinning widely. "He wrote to my son Antoine Jr., and the letter makes his intentions for the estate clear." He looked very satisfied. "Everything we've been telling the court for months is borne out. A.J. has had the document in his possession for almost a year without realizing the importance of it."

They looked questioningly at one another around the table, Philomene to Emily, T.O. to Joe, Mary to Josephine.

"A.J. thought the letter the fond musings of a troubled old man, of no importance to anyone but himself, but when he told me, I grasped immediately its significance." Antoine touched his own temple lightly, as if he were reliving the discovery of that moment. "The letter was written three months before poor Joseph performed those desperate last acts of a disturbed man."

He leaned in to visibly convey his reassurance to his audience on Cornfine Bayou. "My strategy," he said, his voice barely above a whisper, "is to bring these affairs to conclusion, something you can't do for yourselves because of your . . . circumstances. The court would never seriously consider any petition from you directly, so you need someone working for you. Our settlement is your settlement."

"What is it you ask us to do?" said Philomene.

"Nothing, nothing at all," Antoine said. "I just came by to read the letter to you myself, in case you hear of it from others and do not understand the meaning. You know how fond Joseph was of my A.J., like a son."

Emily glanced sidelong at T.O., his face rigid under the reference, and then at the letter Antoine held. Antoine allowed the paper to linger under her nose before pulling it back and adjusting his reading lens over the characters. Emily recognized Joseph's handwriting, the right-hand slant, the cramped letters in French, the signature.

Redemption post office   *Oct. the 27th, a.d., 1906*

My dear Cousin Antoine,

You will excuse me for not answering your letter sooner, I will say to you I have been to New Orleans since you left school. It was on business, and I returned eight days ago. I am very glad to know of your safe arrival at Memphis, Tenn., especially after hearing about the disasters you narrowly avoided. Last Sunday your father and your mother told me that you are at a new school that has been opened and I think that will be a greater advantage to you.

Now, do as I told you at the station when you left. If anything should happen to me, no matter what, take possession of that which I have. I give you all that I have accumulated. That is my will. Not a cent for my brothers, remembering the ingratitude of which you know. Settle my accounts. Above all, do for my children as I said. I transfer to you all my rights. Take care of this letter.

Now, work hard. This will be the last year of hard work for you. Try to work so to be received in the world. You know how difficult the field is, and you have tackled it with courage, and that is what makes me believe in you. As to the examination, you will go out one of the first, and afterwards, you know, if your father cannot afford to do for you what you need, I will. Accept then my sincere friendship. Your Cousin. And if you need anything, write to me.

Joseph Billes

Antoine stumbled slightly at the part referring to his inability to afford to do for his son, but he finished reading the letter with a flourish, allowing a dramatic pause to develop before he went on.

Joseph Billes's last will and testament, entered into evidence, Louisiana Supreme Court.

"So you see," he said, directing the comment to Emily, "this letter makes it clear that Joseph wanted us to handle his affairs, that he trusted us to do the right thing for your children. It's the Grandchamps with their greedy hand out that we need to fight, and with this, I'm prepared to take that hand out of our pocket once and for all."

"What about the will, the one they found at his house?" Emily asked. "It was written after that letter."

Antoine talked directly to Emily, but she saw his eyes slide briefly to T.O. before coming back to rest on hers. T.O.'s face was ashen as he stared down at the table, never lifting his head.

"That was a mistake, never valid," Antoine said dismissively. "And it seems the original has disappeared. Once this letter is recognized as the last will and testament, we can accomplish the same thing. Surely you trust us?"

Emily said nothing, trying to shut out the memory of Joseph's visit to her the night before he was killed. The court would no doubt accept this old, stained letter once Antoine brought it forward, even though they had rejected the later will for not being in the proper form. And it was unlikely this letter would disappear.

"I don't expect you to follow this, nothing to worry about," Antoine went on, "but Joseph gave Lola a great deal of property when they first got married, a donation, like this land you're living on here. He regretted it immediately after they actually married, and he got her to sign it back over to him, in front of witnesses. Lola's people are trying to lay claim to that land as being hers, and rightfully theirs now that she is dead. With this last will and testament, we'll prove that it all comes to us. Then we'll be able to see after you and your share, once the law gets out of it. I just want to make sure there's no loose talk about Joseph and his wishes to have us handle his estate for him. Not that there would be, or that anyone would listen, but the law can be demanding. Better not to tangle overmuch with either the law or the Grandchamps, eh?" Antoine gave a wink. "We can straighten everything out between us later, after it is finished."

They all sat quiet, alone with their thoughts. Emily wondered who there was to truly mourn Joseph, other than his family on Cornfine Bayou.

The trials spilled over into two years of appeals, moving from Colfax to New Orleans, where the Louisiana Supreme Court heard the case without anyone from Cornfine Bayou being involved in any way. Once again the demands of farm life consumed them, and they seldom heard anything about the case or even spoke of it.

T.O. came back from Colfax one day enraged, so filled with disbelief that they could hardly understand him. "It was him," he said. "I heard his voice. I'm not likely to forget that, am I? The voice in the woods. He was in it with Antoine all along, doing the deed and then sitting on the police jury, cozy with the judge."

"T.O., calm down, tell us what's happened. What voice in the woods?" Emily said, but her son wasn't listening.

T.O. paced in the front room, his hands thrust deep into his pockets, his eyes narrow with rage. "Antoine Morat cheated us. He has the court on his side, from here down to New Orleans. He never had any intention to do as Papa wished. They settled with Lola's family already, twelve thousand dollars, and they aren't going to give us anything at all."

Emily tried to make sense of T.O.'s words. Was it all over? "Did you talk to Antoine?"

T.O. curled his lip. "He laughed at me, him and his lawyer, just back from New Orleans and victory. He paid the Grandchamps off, but said we held no such legal claims. Well, I can get a lawyer, too."

"T.O., there's no more to be done."

Emily did her best to soothe her son. Suing Antoine and A. J. Morat was a man's way, full of strutting, with nothing

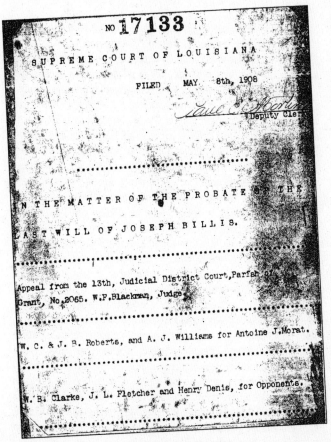

Louisiana Supreme Court record, 1908.

to be gained in the long run. There had been murder over the land already; they weren't going to give it up now to an impotent colored man just because he shouted it was unfair. The women's way was more effective. They might be ignored, abused, or dominated, but in the end the women were more practical, keeping their eye on whatever prize was within their grasp. But T.O. couldn't hear that in his current mood, not from her.

As an emigrant from the old country years ago, Jos. Billis knew the eventual value of American realty and forests, and put forth his hands and with little effort accumulated a competence, becoming with its increased value wealthy. He had little in common with the world, and took small part in its affairs. During all this time there grew up around him quite a brood of children, offsprings of his illegitimate union with a colored woman. He loved those children and they and their mother lived in the house with him. It was in their common dwelling he returned each night after tossing about on the ocean of life, but he never ventured far from the shore. This was the refuge he sought. Here is where his heart was at rest—such rest as a heart could get amid such environments and constant reminders of wrong doing. Here is where if his heart was ever warmed by childhood affection, it was when the thick lips of his dark skin mulatto children pressed his.

We would call the Court's attention also to the testimony of Mr. Raney Antee at page 125 of the transcript, who testified to a number of quarrels and serious altercations between these spouses about the husband's negro wife and negro children. Mr. Pierre Antee at page 127 of the transcript testified to a number of serious disputes between them and from which it appears that she wanted him to give up his negro wife and children, but which he refused to do, declaring that he was going to lose the last drop of his blood before he would do so.

Lawyer's summation and witness testimony, Louisiana Supreme Court, 1908.

Emily couldn't stop T.O. from going to Montgomery to find a lawyer to represent the family. After the case was already cold, T.O. filed suit against A. J. Morat. Emily knew it was as much about wanting to be seen as Joseph Billes's son as it was the land. In 1909, his action was ineffective at best, presumptuous and dangerous at worst. They accepted his petition, then laughed him out of court.

"Bring back a paper saying Joseph Billes married your mama, boy," the judge said, "and then we'll look at your claim."

Philomene carried the food tray down the hallway to the back bedroom she shared with Suzette. The old woman was asleep, breathing heavily. Philomene slid the tray on the bedside table and gently shook her mother awake.

Suzette slowly shifted between sleep and wakefulness, cranky from the start. "I want collard greens," she complained.

"It's not the right season, *Maman*. We fixed up a nice plate so you could eat before everybody gets here."

"I want one of the others." Suzette's voice was a petulant whine. "You drop food all over me on purpose. You do that with Madame and she'll sell you off to the first one passing by, sell you so quick your head spins. Away from everybody you know." She leaned toward Philomene conspiratorially. "You have to be careful, but I spit right in his wineglass. Listen to what I'm telling you. Pick your time.

The rest isn't important, you do what you have to. They're all right, you know, if you know how to work with them."

"Uh-huh," Philomene said. "Sit up a little, *Maman*."

Suzette chuckled. "I changed my name. They can't find me now. You better believe they're out there looking, too, but I got them this time."

"It's hard to eat when you keep talking," Philomene said.

Suzette stopped and considered the plate of cut chicken, rice and gravy, green peas and cornbread. "This doesn't have any taste."

"I'll put some more hot sauce on it for you, *Maman*."

"He up and married a white woman. Those babies have a chance, though."

Philomene studied the hand that gripped the spoon as she moved the food toward Suzette's mouth, and she found surprises there. Light and dark splotches speckled her hands, and the skin sagged around the colony of tiny wrinkles near her knuckles. Her grip was firm, but ropy veins protruded upward from under the skin, as if they were trying to escape their prison. If she didn't look at her hands, she could forget she was a sixty-eight-year-old woman. She had never been vain about her appearance, indifferent until she started to lose the things others envied: her figure, the thin coolness of her hands, the luster of her thick hair, the elegant stiffness of her bearing.

Her mother was petulant today, pushing her to the point where Philomene grew impatient, but she didn't like sending the young ones in to look after Suzette when she got this way. Suzette lived much of her time on the plantation, and there was no point in having them hearing too much of that. They had fought their way beyond it. They had their own

10 2

STATE TAX COLLECTOR'S OFFICE.
NATCHITOCHES, LA.

To *Philomen Dorard* of the Parish of *Natchitoches* Oct* 188*

You are hereby notified that your State and Parish Taxes for the year 1884 are now due and unpaid, and if not paid in Twenty days from the service hereof, I will proceed to seize and sell property to satisfy same, and all costs, as required by law. *See Statement below* *G. P. Trichel, Tax Collector*

☞ BRING THIS NOTICE BACK WHEN YOU COME TO PAY.

VALUATION OF PROPERTY, $ 30

	DOLLARS	CENTS	
STATE TAX, ...MILLS		18	*Colfax*
PARISH		27	
POLL	1		
NOTICE	1		
PUBLICATION		30	
PENALTY			
MAKING SALE AND RECORDING			
TOTAL, ...	1	75	

Red Bayou Feb 14

Hopkins, Printer, 30 St. Charles St.

Collector.

No. *1668* Ward *6*

STATE OF LOUISIANA

TAXES 189*9*.   Parish of *Grant* *Feb 9* ~~1900~~ 189

Received of *Philomen Dorade*

Seven & 93/100 .... Dollars,

Amount of Taxes as itemized for the year 1899 on property described on reverse hereof, in accordance with law

State Tax............	2	88
Parish Tax............	4	80
Poll Tax............		
Levee Tax............District		
Levee Tax............District		
Interest............		
Costs............		25
Special Tax............		
Total............	7	93

M E Swagford
SHERIFF AND EX-OFFICIO TAX COLLECTOR.

Grant .... Parish.

The Taxpayer shall present his Tax Receipt to the Recorder of Mortgages, who shall cancel the mortgage against the property described upon Receipt.

N. F. DUNN & BRO., PRINTERS, NEW ORLEANS.

State of Louisiana tax receipts, 1884 and 1899.

land now and paid their taxes promptly every year. She had never once missed a payment since the time she had almost been late twenty-five years before, in 1884.

In certain moods Suzette stroked Mary's sandy hair with gratitude and longing. "Don't you ever let dark hands touch this," she would say. "You're too good for the likes of that. You come from quality, and you owe it to your children." The problem was that neither Josephine nor Mary had an acceptable suitor, and they were already well into their prime marrying years.

Philomene heard the boastful rooster outside as she fed Suzette her dinner. In her mind's eye she could see the old red cock puff out his feathered chest in response to the first of the family to arrive outside, announcing each batch of visitors as they pulled up to the house. Right alongside, or from a more restful, shady spot, their ancient yellow dog would barely lift his head. The dog was another of the strays Suzette insisted they keep, back when she was still vigorous enough to take care of them. In his day he had been a good watchdog, but now he was blind in one eye, and great patches were gone from his once golden fur. The dog had conceded his custodial responsibilities to the rooster the year before.

Unlike the dog that drowsed in the shade of the gallery, Sunday visiting day on Cornfine Bayou brimmed over with energy, life renewing itself. Philomene's children came, with their own futures in tow. Spouses, live-ins, children, grandchildren, stepchildren, in-laws, so many sometimes that it was hard to keep track. Philomene had borne ten, and six were able to come to her and pay their respects each week. Three dead and buried in small mounds, taken before childhood, and one who had used his light color to run off to Texas and pass from the life they were living in Louisiana.

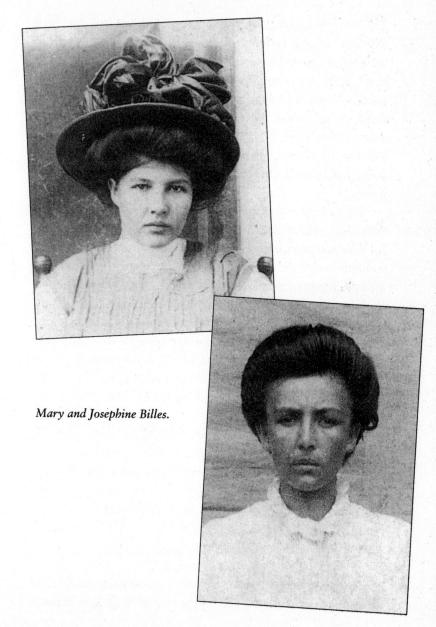

Mary and Josephine Billes.

Bet, the oldest, came with her new husband, the third she was in the process of outliving, in a wagon full of squirming children, stepchildren, and grandchildren. Once her first husband died from fever she had gone on to older men, widowers looking for a strong woman to take care of them, who would adapt to their set ways. Bet was that woman. She seemed to pick the ones too old to outlive her, but not so old that they couldn't give her more children. From hardy, long-life stock, she was no good living without a man.

Philomene's youngest, Matchie, had married and had two quick babies already. He seemed happy enough.

Her son Joseph had always been a ladies' man. There were so many Josephs in the family, they took to nicknames and initials. Philomene's son was Joe F., and he brought his Indian-looking wife, a pretty little thing who always brought to mind her grandfather Gerasíme. She liked Fannie. The girl had been raised right, a pleasant young woman capable of making herself useful, and they already had two children, little Narcease and Gurtie. Philomene knew her son's nature, and she wasn't sure how long Fannie could hold Joe F.'s interest.

Joe F Married Two times His first Wife was Fannie Nash, they had two children Narcease and Gurtie.
--Cousin Gurtie Fredieu, written family
   history, 1975

Nick had taken up with a baby-faced white woman from the hills named Kate, and they had a little girl named

O'Rena who was oh so sweet. Kate wasn't prepared to be a wife. Philomene didn't consider her cooking worth eating, she couldn't dress the deer Nick caught, her garden went to seed from neglect, and she kept a dirty house. She had been cut off from her own family, probably because of Nick, but Philomene didn't ask. The girl pressured Nick until he took her up to Montgomery to get married before the baby was born. They didn't know either of them there, and Nick lied about his color, so they married the couple. It might not be strictly legal, but the girl had her piece of paper, and she convinced herself that the children were going to be legitimate.

Henry married a girl from over Campti way, but there were no children yet.

And, of course, her Emily. On Sundays Emily was the centerpiece in a house overrun with family. She carried on as if she had no cares in the world and refused to allow sorrow to come into her house for too long a stay. She fed everyone, young and old, colored and white. Her rules of conduct were few, but they couldn't be violated. Everyone past the age of crawling had to have at least a sip of her homemade wine shortly after coming through her door. Each mother had to control her own children, make sure they did not act like common riffraff and were respectful of their elders.

And after dinner, when the dishes were cleared and washed and the smallest children laid down for their naps, Nick would pull out his fiddle. Alone in the middle of the front room with the audience clapping and cheering her on, Emily would dance a spirited three-step, as spry as they all remembered. The children were entranced, the adults impressed. No one dared to leave before she tired. No one wanted to. Sundays were the best time they had.

Narcisse's son Edd always came alone to their Sunday

dinners when he could. If he met any of them in town, there would be a curt acknowledging nod, white to color, but in the woods on Cornfine Bayou they met like family.

Joseph was still in the house with them, even though he had been dead for two years. Emily wouldn't speak his name out loud, but Philomene knew that she carried him with her in spirit. Her daughter had lost the freshness that had been captured so well in the oil painting over the mantel of their front room, but she was still a good-looking woman, trim and lively into middle age. She had learned to dance alone and not dwell on the past, a lesson she hadn't been able to pass on to her son.

There was little to be done for the boy. He was grown, but T.O. was one of the many Philomene had seen who took each hurt inside and nursed it until it threatened to rupture. She felt helpless when she thought about her grandson.

Philomene realized that Suzette had slipped into sleep, and she wasn't sure how long she had allowed her reveries to keep her in the bedroom. Certainly longer than she intended. It wasn't in her nature to sit idly. There was always something to be done, some child to look after, a meal to cook, an animal to feed, clothes to mend, her mother less able to do for herself with each passing day, but she caught herself more often drowsing in the sun, taking too long to do too little. Like now.

With Suzette fed and resting, Philomene went out to the front gallery to get some air. Two of the great-grandchildren had spoons from the kitchen and sat in the middle of small mounds of freshly loosened dirt in the front yard, seeing how deep a pit they could dig. Their faces and mouths were striped with the muddy remains of dirt they had eaten.

Philomene swooped down on the children, yanking them

upright by their collars, startling them into bewildered tears. She looked at the unmistakable signs even as she began to comfort the children, blubbering and shaken, but it was too late.

Digging in the front yard meant someone was going to die.

*   *   *

Two weeks later Suzette passed over peacefully, in her sleep.

Eighty-five had been a long, respectable life, and Philomene hoped Suzette was someplace now that offered more than the indignities she had borne in this one.

If Emily was the bloom in Philomene's garden and Elisabeth the root that reached down deep enough to anchor itself and search for nourishment, Suzette had been the soil itself, buffeted by winds, withstanding storms, baked by the sun. Philomene met her mother's death with grim acceptance.

Death would be knocking on her own door soon enough, and she would have to let him in.

She wasn't ready.

J oseph Billes may not have been allowed to leave the inheritance that he intended, but he left a legacy that assured T.O.'s privilege among Negro and colored alike. T.O. himself, along with his brother and sisters, and his mother, for that matter, could have passed for white anywhere in the country, anywhere except for this part of Louisiana. His background dictated that he marry an as-yet-unnamed but clearly defined wife who would bring more of the same to the table. White skin, light eyes, straight hair, Catholic upbringing. And fertile, so the next generation could put even more distance between themselves and Negroes and come closer to white. It was even possible for him to marry white the way his uncle Nick encouraged him to do.

Generations had been sacrificed for his look. The thought filled T.O. with such despair that sometimes he didn't know how he could go on. He spent hours locked in his own mind, playing with ways he could live out his life without this constant coil of hopeless entrapment.

He thought about moving away from Louisiana and passing, like his uncle Eugene, but was sure he couldn't make it on his own. Deep down he didn't think he could carry it off. Everyone would know he was an impostor.

When he looked in a mirror, it was a haunted man who looked back at him; an incomplete man with flat eyes and a crippled soul, inadequate in every way that mattered. A man who stood by and did nothing to prevent his own father from being murdered. A man who couldn't live up to his responsibilities to those he should be able to protect, accepting crumbs instead of finding a way to win the inheritance that belonged to his family.

T.O. despised the man in the mirror, and with an uncharacteristic clarity knew what he needed to do to break the chain. He didn't have the courage or the stamina to go up against Morat again. That was all over. The one thing he could do was to strengthen the blood of his own children. How many times had his mother told him blood was everything? She meant white blood, but he didn't believe in that anymore. He would find a mother for his children who was everything he was not. Strong. Determined. Capable. Unafraid. And not brought up with the same attitudes that in the end would keep the wheel going in the same direction. That meant a woman who had no pretensions toward being colored Creole. A Negro woman. This would be the boldest act of courage he had undertaken in the thirty years he had been on this earth, because it would run contrary to his mother's wishes. He looked again into the mirror.

It would stop with him, and something new would begin again.

"*Maman,* this is Eva Brew," T.O. said nervously in English. Eva was the first girl he had ever brought home, and he counted on Emily's relief to give him an extra measure of forgiveness in his choice. He was thirty, and Eva was nineteen.

T.O. hardened himself, conscious of the half beat too long while Emily digested Eva. Nappy hair parted down the center and pulled back tightly in two coiled braids, accentuating the pretty roundness of her face, her ginger-colored skin, her broad nose, and the freshly starched, ironed, and serviceable gingham dress free of frills. He had expected his mother's unspoken disapproval, but he had not anticipated the clear, level gaze that Eva gave Emily in return, no fluttering hands or averted eyes.

Geneva (Eva) Brew.

"Bonjour, Mademoiselle Eva. Voulez-vous du café?" Emily offered.

"Maman, English, please," T.O. rushed to say. "I told you Eva doesn't speak French."

Emily smiled charmingly at Eva, and T.O. noted it was her polite "because you are a guest in my house and I was brought up properly, I choose to extend you this courtesy" smile she reserved for company. "Welcome to Cornfine Bayou, Mademoiselle Eva," Emily said. "May I offer you coffee?"

"Yes, ma'am," Eva said. "Would you like any help?"

"No, no." Emily kept her eyes on the girl. "Josephine will bring it."

Eva looked around appreciatively. "You keep a lovely home here, ma'am."

"Thank you." Emily sat and motioned for Eva to do the same. "I understand you live in Colfax. Which church do you attend up there?"

"Pilgrim Rest Baptist, ma'am. I go every Sunday."

"Well, here's Josephine with the coffee at last. Shall we pour?"

T.O. thought Eva held up to the rest of the afternoon very well.

The courtship was short. In 1911 T.O. Billes married Eva Brew and moved her into the house on Cornfine Bayou.

In the winter of 1912 T.O. approached his grandmother's room with a feeling of dread. Philomene battled pneumonia and today had called for him by name. It was too much like the summons before *Mémère* Elisabeth died.

She was small against the whiteness of the pillows, but

even weakened she still emitted a potent life force he felt from across the room. Philomene took both his hands in hers, rubbing them gently as she talked. The hands sliding over his own were dry and rough to the touch, but a strange warmth began to generate between them, as if they were building a fire together.

"T.O., I've never told you about the gift I had when I was young, because I thought it had left me for good." Philomene's eyes were bright, almost fever bright, T.O. thought, but unclouded. "I used to be able to see the future. Now it seems to have come back, at least a little, and it concerns you."

T.O. was soothed by the calm certainty in her voice and the heat of her hands.

"I see a woman standing in front of a large room, people as far as the eye can see, young and old, black and white, men and women. She talks, and they listen with their whole minds. There's respect in that room, and the woman in the front comes from us, from you. I tell you this, T.O., so you know that you and yours are going to be all right. Don't waste what came before. Add to it."

T.O. didn't know what to say. He held her hand in his until she fell asleep.

Philomene died later that night. Emily insisted on a family celebration, and then, just as it had been with Joseph, Philomene's name dropped from his mother's everyday speaking as well.

Grandmother Phelman died Nov 1912.
--Cousin Gurtie Fredieu, written family
   history, 1975

On a pleasant evening the following spring, Emily, Mary, T.O., and Eva lingered around the kitchen table after supper. Joe had left the house to go courting, and Josephine had gone off to bed early with a headache. While the dishes soaked in the sink, Emily brought out a fresh gallon of home-brewed muscadine wine. She filled a glass tumbler for each of them, and Mary retrieved the black and white bones for dominoes.

"Do you know how to play, Eva?" T.O. asked, careful in his tone. Since her belly had gone big with their first child, she was less predictable in how she reacted to him.

"I'll be fine," Eva replied. "No need to know French to play dominoes."

It took T.O. by surprise how fast with numbers Eva was. She held all of her bones in one hand close to her bosom, propped up over her smooth, round stomach, carefully watching every play on the table with intense concentration. She won the first game with apparent ease, beaming with delight.

T.O. felt a nice, rosy glow. His wife was happy, he was happy, all seemed right with the world.

"Very lucky," Emily said, mixing up the bones for a rematch.

Eva won the second game as well.

"You need to try a little of my wine," Emily said, nodding toward Eva's untouched tumbler. "Loosen you up a bit."

"I do fine without it, Miss Emily," Eva said. "I'm surprised you can hold so much liquor, you're such a little woman."

Emily motioned for Mary to pour more into T.O.'s glass as well as her own.

"I never have been able to hit one hundred pounds." Emily turned to T.O. and switched to French. "That time, weighing myself on the cotton scales? Ninety-nine. If I had known I was so close, I wouldn't have spit out my tobacco."

It was an old family joke, and they all laughed. Except Eva.

Eva noisily scraped her chair back from the table, took her tumbler full of wine, and poured it out in the sink, then began to wash the dishes they'd set to soak earlier.

"*Maman*, let's talk in English," T.O. interrupted, casting a nervous eye over to Eva.

Emily ignored him and continued on in her silken voice, the strong rise and fall of her Creole patois dominating the room.

T.O. knew that Eva wouldn't think of disrespecting his mother by talking back to her, but the time was fast approaching when he would have to take a stand between these two women, his mother and his wife, before they ground him to dust between them.

"We need to find a place of our own to rent," Eva said.

Their first year of marriage had been a constant battle of wills between Eva and Emily, although harsh words were never spoken directly.

"But there's plenty of room for us here," T.O. protested. "And help with the baby. We don't have enough for our own place."

Eva wore a stubborn scowl, with her lips pursed tight and not open to challenge. "We are both young and strong. It may not be considered proper in your family, but there is nothing wrong in taking in other people's washing and ironing, as long as they pay me for it. And I can take care of Joseph Lee myself."

"I know you and *Maman* don't always see everything the same way, but—"

"T.O., we have another child on the way. I appreciate

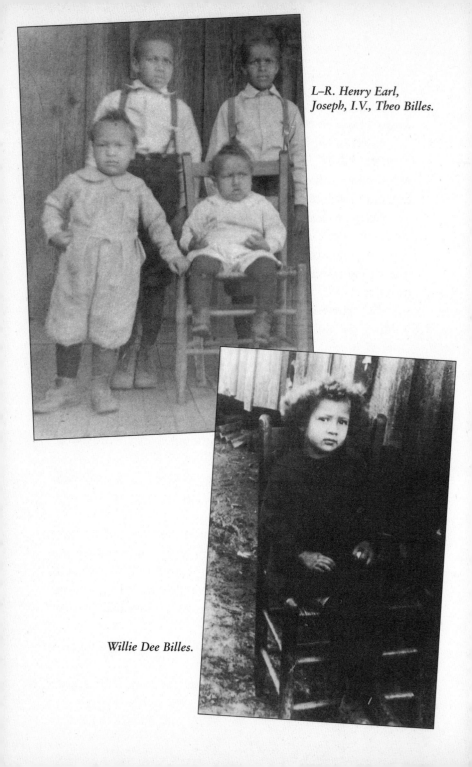

L–R. Henry Earl,
Joseph, I.V., Theo Billes.

Willie Dee Billes.

what your mama has done for us, but I'm raising our children my own way. They *will* be Baptist, and they *will not* speak French."

The years passed, T.O. taking odd jobs and Eva in charge of the family and their small farm outside Colfax. By the time Eva's childbearing years wound down, they had five children. There were four boys, Joseph Lee, Theodore, Henry Earl, and I.V., and the youngest, an untamed girl named Willie Dee. Strict and full of direction, Eva brooked no interference from anyone in raising them to be morally strong, neat, clean, and respectful.

T.O.'s family still spent occasional Sunday afternoons on Cornfine Bayou. After Eva and the children walked the two and one-half miles back from church in Colfax, T.O. hitched the mule and they all drove to Aloha. The young ones loved to visit the farm back in the country with their grandma 'Tite, a spirited old woman who always had an inexhaustible supply of thick-striped canes of sweet peppermint candy.

47

COLFAX, LOUISIANA—1936

Deep in thought, Emily unscrewed the lid from the top of the Red Rooster tin, slowing her pace as she walked to make sure she didn't drop the last of her snuff. Her grip wasn't as steady as it used to be. It was twenty-nine years and four months to the day since her Joseph was taken, and even after all the time without him, lately she missed him with a ferocity that unnerved her. She felt an urgent need to talk to Philomene about her unsettling longings, but Emily had had to do without her mother's council and comfort for twenty-four years.

She took the time to pinch together the final bits of moist dark brown tobacco that remained in the tin, expertly transferring the stringy blend between her inside bottom lip and gum in one fluid motion. A familiar rush hit as the thick, syrupy liquid rose in her mouth. She spat just once, force-

Josephine Billes.

fully, into the fallen pine needles and dirt under her feet, a short, accurate shot. One more spit before getting on the bus, and she would be fine until she got all the way to Colfax. Everyone knew that Emily Fredieu could hold her juice.

Yesterday a mud dauber's nest had fallen from the roof of the house, a powerful and unlucky sign. And then Josephine, in a rare fit of pique over a stuck jar lid that refused to budge, had declared, "If I knew then what I know now, I would have married the darkest man I could find and had a house full of babies of my own." Out of nowhere. As if the fact that neither daughter ever married were her fault. Emily had decided at that moment to come to town today.

It wasn't often anymore that Emily could be persuaded to leave the home place for any reason, even to keep the graves clean, but she had been feeling lately that if she didn't keep moving, God might think she was done and come to collect her early. Besides, wandering through a store would almost be like breathing in Joseph once again. Between the strength of the omen and her assorted pains, she had been able to sleep only fitfully last night and had been up long before the rooster's first crow this morning. She wondered whether this was how her mother, Philomene, had felt at this age. Or her *mémère* Suzette. Or even the dark old woman Elisabeth. The women in her family all had a grip on living they didn't let go of easily, no matter the limitations.

The three-mile walk through the Louisiana piney woods out to the road to catch the bus to Colfax seemed longer than she remembered, demanding more than her knees wanted to brace, more than her heart wanted to sponsor. She could have sent either Josephine or Mary to do the erranding when she saw they were getting low on Red Rooster or waited until Sunday when the relations came to call. They were all willing to do for her if she asked.

Trading her country time for town time put Emily in a reflective mood. Josephine's outburst yesterday notwithstanding, they got on well in the country, she and her daughters, growing most of what they needed to eat, using the muscadine grapes to make their own wine to drink, keeping the farm, having supplies they couldn't grow or make themselves brought in. Joe Jr. had died in World War I, but T.O. frequently brought his children to visit. Despite being off in the backcountry, they seldom wanted for weekly visitors, family of one sort or another from the white side and the colored side both. Going to town usually meant something new and pretty to see, even if Colfax seemed to be shrinking instead of growing. When the sawmill pulled out, the town had gotten a bit of a hangdog temperament to it, as if it knew its best days were behind.

A black squirrel jumped from one tree to the next not far ahead of her, his mouth swollen with nuts. How she still loved her woods, even after all these years, even after most of the virgin pine had been plundered and the sun was free to burn through. It wasn't as if she didn't have other places to compare it with, like most of the untraveled country folks around these parts. She had been sent all the way to New Orleans when she was a girl and had learned to read and write in both English and French. She had tasted the city, the real city. Not many in her circle made that claim.

Emily reached the road that could take her to Natchitoches or Montgomery to the north or Colfax to the south. Years ago gangs of men had carved out the ugly thoroughfare, wide and asphalted. It was convenient, no doubt about that. The world had been a smaller place before these things they called progress reached them, steamboats instead of railroads, horses instead of automobiles, but the improvements tended to be hard-edged and drab, one of the worst possible sins in Emily's book.

She slowed her step and looked in first one direction and then the other. There was no traffic, no other person out walking. The bus line conformed to some sort of schedule, but she knew the bus would show up in its own good time, and all she had to do was wave it down however far she had managed to get along the road. She turned south on the hot asphalt, kept a steady pace until she finally heard the rattle of the bus behind her coming along Highway 71.

As always happened when she knew she would be judged by strangers' eyes, she wished she were taller and more imposing. She was almost five feet, missing the mark by less than an inch. And she still hadn't managed to tip the scales beyond one hundred pounds. Her waist had thickened with the passage of time, but even without her corset she could have invited an admiring arm around it if she had ever so decided. Her hair was pulled back and up, severely, and arranged in a topknot to keep it off her neck in the heat, but if left free it still hinted at the saucy brown color of her youth. It could reach almost to her waist. Sometimes she washed it just to see her old glory turn dark in her hands again while it was wet, before it dried and turned back to grayish white.

She wished she had on one of her serviceable long-billed bonnets, but she wouldn't wear them to town anymore since her granddaughter had told her they weren't fashionable. She wore a smaller bonnet, not as good to keep the sun off, but a pretty little thing. Her feet had spread from a lifetime of work and narrow shoes, but when she bought store-made shoes, she still needed the smallest possible adult size. And seventy-five years old or no seventy-five, she knew the touch of beauty was still with her. The unflawed clear white skin with almost no wrinkles, the sharp but delicate features, the French nose, the beautiful long straight hair with only the insinuation of the natural curl that might start minds thinking about the possibility of café au lait.

The dingy silver country bus distinguished itself from the dust swirls that preceded it, and Emily lifted up her hand in a wave. The driver stopped. It had been over five years since she'd last taken the bus, and it seemed more crowded than she remembered, whites in front, colored in back. She looked carefully at the passengers as she climbed the steps, including the bus driver, and when she didn't see anyone she recognized, she took her place in front and settled in for the ride, grateful to be off her feet. They were all strangers around her, outsiders who would probably never think to stop at Colfax, passing by on their way to some bigger town. Those who carried on conversation did so in English. It was an annoyance, but switching away from the easy Creole

French in her head was one of the prices to pay to go to town.

Someone had left a copy of this week's *Natchitoches Reporter* on the seat beside her, and it was open to the "Letters to the Editor" column. Emily didn't put much stock in keeping up with events reported in the newspapers, even when someone brought one out to the farm for her. They seemed to have so little to do with anything genuine or important, but today she needed to stay alert. It wouldn't do to drift off and miss the Colfax stop nine miles away. She read to occupy her mind.

"They're trying to get the name of Highway 71 changed to FDD Derbanne Highway," Emily said excitedly, pointing out the article in the newspaper to the woman sitting across the aisle from her, a bosomy matron in a flowered dress, white-gloved hands clutching her purse. "These are my people they're talking about."

The woman smiled at her politely, indulgently, but didn't encourage further conversation, leaning back and closing her eyes to signal that she was resting and unavailable.

The words had come out in French. Just as well, Emily thought. It had been both foolish and dangerous to talk to a stranger in the front of the bus.

Emily sat back and read the article through again. François Dion Despres Derbanne was a distant ancestor who had helped set up Natchitoches as a trading post years before New Orleans existed. Her Joseph had told her all about the explorer when he had laid out her father's bloodline for her, and she had spent countless hours as a teenager rolling that beautiful name over her tongue and begging him for more stories. François Dion Despres Derbanne. It had to be the same man, and it was his same blood running through her. She folded the newspaper carefully and pushed it deep into her bag.

The bumpy ride of the bus on the country road created its own rhythm, and Emily relaxed into it. She had become much more dreamy of late than she could ever recall being before, and often sharp, fresh memories of fifty or seventy years ago crowded out the necessities of today. Sometimes they gave her great pleasure, like good friends come calling.

The bus shifted gears abruptly, and Emily looked out the windows at the thinned woods on each side. Joseph had owned all of this at one time, and she had helped him get it.

The Colfax stop was close.

Good thing.

She needed to spit.

Emily stepped off the bus. Colfax, Louisiana, the sign said, population 1,400. The weathered sign hadn't changed for at least twenty years that she knew of, and it was already 1936. She still had a long walk down the wide, dusty road to the other side of town.

Across the street from Tumminello's general store, a loose knot of men idled around the grandstand, swapping stories, and Emily heard a short burst of laughter behind her as she entered the relative darkness of the store. Some of the men were old enough to know who she was, but she felt a little reckless today.

The very smell of the place assaulted her, triggering memories, good and bad. The store was empty except for the bored-looking young white man behind the counter. This young one didn't know her. She always sent someone else in to pick up supplies, but Colfax was a small town, and her story might be known, if not her face.

510 Lalita Tademy

She wandered around the store, drinking in the remembered magic of places like this while the boy eyed her.

"Can I help you, ma'am?" He had round owl-like eyes, dark slick hair, a thin nose that took a sharp downward curve near the tip.

She could see herself through his eyes, another old-line Frenchwoman come down from the country, dressed better than most, back straighter than most, who might not have enough money to buy the goods on the shelves. Many of the folks around Colfax didn't have much, and he had a right to be suspicious. Why should he know about the $1,300 in cash she had sewn in her mattress, more than some of these farmers had seen in a lifetime?

"Thank you," Emily said to the boy. "I need to browse a bit before I'm ready."

She wandered down the two aisles slowly, and after she filled up on the sights and sounds and smells of the store, she got down to business. She needed a new pair of shoes. Riding in the front of a bus where no one knew her was one thing. Trying on a pair of shoes in a general store where she could be recognized at any moment was another. She wasn't feeling that rash. She picked out the smallest pair of women's shoes she saw, matching their general outline to the bottom of her own overrun shoes, and carried them up to the front of the store.

"I haven't seen you in here before," the boy behind the counter said, taking the shoes from her. "You from Colfax?"

"I'm from up the road. Aloha. It's been a long time since I was here. My name is Emily Fredieu."

"Glad to see you in the store, Mrs. Fredieu. I just started here not too long ago myself. I'm still getting to know everybody. Will this be all for you today?"

"Add five tins of Red Rooster snuff, please."

Willie Dee Billes Tademy, Nathan (Ted) Tademy.

"Yes, ma'am. Anything else?"

"Eight . . . no, ten sticks of peppermint candy. My granddaughter is coming to visit this afternoon, and she has a sweet tooth as demanding as mine."

"A little girl?"

Emily laughed, thinking of how her outspoken granddaughter, Willie Dee, would react to the question. Willie was high yellow, her brown eyes always seeming to blaze with curiosity, reminding Emily of T.O. in his youth. That and her long, slender fingers. But she had also gotten a heavy dose of spunk and her big feet from Eva. Her granddaughter considered herself fully grown, with a quick tongue and the sassy arrogance of a fifteen-year-old accustomed to being chased by all of the local colored boys. "Not so little any-

Nathan Tademy and Willie Dee Billes with daughters Joan and Theodorsia.

Willie Dee Billes and Nathan (Ted) Tademy.

Eva and T.O. Billes, front. Children L–R. Henry Earl, I.V., Willie Dee, Theo, Joe.

Billes children.
L–R. Henry Earl,
Theo, Willie Dee, I.V.,
Joe. Lalita Tademy off
to side.

Emily Fredieu and
daughter Mary Billes.

Nathan (Ted) Tademy.

Eva and T.O. Billes (back) children and grandchildren, 1954. Lalita Tademy, far left, hands on hips.

more. She's bringing her latest beau out to see me. One of the Tademy boys."

"Another family I don't know."

The boy stacked her purchases on the counter. He took his stubby pencil and began to add up her total as he talked. "You picked a good time to come in. There's going to be a rally across the street starting soon. Jim Fletcher running for police jury."

Emily was suddenly wary and anxious to be back home. "How much is it going to be?" she asked.

The bell over the front door of the store shrilled loudly, and Emily startled. A well-dressed but overly powdered older woman entered, dominating the room. She eyed Emily sharply and then turned to the clerk.

"Five pounds of flour and two pounds of coffee."

"Let me finish up here with Mrs. Fredieu, Mrs. Fletcher, and I'll get right on it."

"Excuse me? You'll help me now. Miss Emily will be glad to wait."

The boy looked closely at Emily, as if memorizing her facial features, and back to Lucille Fletcher's unyielding expression. "Step aside, Miss Emily." His tone became curt, full of authority. With a sweep of his hand he pushed aside her items to clear space. The lid from one of the tins of snuff loosened, and a dark sprinkling of brown tobacco spilled on the counter. "The order for Mrs. Fletcher is next."

Emily concentrated on the rich, sour smell of the snuff, wanting the potent comfort of it in her mouth, even thinking for a reckless moment of reaching out to take a pinch. She backed away from the counter, one small step, then two, and stood quietly while the boy retrieved the white woman's order.

The bell rang again, and a young woman with dark unruly hair came into the store. The woman stood by and waited patiently for her turn at the counter. When Mrs. Fletcher left, the boy turned his attention to the newest arrival.

"Something I can help you with?" he asked her politely.

She nodded toward Emily. "I think she was here first." Her words had a strange, flat tone.

"She knows her place. I can help you next. You from around here, ma'am?"

"I'm from Oklahoma, visiting my aunt. My name is Sarah Feraldo."

"How can I help you today, Miss Feraldo?"

Emily calculated the distance between the counter and the entryway, allowed herself one last look at the snuff tins, and eased toward the door. Careful not to make any sudden motions, she opened it slowly. The bell rang out as if she had yanked it.

"Hold on. What about these things you picked out?"

Emily gave a small weak smile as the old familiar queasiness gnawed. "I don't need them after all, thank you kindly."

She walked away from the store empty-handed, listening for angry steps in pursuit behind her, and began to breathe more regularly when there were none. The wind carried bits and pieces of the politician's words as they spread over the small crowd gathered around the grandstand.

"It's up to us to teach them how to accept with humility the limitations placed on them. They must always remember to accept with grace their inferiority. If you elect me, I'll protect our way. . . ."

She didn't look back. She walked on, past the café to the bus stop, and settled herself to wait for the Montgomery local.

Cooking smells from the café wafted up as Emily waited for the bus, and her stomach complained in response. It had been a long time since breakfast. The sun beat hot directly overhead, and she felt a powerful need for food, water, or snuff. A tall white farmer in dirty overalls and a wide straw hat approached the café. From the shade of the café's doorway, the owner beckoned.

"Come on in out of the hot sun," the man said to the farmer. "We have a special that looks mighty good today, and a breeze to help you enjoy it."

The men disappeared into the cool of the café. It was the dinner hour, and while Emily waited, a pair and a few singles entered the diner. A man the color of strong coffee in a well-worn jacket and trousers went around to the back door and reappeared later with a brown bag. He found a thin patch of shade under an elm tree, sat on the ground, and began to eat.

I'll never be hungry enough to go to anyone's back door, Emily thought.

When the northbound bus finally came, emitting its noxious fumes as it slowed to a halt, Emily was the only passenger to get on. She shook off the dust of Colfax, raised her chin slightly, dropped her nickels into the driver's waiting palm, and walked deliberately to the front seat, composing herself for the ride home.

Emily died sept 13, 1936, She had $1,300.00 in Her Bed. Josephine and Mary both died Old Maids.
--Cousin Gurtie Fredieu, written family
  history, 1975

ACKNOWLEDGMENTS

I have been truly fortunate in having Jamie Raab of Warner Books as my editor. Her insightful editing and unruffled navigation through a world foreign to me has made the adventure productive and fun. Thanks to Donna Levin, both for suggestions in her Novel Writing Workshop at UC Berkeley Extension, and for leading me to my most amazing agent, Jillian Manus. Jillian has been exacting in her expectations and tireless in her efforts on the novel's behalf, a wonderful combination.

I am grateful for the safety net woven by my own coterie of early supporters. They each started their long-haul work of encouragement when the novel was still fragile and unpredictable, keeping me moving forward more often than they knew, giving help in any form I asked. They read, critiqued, listened, suggested, hand held, strategized, but, most important, they believed. Thanks to Anne Adams, Randy

Adams, Dori Ives, my sister Joan Tademy Lothery, Susan Orr, Judy Squier, Carole Straw, and big brother Lee Tademy.

From the moment she took me on my first tour down in the Louisiana countryside, helping to turn my research into real places and people, Vicky Martin has been invaluable as my personal "step-on" Natchitoches guide, providing local history and background for *Cane River*. Also thanks to Rachal Mills Lennon, a certified genealogist, for being both skilled and persistent enough to find the plantation records, in French, for all of my Cane River women.

My mother, Willie Dee Billes Tademy, deserves special thanks, for tolerating my constant questions and tests of her memory, even when my obsession with the past was baffling and unsettling to her. She indulged me in this as only a mother would, and was the gateway to the remarkable women of Cane River.

Lastly, I thank Elisabeth, Suzette, Philomene, and Emily. Getting to know each one of them has made me stronger.

THE INEVITABLE TELLING OF CANE RIVER

My great-grandmother Emily was born a slave in Cane River, just as the Civil War was beginning. Her mother Philomene and her grandmother Suzette were also born there. Emily's great-grandmother Elisabeth came from Virginia, not Louisiana, according to records I found, and she appeared in Cane River some time before 1820, when she was still in her teens. *Cane River*, the novel, is an attempt to capture the stories of these remarkable women.

A few years ago, after a long search, I found the Bill of Sale of my great-great-great-great-grandmother Elisabeth. In 1850 she was sold for at least the second time, away from her Cane River family, for $800. Holding a copy of that Bill of Sale in my hands was a life-changing event for me. By then, I had already left my very good job as a vice president for a high-technology Fortune 500 company, for reasons I couldn't explain to anyone, even myself, and I was spending a majority of my time poring over old records and making research trips back to Louisiana from my home in California. I had spent almost two years obsessively researching my family tree. After finding that Bill of Sale, what had started as an absorbing and interesting project to chart my family's lineage suddenly became even more personal, in ways I could not have anticipated.

Looking back, my writing of *Cane River* seems inevitable, but in the beginning I had no intentions of writing a book. But the more I dug and the more facts I uncovered, the more the women of Cane River began to speak to me, one at a time. I had been toying with the idea of putting something down in print about my ancestors, but the Bill of Sale changed my internal debate away from whether I should write a book, and directed it toward how to tell the stories.

Cane River covers 137 years of my family's history, written as fiction, but deeply rooted in years of research, historical fact, and family lore. In piecing together events from personal and public sources, especially when they conflicted, I relied on my own intuition. There were gaps I filled in based on research of the events and mood of the place and time. I presupposed motivations. Occasionally I changed a name, date, or circumstance to accommodate narrative flow. I tried to capture the essence of truth, if not always the precision of fact, and trust that the liberties I have taken will be forgiven.

I hope *Cane River* touches readers as a universal story of resilience and strength. I am especially pleased with the cover of the book. The woman standing beside the oak tree staring out to the future is my great-grandmother Emily. I think she, and the others who came before her, would be honored to have you hear her story.

READING GROUP
GUIDE

QUESTIONS FOR DISCUSSION

1. Philomene says that to be a slave was to have nothing but still have something left to lose. Discuss the profound but different losses suffered by each generation of women.

2. The relationships between Suzette, Philomene and Emily, and the white fathers of their children range from flat-out rape to calculated financial arrangements cemented by childbearing to real, if forbidden and dangerous, love. What did you find most surprising about these often complex relationships?

3. Do you think Doralise was in a position to help Suzette and Philomene more than she did?

4. *Cane River* dramatizes the roots of turmoil within America's black community on issues of skin color. Emily, for example, is described by the author as being color-struck. In what ways does color consciousness continue to afflict

black and mixed-race societies today? How, in *Cane River*, was the color-struck attitude a help or hindrance in successive generations' rising fortunes?

5. During the course of researching *Cane River*, as she kept unearthing tender relationships in unexpected situations, Tademy found herself frequently being forced to rethink some long-held beliefs about slavery. What, if anything, surprised you most about the relationships described in the book? In which ways did you find Tademy's depictions believable? Upsetting? Eye-opening?

6. Cane River was a community made up of French planters, slaves, and *gens de couleur libre,* or free people of color who had accumulated a great deal of land and wealth and were just as likely to be slave owners as their white neighbors. How do you think the free people of color justified playing a willful role in their kinsmen's oppression?

7. The free people of color considered themselves neither black nor white. Can you think of any parallels in today's society?

8. Each of the four women in the book approached life differently and handled their relationships to the men and children in their lives very differently. Discuss the differences.

9. Do you think that each of the women was a good mother? Was there more that any one of them could have done for their children than they did?

10. How—or did—each of the women fight against the oppression of their lives? Do you think there was more that Elisabeth or Suzette could have done?

11. Philomene seems to be the strongest of the women. If you agree with this statement, what do you think accounts for her unusual strength? If you disagree, why—and who do you think was actually the strongest? The weakest?

12. Philomene coldly made a choice to stay with Narcisse Fredieu after he returned to Cane River following the Civil War. At this point, she was now free. Why, then, would she make this decision?

13. Suzette changed her last name three times. Why was this so significant to her?

14. Did Joseph Billes do everything he could to protect Emily and their children? Did Emily do everything possible to protect her children?

15. Elisabeth called all of her descendants to her bedside when she knew she was dying. What were the long-term repercussions of this act for her family?

16. Sunday dinners were a major event in *Cane River.* What made them so important? Family dinners, in which generations come together on a regular basis, seem to be a dying tradition in this country. What effect do you think this has on families today?

17. Cane River was a community with both rigid hierarchies and notable exceptions to these hierarchies. Do you think that Cane River's historical divisions of class, race, and gender have contemporary parallels?

18. What are the similarities and differences between Cane River of the 1800s and the United States today?

19. In many ways Cane River, a rural farming community established by French Catholics, was unlike other southern communities of the time. What did you find most surprising about the community and its leading citizens?

20. Each of the four major women characters in Cane River was born a slave, but even so, each made distinct choices regarding how she was going to live her life. What were their choices? What were the other options they might have chosen?

21. When Madame slaps Suzette in the cookhouse Elisabeth doesn't interfere, nor does she have a heart-to-heart conversation afterward with her daughter about what happened? Why not? Was this realistic?

22. What do you think would have happened to each of the main characters if they had not been so deeply rooted in family?

23. Which living situation do you think was easier, big house or quarter?

24. Emily, in the very last scene in the book, takes a seat in

the front row of the bus to return home from her trip to town. Is this something you believe she would do? Why or why not?

25. Elisabeth, Suzette, and Philomene don't talk about slavery with Emily, who was too young to remember slave life. In fact, they don't talk much about those times with one another. How does this avoidance shape them and affect the younger generation?

26. When Joseph moves Emily out of the house where they raised their children in order to marry a white woman, Emily asks to take only those things she considers to be her possessions. Was this foolish pride that possibly deprived her children of a larger inheritance?

27. Joseph stays close to Emily in his later years. Why do you think Emily continued to allow Joseph into her life after he kicked her out of their home and married another woman?

28. Emily's daughters Mary and Josephine never marry, and her son T.O. married a woman radically different than his mother. What do you think this says about the long-reaching effects of Emily's choices and behavior as a mother?

29. Elisabeth says that everyone along Cane River was "waiting for the spider to come home." What did she mean?

30. The author of *Cane River* made the decision to turn her family's story into a work of fiction rather than nonfiction? What do you think motivated her to do so, and do you think it was the right decision?

to
Shreveport CAMPTI
NATCHITOCHES ⊙
Red River

Cane River → MONTGOMERY
CLOUTIERVILLE ⊙ ALOHA
COLFAX

ALEXANDRIA ⊙

N

MILES
0   10   20   30   40   50   60

Cane River

(after the Civil War)

NEW ORLEANS

The Bondwoman's Narrative
by Hannah Crafts
edited by Henry Louis Gates, Jr.

A historical and literary event, this recently uncovered tale written in the 1850s is the only known novel written by a fugitive female slave and, by all accounts, the first novel by an African-American woman. The riveting story recounts the adventures of a young slave on a southern plantation as she escapes and makes her way to freedom. From a manuscript discovered and edited by noted African-American scholar Henry Louis Gates, Jr., this book also features research notes by Dr. Gates on Hannah Craft's remarkable life and the history of her fictional work.

Out of the Night That Covers Me
by Pat Cunningham Devoto

John McMillan was only eight years old when his mother died and he was ripped from his sheltered world. Abused by his alcoholic uncle, John longs for escape. A twist of fate will bring him to the Bend, a black settlement that has become a refuge for outcasts, where he'll join Tuway, a black man who helps others leave the

South. But neither will be ready for the brutal confrontation about to change their lives, challenge the prejudice of an era, inspire the courage of a people, and most of all, touchingly reveal the secrets of one boy's heart.

"Wholly convincing. . . . [John is] a terrific and totally believable little kid. From his point of view we see an entire society beginning to implode."
—*Washington Post Book World*

The Curing Season
by Leslie Wells

In 1948, on a tobacco farm in southern Virginia, book-smart but naïve Cora Slaughter struggles to rise above her hardscrabble existense and her father's alcoholic rages. Hungry for affection, Cora marries handsome drifter Aaron—but soon learns that being with him is nothing like she imagined. Her only joy will be the moments of happiness she snatches with her young son, and the African-American woman whom she meets and befriends. Soon, in a racially divided South, Cora must make a courageous—and dangerous—choice.

"Stunning . . . compelling and triumphant."
—Terry Kay, author of
To Dance with the White Dog